THOSE
HAMILTON
SISTERS

Averil Kenny grew up on a dairy farm and began work in the tourism industry at a young age. She studied Education at James Cook University, before completing a Bachelor of Journalism at the University of Queensland. She currently lives in Far North Queensland with her husband and four children. When not dreaming up stories, she can be found nestled in her favourite yellow wingback chair reading and sipping tea, in her library overlooking the rainforest. *Those Hamilton Sisters* is her first novel.

THOSE HAMILTON SISTERS

Averil Kenny

ZAFFRE

First published in the UK in 2021 by
ZAFFRE
An imprint of Bonnier Books UK
4th Floor, Victoria House, Bloomsbury Square, London WC1B 4DA
Owned by Bonnier Books
Sveavägen 56, Stockholm, Sweden

A CIP catalogue record for this book is
available from the British Library.

ISBN: 978–1–83877–306–9

Also available as an ebook and in audio

1 3 5 7 9 10 8 6 4 2

Typeset by IDSUK (Data Connection) Ltd
Printed and bound in Great Britain by Clays Ltd, Elcograf S.p.A.

Zaffre is an imprint of Bonnier Books UK
www.bonnierbooks.co.uk

For Liam,
the boy who saved me a seat every day on the school bus,
and for the beautiful stories we started together:
Dash, Aurora, Eleanor and Teddy

PART ONE

'Look like the innocent flower,
But be the serpent under it.'
William Shakespeare, *Macbeth*

CHAPTER 1
TO NOAH VALE

1955

The Sunday train which snaked into Noah Vale that verdant, midwinter afternoon brought with it fire, sending an inferno of small-town gossip roaring up the valley.

Olive Emerson, a sprightly middle-aged figure on the crowded platform, shot off one last fretful prayer as the train jerked to a stop, then wandered slowly along its length, scanning each carriage for the first glimpse of her nieces – three newly orphaned girls come home to their outcast mother's birthplace.

And here they were. The fifth carriage was set to burn, flaming with redheads: the first, richest red, hauled back in an austere bun; the second, flowing strawberry flames striated with gold; and lastly, the burnished auburn curls of a clinging three-year-old. Olive marvelled at how Esther's radiant colouring had filtered down through her daughters. Each girl carried that wild, red streak in her own way – enough of their tragically beautiful mother to bless or curse, accordingly.

Superstitious fool, Olive rebuked herself. She'd vowed to wipe the slate clean with her nieces – a mercy Esther was never afforded.

Olive's eyes fixed on the carriage window, imploring the girls to acknowledge her before the murmuring crowd. She was acutely conscious of her assumed status here as rescuing aunt, when, in truth, she was naught but a stranger to these girls.

Olive had *heard* the voices down Main Street dripping with scorn over the latest Hamilton tragedy: the long-ostracised daughter of Noah Vale finally getting her comeuppance, and Esther's bastards coming home in repentance for her.

Even after all these years, Olive could not stomach what had happened to her kinfolk. The Hamiltons had been a founding family of this insular rural valley and, for generations, bastions of respectability in church, school and farming life. No one would have predicted it – least of all themselves.

Malcolm and Lois Hamilton, coming late to parenthood, had raised two girls who would take vastly different paths in life. Olive, the eldest, had finished school at fourteen, married a nice local boy and settled into her expected place. Though Olive and Gavin Emerson had produced no children of their own, they'd always given back to the community, and tried to be a light to others. Side by side, their shop shingles proudly hung: EMERSON'S HARDWARE, and EMERSON'S FASHION AND FABRICS.

Then there was Esther.

A change-of-life baby, born more than a decade after Olive, Esther had been an aspiring writer, with a bright intellect and astonishing beauty. The most promising debutante to have ever graced the stage of Noah Vale School! Or so they once had said. Esther Hamilton was only remembered now as a ruinous Jezebel.

The Hamiltons had lived with that shame chafing their infamous family pride for nearly two decades. But Lois and Malcolm had both passed away in recent years, unreconciled with a daughter who'd proven herself, time and time again, a woman of ill repute.

4

For twenty years, Olive had borne the comparisons between the Hamilton sisters, suffered their estrangement, and prayed unceasingly for little Essie to be brought to her senses and home to the family fold. But pride on one side, and shame on the other, had proven insurmountable on both counts.

Of the Hamiltons, only Olive had sustained tenuous contact with Esther. Odd letters and birthday cards, occasional phone calls, all attempted gently, through indirect routes. Mostly they went unanswered, or took so circuitous a journey back, they were hardly relevant anymore. But what more could Olive have done?

The question haunted her.

The Hamiltons' last contact with Esther, eight years ago, had been to inform her of Lois's funeral arrangements. What daughter *wouldn't* come home for her mother's funeral? Well, Olive knew now: the one who was telephoned for the first time in twelve years by her gruff-voiced father and expressly forbidden to attend, lest she bring shame on an honourable woman's memory. There was no question of Esther coming home for her father's funeral a few short years later.

Banished Esther had stayed, until her own wretched end three months ago – in a red Hillman Minx skidding across a wet, lonely road, with Japanese maples raining down. Drunk, as far as Olive could determine. What an ignoble ending for the girl who'd seemed likely to outshine them all.

Olive winced as the foot worrying at her calf began to cramp. She hadn't even received news of her sister's death until two months ago. There she was going about her quiet, orderly life for weeks with no idea her baby sister had been wiped from the face of the earth.

And here, now, were Olive's homeless, fatherless, friendless nieces: Sonnet, Fable and little Novella Plum, whom they apparently called Plum.

Unease prickled beneath Olive's collar. Perhaps she should have been more forthright on the phone with Esther's girls about their mother's history in Noah. It had been on the tip of her tongue, burning. But how *did* one initiate such delicate topics with grieving girls? And what right did Olive think she had to tell them anything?

No, they would have to take it one step at a time, together.

Finally, her eldest niece turned to the train window. Her weary gaze swept over Olive, taking in the sea of peering faces. Olive raised a shaky hand. Sonnet's eyes settled on her with an unsmiling nod before she turned away to snap shut Plum's tiny suitcase.

Olive wondered if she had time to swallow an aspirin before the girls disembarked.

First was Sonnet, new legal guardian, who, twenty years earlier, had caused her mother's belly to swell beneath her school uniform. Sonnet had never stepped foot in Noah Vale, yet she'd been the talk of the town for decades. Olive shivered. Unlike her willowy mother – all curves and slender limbs – Sonnet was tall and toned, matching a queenly athleticism to her mother's generous bosom. The severe hairstyle did nothing to flatter her strong features, but she was undeniably striking with her sharp green eyes.

Following close in Sonnet's wake was Plum. Olive's heart squeezed at the sight of the chubby girl cleaving to her sister's hand. To her chest, she clutched a comfort bear. Ringlets framed aubergine eyes, a heart-shaped face and full cheeks.

Twelve-year-old Fable was last to step down from the train, and when she did, Olive's lungs faltered on a disbelieving breath.

It was Esther in the doe eyes and full lips. Esther in the long, spilling mane, Esther in the slender limbs, and Esther plastered all over those fine features. Only the hair was different. And while Esther's eyes had shone vixen green, Fable's were a sunlit amber floating in a pool of violet shadows.

This young girl was lovelier than even her heartbreaking mother had been.

Four Hamilton women stood in silent regard of one another. All around them, curious eyes and ears strained; whispers crackled.

Blood of my blood, Olive thought, scouring her nieces for traces of herself.

She stepped forward to embrace the girls, and was rebuffed. Sonnet bore a frown that would intimidate the best of women. Fable, poker-faced, glanced rapidly between sister and new aunt. Plum quaked against Sonnet's skirt, reaching and mewling to be carried.

This was no place for intimate first meetings.

'After all these years, you've finally come to Noah Vale!' Olive said. 'I can't tell you how glad I am to have you here.'

She extended a hand to Sonnet. Instead of taking it, Sonnet leaned forward in tight-lipped appeal. 'Can we go straight to your car? This is too much. The girls are exhausted.'

Olive reached for the first of three shabby suitcases. 'Follow me!'

Sonnet heaved the last suitcase into the back of the Holden, then hurried an escaping red tress back into her bun. Olive straightened the smallest bag. Both women stared at the suitcases for a strained moment.

'Okay, then,' Olive said, slamming the boot. 'Let's get you girls home. I've got lovely chicken soup on the stove.'

Sonnet dallied, hand on boot.

Olive paused. 'Sonnet?'

'We'll go directly to the cottage.'

Olive made for the car door. 'Oh no, it's late. Gav and I will take you over in the morning. First thing.'

'We want to move in immediately,' Sonnet said, with eyes fastened on two small redheads through the back window.

'Goodness, we haven't prepared the cottage. It's not fit for living in – the electricity hasn't even been restored yet.'

'Not a problem.'

'No, dear, it needs plenty of work first,' Olive said. 'Gav was going to look at all that for you.'

Sonnet's jaw jutted. It was an expression Olive suspected she would come to know – and resign herself to.

'I told you on the phone, we intend to move straight in. I won't camp out in a stranger's home.'

Olive's forehead puckered. 'But we only want to take care of—'

'I've been caring for my sisters since they were born, and exclusively since our mother's passing. We don't need *taking care of*.'

Oh yes, Olive could only imagine how it must have been, living perpetually in flight – switching cities, homes and friends at their mother's whim. How could this young woman be anything but fiercely independent?

Olive was torn. Pursue, or let them be? 'I fear you'll be disappointed, dear. The cottage is run-down and infested with pests – gecko poo everywhere! Rainforest rats, too.'

'It'll be fine for us.'

'But it's hardly proper for young girls to be living all on their own. We've plenty of room at the main house. You'll hardly know we're there—'

'It's not up for ruddy discussion,' Sonnet snapped, 'I outlined my plans specifically before we left Canberra.'

'Yes, I recall. But, by golly, you must want a break? You've had so much to bear. Surely we could help shoulder your burdens?'

But she'd pressed too hard. Sonnet was about to blow her top.

'As you wish, then, to the cottage we'll go. I'll let you see for *yourself* the condition it's in.'

'You've arrived at our mildest time of year,' Olive intoned as the car began a steep ascent from the station. 'Winter in the tropics is paradise: picnics and swimming every day. We love life away from the big smoke. And we're a close-knit community.'

In the passenger seat, Sonnet sat in taut silence.

'Noah Vale is an old sugar town. You'd have seen our mill as you came into the valley. Cane all round these parts, but we can also boast of our tobacco, mango and banana plantations. Lots of historic properties.'

They emerged on a wide curve. Below, within a steep bowl of mountain ranges, atop a rolling patchwork quilt, lay Noah Vale.

'*This* is our town.'

Late-afternoon sunlight, having loitered all day behind blanketing rain, broke forth at the mountain rim now, sweeping golden beams across the misty vale. It was a technicolour scene; overblown hues slickly accentuated by rain.

Olive cast a glance at the back seat and saw Fable's lips part wide. Plum, straining to see, was so bug-eyed as to be comical. Only Sonnet remained rigid, unreadable.

They began the descent into Noah Vale: past a tractor idling in a freshly tilled field, with egrets strolling the red rows; along an avenue of vermilioned mango trees; and onto a bridge spanning a wide, shrouded creek gorge.

'Serpentine Creek,' Olive said, nodding below. 'Winds right through the middle of the valley.'

'*Oh*,' Fable breathed, rousing from her slumberous enchantment. 'Sonny, it's *Mama's* creek! Remember? How she always talked about her Serpentine Spells . . .'

Olive tsked. 'What nonsense. Esther barely looked up from her books to notice the creek existed! And if she loved the creek so much, then why did . . .' Seeing Fable's face shuttering up, Olive halted. Tension infused the air.

Olive momentarily removed her hand from the steering wheel, to touch the foil of tablets in her skirt pocket. She'd make a cuppa for the girls once they arrived at Heartwood, and take a couple of aspirins then.

'Well, never mind,' Olive muttered. 'You'll be close to the creek at the cottage, so you'll see for yourself: it's just an ordinary, non-magical watercourse. At least until the wet season – then we have our own raging river!'

Plum's small face pressed worriedly against the window.

'The bridge into Noah floods over each year. All our bridges do in the Wet, cutting us off from the outside world. Wettest region of Australia, we can go weeks without a ray of sunshine. Practically need an ark!'

They were entering Main Street now. Impeccable art deco buildings with pretty, rustic facades lined the street front. Veritable institutions presided proudly: the Post Office, the Canecutter's Hotel, the Paragon Cafe – all respectably closed on a Sunday afternoon.

'There are our shops,' Olive said, slowing the car to a mere putter, as they passed the adjacent stores.

Olive admired her shop-window mannequins, garbed in modest, ladylike dresses for the occasion of her nieces' grand arrival. 'Not quite what you're seeing in winter fashion down south, I imagine, but we don't really *do* winter here.'

Seeing the wrinkle between Sonnet's eyes, Olive added, 'I'll be glad to have young women to inspire me now. My largest demographic is our middle-aged ladies, and I lose many debutantes each year to the big department stores in Cairns. I've got plenty of work for you girls in my shop . . . if you're interested.'

Sensing Sonnet bristling, she pressed her foot on the accelerator, leaving behind, for now, her dream of graceful nieces swanning between clothing racks, sprinkling youth and vivacity all about.

Main Street forked out around a large park, fronted with a wrought-iron gate. The giant trees within, their branches spreading so widely they might have roofed a house, seemed to pique Sonnet's interest.

Olive quickly resumed her tour guiding. 'Rain trees. They've been in Noah Vale since we were settled. In winter, our church – you see, just over there – hosts a Sugar Festival in the park, to kick off the cane-crushing season. Every family in town has a table. There are rides and stalls – you girls will love it!'

She'd lost Sonnet, however, to glazed indifference at the first mention of 'our church'.

They wound over another hillock, blanketed in banana crops, passing a school on the crest. Fable wound down the window.

'Is this my school?' she asked, eyes combing old timber buildings and the banyan trees spilling their long tendrils.

'Yes, primary and high are both together here. You'll be the fourth generation of Hamiltons to step over the threshold of Noah Vale School . . .' Olive paled, the rest of her story unuttered. . .

But the last Hamilton here was howled off the school grounds.

The journey continued where the proud commentary did not, as Queenslander homesteads spread out between farmland. The valley narrowed and deepened; looming mountains, implausibly green, enclosing them. Through one last grove of rainforest and there, proudly overlooking flowering cane, was the Hamiltons' colonial-style plantation house.

'This,' Olive said grandly, 'is Heartwood.'

Olive heard Sonnet's intake of breath as she clapped eyes on the sweeping veranda and hanging ferns, white shutters open to the bending pawpaws, coconut palms standing sentry around, and showy tropical gardens bursting against the white wood.

'It *is* nice,' offered Sonnet. 'I can see why you're keen to host us.'

'Gav and I inherited this home from your grandparents. The very land I was born on. It was a working cane farm back then, but most of the cane I roamed as a young girl is now farmed by the Hulls on one side of us, and the Lagorios on the other.'

The Holden pulled to a stop.

'And now,' said Olive, 'we make the short trek to your new residence.'

A golden retriever bounded over the grass towards the newcomers. Plum screamed, throwing herself onto Sonnet.

Olive tutted as the dog gambolled around them. 'Oh, never mind Zephyr, he's friendly.'

Plum wailed while Sonnet bobbed a hip to hush the crying. 'Olive, Plum's terrified of dogs!'

'Oh dear,' Olive said, with more peevishness than intended. 'Zeph adores everyone, so don't take his enthusiasm too personally. Down, boy, down!'

Zephyr sat with a grin and Olive shrugged. 'She'll get used to him quickly enough.'

'Or maybe we'll have to steer clear of his house.'

Zephyr was promptly removed to the veranda. His gaze followed the Hamilton sisters longingly as they girded themselves with suitcases.

Bypassing the main house, they climbed an orchard hill filled with exotic fruit trees. Fable reached out to touch a swollen fruit with reptilian skin.

'My custard apples,' Olive began. 'And wait till you try . . .'

But Sonnet wasn't stopping for anything now.

Atop the hill, they gazed over a flood-plain paddock stretching to a thick remnant ribbon of rainforest-shrouded creek. Nestled at the base of the slope was a ramshackle wooden cottage encircled by trees and a garden choked with allamanda shrubs, molasses grass and climbing mandevilla. In the falling darkness, the cottage was a beacon of homeliness against lush, dark forest.

Fable sighed.

'The cottage is Edwardian era, built by your grandparents,' Olive explained as they trotted, with increasing momentum, down the hill. 'I lived in the cottage myself during my early married life, and after me, it was always promised to your mother. Even after she . . . left Noah Vale, it was still hers. We've used it as a guest house, and more recently as a storage shed. But now, it's yours.'

As the younger girls streaked off ahead, Olive stopped. Sonnet turned questioningly.

Olive sighed, long and hard.

'Here,' she said, pressing her key into Sonnet's hand. 'You go ahead, make yourselves at home. I wish you'd believe me – it's really quite unliveable. But at least there are clean sheets on the beds, hurricane lanterns, and on the bench you'll find sugar bananas, fresh bread and passionfruit curd for your supper. I had suspected you'd insist on staying here tonight. You are your mother's daughter, after all. It will be rough for you, but if it's what you really want . . . ?'

Sonnet was a horse, already bolting.

Fable was first to step through the rickety gate and under the rotting arbour. She paused to admire the crumbling gables and attic windows winking in the last golden light; lifted her nose to receive the scent of gardenias blooming in the wild overgrowth; tiptoed over frangipani blossoms scattered on the stone pathway; and, hearing the creek song, felt her pulse beat double. Here was more beauty than she'd ever beheld in her young life. Here, her broken heart could heal.

Sonnet, striding up the stairs, picked at the peeling clapboard paint as she entered the fusty darkness, and began her inspection with a mental spring cleaning – obliterating years of dirt by force of imagination. She scoured the claw-foot tub in a mould-acrid bathroom, swept cobwebs from the exposed beams, chased dust bunnies down the long central hallway, banished clutter from the window seat in the sunroom, excavated furniture from debris, and scrubbed grime from the front bay window. She traced a finger along a grimy bookcase, counting spaces for each book she might one day display, and nodded approval at a simple, albeit cluttered kitchen. She finished her inspection with a sigh, as if after physical work. In all, she saw potential for a real home at last.

CHAPTER 2

HEARTWOOD

The greasy sizzle of eggs, announced by an insistent rainforest dove call, brought Sonnet, stomach clenching, to consciousness. Her eyes panned the attic bedroom, waiting for any of it to make sense: faded chintz curtains at the dormer windows letting in warm light; lumpy, left-sliding bed; vintage tallboy and dresser buried in bric-a-brac; and, in an imposing wardrobe, floral dresses and beaded gowns hung like limp, grandmotherly wraiths. Sonnet was home.

But without Mama, how could it ever truly be home?

'Saudade,' Sonnet whispered into the musty air – one of her favourite words from her collection, and lately a lifeline. Nothing else came close to describing this new existence: the presence of absence.

Now she had an aunt, and endless work ahead of her. Sonnet cringed to recall the tension of the previous afternoon. She hoped she hadn't put Olive offside already, but the woman was persistent as hell. Something about Olive's earnestness had immediately irked her. Though to be fair, many things annoyed Sonnet about many people. She should wait to see exactly what Olive had to offer them before she wrote her off completely.

Surveying the mess around her, Sonnet felt a spasm of panic in her gut, remembering the tiny, neat rental they'd left behind in Canberra as something like a castle. That flat had housed them longer than any other – three whole years – and was the only home Plum had ever known. There, for the first time, life had been stable, even bright; as if a shadow had fallen away from all of their lives.

Sonnet had spent her senior year at a single high school, a miracle itself, graduating with excellence. Not that there was much point in academic overachievement, or secret dreams of attending university. Straight out of school, Sonnet had eschewed higher learning to join Mama in her dressmaking work. It was the least Sonnet could do to help support the girls, and she'd suspected it was her destiny since the first stitch Mama insisted she sew in girlhood. Fable, nearing adolescence, had been thriving too – cherishing the new private art classes Mama scraped every last dollar together to afford. Plum, meanwhile, had been lovingly cared for by Esther's new friend, Maria, who lived across the hallway.

Plum had always known a different version of Esther Hamilton from the one Fable and Sonnet were born to. That dimpled darling had heralded such change in their mother, it could scarcely be believed. With Plum's arrival, Mama had finally seemed ... well, you could never say *content*, but something like settled. Sonnet supposed much of it owed to Esther's close friendship with mother-of-five and devout Christian, Maria. Despite Sonnet's distrust of religiosity, she conceded to Maria's calming effect on their mother. Life had been conventional, even banal. Almost forgotten were the days when Mama would uproot their lives without notice, desperate to outrun something, or someone.

Had Mama managed to stay ahead of her demons in recent years? Sonnet wanted to believe so. There had been less of the chaos and calamity of earlier years. No more of the month-long periods tiptoeing past the door as Mama tried to sleep her way out of hell. And none of those mystery lovers, experienced only in fragments – a sonorous voice on the telephone, a familiar scent on Mama's skin, the shadow passing their window in the wee hours. There had been more of Mama's buoyant, creative episodes, her literature quoting, that folksy alto drifting through the flat. Mama had still dripped with turquoise, incense and allure, but there had been maturation, at last.

Normality and predictability, after all, had always been hard won with their quixotic mama: vivacious and ferociously loving one moment, the very next blankly distant and overwrought. No one else seemed to have a mother as young and beautiful – or as sad. Esther was the girl play-acting a mother's role, and forgetting her lines. She who dragged them out to art galleries and literary festivals at late hours, though it always ended in tears – her own – yet avoided the school gate, school parents, schoolwork, even the mere mention of school itself. Esther would happily live in domestic squalor for months on end, and then embark on manic cleaning enterprises as if she expected any moment to entertain royalty. Perpetually tired, Mama could rarely muster the will after a long shift to make lunches, serve supper, or indeed provide nutrition at all. Her 'nerves', Mama described as constantly 'afire'. Sonnet might have corrected: *No, Mama, burning out.*

That was where Sonnet had always stepped in, wasn't it? She'd tried her hardest to lighten Mama's burdens. Sonnet: cook and cleaning lady; clothes mender; grout scrubber; school-bag packer; grocery shopper. Sonnet had realised at a young age what sort of girls they were – poor and fatherless, the kind to pity. Shrewdly, she'd learned to decode the prying aid of neighbours, and the recruiting charity of churchy do-gooders. Each claiming concern for the 'safety' of young girls left alone while their mother worked long days and nights to support them, with no father to guarantee moral decency – or rent, paid in full, and on time. Sonnet had learned, like Mama, to reject such charity with scathing pride. She'd embraced the lesson Esther had imparted in word and deed: 'We don't need anyone else; we Hamilton girls will always have each other.'

Until death came romping in and, suddenly, we didn't.

Plum seemed to suffer most, keening for weeks on end for the mother who would never, this time, come home. Plum had spent her infancy attached to Esther whenever she wasn't working. She was carried constantly, loved desperately and slept curled around Esther's breast.

But Plum had also adapted most quickly, scrambling for what she needed from Sonnet. She slept in Sonnet's bed by night, and clung tenaciously to her by day. All her pain was visible, treatable.

It was Fable, unnervingly serene since Mama's death, who kept Sonnet frozen awake at night. Fable was a smooth, mirroring pond of unfathomable depths; hidden waters always unplumbed. Mama always had a special way of reaching Fable there. But would Sonnet? Wailing and railing Sonnet might have soothed, but inner turmoil would go unchecked. And long had Sonnet vexed over Fable's propensity for secret worlds that could not be guessed at or entered into.

Fable Winter had arrived at a heartbreaking time for Esther, abandoned by another mysterious lover, who, in his absence, managed to fill their lives entirely. Fable's absconding father stole away with him most of Esther, too. The petite baby girl with the dark violet eyes, who rushed into the world one August morning, was placed into the arms of a hollowed-out mother. Sonnet was only eight at the time, but well she remembered the heavy-hearted mother who drifted from room to room with her bundle of strawberry-gold held near, yet so far. She had insisted Mama should 'send back' the baby who'd brought such sadness with her.

Fable seemed to know, from the moment she was born, that she ought not to make a fuss; rather, to soothe herself and be thankful for the smallest ministrations. Where Sonnet before her had been fractious and demanding – still *was*, she could admit – Fable was an obliging, placid child. She was also the sole recipient of Mama's creative passions; an avid writer, and a precociously talented artist. Yet while Esther's literary endeavours were frenetic and dispirited, Fable's artistic heart was sweet, steady and dreamy.

Or had been.

Frighteningly, Fable hadn't touched brush or pencil since the day Mama had died. The stillness and cleanliness of Fable's hands terrified Sonnet. It was for Fable, more than anyone, Sonnet had brought them here. Fable, heading into the tumultuous last years of girlhood, needed stability, quietude, security – all of which Noah Vale offered. From Sonnet's research, this valley sounded like an idyllic Eden.

In bittersweet irony, Mama's passing had presented the girls with a new station in life. Two unexpected treasures arose from Esther's carefully structured will: a cottage of their own and a generous fund for the girls – an inheritance Esther apparently had been too proud to spend on herself. Enough to set them up independently, in a real home, within walking distance of an aunt, who, by their mother's vague testimony, had a 'good heart'.

Too right Sonnet had jumped at this opportunity! Whatever the reasons Mama had come to despise her family and community, they were not Sonnet's. Mama was fond of saying, 'small towns breed small minds', and she'd avoided ever stepping foot outside a city again. But as the daughter of an unwed mother, even a seasoned city-dweller, Sonnet knew all too well: conservatism reigned *everywhere*.

How much worse could a small town really be?

Sonnet was pinning a nomadic lifetime of hopes on this move north; a clean slate and brand-new life for the Hamilton sisters. She had it all mapped out: do up the old cottage, ease the girls into the local school, get herself work, save like the dickens, and send the girls off to join the ranks of aspiring modern women at university.

Then it would finally be Sonnet's turn, too.

That, after all, was the one personal thing this regional move had cost Sonnet, at least in the short term: the tertiary education she'd long coveted. Sonnet had no intention of fulfilling the prescribed house-wife's role; counting children instead of accomplishments.

But there was no way she could leave her sisters now. They needed her, as they always had. Sonnet's brilliant career would have to wait – but not forever.

No one was promised forever.

Her gaze went to the urn set gingerly last night on a grimy shelf, releasing Mama from her crude travel arrangements – the socks and undergarments that had protected her from bumps.

You'll be free soon, Mama.

It was a priority to choose where her ashes should be spread. Their mercurial mama would never be at rest in a ceramic urn.

Plates clattered, jarring Sonnet from her ruminations. She swung legs out of a bed conspicuously empty of the smallest Hamilton, and headed down creaking stairs to investigate.

Olive was in the kitchen, salted-ginger head bent over the gas stove, with an unlikely audience at her side. Timid, terrified-of-strangers Plum stood on a chair beside her, gripping teddy bear to baby cheeks. Outside the front door, Zephyr rested in panting silence.

Plummy, calm in the vicinity of a dog *and* keeping company with a virtual stranger? They'd been here all of five minutes and already Olive was trying to change things.

'Good morning, sleepyhead!' Olive called. 'Knew you'd be hungry after your light supper, so I let myself in. Thought I'd cook something nourishing.'

Forced breeziness poorly covered the absurdity: Olive sneaking into the cottage she'd always known as her own, to minister to nieces she knew no better than strangers.

'Who collects newspapers?' Sonnet asked, pulling up a chair at a Formica table cluttered with paper stacks and empty jam jars.

'My Gav,' Olive replied, cracking another monstrous egg into the pan. 'Uses them for gardening mulch.'

'Yours are the jars, then?'

'Yes, I'm a keen jam maker, well known in Noah Vale, if I may be so bold, for my pineapple butter and mangosteen chutneys. I'll clear up this clutter. In fact, I was thinking of shutting my shop for a couple of days, to help you.'

'Oh, no thanks, we'll manage.'

Olive flipped an egg expertly. 'Plum was telling me about your train trip. Certainly has been a long journey for you girls, coming all the way from Canberra.'

Plum *talking*? The line between Sonnet's eyes deepened. 'Yes, it took us half a week.'

'You must have been glad to sleep in a stationary bed last night.'

'Sure was. Still felt like I was rattling along, though. Or maybe it was the general slide of my mattress.'

Olive pounced. 'Quite dilapidated here, isn't it? Surely you'd be glad to shift to Heartwood and try some modern hospitality now?'

Sonnet gave the woman credit for her pig-headedness, if nothing else.

'The cottage has everything we need.'

'Well—' Olive sniffed '—it doesn't have cutlery, for a start. I had to bring these down. And good luck trying to take a hot shower this morning without electricity!'

Sonnet smiled, in spite of herself. Olive smiled because of herself. Plum looked warily between aunt and sister.

'I want to make you a deal,' Olive said. 'Or at least try to.'

Sonnet braced.

'How about you come stay with us for a few days while we fix up the cottage. We'll connect the electricity, and Gav will attend to the maintenance issues. We can clean this whole place out, top to bottom, and then—'

'Olive,' Sonnet interrupted. 'I appreciate your offer. But I'm worried "a few days" will turn into a week with some problem or other, then a month, or six, and so it goes until we're permanently leeching off your charity.'

'Oh, would it be so terrible living with Gav and me?'

'I'm not going to waltz into Noah Vale and abandon my independence.'

'Not abandon it – just lay it down for a rest.'

'No.'

Olive turned away to scrounge in the pantry, sighing. She returned with a vintage salt-shaker, and banged it hard against the table. Salt was not forthcoming. Sonnet watched all of this pensively.

Stay strong! If you give in now, your life here will be a series of concessions to the woman.

'I hope you like your food bland and unflavoured,' Olive said, pushing a plate of eggs in front of Sonnet.

'My favourite, thank you.'

At the stove, Olive's back twitched with words unsaid. Sonnet raised her eyes to the heavens, stifling a groan.

Maybe this one time?

She eased out a quiet huff.

Just this one time.

'Fine,' she said, tone indicating otherwise. 'We would be willing . . . glad, to stay a few days at Heartwood.'

Olive turned, brows lifting.

'School starts back in two weeks,' Sonnet said. 'I want to have a comfortable home by then.'

'Oh good, I love a deadline!'

'But you have to promise you'll let us move back to the cottage by week's end.'

'Promise.'

Sonnet nodded dubiously. 'Okay, thanks, Olive.'

'Would it be too soon to petition for the title of "Aunty"?'

'Let's not push the friendship. And what *is* that blasted bird carrying on outside my window?'

'Wompoo fruit dove.'

'Right, first up I'm going to need a slingshot.'

Sonnet was a woman on a mission, ever mindful of the urn awaiting the cottage's resurrection to its former glory. Olive worked alongside her for a solid week, proving herself indefatigable. Sonnet was beginning to see how her aunt had developed those strong calves and arms – the woman was a powerhouse, tackling every task with grit. Grudging collaboration slowly softened into something almost like respect.

Not that Sonnet had any intention of Olive knowing it.

'I don't want that bookshelf there,' Sonnet would snap, ignoring how it now gleamed with polish. 'Leave it, I can handle it,' she might bark, meaning: *Thanks, good job, how would I have managed this without you?*

Fable was only a capricious help, flitting between exuberant cleaning efforts and dreamy amblings over the farmland, murmuring under her breath. Home she came at dinner time, with pink snakeweed flowers in her waistband, purple princess blooms behind her ears, Singapore daisies crowned around her forehead and sun-warmed exotic fruit in her pockets. Oh sure, when it was *Fable's* room getting a facelift, *her* bookshelf stacked with much-loved novels, she was willingness personified. Any other task, though, and Fable was a speck roaming in the distance; uncontainable.

'*Solivagant!*' Sonnet hissed after Fable's fleeing figure each day, like a witch's curse. It was impossible not to resent her sister when Sonnet was up to her neck in decades of grime.

Plum was a shadow at Sonnet's side: eager to help, incapable of offering real assistance. Occasionally, she sidled up to Olive – skittering away when addressed directly. To Sonnet, Olive said nothing of the increasing attention, accurately perceiving her possessiveness. Nevertheless, there was an ever-growing confidence in Olive's stride.

Their new uncle, Gavin Emerson, ever redolent of pine and diesel, had requested on their first meeting that they only call him Gav. He was proving a stumbling block for Sonnet, who struggled to command an avuncular figure. Gav was a keen jack-of-all-trades, the perfect asset, yet Sonnet refused to hand anything over. Too often he caught her in compromising positions, popping the veins in her neck to push heavy furniture, or teetering off the edge of a ladder to clean cornices and exposed beams, and he would dive right in – after a muttered comment about 'Hamilton pride'. It was maddening, but Sonnet was also immensely grateful. Gav's manner was refreshing. He suffered no fools, offered no platitudes.

The younger girls watched Gav with such wide eyes it made Olive chuckle, and Sonnet chase them away to spite Olive's enjoyment. Never before had they seen a male relative in such an intimate setting. Look, an uncle sweeping a floor! Look – an uncle playing with a dog, tinkering with a tractor, hammering a nail. Look: an uncle changing a light bulb! No wonder their eyes boggled out of their heads.

'Flat out like a lizard drinking,' Gav exhaled whenever he chugged back a glass of water – first, to the girls' bewilderment; later, to Fable's mimed impersonation and silent fits of laugher.

Work began with the rooster's crow at daybreak and ended with the arrival of the bats. On the first evening, that dark legion swarming across the purpling vale had sent a shudder up the nape of Sonnet's neck. She *loathed* things with feathers, or wings.

'What are they?'

'Bats,' Olive explained, with nary a gaze to the sky. 'They come from the colony in Cairns at sundown, and spend the night fertilising and pollinating the rainforest.'

Fable snorted. 'They what?'

'Poop, dear. They eat all the rainforest fruits, then poop everywhere. They're called spectacled flying fox. Noisy, disease-ridden things, and they're always after my orchard, but the rainforest surely needs them.'

'Flying foxes in glasses with diarrhoea!' Fable whispered, eyes glazing over with wonderment.

Sonnet did not share her sister's marvelling at every weird facet of tropical life – for starters, the size of the blasted huntsman spiders she was chasing out of this cottage! Things, people, places all had to grow on Sonnet – especially wishful aunts.

Midway through the week, Sonnet spied her sisters out beyond the garden gate, twirling with arms and faces lifted to the sky, and Zephyr barking at their heels. Their excitement brought Sonnet down from her ladder, duster in hand, to investigate. They were catching large curls of dark ash floating from the heavens. Sonnet stretched out a hand to catch a flake, and was turning the disintegrating whorl over in fascination when she heard Olive's shout from behind the cottage.

Sonnet tore around the back to find Olive at the clothesline pulling washing into the trolley.

'Oh, Sonnet, help me, quickly! We're about to lose an entire day's washing!'

'What is this ash?' Sonnet asked, working rapidly.

'Sugarcane fire at the Hulls',' Olive said. 'You're going to get ash falling in crushing season. Best to keep an eye on the skies when you've got washing out.'

'So, it doesn't snow in the tropics during winter, it rains ash, instead?'

Olive laughed.

Now Sonnet could see the black plume of smoke rising beyond the wall of rainforest.

'They set fire to their own crop?'

'Surely do,' Gav answered, arriving to help. 'Burns off pests and readies the cane for harvesting. 'Tis a beautiful sight to see a canefield aflame on a dark night. Nothin' like it when we were still farming. Got ash on your forehead, love!' Gav added, chuckling at Sonnet as together they carried the linen over the back stoop.

Sonnet wiped the ash away with a scowl.

It took six days to restore the cottage. On the final day, as had quickly become their evening habit, they gathered around the table on Heartwood's wide veranda to enjoy the spoils of small-town life: casseroles arriving daily from Olive's church friends; home delivered, in Sonnet's opinion, simply for the thrill of eyeballing Esther's lookalikes. These charities were endurable for their limited scope: soon she'd be in her very own kitchen, and she'd never have to accept the handouts of nosy strangers again.

A full moon had risen over the valley and a breeze came softly over the canefields to tease tendrils from behind Sonnet's ears. The younger girls were asleep in a four-poster bed draped with mosquito nets.

Gazing over the shimmering sea of cane, Sonnet took stock of all they had achieved in a week: a trailer-load of junk bound for the dump; and a home de-roached, de-webbed and de-cluttered, ready for the Hamilton girls to claim as their own.

She sank back against her rattan chair, pleasantly full. Olive had gathered up the bowls as quickly as they were emptied, sweeping off to the kitchen. Gav and Sonnet were left in silence.

'Why did you call the place Heartwood?'

'The Hamilton property has been called Heartwood as long as I can remember,' he told her. 'But this was Aboriginal country first. Always will be, if you ask the heartbroken people Sergeant Windsor regularly hounds out of Raintree Park. Used to be a Heartwood sign on your front gate, before the original cottage was wiped out in 1918 by a Cat-five monster called the Great Northern Cyclone. You can't wipe out a name, though.'

Gav leaned back to consider Sonnet as she fixed on the rattling approach of a large vehicle or small train through the canefield. A haunting blast confirmed it was the latter. Sonnet strained forward in her seat, peering.

A tiny steam locomotive hurtled out of the darkness, hauling a long line of bins loaded high with vegetation.

'What is it?' Sonnet asked, standing for a better look over the balustrade.

'Cane train,' Gav said, joining her.

'Didn't even know there was a rail line on the property!'

'Well, you've hardly stepped foot outside the cottage. Now you have time, you'll find plenty to impress. During the crushing season, cane trains come across the creek, over yonder, where a bridge joins our land to the Hulls'. Then she goes through these fields, once proud Hamilton land, but now the Lagorios' cane, down to the sugar mill near Cairns.'

The train puffed out of sight, leaving the scent of smoked molasses in its wake.

Sonnet smirked at the inanity of it all.

'Do you want to taste some fresh cane juice?'

'I don't have much of a sweet tooth.'

Gav grabbed a machete and thumped into the cane. Olive wandered onto the veranda, wiping sudsy hands on her apron. 'Getting you some liquid sugar to sample, is he?'

'With his big scythe, apparently.'

Gav was boyishly proud as he sprang back onto the veranda, holding a section of cane. He twisted the fibrous innards of the stalk into Sonnet's glass, thick, sun-darkened muscles rippling as he worked. A stream of pale juice trickled into her cup.

'Give that a try!'

Sonnet sipped cautiously. It tasted as she might have anticipated: brown sugar top notes, grassy finish on the palate.

'Refreshing,' she said, placing her glass down, barely touched. 'You'd better watch Fable round these parts, she has an insatiable sweet tooth – your neighbours will lose half their fields.'

'Wait till she tries my chocolate fruit, then,' Olive said. 'Or better yet, my miracle fruit; can turn the bitterest dish sweet!'

Sonnet snorted. 'It's like another world out here. The girls are particularly going to love the miniature trains.'

'Mind them in those fields, though,' Olive said, 'particularly Fable, with the way she swans about. Cane tracks are no place for children during the crush. And big taipan snakes live in those fields – they're quick as lightning, and deadlier still.'

'Fable's not stupid,' Sonnet snapped, the cane juice suddenly sour on her tongue.

'So,' Olive said, glossing over this remark, 'you're all ready for a brand-new life in Noah Vale?'

'Ready as we'll ever be.'

'And how are you feeling about Fable starting school next week?'

'Looking forward to it. It'll keep her mind off Mama, and the structure and routine will offset her dreamy ways.'

Olive cleared her throat, flicking glances at Gav. 'Sonnet, it could be . . . daunting for Fable, to begin with. Might take her some time to . . . find her place.'

'No, Fable is well accustomed to being the new girl in class. We spent our childhood moving. She is reserved, but also desperate for friends.'

'But Noah Vale isn't like the big cities you've lived in. Here, people talk. Memories go back a long way.'

'What's *that* supposed to mean?'

'For a start, there's how much Fable looks like her mother. It'll be like the spirit of Esther Hamilton walking back into school.'

'Fable is her own person.'

Olive nodded, though the worry did not abate in her eyes. 'I only mention it in case you want to prepare Fable for people being initially . . . standoffish. Your mother did have . . . a reputation . . .'

There it was.

'Fable doesn't!'

'And there were circumstances.'

'By which you mean me.' Sonnet felt her face grow ugly.

'I'm sorry. I don't mean any insult; just don't know how to broach . . . what happened with your mother.'

Gav interjected then: 'Esther was seen as the town trollop.'

Olive raised an arm, too late, to shush her husband. Tears burned behind Sonnet's eyes. She rose from the table, seeking escape. Gav's big hand took her much smaller wrist. 'Don't run off on account of my boorishness. We only want you to know how the town saw Esther, not what *we* think.'

Sonnet sat. Wrist released, she crossed her arms, fixing on the couple with a frown. 'Well? What?'

Olive's reply came with a quaver. 'I loved your mother dearly, and nothing in my life has ever hurt more than our estrangement. She made . . . mistakes.' A consolatory grimace at Sonnet here. 'But she deserved to be forgiven. It's just – she could never have come home to Noah again, not with her . . . reputation.'

'Her "reputation" as a single mother?'

'That's part of it. And her reputation for being . . . unstable.'

'Folks said she had a problem holding on to both men and mood,' Gav threw in, still chewing at his cane.

Sonnet sat pinch-lipped, refusing to let agreement show.

'Essie was wildly poetic and irresistible,' Olive said. 'But stubborn, contrary, and just *too much* for most people – felt too much and wanted too much and said too much. You had to live every emotion with her, and she wore us all out with her mighty swings, from big passions to big tragedies. She got snagged on things, too, couldn't let go of a feeling, once she had it. Yearned for love—'

'Craved it,' cut in Gav.

'Oh hush, you,' Olive said. 'She *needed* love – and there wasn't much of it from Mother and Father. As she got older, she seemed better able to manage her intensity . . . but in the end, perhaps not?'

Silence sprang up between them.

The first to break it was Sonnet – startling herself. 'Mama used to say: "My heart goes in and out of season, and I have borne the fruit of those transgressions." I knew she meant us girls, as much as the bleak episodes which plagued her.'

Olive had no difficulty making her segue. 'Did you have many stepfathers, Sonnet?'

'*Stepfathers*? There were never any fathers at all. I suppose you have this idea of us enduring a carousel of lovers. Well, you're *wrong*. You don't know anything. Mama was fanatical about keeping us apart from her beaus. Never saw them! As I grew older, I could tell when she was in love. Those were her shining highs. And I always knew when her latest affair had ended. She'd come spiralling down, sometimes for months.'

Olive was struggling with something yet unsaid. Sonnet wasn't waiting for it, though; it was like her brakes had failed. 'But paternity was a lost art with Mama. None of us have a father listed on our birth certificate. We might have been sired by ghosts.'

Gav clucked.

Sonnet glared. It was one thing for her to bare something of their lives; it was another thing entirely for this man – a *stranger* – to punctuate it with his opinion.

'And what do you know of . . . your father?' Olive asked, delicately as one picking through a basket of pins.

'I know enough.'

Olive probed her face. Sonnet thrust forth her chin.

31

'Is there something you'd like me to tell you, dear?'

Sonnet struggled against the need to possess, here and now, every-thing this woman knew about the man who had fathered her. Olive might finally plug every sorry gap in her heritage she had been, at varying times, consumed with, or humiliated by.

But Olive's fawning pity was too much. In an instant, rankled pride swallowed curiosity whole. Sonnet had been ensnared, unwittingly.

'I don't have *anything* I want to ask you or anyone else in this town about him.'

CHAPTER 3
THE GLADE

'What *snakes*?' Fable griped, slamming the cottage gate behind her. She gazed wistfully at the canefields from which she had been unequivocally banned. In the fortnight they'd been in Noah Vale, her wanderings had led her to a plethora of delights, hours of imaginings. This morning, however, she'd been ordered out of the 'taipan-filled' cane by Olive and Sonnet, who'd sat her down in a show of faux solidarity that Fable hadn't bought for a second.

'I don't need two play-acting mothers!' said Fable, shooting a filthy look at the cottage. Inside, Sonnet was prancing around neatening edges and straightening corners. They'd only just settled back into the cottage, but already Sonnet had crowned herself queen of *their* new kingdom.

Fable was thankful for small mercies, however. She had a bedroom to abscond to, even if it *was* an addendum sunroom, hastily constructed on the cottage when baby Esther had arrived. How Fable loved that forest-facing sunroom! The first space she'd ever had to call her own. New lace curtains framed her bay window, a white quilt lay over her stubbornly unmade bed, shelves and dressing table gleamed enticingly, and frosted French doors offered long-wanted privacy. The room was a

blank, waiting canvas. She wasn't ready yet to bring colour and detail –
herself – to this new setting.

Fable was convinced the room possessed unearthly power, perhaps
even Mama herself. Since arriving here, she had felt closer to Mama
than any time since her passing. Some nights she woke from dreamless
sleep to, she *swore*, a warm, radiating presence beside her. If she lay still,
without opening her eyes or moving or even breathing, Fable could
smell her mother's Femme Rochas perfume, and feel her silken touch,
sweeping the strawberry wisps from her forehead and nape of her neck,
as she'd always done at bedtime.

Fable sighed, turning her amber gaze on the dark ripple of rainforest
neatly dividing farm from farm. Never mind the canefields, then, there
was a creek to explore. *Mama's Serpentine.*

Over the paddock she tramped, careful to make her footsteps plainly
felt to both taipans and sisters alike.

Oh, this heavenly winter's morn! How easily they had been trans-
planted from a bleak and frigid Canberran July into this halcyon vale.
Fable hated the name 'Noah Vale', though. Whoever he was, Noah had
no right to claim the valley. Fable had decided to call it Rainbow Valley,
after both the musty Montgomery novel she'd found in the cottage bookshelves and the sky miracles which materialised so flamboyantly here.
Sometimes Fable felt there were not enough elegantly named colours in
the world to cater for the abundant hues of the tropics.

Approaching the creek, the rainforest wall became a living body. A
thousand permutations of green separated, one from the other, leaves
taking their unique shapes. Cool, pungent air emanated forth, river
ripple rose up in greeting. Fable charted her course towards a break in
the tree line where she supposed the cane bridge must lie.

She found the narrow-gauge track, hidden in volcanic soil, and
followed the sleepers to an old train bridge spanning the waters of

Serpentine Creek. Without hesitation, she cast off her sandals and stepped carefully onto the bridge slats. Dead centre of the bridge she stopped, legs akimbo, to survey the thickly overhanging trees, spanning to touch across the creek. Sunbeams speared the canopy, as through stained glass windows. The gilded-turquoise creek slid sinuously beneath her feet, curving away around an S-shaped bend.

'Line of beauty,' Fable whispered, hearing again her art tutor's voice. She exhaled, grateful for the sudden creative ache sparking deep in her chest, heart-side. *Ah, there you are, little glow.*

It was an urge so long missing; Fable had been afraid she'd misplaced it forever. Convinced, even, that Mama had taken it with her. After all, no one in the world had loved and praised Fable's art as Mama had. Mama could sit for hours just watching Fable draw, tears streaming, unchecked, down her face. Always such a lovely hurt, being able to make Mama cry like that. The memory of her mother's stricken face now, however, made Fable cover her own. It took thirteen breaths to quell the emotional uprising.

Why hadn't she come here sooner? The tremor in her fingers grew insistent. She longed for her sketch pad and ribbon-bound pencils, hidden beneath the loose board she'd found in her new window seat. But no way was she going back home to 'make herself useful' in Sonnet's eyes.

What would she give for a new tin of watercolours to do justice to this scene of light and shadow and ancient, breathing stillness? Her soul, she'd sell her very soul!

Fable groaned with the knowledge she'd have to approach Sonnet directly for better art materials. In Sonnet's current frame of mind, that would inevitably entail 'establishing chores' and 'being a help' and 'earning pocket money'. These precious last days before school started were Fable's alone to squander. She would not waste them trying to earn her keep, or being kept!

Fable considered the eastward direction of the creek. Olive said the creek meandered all the way through Noah Vale, meaning if Fable followed it, she had access to any place she desired.

Continuing over the cane bridge and through the opposite tree break, she discovered another sprawling cane farm. Atop the rise was an elegant plantation house, surrounded by mango trees. The Hulls' property was even grander than Heartwood!

Whistling appreciatively, she drew back into the forest to contemplate the winding path on the Hulls' side. It was still part of the creek – surely she wouldn't be roused on for trespassing by some slack-jawed, dull-witted, rifle-toting farmer? Well, the Hulls would have to get used to Fable Hamilton's daily incursions.

Fable drifted on. The creek's curving course alternated between stretches of rapids and languid pools of glassy perfection. Fable began to catalogue in her mind's scrapbook. She bent to heart-shaped leaves, soft as velveteen, smiling as raindrops skittered off like marbles. Softly, she pressed the image onto the imagined page. She lifted her eyes to a waxy globe of leaves dangling like a forest lantern. Nasty green ants swarmed from the sphere when she poked it, but Fable dashed away with a mental duplicate stored. She rescued glossy fallen leaves in commingled hues of crimson, saffron and teal, holding them against flaring sunlight to reveal their complex inner veins. She needed a fine black ink, and pronto!

Soon, the rush of a waterfall could be heard and, over it, voices raised in youthful abandon. Fable slowed, wary of revealing herself before she'd had a chance to spy. At the next corner, the creek narrowed into a rocky gorge, the path winding steeply out of sight to the source of the commotion. With hammering heart, she descended a natural staircase formed of stone.

She came upon a swimming hole, surrounded by steep, mossy walls, fed by a waterfall rushing into a deep amber-lit pool. Mirrored light danced on the cliff faces. A young boy hurtled across the water on a rope swing. On a wooden cubby-house deck jutting out of the rainforest was an elfin-faced, raven-haired girl of her own age, hollering shamelessly. Two dark-haired boys, twins, bobbed out under the waterfall from a cave hidden behind the curtain. At positions around the pool, jumping from rocks or boulders, were children of varying ages. They might have been water nymphs at play. It was an otherworldly scene, more idyllic than any vista she had ever dreamed up.

Delight was quickly eclipsed by covetous sorrow. How unbearable that this place had already been discovered, and claimed. Fable was about to slink away when she was spotted. Silence descended on the pool, all eyes trained on the strange, strawberry-blonde girl unexpectedly in their midst.

The elfin-faced girl stepped forward on the high platform, face exultant as though espying a great prize. She executed a pert dive and leapt out to stand before Fable, dripping prettily.

'Who are *you*?' she cried, blue eyes devouring Fable. Everything about this ravenous girl made Fable want to back away.

'My name's . . . Fae.'

'I'm Adriana Hull. Are you here on holidays?'

'I'm just up from Canberra.'

'How old are you?'

'Thirteen next month.'

'I'm turning thirteen in October,' Adriana said. 'Having a huge party. *Huge.*'

Fable found herself surrounded by young people now.

Adriana motioned grandly. 'This is *our* waterhole. We call it the Glade. And this is our Glade Gang. We're mostly all cousins, except for Christy; she's my *best* friend. And the Lagorio boys, they're identical twins. Can you tell them apart?'

One Lagorio boy grinned at Fable. 'I'm Marco, and that mop's Vince.' His mirror image nodded, not looking at her.

A young woman, of Sonnet's age, grinned from the shallows. 'Howdy! I'm Kate Hardy, a cousin. This is my kid brother, Eddy.' A young boy stared beside her. From a cliff ledge, a teenage boy sang out, 'Hey, I'm Ben! The best-looking Hardy.'

Kate chortled.

Two boys at higher jumping positions offered no greetings.

'Oh, the Ravellis are here, too,' Adriana said, nodding in their direction.

Flanking Adriana now, a slim girl eyed Fable charily. 'I'm Christy *Logan*,' she announced.

Fable's hand lifted weakly.

Adriana moved closer still. 'I have two older brothers as well. Rafferty lives in Brisbane, he's at *university*! And my other brother is Eamon. He's fifteen. But he's working on the harvest today.'

Fable's gaze slipped free of Adriana's. She dipped a toe in the water.

'Got your togs on underneath?' asked Adriana.

Fable shook her head, patting her blouse; perfectly pressed by Sonnet.

'Bring them tomorrow then! We'll be here. But you can stay now, watch us do some dives.'

With that, the ruckus resumed. A series of dives followed. Fable smiled courteously at each diver, eyes darting away between performances to study their Glade. Adriana saved her dive for last, pulling it off with elaborate flourish, to Christy *Logan's* enthusiastic albeit unsmiling applause.

The next morning, Fable raced out of the cottage straight after breakfast, togs beneath plaid shirtwaist dress, well-worn towel under her arm, and an exasperated Sonnet waving a ladle at her from the stoop: 'Be home for lunch!'

For an hour she sat and stewed at the waterhole, ears pricking over the waterfall rush for approaching children, hesitant of shifting a leaf out of place before the Glade's rightful owners had returned.

Then, with gust of laughter, the Glade was filled again. Not a person looked surprised to see her there, especially not Adriana.

'Can you swim, Fae?' she asked, tossing an apple core into the forest deep. 'Come under the waterfall with me!'

Together they stroked towards the curtain of water.

'Deep breath on three and follow me under!'

Heart pounding, Fable copied Adriana's dolphin dive. She surfaced in a cavernous hollow where Adriana waited, eyes agleam. They scrambled up onto a rock plateau, wider than a bed, and sat blinking wetly at one another behind the sheer, backlit screen of falling water.

'This is *our* cave. When I was little, I'd bring my baby dolls in here and play mums and dads. Eamon used to hide out here when he was going to get another flogging from Pa. But you can't get under here in the Wet when the creek floods. Even Raff can't, and he's a top-notch swimmer!'

'It's more magical than anything I've ever seen,' Fable said, hugging her legs.

Adriana nodded, as though it was exactly what she'd expected to hear. She slid from the rock. 'Can you high dive? Come and have a turn from the tree house!'

Fable followed her obediently out into the pool. They came to a floating stop beneath the platform.

'Oi! Ladder!' shouted Adriana.

A handmade rope ladder fell, uncoiling, for the girls to climb. At the top, Marco Lagorio greeted Fable with puppyish cheer.

'Hullo, newie!'

She grinned.

The wooden tree house, cantilevered over the creek from the cliff, had huge windows open to the forest and a tiny veranda, complete with handrails. Fable felt as though she were shrouded in the canopy itself.

'This is gorgeous,' she breathed. 'Who made it?'

'My brother, Raff. Designed it all himself,' Adriana said. 'Now, watch me jump!'

She scaled the handrail and took hold of a rope dangling by. Seconds later she was whooping out over the pool, and plummeting down.

'She's so brave,' Fable gawped.

Adriana surfaced on a shout. 'Come on, Fae! *Jump!*'

'Ah, Adriana likes to show off,' Marco said, coming to stand beside her. 'But tell her to jump off the top of the waterfall – she won't do it! We call that jump "No Fear",' he said, pointing to the name painted on the cliff face.

Even as they watched, an older boy was scaling the cliff to the No Fear ledge.

'That's Eamon,' Marco said as a cocky, dark-haired boy executed a perfect backflip from the towering rock.

Fable covered her mouth, and Marco chuckled. 'They're *all* show-offs in that family. Eamon's been known to do it blindfolded before.'

'*Fae!*' Adriana hollered, splashing impatiently. 'Hurry up and jump, you big chicken!'

Fable backed away from the edge. 'I can't.'

'You don't have to,' Marco said, gesturing at the forest path behind. 'That way takes you back to the pool. Try one of the baby jumps first.'

Baby? Fable was affronted. She was on the railing and sailing over the edge, before she'd even processed her intention. The surprise of cool water registered simultaneously with the shock of her impulsivity. She surfaced to rousing cheers and whistles.

Only Marco, still standing on the platform, witnessed the splash of rage across Adriana Hull's pretty features.

Fable returned each day to the Glade, and her new gang. On the last Saturday morning before school, a fractious Sonnet – fed up with the daily disappearing act and the accumulation of rocks, berries and seeds along Fable's window seat – detained her for a morning of chores.

Fable was standing on a pile of encyclopaedias in a second-hand school dress with Sonnet kneeling at her ankles, pins in the corners of her mouth, when Adriana announced herself loudly at the screen door. Both Hamilton sisters looked up in startled unison.

'So much for taking a while to fit in, *Olive*.' Sonnet smirked, elbowing Fable forward.

Adriana was their first official visitor and Sonnet sprang immediately into the kind of saccharine hostess-playing Fable thought only little girls disposed to. She bit her tongue, following closely behind Adriana.

'I've never been inside the old Hamilton cottage,' Adriana said, eyes scouring their humble abode.

Sonnet peppered Adriana with a thousand questions on Noah Vale and Adriana answered it all in her self-aggrandising way. Fable was thrown into toe-curling discomfort by the unexpected meeting of no-longer-secret friend and nosy sister, unease only intensifying when Adriana slipped an arm through hers in a show of alliance. The revelation of her real name by an oblivious Sonnet passed uneventfully, with only the barest flicker from Adriana betraying intrigue.

But the interview, however cringe-worthy, had the desired effect: liberation!

CHAPTER 4

SUMMERLINN

A cloudless bowl of cobalt blue arched overhead as Sonnet walked Fable to the quiet country road along which the Noah Vale school bus trundled each morning. Plum stumbled along beside Fable, pulling at her hand.

Fable sat on her school port beside the row of barrel mailboxes doubling as bus stop, and fixed her impassive gaze on the bend in the road. With every whimper from clinging Plum, Fable stilled further. Only the quiver of her chin hinted at hidden turbulence.

Olive had insisted she could drive the girls into school for Fable's first day, and had been rightly spurned. As if Sonnet was letting *her* take control of this momentous occasion!

The school bus rumbled into view and instantly Fable was on her feet, straightening her faded uniform and scanning the windows for Adriana's face. There she was, on the back row, waving Fable imperiously to a saved seat. Fable darted out of Plum's crying grasp and in the clatter of a door was gone.

Sonnet waited until the red dust had settled, before the smile fell from her lips. For the first time since Mama had passed, the Hamilton girls were going their separate ways. Sonnet swallowed a lump, scooped a protesting Plum onto the angular jut of her hip and turned for home.

The morning dragged, plagued as Sonnet was by a gnawing disquiet. Plum wandered forlornly around the house, asking for her sister.

Sonnet busied herself getting to know the ancient Singer lugged out of the hall cupboard. By afternoon, she'd mastered the tetchy machine, even running up some skirts for chubby-kneed Plum, who was now engaged with a grand heirloom doll's house given over, reluctantly, by Olive.

Mama had purportedly played happy families with the Victorian doll's house for many years – far longer, Olive had murmured, than most girls were wont to do. Plum had fallen in love with it, too. And each time Sonnet glanced at Plum sitting with the doll's house in a pool of lacy sunlight, she nursed a glow of smug victory: Olive thwarted yet again.

Olive had originally shown Plum the doll's house at Heartwood, knowing full well that Plum would demand to stay and play with it in her newly kitted-out playroom.

'Let her be with us for a few hours,' Olive had petitioned, as Plum was dragged away, wailing, to the cottage.

Handing Plum over for *any* length of time was a step too far. Plum had sobbed for the dollhouse each time Olive had visited the cottage – which was, much to Sonnet's chagrin, still every day.

'Just checking how you girls are getting on,' Olive always said, expertly manoeuvring herself in between screen door and frame. After each visit, Sonnet cursed Olive's name louder still.

I see you chipping away at Plum, at all of us!

Eventually, Olive had confronted Sonnet directly about her unwillingness to relinquish Plum. And Sonnet had replied from the heart.

'I'm scared of anything happening while I'm not there to protect her. I can't lose anyone else – the girls are all I have left.'

'Oh, Sonnet,' Olive had cried, reaching for her. 'You're *not* alone anymore, you have us!'

'No, we're only neighbours,' Sonnet had retorted, moving safely away. 'All we Hamilton girls have is each other.'

Nevertheless, the following day, Gav had helped Olive carry the doll's house down to the cottage for the girls to keep. Conceding defeat, as far as Sonnet was concerned.

Sonnet was putting the final row of rickrack on a basic apron when, through the window, a figure in a blue pinafore caught her eye: Fable, plodding slowly down the hill, afternoon sunlight glinting off her strawberry locks. Imperceptible to another, but not Sonnet's keen eye, was the dejected stoop of Fable's shoulders. Sonnet stood for a long moment considering this, as Plum swooped out of the door to meet her sister.

She watched Fable squeeze her baby sister, face contorting against tears. But by the time Fable reached the cottage, and Sonnet, calm had descended over her delicate features.

Fable was largely non-communicative for the remainder of the evening, and the rest of the week. Her teacher was fine, her class was fine, her lunch was fine, her friends were fine; everything was *fine*. And yet, each day, that shining head dipped a little lower, her shoulders hunched further over as she traipsed down the hill.

When Fable slouched through the door on Friday afternoon, head sunk to her chest, the fist around Sonnet's heart clenched too tightly to be borne a moment longer. Enough! Outright interrogation might push Fable further into her shell, but it was a risk that must be taken.

Sonnet forced Fable onto the couch as she tried to slink by. 'Fable, this can't go on. I know you're hurting – and I want to know *why*. Is it Mama? Or is it something else? Are you not fitting in at school?'

Silence.

Masked amber eyes.

More sisterly pleas.

Then, with a wail, the dam broke – dignified guardedness crumbling all at once. Fable wept, face buried in the upholstery, shoulders heaving.

'Oh, Fabes.' Gentle now, stroking her arm. 'I'm sorry, sweetheart. I knew you were upset, but I didn't want to make you *cry*. Please tell me, Fable.'

Muffled sobbing continued unabated for several minutes. Plum sat transfixed nearby, mouth lolling open.

'I'll get you some tissues,' Sonnet said, watching tears and snot coagulate on the old couch. As she rose, a slim arm flew out to stop her. Sonnet eased back down.

Fable began on a sob. 'They say Mama was – oh I can't!'

'She was *what*?'

'They're all saying she was the . . . "town floozy".'

Shock slammed Sonnet back against the couch.

'That she seduced a married man. And you, Sonnet, you're his bastard. We're all bastards!'

Guttural sobbing took over.

'Who says this!'

'*Everyone.*'

'No, be specific. It's a vicious lie. *Who?*'

Big, glittering eyes locked tragically with hers. 'Christy Logan to begin with – she spread it round the first day of school. Then she and Adriana ganged up on me, and now they're all saying it about Mama . . . and us. No one wants to talk to me, they all hate me, and Adriana won't even look at me, except to sneer. The story's been getting worse every day – we're homewreckers and Mama was a harlot! I didn't even know what that meant until I found it in the dictionary . . .' Her face coloured.

Rage blew Sonnet physically from the couch. 'That snake in the grass! How *dare* she come round here pretending to be a friend then spread *such lies*! Backstabbing, malevolent little—' She checked herself. 'Well, it's not your problem anymore, Fabes.'

She considered her sisters for a moment, already decided. 'Fable, dry your eyes. I want you to take Plum to Heartwood. Stay with Olive while I sort this out!'

Fable snivelled. 'But where are you going?'

'To the source of the rumour. I'm going to squash her . . . *it*, for good.'

Sonnet hurried the girls up the hill muttering perfunctory directives on safe passage and best behaviour, even as her eyes were making a head start for the creek, and the family living beyond it.

'Quick, on you go! I'll see you in a sec!'

Sonnet swivelled towards the cane bridge crossing. Swelling rage had become a flood, which could not be contained.

The Hulls' grand homestead, proud and regal in the slanting light, was surrounded by mango trees and encompassed by a full-length veranda. A hanging sign announced the property as Summerlinn.

The woman who stepped out to greet her at the top step was handsomely statuesque, with dark hair swept into a French roll. Still on the bottom step, Sonnet was at a distinct height disadvantage.

'Are you Adriana Hull's mother?' Sonnet blurted in her rush to expunge indignation.

'I am indeed,' she answered, blue eyes scouring Sonnet with the same avidity as her daughter. 'I am better known, however, as Delia Hull. And there's no mistaking who *you* are. You have Esther Hamilton written all over you.'

'Sonnet Hamilton,' she said, fist clenching by her hip.

'We wondered when we'd finally meet the daughters Esther kept hidden away. I called by Olive's the other day to see you, but she told us you needed more time, apparently, to settle in. Come inside, won't you,' she said, indicating her stylish front parlour.

'No. I won't stay. I came to voice my disgust with your daughter's behaviour at school recently, as it concerns my younger sister, Fable.'

Finely shaped brows arched high. 'Whatever could you mean?'

Sonnet stepped onto the veranda and straightened to full height, rectifying the customary stoop of a tall girl accustomed to lowering herself for others.

Delia waited; a shrewd silence, meted out with expert patience.

'Mrs Hull, your daughter has been waging a campaign of lies against my sister at school. Fable so recently lost her mother – she's a grieving girl, who only wants to fit into her new school – and to have some chit spreading such rumours about our mama is beyond cruel. I insist you stop her.'

Delia's eyes widened. '*Our* Adriana would never condone such maliciousness. What sort of things could you possibly have heard?'

'I think you already know.'

'I assure you, I have no interest in petty playground squabbles. I suggest you rise above it, too.'

'I wouldn't call the kind of slander your daughter's been spewing a "playground squabble"!'

Delia gave a curtly dismissive wave.

Sonnet took full measure of the woman before her: no one challenged Delia Hull. Her voice shook. 'Calling our mother the town harlot, accusing her of being a whore and a homewrecker – I can't imagine where a supposedly well-to-do girl would learn such foul language. Perhaps you can enlighten me?'

Delia's eyes flashed. 'If, as *you* claim, my daughter had been using such terms, she could only be repeating the general gist of what's being said all over Noah. What's been said for years now—'

'How *dare* you!'

'Lower your voice.'

'Don't tell me how loud I can be! You don't even *know* my mother!'

'Ha! I knew your mother all right. She was in my sister Beth's grade at school' and we grew up together, playing by Serpentine Creek. I knew Esther extremely well – though none of us could have guessed what she was truly capable of. More importantly, the Brennans were our *dearest* friends. Esther Hamilton was everything you've heard. And if your sister's feelings are hurt by that truth, remember your mother brought it all on herself, and you, too.'

The Brennans? No, don't get out of your depth; do not give her the upper hand!

'I am telling you: control your vicious little viper!'

A hard smile twisted Delia's lips. 'I can't prevent my daughter hearing what she hears. All of Noah is abuzz with the news – how can Adriana be expected to think any differently?'

Sonnet felt the snarl rising in her throat, and did nothing to stop it. '*You* set the right example, that's how! *You* refrain from being a spiteful old gossip. Teach her to think for herself without parroting the stupidity of others.'

Delia drew back as though whipped. 'Believe me; Adriana will keep her distance from you *Hamiltons*. I will personally see to it she has nothing further to do with a ruined woman's trashy daughters.'

The front door slammed, stained glass roses reverberating.

Sonnet thundered from the veranda. She turned back, only once, at the border of mango trees, to holler at the quiet facade, 'With families like *yours*, no wonder my mother left this bloody town!'

CHAPTER 5

SINS OF THE MOTHER

The moment she was on the Hamilton side of the creek, Sonnet collapsed. She slammed fists and tears into the peaty earth.

'Damn the Hulls, damn them all to hell!'

Sonnet picked herself up and sprinted until the tears sluiced clear, and exertion began to purge angst – never before had running felt quite so much like prayer. She did not stop until she'd reached Heartwood.

Olive hurried down the stairs, arms open. 'As soon as Fable said where you'd gone, I just *knew*!'

Sonnet pushed her embrace away, gasping for air. 'Why didn't you *tell* me what this town's like? Where was the forewarning?'

'I tried, Sonnet, I did! On the phone, when you were first trying to decide whether to come to Noah, and the other night over dinner, I tried again.'

'Not hard enough! I let Fable walk right into it, with no preparation! She's *gutted*. How could any young girl bear to hear her mother crucified like that? I can't believe I brought her to this hellhole!'

'I didn't know what your mother had already told you, and you made it abundantly clear it wasn't *my* place to pry. You've been so determined and self-assured. I tried to not interfere. It's what you wanted.'

'I feel like you tricked me into coming to Noah Vale! And right now I don't know who to believe, or *what* to think!'

Olive's eyes glistened. 'Come up and have some dinner, then we'll talk. I'll tell you anything you want to know.'

Merely picked-at dinner sat in Sonnet's stomach like a rock as she hunched over the table, waiting for Olive to begin. Across the valley, a cane fire raged against the darkness. From within the house, came the sound of Plum's squeals and Fable's restrained giggle as Gav guided them through a comedic washing-up routine, while reciting 'Mulga Bill's Bicycle'. Zephyr's barks completed the cacophony.

'Your mother's history,' Olive started, 'was partly why I pushed so hard to have you girls staying here with us, to cushion your arrival against any reproach.'

'About the Great Big Dirty Secret, you mean? The one you deliberately kept from me before I uprooted my grief-stricken sisters from their home and dragged them to the middle of Woop Woop? The truth you could have given me over the telephone instead of tricking me into accepting our inheritance?'

'You have no idea how I struggled with that decision. You don't broach the topic of a young woman's controversial paternity over the phone, so soon after her mother's tragic passing.'

Sonnet folded her arms. 'Get on with it!'

Olive poured herself a cuppa with a trembling hand, and was waved away when she moved to fill Sonnet's cup.

'Who had you been led to believe your father was, Sonnet?'

'An itinerant fruit picker, couple of years older, not from Noah.'

Olive's face was expressionless. Sonnet hurried to add bolstering detail. 'It was a brief thing and he bolted when he found out I was on the way. Mama didn't even know his last name if I wanted to track him down one day. But my loyalty is to the parent who *wanted* me. The shame of being a "bastard" is always there, but when you spend your whole life pretending your father doesn't exist, paternity eventually ceases to be an issue. Until suddenly it is for a whole *town*!'

Olive didn't reply for a long time.

Sonnet felt incalculably childish, sick with expectant fear.

'First,' Olive said quietly, 'you must understand how Essie came to be in a ... vulnerable position. Your mother, as you probably know, was terribly bright. Our father often said, "too clever for her own good". He tried talking her out of continuing her education, after she turned fourteen. What good are *books* to a girl that beautiful, he reckoned. But Es's ambitions went beyond us all. She was a talented writer – good outlet for the feelings she couldn't contain, actually. And she had such *dreams* for herself. Wouldn't let anyone tell her to keep her feet on the ground, much less abide Father's refusal to send her to university. Declared she was going to "write her way out of this damned valley!" And to that end, in her final year of high school, Esther was being tutored for a scholarship ...'

Olive veered away, regathering herself.

'Maybe if I'd still been living at home, I'd have seen warning signs in your mother, before it was too late. But your grandparents never suspected a thing. When she wanted to, Esther had a way of dazzling you – like light shone in your eyes, big shadows behind it.'

Sonnet shivered, thinking of another Hamilton daughter, and her adamantine mask, both light and shade hidden.

'No one saw it coming. I was newly married to Gav in those days, and we were living above his shop. I was wrapped up then in my own ... troubles.' Anguish twisted Olive's face.

Sonnet had no sympathy – only impatience.

Olive took a breath, and launched. 'Sonnet, I'm sorry, your mother was not involved with a fruit picker passing through. In fact, he was one of our best-loved townsfolk. Esther was having an affair with her vice-principal. He was ten years older. And married, with young children, including a very complicated boy who required constant care and supervision.

'The affair was finally revealed in the most appalling circumstances. They were discovered at the Graduation Ball doing . . . that . . . on the school stage. Someone had . . . the curtain was pulled back.'

Sonnet looked away, fixing her gaze on the firelit horizon.

'It was a shocking scandal. Just *shocking*.'

'And then I came,' Sonnet said, voice leaden.

'Not straightaway, no. The fallout from the affair was bad enough. One of our best-loved teachers sacked! The family left Noah Vale. Within weeks of the affair being revealed, they were gone. But he was the fortunate one – disappearing into the big smoke, where he was anonymous. Your mother, meanwhile, was left pining for her lover, thrown out of school, reviled by her parents, and trapped in this town with all the judgement and outrage. And then she was sporting a swollen belly on that tiny frame of hers.

'It wasn't long before Esther got wind of Father's plan to send her to a home for unwed mothers. She wouldn't hear of it! Father was offering her the opportunity to shed herself of . . . the very stain of sin. But Es would never surrender when she took her mind to a thing. Said they'd have to pry you from her dead hands first. Father called her the "valley whore" and threw her out. Not long after, Esther fled, never to return . . .' Olive's tale ended on a low, weak note. She studied her niece for a reaction, but Sonnet was a cold, carefully blinking statue.

Within: a blizzard.

It hurt Sonnet to utter a single word. 'Is that the sum of it?'

'The whole sordid tale.'

52

Sonnet had an extraordinary urge to pick up Olive's cuppa and dash it in her face. 'So, you're saying my very existence was the end of an esteemed teacher's career, presumably the finish of his marriage and family, too, that Mama spent the rest of her life alienated from her family, wandering the earth like some leprous biblical prostitute, and as if that weren't awful enough, I have come to the one priggish place on earth where I am most despised for it?'

Olive reached to take her hand, but Sonnet was faster to withdraw. Olive did not, Sonnet noted, deny her summary.

'That's it – we're leaving!' Sonnet cried, pushing back her chair, ready to fly away and pack.

'No, no, you mustn't blame yourself! Your mother's mistakes were her own; no one in this town will blame you.'

'That's funny, Olive. Because it sure seems like they do!'

'They can be judgemental busybodies, but they don't blame you girls. Memories are long in this town, but forgiveness, no, *acceptance*, will come quickly despite this initial reception.'

'It doesn't look promising from where I sit.'

'Be patient, and you'll see. *I* promise.'

Sonnet ground her teeth, gauging the weight of Olive's assurance. 'So, what, I'm supposed to lie low, and just wait for them to get over themselves?'

'Something like that. Have you heard the saying: "You catch more flies with honey than vinegar"?'

'In other words, be *nice* no matter what? I doubt you'd be giving the same advice to a nephew. Only women are expected to be *nice* all the time. Don't think this comes as a surprise to you, but I'm not a laying-low kind of girl.'

'Think of it as "killing them with kindness" then.'

'The killing I can do.' Sonnet matched Olive's pursed lips with thrusting chin. 'I mean it! The next time someone humiliates my sister, they'll have *me* to deal with!'

'I can understand the impulse, even if it's counterproductive. If you flounce around Main Street ruffling feathers everywhere, you'll only breathe new controversy into the memory of Esther Hamilton, make it harder for them to see you girls in your own light.'

'If this town is hell-bent on making us feel unwelcome, I'm taking the girls out of here.'

'Give us a try, that's all I'm saying.'

'I already did!'

'A proper try, dear. Don't *quit* at the first hurdle.'

Sonnet glowered. How quickly this woman had learned her tender spots.

'Look,' Olive said, placating now, 'you've claimed your inheritance, you've got enough money to set yourselves up wherever you please. You don't *really* need us, or this town. But give us a chance. We are family, like it or not, and I think we'll be good family to you. Don't cast us in with the sneering gossips – let us prove we're different. In the end, this *was* Esther's home.'

Sonnet mulled this over. She truly wasn't indebted to this town, but she was hungry, after so many rootless, roving years, for a home and community of her own. Noah Vale had offered a place of belonging, at last. And maybe waiting out small-town prejudices was a bearable price to pay.

She sighed. 'So, I'm supposed to take the bad with the good, until the ruckus dies down?'

Olive nodded, hope gathering at the corners of her mouth.

'But *then* they'll forget about Mama?' It was a warning, more than a question.

'I promise. You won't regret it, Sonnet. Hang in there, and you'll come to love Noah Vale as much as we do.'

Sonnet did not look convinced. 'There's one more thing. Then I won't *ever* speak of this with you again. I want to know that *reprobate's* name.'

Olive flinched at this insult. Sonnet enjoyed the effect.

That's right, you heard me: reprobate!

'His name was Archer Brennan,' Olive said. 'He came to Noah Vale as a new teacher, fresh from college. Was meant to be a short-term rural posting, but the town and students adored him. Then he married a much-loved local girl – one of the Logans. Archer was made vice-principal by the time he was twenty-six.'

'And he had children?'

'Two boys. They'd be, oh let's see, a few years older than you. Their younger boy was born with severe issues. I've often wondered how they got on with that poor lad. Archer was devoted to him – as wonderful a father as he was a teacher. That's why it was so shockingly out of character for him to have taken up with a schoolgirl, why people accused Esther of having bewitched him. And for Delia Hull, it was quite personal. She was—'

'Stop! I don't care what that harpy thought of Mama! I only wanted his name so I don't have all Main Street laughing at me as I run smack bang into the man who sired me.'

'There'll be no chance of meeting Archer. I'm sorry to tell you he passed away about two years ago. Cancer – he was riddled with it. The funeral notice appeared in our paper. It was tragic to see your mother's name in the same column only a year later, like a sad epilogue.'

Sonnet extended her chin. 'Enough. Don't ever mention him again.'

'You're a brave girl,' Olive said, 'stronger even than I first gave you credit for. I think you'll lead the next generation of Hamilton girls into a beautiful new future in Noah.'

Sonnet harrumphed, shrugging off Olive's mawkish words. But that was exactly what she planned to do. One of Mama's favourite quotes drifted to her then, as though carried on the breeze of burnt molasses: 'My drops of tears, I'll turn to sparks of fire.'

Yes, Mama. We'll show them all, the whole bloody lot of them!

Unseen and unheard on the veranda, Fable's slim shadow eased away from the open shutters.

PART TWO

'But I hate to hear you talking so like a fine gentleman, and as if women were all fine ladies, instead of rational creatures. We none of us expect to be in smooth water all our days.'

Jane Austen, *Persuasion*

PART TWO

CHAPTER 6

THE GREEN WOMAN

Winter 1955

After that night, Fable knew what she must do next, though it took four weeks to summon the courage. Four long, lonely weeks, in which she came to imagine herself as a tiny crustacean stripped of her pearlescent shell, and left under the white-hot tropical sun to bake alive. The glare of peer opinion and recrimination was unbearable, yet bear it she must.

Each day, Sonnet dragged her out of bed and marched her bodily to the bus stop. Each day, Fable made herself as smooth and flat as a creek-polished stone. And it worked – the insults appeared to roll right off. In fact, with her aloofness and eyes shaded like lamps, Fable was deemed 'stuck up!' by her detractors.

Her critics were many, and strident. Adriana, the ringleader, Christy, her loyal, rapid deputy, and a gaggle of she-geese honking after them . . .

'Bastard!'

'Fable's got her mother's legs, easily spread!'

'Your mother's the town bicycle – everyone's had a ride!'

'Daughter of a whore!'

'Home-wrecking Hamiltons!'

And, much to the amusement of the teachers who had caught wind of the latest slur: 'Aesops!'

Well, at least *that one* was witty, they concurred in staffroom whispers, and proved the little blighters paid attention some of the time. Besides, anyone who gave their daughter such a ridiculous name should also have equipped her with the backbone to handle it. Everyone knew kids were bound to be cruel.

All the while, Fable had Sonnet's bustling bravado in her ear: 'If you hit back, they win. They're just bullies, ignore them and you take away their power. Don't let them get to you. They'll soon forget about it.'

Fable looked stubbornly away from her sister's piercing gaze, and past the hate-contorted faces greeting her at every bend, as though they were gargoyles fashioned into the buildings themselves.

Nightmares plagued her. Haunting visions played out across the unfamiliar tropical landscape, filled with the terrible unravelling of family, love and safety. Always, in every dream, Fable was searching for a mother locked away in an unseen room, Mama's voice fading out as Fable scrabbled desperately to get a foothold, or move an inch forward.

In her waking hours, she chased the face of her mother – and it eluded her there, too. She could summon any other face – imagined or otherwise – yet her mother stayed a darkened silhouette.

Fable blamed herself. She had rejected her mother's memory, and spurned those ephemeral sunroom visits when she turned her ear to the malicious slander of these Noah Vale children. She had let them make her mother a stranger.

But no more! If she had a hope of seeing her mother's face again, or feeling her presence in the near-waking veil, then dull their voices she must. She would find that beloved face and never let it go.

Yesterday afternoon she had evaded Sonnet's supervisio
to Heartwood. Olive, weeding her pineapple patch, squi
ingly at the young niece who appeared before her, backlit by io.
Fable offered a weak pretence about needing to consult an encyclopae-
dia from the living-room library, and Olive waved her inside without
probing.

Fable had spotted a row of photo albums in Heartwood's towering bookshelf weeks ago. They were heavy, formal and bursting at the
seams with old photographs. Each time Olive attempted to bring out
the albums at the Heartwood dinner table, Sonnet terminated the
conversation. She would tolerate Olive's Hamilton stories only so far,
and photos were overstepping by leaps and bounds.

Fable knew it was a betrayal of her older sister to seek the albums.
Guiltily, she pulled a pile onto her lap, hands tripping over each other
in her flipping rush.

The albums lost their illicit pull almost immediately. The faces and
houses and landmarks were alien to her. She was flicking through
strangers' lives, rendered in washed-out sepia, and black and white
tones.

A lump formed in Fable's throat as she realised she'd reached the
second-last album without spotting a single image of her mother –
only empty, yellowing slots where her mother's luminous face must
once have beamed. The Hamiltons had expunged all evidence of their
daughter when they expelled her. What kind of person tried to wipe
out even the memory of their child?

On the very last page, beneath tissue guard, Fable found what she
was looking for. Young Esther, in grainy black and white. She was not
much older than Fable now, albeit curling at the edges, and fast fading.
But it was *Mama*, all the same.

With immense relief, Fable rested her eyes upon the image of her mother: heart-shaped face of gentle slopes, wide-set eyes, Cupid's bow on full, pouting lips, and fine, small nose.

Fable slipped the photograph from its corner mounts and pocketed it, before streaking out of Heartwood past Olive's carefully turned back as she stood chopping at the kitchen bench.

A week later, the photo was a talisman hidden in the pocket of her school dress, as she nestled high within the shadowy heart of a banyan tree. Under the school building, boys were playing 'Beamey' – lobbing tennis balls against the bearers.

The school library sat on the opposite side of the quadrangle, waiting. No one frequented the library at lunch, and none of the Beamey players paid her any heed. For a week running, Fable had returned to the banyan, ready to enact her plan; unable to cross the last fifty yards. Now, it was *time*.

With a decisive jolt, Fable slid down the root tendrils, determined not to baulk again. Inside the library, all was silence. A ceiling fan stoked the warm air. The librarian, looking up from a sandwich, shot her an obligatory glare, accompanied by a shushing finger.

Fable nodded meekly, making straight for the wall of gilt-framed photographs beyond the concertina door of the study annex. Decades of staff, graduating classes and school captains adorned this glory wall.

He was sure to be here, somewhere.

Fable cast a look over her shoulder, but Mrs Kent, back still turned, was busy catching sandwich debris.

First, to find Mama. Quickly, she scanned the years until she found the Graduating Class and Staff of Noah Vale School, 1935. She skimmed across the many rows of clean-cut, grinning boys to the single row of primly seated girls; all gangly and ungainly, still not grown into themselves. Except for one.

Esther.

She glittered within that line like a crystal caught in a blade of light; natural sensuality and poise combining to alluring effect. In the midst of those adolescent girls, Esther alone was a woman. Even in black and white, she was no less startling.

Fable had to force her eyes away, resisting the urge to sink against the glass itself. She hadn't come for Mama, not this time. It was *him* she was after. She searched the staff names listed below, locating the face matched to 'Archer Brennan, Vice-Principal'.

He stood as the tallest of the male teachers, in the centre of the back row – blindingly handsome, blond and young. Fable studied his face for Sonnet and found her there in his height and posture, the attractive angularity of features, the athleticism of his form. This was where the strength of Sonnet's presence came from.

Sonnet's *father*, Fable mouthed incredulously. The very concept of belonging, by blood, to a man was outlandish to her young mind. Her whole life, all she'd known was the bosom of sisterhood. Here, at last, was a male wellspring.

For the longest time Fable simply stood, beholding his proud face, seeking to understand it all. She thumbed tentatively back through the pages of an imaginary family photo album – the only one the Hamilton girls had ever known – seeing, with dawning clarity every gaping, ugly hole Archer Brennan might have filled.

Slowly then, softly, revelation came to settle upon her heart.

When finally she turned and left the library, it was into an entirely new world.

For the first time in a month, Fable slept dreamlessly. In the wee hours, she awoke with a ragged start, aware of a presence hovering inches above her own. The floating weight seemed to draw back as Fable opened her eyes. She clutched at empty air and fell back against the pillow, surveying her dark bedroom. The moonlight filtering through her curtains offered insufficient illumination of the mysterious hollows and shapes of this yet-unfamiliar room. There was a flash of movement, near her armoire. Were her eyes deceiving her, or was that not the trail of a green gown susurrating away through the French doors?

Fable flew from the bed, knocking her bony elbows against the dresser in her rush to catch the dress, and its wearer. The hallway was empty; moonlight through the front door lay as a long bar over the wood floor. A shadow moved across the pane of glass.

Fable hurried up the hallway and eased out of the door, breath held in anticipation of its telltale screech.

Night air hit with unexpected chill. She paused, rubbing goose pimples away, her thin nightdress proving inadequate for the first time in this tropical winter.

The garden gate squealed ahead, and the cold was forgotten. Fable surged down the stoop and across the garden path, certain now of what she could see, melting into the darkness of the creek: a barefoot, fleeing woman, wearing a beaded ballgown.

'*Mama!*'

Heedless of wakening Sonnet, Fable threw open the gate and tore into the gloom. The grass was cold and slimy underfoot. The forest wall rose out of mist, a looming blackness in the pale moonglow.

Fable strained for Mama's fleeing figure. She was heading, by instinct, for the train bridge when she espied a glimmering further north: moonshine catching shimmering peridot, as the woman faded into the forest. Fable turned smoothly in a northward direction, and into the thick fortress of trees.

A scream rent the predawn darkness apart, tearing Olive from slumber. She was out on the veranda, chest thumping, in what felt like a single leap. Behind her, Gav crashed about for a flashlight. Zephyr's paws scrabbled madly at the door, seeking release.

'Olive! Gav!'

Olive scoured the darkness. The scream was coming down Orchard Hill.

'Sonnet?!'

The veranda light flipped on, and Gav arrived at her side with a flashlight. The light arced into the garden, striking upon Sonnet, sprinting across the grass, with Plum wrapped around her waist.

'Sonnet!'

Olive and Gav banged down the stairs and Sonnet came slamming into them, throwing Plum into Olive's arms.

'Fable's disappeared! You have to take Plum for me!'

'What do you mean she's disappeared?'

'I don't know – she's missing!'

'Could she be curled asleep under something?'

'No! I've checked everywhere – she might be drowning in the creek! Just take Plummy!'

'Don't get ahead of yourself,' said Gav. 'Sure she's not in the loo?'

'I searched there straightaway.'

'But why would she go outside?'

Sonnet gave an exasperated scream. 'Olive, she's *gone*, I need to search! Will you help me or not?'

Gav thrust a flashlight into Sonnet's hands. 'Here. I'll grab another. Fable can't be far, we'll find her together.'

'Hurry, Gav.' Sonnet turned despairing eyes on Olive. 'I heard *screams*. That's what woke me. I couldn't bear the sound. I went to check on Fable, and she was gone. Even when I was running up here, I heard them again – such God-awful screams.'

'You need to calm down,' Olive said, covering Plum's ears. 'You're scaring her. If Fable's screaming and you can hear it, she must be close! We'll follow the sound.'

'She sounds so heartbroken.'

Gav walloped down the stairs, Zephyr hot on his tail.

'Let's go. Olive, you wait at the cottage for her.'

Up Orchard Hill they charged, voices impeaching Fable in unison, torchlight raking black foliage. Down the slope they ran, bellowing, to the cottage. Olive ducked inside while Sonnet and Gav turned towards Serpentine Creek.

'It's going to be morning soon,' he soothed.

Sure enough, profound blackness was lifting to grey; shapes separating out. Even as she watched, the dark vein of creek distinguished itself from the void.

'It's those screams. I can't get them out of my head.'

Gav pulled her into his large armpit. 'Don't immediately think the worst, pet. She can't be too lost, she's a Hamilton; this land's in her blood. We'll make for the train crossing and check the bottom of Hulls' first.'

Their shouts seemed to chase the night away, light hastening into the world to aid their search. Crushing dewed spider webs underfoot, they charged across the paddock. Nearing the creek rush, the plangent keening started again.

'Oh, Gav!' Sonnet cried, clutching at him. *Don't take her too. I won't survive it!*

Gav gave Sonnet a squeeze. 'Pet, that's just the curlews calling. "Wailing Women" they call them. Flamin' awful-sounding birds they are at night, don't blame you for thinking someone's being murdered—' He cut off, abruptly. 'Come on, we'll find her in a flash, safe and sound.'

For an hour they searched the track along Serpentine Creek, until the trail turned away into canefields and, ultimately, the road into town.

'If she's gone that way, a car will spot her soon enough. Best we double back up the creek,' Gav said.

North of the train bridge, Gav led Sonnet up an overgrown trail running along the Hamilton side. Branches thrust into their faces, tree roots slithered over each other in the rush to topple them. Sonnet yelped as a viciously barbed vine tore into her limbs.

'Get it off me!'

'Flamin' wait-a-while,' Gav cursed. 'No time to wait today.' He ripped her free. Blood beaded along her skin.

Panic sought to choke Sonnet. How could Fable possibly have found her way along this twisting, jarring path, in the black of night, with unearthly birds screaming at her? She looped her arm through her uncle's. Gav knew what to do. She wasn't alone in *this*, at least.

The path narrowed further, funnelling the pair into a shadowy, circular grove formed by a leviathan tree. Mossy buttress roots rippled out from the trunk, forming a skirt of deep valleys and hollows.

And there in a curving cleft, like a foetus within womb's embrace, or a faerie fallen from her sky, lay Fable Winter.

'*Fabes!*' Sonnet cried, lurching forward.

Her sister stirred, whimpering.

Sonnet's hands ran all over Fable. 'Are you hurt? Where are you hurt?'

Fable grimaced, fingers going to her neck. Recalling herself, she cast about wildly. 'Where is she? Where's Mama?!'

Sonnet exchanged a glance with Gav, who'd come to kneel quietly at her side.

'Fable, she's gone. Remember, sweetie?'

Fable struggled out of her embrace. 'No! I followed her last night!'

'Is that why you came here? Looking for Mama?' There was pity in her voice and Fable recoiled from it.

'I'm not an idiot, I *saw* her! Mama was in my room. I followed her until she stopped. She was standing here, just looking at the water – so still. I was waiting for her to turn and speak to me. I didn't want to frighten her away. Then I must have fallen asleep. But she was *here*, Sonnet!'

Gav had whitened, but said nothing.

'Fabes, Mama's not here anymore. She's just not here.'

Fable pushed her mollifying hand away. She rose unsteadily, scanning the grove. Sonnet stepped back, arms aching to grab Fable near. Water rushed callously by.

When Fable turned back, it was with a countenance laid bare; bereft. Tears seeped long down her cheeks.

Sonnet stepped forward, but Fable's gaze travelled beyond her to the giant tree. A strange smile, wise beyond her years, lifted her lips. She pushed past Sonnet, reaching for the tree. She stood, hand to tree, and then, placing her forehead to the bark, she whispered, 'Mama.'

Mama? It's a ruddy tree! Sonnet fought the urge to correct. Even in her cynicism, she could admit the tree's eerie resemblance to a woman, one sheathed in a trailing gown. No wonder Fable had been mistaken in the moonlight. Eyes playing a trick, that's all there was to it. She could say nothing this minute to ease the stricken horror on Gav's face, though.

Fable's lips moved again; a little broken murmur: '*She is not thou, and only thou are she.*' Finally, she turned. There was a wet blaze in her eyes. 'Here. This is where we have to scatter Mama's ashes – under the Green Woman.'

CHAPTER 7
SECRET GARDEN

September 1955

The bright yellow paint of her bicycle gleamed as Sonnet sailed, red strands whipping loose, down the row of towering sugar-cane, their silvery-pink headdresses resplendent in the spring sunshine. In her wicker basket jiggled a string bag filled with fresh fruit and vegetables. The cloying odour of the crowded farmers' market still clung to Sonnet. She had procured a dragon fruit for Fable to sample, and she couldn't wait to see her face when she cut it open to discover the outlandish hot-pink flesh.

Olive wasn't the only one who could impress Fable!

Sonnet's heart was light. With happiness, perhaps; or something so much like it she didn't care to analyse the difference. Here was a morning alone for the first time since her mother had passed. No pressing cries or cleaving hands, only the simple pleasure of gathering food for her family.

The solitary outing had been Olive's idea, but even she must have been surprised by the speed at which Sonnet had accepted the offer. And who could blame her? For every two steps Olive made into their lives, Sonnet beat her one step back. Even as Sonnet chafed at Olive's doggedness, she recognised herself in it. Sonnet would never admit it to Olive, but she *was* relenting. The fear and powerlessness of the dark morning Fable disappeared had softened something in her.

It was Gav who had carried Fable home to the cottage from that creek-side grove. Olive who had bathed her slender feet and hands, made Fable a warm breakfast and sweet milky tea and administered an aspirin from her pocket – as an anodyne placebo, it seemed. Gav, again, who sat Fable at the kitchen table and explained just how many aspects of the rainforest conspired to harm her during a midnight foray.

The highlight of his lecture was the Stinging Tree, bearing large heart-shaped leaves covered with tiny, toxic hairs which caused excruciating pain once embedded in human skin. Gav's tale included a graphic description of early European explorers in the valley who'd wiped their arses with those conveniently large leaves and suffered such agony, they'd leapt off a cliff trying to escape it.

Fable must have been convinced, even if she'd remained stone-faced, for there had been no night vanishing incidents since. Days were another matter, though. Whenever Sonnet's back was turned, Fable still slipped away to the 'Green Woman's Grove', which didn't seem healthy, frankly, but instinct told Sonnet not to interfere. She couldn't fathom what Fable actually did all day in that grove, since she still hadn't picked up, much less used, her sketchbooks. Perhaps she dreamed away the hours there, and maybe that was enough, for now.

Thoughts having turned once more to her responsibilities waiting at the cottage, Sonnet thrust harder on the pedals towards Heartwood. She couldn't wait to show her new bike to her sisters – they had begged to come along when Gav had dropped Sonnet into town for the daunting purchase.

Never before had Sonnet spent so much money on herself. It was her first official purchase using their inheritance funds, and although some transport was justifiable, guilt at using Mama's money had nearly outweighed the pleasure. It was money Mama had never dreamed she'd see from her parents. And even when Esther had received the windfall from her father, big-hearted only after death, using a cent of it had apparently proved too much for her Hamilton pride.

If Mama couldn't bear to spend Malcolm's money, how could Sonnet? It had taken persuasion on the part of Olive and Gav, for starters, followed by some hard soul-searching. Mama had expressly willed the money to the girls, placing no restrictions on its immediate use. Esther might have shunned the money herself, but she'd wanted the girls to use it when the time came. And the time had definitely come. Sonnet *refused* to rely on Olive constantly for transport; the less time spent captive in her car the better.

Even then, it had taken serious haggling over the counter of Ryan's Wheel Lot, until Sonnet was satisfied she'd spent Mama's money well. She resisted the eponymous Ryan's suggestion that a dainty pink bike with floral basket was more appropriate for her 'feminine needs'. Sonnet, noting the predominance of tractors and trailers in the yard, decided Ryan wasn't as well acquainted with 'feminine needs' as he insisted.

Besides, she'd fallen head over heels for this sunny bike the moment she spotted it shining in the lot. It was bold and brave and tenacious – everything she wanted in a bike, and herself. She'd named her bike Freya.

On a wave of euphoria now, Sonnet soared, legs splayed, down the last hill to the cottage. Hair flew about her face. She arrived at the gate in a skidding, exultant rush.

Gav and Fable were hard at work in a garden which had changed dramatically in the few short hours Sonnet had been in town. Giant tropical butterflies flitted around the flowers emancipated from choking weeds. Fable's pleas about redeeming the garden had apparently been taken up this morning.

Her uncle and sister scrambled up as she clattered in, their beaming faces mirroring hers. Fable admired the new wheels as Gav ambled over with an appreciative whistle. 'What a beauty! How does she ride?'

Sonnet patted the bike. 'Like a dream. Haggled Ryan right down, too. Want a ride?'

Gav took the handles from her, chuffed grin on his weathered face as he circled out into the paddock. His oversized bulk was ridiculous on the yellow frame. Fable clapped with a girlish cheer, and then clutched Sonnet's arm.

'Sonny, you have to see what Uncle Gav and I unearthed in the garden – it's all so *magical*!' She led Sonnet along an uncovered pathway. 'Look, our own wishing well and it still works! All this time it was hidden here. Uncle Gav says our grandpa built it!'

Sonnet grimaced at 'grandpa', peering into the dark well.

Gav came up behind them, puffed and smelling of the strange maleness the girls were still adjusting to. 'Now don't have a hissy fit, Sonnet,' he said. 'It's fake. Doesn't go deep.'

'Am I so transparent?'

He slapped her back. 'You're a worrier, pet.'

Fable was already pulling her away along another pathway. 'And it gets even better, look what *else* I found!'

Under the dappled shade of a frangipani tree, where flowers lay scattered on the red earth, Fable presented a neat circle of river stones, set around the trunk. Each stone was unique; some polished painstakingly, others coarsely shaped by nature itself.

'It's a faerie ring!'

Sonnet crouched to examine the stones. There were a dozen or more, spaced evenly and purposefully apart. 'You're too old for believing in faeries, Fabes,' she said absently, tracing a barely distinguishable name and date carved into one stone.

Fable snorted. 'Oh, come on. I'm saying, imagine! This could be our faerie garden. Plummy will love it. She can bring Mama's baby dolls out here and I'll make signs and pebbled paths, and paint the stones to look like houses.'

Sonnet felt Gav's shadow fall across the stones in the same moment she comprehended exactly what she was looking at. She paused, sickened. 'I don't think this is a play area, is it, Gav?'

Something not-quite forgotten flared in his eyes. His face slackened. 'They were . . . something Olive lost, when we lived here.'

Fable looked at her uncle in confusion. 'Doesn't she remember she left them here?'

Gav grimaced.

'But there are so *many*,' Sonnet said, quite staggered.

'Yep. There were – so many.' Gav shrugged. 'Look, you girls can do whatever you want with the garden, it's yours now. I've neglected this place far too long. If you keep it neatly trimmed back from now on, you can do as you like.'

Sonnet stood, brushing earth off her capri pants. 'Fable, these are Olive's stones. I don't want you to disturb this circle, and I certainly don't want you painting anything here.'

Inside the cottage, Sonnet came upon Olive and Plum in silent repose. Olive was pinned to the couch by the sleeping girl, and surrounded by hardcover Enid Blyton books. A hand drifted slowly over burnished auburn curls, as Olive stared through the window. Sonnet stopped for the uncomfortable ache striking up in her heart.

Unutterable questions beset her. *How could you bear it, Olive, when children came so carelessly to Mama? Was this why you stood aside and allowed your own sister to be driven out of town? When did you finally rise from your bed of perpetual miscarriage to admit your stubborn God had never intended to answer your prayers?*

Olive's face turned and the sorrow exposed there, in the instant before dignified veneer re-formed, revealed more than Sonnet could ever have wanted to know.

Olive moved to shift Plum off her lap, and Sonnet quickly bade her to stay. 'She'll be awake soon enough.'

'I'm sorry,' Olive whispered, settling back uneasily. 'It was the only way she'd nap. She refused to stay in bed, wanted me to read her all these books, and when she finally fell asleep I didn't dare move her.'

'She doesn't like to sleep alone. You did the right thing.'

Embarrassed by Olive's relief, Sonnet busied herself in the kitchen. The bench was buried under fine bone china.

Sonnet turned, mystified. 'Is this your collection?'

'No, it was your grandmother's. I thought you might be interested in it. She collected Shelley china. I'm not into crockery and such. But Essie had been asking for it ever since she was a girl. She'd sneak into Mother's cabinets, take her favourites and set up these elaborate tea parties for her book characters. She'd get such a whipping – but it never stopped her. She loved that china more than Mother herself. When Mother finally passed on, she left the whole collection to me. She *knew* I'd never liked it. Always troubled me that she did that. I'd been keeping it stored here, waiting for Es.'

Sonnet rotated a delicate teacup in her hand. 'I'm sure Mama would be glad to know her own daughters will have them now.'

Olive was chuffed – way too chuffed. Sonnet looked away.

Her next words, then, amazed even herself. 'And listen, about your offer a while back: helping you out with some alterations in the shop? I might be willing to give it a trial.' She busied herself stacking plates, rushing on lightly, 'And if you wanted to watch Plum for me, maybe I can have a go at minding your shop. Could be a way for me to get to know some of the local ladies . . .'

CHAPTER 8

CHRISTMAS COMES TO NOAH VALE

Warm winter rolled into scorching dry spring. Yellow and pink *Tabebuias* burst into vibrant bloom against grass baked brown and air hazy with smoke from back-burning. As the sunshine intensified, the heat at Noah Vale School began to simmer down. Cold, calculated indifference took its place, after the steeliness of Fable's quiet self-possession proved, ultimately, dissatisfying. She was still a loner at school, but, more importantly, was now left alone. Fable clung to this small victory.

School days fell into their inevitable rhythm, within which even alienation began to feel humdrum. But weekends held compensatory joy. Away from school and the omnipresent eye of her older sister – now gainfully employed at Emerson's Fashion and Fabrics on Saturdays and two weekdays – Fable found her bliss in the forest deep.

The grove of the Green Woman had become her secret hideaway, and although she had not once heard the siren's call since they'd spread Mama's ashes there, she was inexorably drawn to that otherworldly coppice. She could not yet muster the prose or pen stroke to capture how she felt in her sacred grove. Nevertheless, each day she trekked faithfully there, sketchbook and pencils tucked under her arm.

Creativity would find her and flow through her again. She simply had to wait.

The first time Fable encountered Marco Lagorio at the cane bridge on her way home from the Green Woman's Grove, she shied regretfully away from his invitation to rejoin the Glade Gang. Though still only spring, it was already as hot in the tropics as any summer she'd known before. She longed for the waterfall's cooling reprieve, and cursed Adriana's name.

Over the following weeks, Marco continued to arrive at the cane bridge simultaneously with Fable; luck inferring both purpose and planning. Each time, his invitation was rebuffed.

On the Saturday Fable finally caved, she approached the Glade on Marco's heel with fear rioting in her chest. Hearing Adriana's strident voice ahead, she stopped, unable to continue. Marco motioned her forward, smiling.

Fable had looked into that hopeful, open face and felt gratitude laced, disconcertingly, with queasiness. Glimpsing, perhaps in the faint future, a time when she would lament ever having stepped foot in their Glade.

At her arrival, Adriana and Christy rolled their eyes nearly right out of their heads and beat an elaborately offended exit from the Glade. Kate waved them dryly off. The remaining boys, unperturbed by the female machinations, accepted Fable's presence without blinking.

The following weekend, she approached the Glade with an air akin to confidence. Adriana and Christy maintained the silent treatment for a protracted hour before making their disdainful withdrawal.

On the third Saturday, they didn't bother appearing at all, but sent a message, delivered with swaggering air through Eamon, elucidating all their reasons for not showing this day. Chiefly: they had better things to do, with better friends, and Fable was to cease and desist from her visits so they might enjoy *their* Glade Fable-free upon their return.

Fable took this as encouragement, and when Marco slumped into the Glade alone the following weekend, convinced he'd been forgotten by his strawberry-haired friend, he found Fable already there with the Hardy kids; sailing through the air from the tree-house platform.

Summer *seethed*. Fable had never, in all her life, known heat like it: an oppressive humidity that sucked the very breath from her lungs. A clinging python's skin she could not shed.

The infamous tropical heat they'd long been warned of, had finally arrived.

'It's hotter than *hell*!' Sonnet was heard constantly to say, as she tried to locate the mythical spot in which a single pedestal fan might cool an entire house. 'Where's the blasted monsoon?' Sonnet raged, as the sun set each day, in fire and charcoal. Olive and Gav had sworn the airless, spiralling heat would soon give way to months of the Wet.

For Sonnet, who felt heat far more irritably than others, it was promised respite, denied. She wanted to cash in her coupons for their Wet on time, with no delays. For Fable, who simply loved rain, the idea of near-constant precipitation was tantalising. She was finding Sonnet more intolerable than the humidity. It was all that pressure Sonnet was putting on herself to manufacture the 'perfect' Christmas for their first year without Mama. Fable evaded Sonnet daily, fleeing into the buzzing shade of the rainforest straight after brekkie – not a minute too soon.

As Christmas loomed closer, and the air thickened to near liquidity, all eyes were on the skies. The golden chain trees encircling the cottage burst now into bloom; grape-like clusters of pure sunshine dripped from branches, carpeting the garden.

On Christmas Eve, Fable hurtled outdoors the moment Sonnet started stressing over the last-minute procurement of a gift for Olive, after the cantankerous sewing machine ate her tea-towel set.

There was no way she could stomach Sonnet's festering mood on what was shaping up as one of the hottest days of the summer. Fable had been sweating since dawn. Her skin crawled for the Glade waterfall. All the gang would be there this morning – except Adriana and cohort, who had responded to Fable's persistent presence with a proclamation of being too *sophisticated* to hang out at the Glade anymore. And besides, there were the St Ronan's boarding school boys, home for holidays, to chase after at the Noah Vale Public Baths.

Imagine Fable's bemusement on this morning, then, to find Adriana, Christy, Megan *and* Isabella mucking about at the Glade with as much horseplay as any other unsophisticated thirteen-year-old. Descending the rock staircase, Fable was greeted by all the familiar faces, but was surprised to see several new kids.

She plopped her towel on the ledge, and took a quick, under-lash inventory of the intruders. Eamon was jumping with some boys his own age – St Ronan's boys, Fable deduced – which accounted for Adriana's vivacious attendance this morning.

On the opposite side of the Glade, however, leaning against the moss-covered cliff face, was an older boy, much taller than the rest. A young man, compared to the others.

He stood quietly, arms crossed, surveying the cliff jumping with a supervisory air. He was strong and golden-fair, with a broadly handsome profile, thick brows, and full, serious lips. Sensing her examination, he turned.

Cerulean eyes, blue as a Ulysses butterfly, alighted upon her – and the very air went out of Fable. Cicada hum filled her ears, laughter and splashing faded away.

Their gaze held across the water.

Beneath a rutted brow, his stare was thoughtful. Fable floundered, unable to breathe or move or think.

'Raff! Watch this one!' came a shout from the No Fear ledge. He looked away, and Fable sagged to her knees with relief, and a strange new sense of dismay. She fussed with her towel, summoning back her thoughts.

So *this* was Rafferty Hull, come home at last for his university summer holidays. Raff: legendary tree-house designer and waterfall kayaker and mountain hiker and cliff jumper, referenced constantly by the younger boys in their daring exploits. The famous brother, of whom Adriana spoke with a smugly possessive air, had finally appeared.

His figure burned in her peripheral vision.

Marco splashed her from the water. 'Coming in, Fabes?'

She flinched, caught in the act of something she couldn't quite understand. She looked at Adriana and crew cavorting in their bright new togs – flashing smiles and neat breasts – and withered. Her sage swimsuit was dowdy and pilled; her slender chest still budding. Fable shrugged off her corduroy pinafore reluctantly. Shame seared. Fleetingly, she thought of Plummy, left sitting before their make-do Christmas potted palm at the cottage, and wished herself desperately back *there*.

Marco called for her again, and Fable decided the water offered better cover than this exposed ledge. She plunged long into the water, not surfacing until she was behind the waterfall. Safely hidden by the curtain, she pulled herself onto the wide shelf, ears straining for Raff's voice over the falls. She could just make out his figure through the silver veil.

His voice, heard for the first time cautioning rock jumpers to mind the swimming kids below, was gentle and measured. She would scale No Fear just to hear it again.

Now, what to do with this aching breathlessness? How to act like herself when she'd never felt such a foreigner in her skin before? But she already willed herself daily to survive Adriana's spite and Eamon's arrogance with feigned indifference – she would somehow survive their brother's blue gaze with grace, too.

It was afternoon before Fable finally drifted home from the Glade. The Hulls had retired to their house for a late lunch, taking the rest of the gang with them. At the cane bridge, Adriana's invitation purposely excluded Fable, and she alone – earning Raff's brotherly rebuke. Adriana dutifully rectified her invitation, but garnering Raff's notice as an object of pity wouldn't do at all.

Fable looked straight past Adriana's dissembling graciousness, ignoring Kate's wry grin, Jessica's rigidity and Eamon's smirking, to meet Raff's gentle smile.

'I'd rather wash my hair,' she said, shrugging.

Fable crossed the bridge to Hamiltons' then on light feet, with Kate's chortle resounding in her ears, and curious eyes burning a hole in her back.

Sonnet, hunting Fable for Christmas Eve preparations, found her sister in the garden; face uplifted and arms outstretched to the golden shower blooms falling like yellow rain on a sultry breeze. The trees hummed with native bee song, as though creation itself were carolling.

Joie de vivre, Sonnet sighed, followed by a sucker punch of realisation: *These are the waning moments of girlhood.*

CHAPTER 9

PERSUASION

Christmas 1955

Their first tropical Christmas was, even by Sonnet's exacting standards, a success. The sun blazed; their only Christmas record played ceaselessly on the old gramophone from the hall cupboard; and each of the stockings Sonnet had managed to fill on Mama's behalf, with much thoughtfulness and creativity, had been gleefully received by her younger sisters.

Even Sonnet's contribution to Christmas lunch had turned out perfectly. It was with a proud heart that she ushered the girls up to Heartwood, arms laden with brown paper-wrapped gifts and Pyrex dishes, warmly filled with roast lamb and vegetables, and caramel dumplings.

As the day roasted on into afternoon, the new Hamilton–Emerson clan gathered in the lounge room, nursing full bellies, to exchange gifts. Sonnet suppressed a smirk as Olive and Gav traded a nose-rubbing kiss with their presents. It was all so *conventional.*

The Mateus Rosé, served graciously with lunch by her teetotal aunt and uncle, had loosened Sonnet's shoulders. She basked in the two-glass afterglow. A year ago, alone in their tiny Canberra flat, they could never have imagined such a Christmas.

On her wrapping-strewn lap, Sonnet held a hardcover edition of Jane Austen's *Persuasion*, given to her earlier by Olive. Seeing Sonnet's shock, Olive had rushed to explain, 'It was your mother's favourite book.'

'Yes, I know. I've never wanted to read it, though. But this is a beautiful edition, thank you.'

'I tried to get you a special book. I'm not into fiction myself, but Alfred said this one was perfect for you.'

'Who?' Sonnet asked, glancing up sharply.

'Alfred Shearer, he has Shearer's Books on Main Street, opposite Raintree Park.'

Sonnet tried and failed to visualise the store. 'And how would Alfred Shearer know my reading tastes?'

'Not yours. Esther's. Alfred knew your bookish mother very well. He's been the town's only link to literature for years. Had that bookshop as long as I can remember, and he was the school's librarian for decades.'

'I'm surprised he remembers what she borrowed twenty years ago.'

Olive seemed to choose her next words cautiously, and as was their customary dance, Sonnet felt her temper rising in expectation.

'Alfred was a great champion of your mother's. He would love it if you popped into his shop one day. I think you would both benefit from a chat.'

Sonnet snapped the book closed. 'I'm sure I'll get into the bookstore – eventually.'

Though Sonnet had quashed further talk of Alfred Shearer, the thought of him weighed heavily. She had watched the girls unwrapping their remaining presents unseeingly. Only Fable's delighted gasp – a rare sound indeed – wrenched Sonnet back now. Fable had received an extensive set of watercolours, boasting every imaginable hue. Olive beamed in Fable's embrace.

Sonnet smiled too. She had been overjoyed to discover Fable buried under a torchlit blanket fort on Christmas Eve, sketching again after months of dispiritedness. When Sonnet snuck in, much later, to place the stocking, she found Fable asleep, clutching the book to her heart. Sonnet dallied for a moment to stroke Fable's forehead, comforted that, in slumber, she still looked like a slip of a girl. Sonnet paused then, trying to make out the picture under her splayed fingers. Ever so gently, she shifted Fable's hand, admiring the blue eyes beneath. The intricate detail was *splendid*. If it were possible, Fable's talent had only improved in the interlude.

Olive drew back from Fable to pat the watercolour tin. 'Perhaps you can test out some of the colours tonight and paint the fireworks for us!'

'What fireworks?' Fable asked, wide-eyed.

'The Hulls put on a firework show for Christmas. You'll see them from our deck.'

Plum scaled Olive's waist. 'I want fireworks, Aunnie Ov! Fireworks, Aunnie Ov!'

Olive laughed, enfolding Plum in her arms. 'Darling girl, you have to wait until it's dark to see the fireworks.'

'Sounds a bit flash for Christmas,' Sonnet said. 'Pun intended.'

'It's a Hull tradition – every year since their children were young. Christmas is quite the affair at Summerlinn, even more so now their eldest boy lives in Brisbane. Rafferty always comes home for Christmas.'

'So, they roll out the fireworks for him – like your regular low-key family?'

'Oh, you're not far off the mark – Delia talks of nothing else but that golden boy of hers, from January to November. I'm surprised she hasn't been in the shop chewing your ear off about him.'

'Ha! Delia hasn't stepped foot in Emerson's since I've been working there for you.'

'She'll get over it. Our Delia's a quilter, so unless she's willing to drive to Cairns each time she needs fabric, she'll be back.'

'Grovelling?'

'Bragging!' Olive laughed. 'Delia would get over any grudge when it comes to lording it over us with her perfect boy. You can't blame her, though. He's a fine, strapping lad, that one. Rafferty's had every girl in Noah after him at some point or another. He's got it all – good looks, nice manners, not to mention the property he'll one day inherit from his father. Has to be the valley's most eligible bachelor.'

'He'd be a mighty fine match for you, young Sonnet,' interjected Gav.

'Too right!' said Olive. 'And he's about your age, maybe a year younger. Of course, Delia would see that happen over her dead body. No woman's good enough for her Rafferty.'

'What a shame, sounds like such a *catch*, too, with a mother-in-law like that.'

'Oh no, he's a dear boy. Not cut from the same Hull cloth.'

'Used to work for me at the store when he was a young 'un,' Gav said. 'Saturday mornings religiously – much to William Hull's chagrin. Didn't want any son of his working in a shop when he should be learning the family business.'

'He's a reluctant heir,' Olive added. 'Got all that prime farming land coming to him one day, yet he doesn't show any interest in it. William was horrified when Rafferty chose that architecture degree of his. Waste of time for a future canegrower.'

'Heaven forbid some chump might want an education,' Sonnet snorted. 'How embarrassing for the bloody Hulls!'

Olive jerked as the curse slipped out in earshot of the younger girls. 'Language! Goodness.'

Sonnet glanced at her sisters. Plum was unpacking her new puzzle, oblivious. But Fable was sitting close by, unnaturally still, lashes kissing her cheeks. Sonnet frowned.

'Well, Rafferty *is* his mother's boy,' said Olive. 'No reluctance on his part to assume the mantle could ever offset *her* favouritism.'

'Or,' Sonnet added, 'maybe he'll escape the clutches of this town and his dragon mother, and make something of himself.'

Sonnet returned her frowning gaze to Fable, thinking they needed to be more careful not to discuss Adriana's family in front of Fabes. The mere mention of the Hulls seemed to disturb her. 'Anyway, who cares about the Hulls? Olive, I have something, and I'm sorry it's not much, that I made for you . . .'

Beneath the epiphyte-festooned branches of the rain trees sat a tense figure, with sensible navy blouse tucked into her capris, and her mother's pearls at lobes and clavicle. Freya rested against the massive trunk. Sonnet's gaze was fixed upon the bookstore opposite Raintree Park, wherein resided the Alfred Shearer she had yet to meet.

In her gripping hands was *Persuasion*, the book she'd read, cover to cover, in one late night. Fancy discovering she actually could *enjoy* an Austen novel – she who didn't have a romantic bone in her body!

Sonnet had ignored the novel for a whole week after Christmas; Alfred's conveyed insistence that *Persuasion* was perfect for her, serving only to repel. But in some instances, Sonnet could admit she'd been wrong. Discovering *that* line – 'facts or opinions which are to pass through the hands of so many, to be misconceived by folly in one, and ignorance in another, can hardly have much truth left' – had convinced her: this was a man worth becoming acquainted with. So, here she was, braced to meet yet another bearer of *her* history, with all the revelation that entailed.

Everywhere she went, Sonnet parried yet more versions of Esther Hamilton: in the General Store, at the back of the baker's truck, at Heartwood when so-and-so dropped by for a chat about such-and-such, and over the counter at Emerson's Fashion and Fabrics, where women were determined to reopen more than just seams. Sonnet's appointment to part-time assistant had drummed up a surfeit of business; local ladies keen to have their gawk, and their say. Most times, the memories of Esther Hamilton were shared with grating pity, assumed intimacy, and such embellishment; it took every modicum of willpower for Sonnet to keep her lips zipped.

Then there was the cruel candour of older folk down the street who spoke before they thought. Oh, the things they said ... 'You've got Esther's dreadful red hair!' Or, 'You look so much like poor Archer, my word your mother did a number on that family!' And, 'I can see Esther kept her beauty for herself, always was a selfish girl.'

It was pure *Schadenfreude*. Never had Sonnet collected a word more apt for this town, and these people. At holding her tongue, Sonnet was becoming uncharacteristically proficient. Such martyrdom didn't suit her and felt, frankly, appalling, but Olive had promised: if she waited them out, they would tire of the Hamilton story. So long as she didn't provide fuel for the fire.

The first fat plop of rain that landed on her book, Sonnet wiped away without a glance. The second and third, she noted distractedly. The following drops, she moved to quickly erase. Then, abruptly, the raindrops were indiscernible one from another. With a roar materialising from thin, or rather, thick air – the sky was rent apart.

Above her, the rain tree folded up its leaves.

Sonnet flew for the bookshop with a yelp; book shoved under blouse, bike clattering along at her side. Into the bookstore, on a gust of rain, she swept. A bell clanged as she slammed the door and pressed back against it breathlessly.

Slowly, her eyes adjusted to the gloom of the overcrowded store. High, dark shelves lined every wall, heavily loaded. Even the leaning book ladders had become makeshift shelves, piled with books. A musty, stagnant odour of books enveloped her.

Toiling down a spiral staircase at the rear was an elderly man.

'Oh, lass, smell that! You've brought in with you the first scent of the Wet hitting dry earth. Might be my favourite smell in the world! "Argillaceous odour" the mineralogists call it, meaning . . .'

He stopped on the final step, voice trailing off. Sonnet sluiced water from her arms. Slowly, silently, he came towards her, arms outstretched. She stiffened. When he was within a few paces of her, he stopped.

'Esther's girl.'

His eyes were spilling over with moisture, whether tears or simply rheuminess, she couldn't tell.

'Sonnet,' she supplied. Tears pricked in her own eyes.

'Sonnet.' He held out his hands, and she placed hers there. For a long, shaking moment, he beheld the flame-tressed girl before him.

'Oh, it's so good to look at you.' Alfred said. 'I've been waiting to meet you for twenty years. Watching that door, hoping your mother would walk back through it one day, with you in tow.'

'Yes, I wanted to come and see you because . . .'

He waited.

'Because I need . . . a book. I was pleased with your suggestion of *Persuasion*. And I think you might be able to help me find something.'

Alfred smiled. If he was disappointed she'd resorted to a cover story, he was too gracious to show it.

'I'd be honoured to help you. Come, I'll make you a cuppa and you can tell me what you're after.'

Sonnet's face burned as the bookstore door rattled closed behind her. That old man had sat with inestimable patience, nodding kindly through her waffling lies about the rainforest trees and *birds* she wanted to learn about, never once questioning her true motives. Nursing her cuppa, comforted by the smell of old books and torrential rain, Sonnet had felt more at peace than she had in years. And yet, she evaded Alfred's eyes, focusing instead on his soft-grey knitted vest. She sat in selfish enjoyment of Alfred's hospitality, silently beseeching him to speak of her mother, without having the gumption to ask a thing.

Sonnet heaved the tomes of rainforest flora and fauna into her basket and pushed away from the kerb with a sigh.

'You gutless wonder!' she fumed as her tyres splattered along the rain-slick road. 'Sonnet Arden Hamilton, you'll go straight back tomorrow, and you'll look Alfred in the eyes and ask him to *please* tell you everything he remembers about Mama.'

Hope of redemptive return to Shearer's Books the next day was thwarted, however, by a rain depression which settled over the valley. The Wet had finally arrived.

'Send 'er down, Hughie!' Gav cried, gleeful as a boy, with both weathered hands outstretched over the veranda, to receive summer's long-awaited due.

'Who?' asked Sonnet.

'Hughie!' Gav shouted, shaking a triumphant fist at the sky.

'You'll soon learn how to talk to Hughie,' Olive said, making eyes at Gav. He came then, with fresh stubble, to nuzzle the Gav Spot behind her neck.

Sonnet scowled. Their conspiratorial intimacy irked her no end. What kind of madness *was* this married-for-umpteen-decades business?

Uxorious, Sonnet mouthed, *showing excessive fondness for one's wife.*

For a fortnight, it rained – though it was not rain as the Hamilton girls had ever known it: thunderous walls of solid white, obliterating all. Serpentine Creek was a distended, all-devouring torrent, severing the narrow gully pass into town, cutting them off from the world. The open field surrounding the cottage became a pulsing brown river, pushing debris the size of telephone poles along with it.

'Looks like we're waterfront acreage now,' Sonnet told Gav with a laugh. Humour belied the twist of fear in her belly.

Gav spoke directly to her hidden dread. 'Stop fretting, pet. You're sitting at the hundred-year flood level. Cottage has been there safe and sound, for generations.'

Sonnet was not appeased. The underworld crept over Noah. Mildew flowered across the ceiling; algae grew in opportunistic frond pails; mosquitoes swarmed forth; long-dead smells leached out of dank fabrics; red devil's claw rose from the earth; and dark mould grew on everything, even a person, should she stay sitting long enough.

Not that Sonnet was in danger of that.

Olive smiled at Sonnet prowling the rain-shrouded deck, swatting at her arms. Sonnet's face would brighten as each rainbow formed, only to fall into despondency as yet another pounding wave swept across the vale.

'It never *ends*!' she cried in disbelief.

'You'll get used to it. It's always a shock to newcomers finding themselves flooded out of civilisation.'

Sonnet slumped at the table.

'Before you know it,' Olive added, 'you'll welcome the rains. It's good to have an enforced holiday, put your feet up for a bit.'

Coming from Olive, with her indefatigable work ethic, this was a revelation.

'Why don't you get stuck into some of those books you brought home from Alfred's?'

Sonnet snorted, jabbing a thumb over her shoulder at the girl curled on rattan settee, sketchbook splayed open beside hefty tome, and a long strawberry plait being masticated between murmuring lips.

'Fabes nicked them. She's been drooling over those dry flora books. And the way she moons by the windows, I think she's infatuated with the damned rainforest!'

Olive noted the withering amber scowl directed at the back of Sonnet's head and grinned. 'Perhaps next time you'll ask Alfred for something *you* want, then?'

The next Hamilton glare thrown was a green one, from Sonnet herself.

CHAPTER 10

SHEARER'S TALE

January 1956

A week passed in sequestered resentment. The first indication that the floodwaters had receded was Fable flapping out of the cottage door with a towel around her neck, and sandals thrown on so hastily they weren't even buckled.

Sonnet lobbed a sigh after her, but turned just as hurriedly herself in search of Plummy's port. Thank goodness Olive was due to mind her today.

Sonnet's morning at Emerson's Fashion and Fabrics crawled by. At the stroke of midday, she locked up and hurried down to Shearer's Books. Alfred's SORRY, WE'RE CLOSED sign was no impediment to a woman on a mission such as this.

At her jangling entrance, Alfred looked up from his newspaper and aromatic steak and kidney pie with a smile so hopeful she wanted to weep.

He too had been waiting, then.

'I want to know,' she blurted, 'why you are the only person in the world anyone has ever called an "ally" of my mother's. Why *you* were her friend when she was friendless.'

Alfred wrapped his pie back in its paper bag. 'That's a story I've been waiting a long time to tell. Come upstairs, we'll chat over a cuppa . . .'

Up the spiral staircase they went, into the overcrowded, odorous heart of an old man's dwelling. Alfred's flatlet above the shop overlooked Raintree Park and the green mountains beyond, sharply defined as cardboard cut-outs. The august view and hot cuppa softened the last residues of tension. Sonnet sank back into the overstuffed armchair. Alfred patted her shoulder as he shuffled to the seat beside her.

'I haven't anything alarming to tell you, Sonnet. You'll have heard the worst of it from the meddlers round these parts.'

But she couldn't look at him while he told this tale. Sonnet picked out a rain tree, the largest, making it her single point of focus.

'I'd known Esther since she was a girl in the Young Readers section of my library – she was my library monitor for years, and I cherished our lunchtime chats. When she wasn't in my library she haunted my bookstore. I used to call my back corner under the stairs "Esther's Corner". She was always starving for stories, like life just wasn't enough for her. And when the bookshop and library were closed to her, Esther had a secret waterfall, somewhere up beyond Moria Falls, couldn't tell you exactly, where she'd hide out with all her stories and dreams.

'Esther lived for her books, or maybe lived *in* them – I've since thought perhaps it set Esther too far beyond her peers, made her yearn for someone who could equal her intellect and imagination, and that passionate heart of hers! And there were none in Noah like that.

'Over the years, I watched Esther grow into a beautiful young woman, with a splendid mind on her. Oh she could *write*! I don't think anyone doubted what Esther swore she'd make of herself. She had such determination about her, always demanding more than this valley could give her. But I sometimes thought Esther was frightened by the intensity of her own wanting. The idea that life might not ultimately live up to her expectations seemed unbearable to Es.'

He broke off, sighing.

'Then along comes Archer Brennan. And who could blame Esther? *Everyone* loved him. Such a handsome man, and an ambitious and charismatic teacher, with artistic talents. Archer was a painter, a mighty talented one. Just a newcomer to Noah; yet he made Vice Principal in no time, married the town beauty, and they had two lads in quick succession. He was a tremendous father, especially considering young Edmund's state.'

Tremendous father hung in the air, heavier than the humidity around them. Seeing her sneer, Alfred hurried on. 'Archer had a passion for art and literature like we'd never seen in this town, and that tiny school. Believe me, I was the school librarian and the only bookseller, I knew! There wasn't any genuine appetite for books here. I saw how Archer tried to whet their desires with his own zeal, a losing battle in this sugar-town backwater. He was too earnest. People didn't want Shakespeare; they wanted to escape the slate as soon as possible, get back to the land or mind a steady income, and keep their heads above water when the floods arose.

'Esther first came under Archer's notice in her senior year. Well, we hope it wasn't before. She always was a precocious beauty, though.' Alfred cleared his throat. 'He saw a promise shining in Esther he couldn't believe, wouldn't leave alone. He should have damned well walked *away* from the things she ignited in him! Archer fancied himself her sponsor – the one who was going to liberate her from small-town life, put her on the world stage. He was working hard to get her into her dream arts course. She had her sights on multiple university scholarships before they threw her out of school. You see? He *ruined* all that potential in his very attempt to possess it.'

Sonnet put her teacup on its saucer with a clatter, no longer trusting herself not to take a bite out of the china.

Alfred sighed. 'Look, I can't lie and say she did the right thing, either. Because she surely didn't – he was married, he had those poor boys. But she was too green to understand the consequences. He was worldly-wise, he was her principal, *he* should have known better!'

Alfred's own teacup came to rest, trembling, beside hers.

'*I* should have stopped it – somehow! All that time he spent with Esther, hidden away in the study annex of my library, the two of them setting my books alight between them. That none of us ever saw it until it was done, that's the part that always confounded me. Then the terrible way they were found out on that school stage, *in flagrante delicto . . .*' He trailed off.

Raintree Park was a burning blur of green for Sonnet.

'I was the only bloke in town who said it wasn't Esther's fault, that *he* bore the responsibility. She might have been eighteen, but she was still a *girl*. I copped plenty of flak, still do, for saying it.

'And that was the worst of it. She was so much bigger than this town, yet they made her small by their shaming. And the graduation they denied her cost that girl her chance at university.'

'Then I came along and spoiled any chance she had left. I don't mean to be rude, but I've heard the rest of this story already.'

Alfred shook his head, voice earnest. 'Now, Sonnet, don't you blame yourself. You were the after. Esther and Archer made their own bed and none of that is your fault. But your mother wanted you more than anything in the world. This is the part of the story you don't know, how she gave it all up – her home and reputation, family wealth and security, all her education dreams – to keep you.'

'I know precisely what she gave up. They were the very things we went without.'

'She had no other choice! They gave her none. Sonnet, I sheltered Es in my home here for a month. I was her last stop on the way out of town, and the only door open to her after your grandfather threw her out, hoping to drive her to her senses. Of course, I only took her in because I was in love with her myself – or so said the town gossips.'

'Were you?' There seemed no reason not to ask.

'She was the daughter I could never have. But no, Esther was never going to be in danger of that from a man . . . like me.'

Alfred stared at his teacup, not meeting her eyes. Sonnet kept her gaze on his aged planes, until he looked up. Her eyes were soft with comprehension, and his grew wetter.

There was a tiny catch in his voice as he went on. 'I imagined I saw myself in Esther – being cast out like that by her family. I would have done anything for her. Least I could offer, though, was to keep her away from the pitchforks, while she planned her escape. Gave her whatever I could, as much money as she'd accept, and connections – old friends of mine in Sydney, good people who took her in, fed and sheltered her until she was ready to give birth. She had you in a tiny back room at their home, safely hidden away from the greedy hands of the state. When she was ready, they helped her on to her first home.'

'She must have been *terrified.*'

'Oh *yes.* If you could have seen her little face! She launched herself into the world at the same stage women were once retiring to their bedrooms for their lying-in. That kind of courage doesn't come along very often. And she did it to keep you.'

'To keep me from *what*?'

'If she'd stayed, Sonnet, if she'd let your grandparents have their way, the doctors would have dragged you out of her womb and off for adoption before she could clap eyes on you. Most likely they'd have knocked her out first. You'd never have seen your true mother again.

The government's long been in the hidden business of stealing babies from "unsuitable" mothers. They'd already been flogging children from Aboriginal mothers for years. Then they set their sights on the white bastard babies. It made good sense to the do-gooders: rob the disreputable unwed mothers, to fill their adoption quotas for respectable married couples. There were dibs on Esther's baby already.'

Sonnet shuddered.

'So she ran. Right out of my front door that wet September morning, heavy with child, determined to save you. And I never saw her again.' He paused, gathering himself.

'Initially, she sent me word of her safety, and yours; then precious titbits on postcards dashed out – though even they fizzled out after the first year. My friends kept me abreast of how she was going so long as she stayed in their district. But once Esther moved on, she severed those ties. She was done with us. The odd postcard graced my mailbox from time to time, and I was able to pass back some of your aunt's letters, too. But we knew next to nothing about what happened to our Essie.'

Sonnet exhaled. 'And that's what I owe you. The truth of what Mama did next.'

'No, Sonnet. As much as I would love to hear about Esther's life after Noah, that would make me no better than any busybody up the street.'

'You must have questions? I'm sure Mama wouldn't have minded – you helped her escape. What would she have done, and where would I be now, without you?'

Alfred smiled. 'If there's one thing I've always longed to know, it's whether Esther kept up her writing? I always hoped I'd see her name writ large across a novel one day. Imagined I'd crack open a new box of books, and there she'd be: Esther Hamilton, published.'

Sonnet mulled this over, wishing she had better news. 'I guess she still wrote, but only when life was ... light for her. And that wasn't often. She seemed to have endless phases of despair. You know, Mama called us her "Story Girls", she *named* us for her love of writing, and yet we cost her that very aspiration. Who has time for writing while single-handedly raising three children and eking out a meagre living with factory work and seamstress jobs when she could barely raise her head from the pillow for anguish? She had to take her hand off the quill and put it to hard labour, instead.'

Alfred's eyes brimmed. 'I'm sorry to hear those tempests followed her. Poor Essie, nobody to steady her; all those intense emotions hers alone to bear.'

'I often wondered how much happier she might have been without us.'

'Oh, she'd never have survived losing you, Sonnet. She gave up a lot for what she wanted most of all: *love*. You were the best thing in her life.'

Sonnet couldn't pretend to agree. 'Not saying much, is it though?'

They fell into a dense silence. Alfred shook himself, as though to cast it off. 'And do you write yourself, Sonnet?'

'Not a sentence. I'm starting to feel I missed out on some impressive talents. Daughter of an artist-cum-literature-lover and his protégée-turned-mistress. And here's regular old me, no artist at all.'

Sonnet looked away to the mountains, afraid of seeing disappointment on Alfred's face. 'But I *do* love reading. Mama used to call me her *logophile*, because I could spend hours with a dictionary.' Oh, listen to her vain posturing! Never before had she so wanted her mother's talents. 'I just like to collect words,' she corrected lamely.

But Alfred was nodding intently. 'Ah yes,' he said, 'you're a *lexiconophilist*.'

Sonnet wanted to grin like an idiot. 'But Mama's creativity is alive and well in my younger sister. Fable can write like a dream, yet she's not quite thirteen. And you should *see* her watercolours!'

'She paints?'

'Yes. She's astonishingly talented for one so young. I say that with the bias of a proud sister determined to see Fable make something of herself.'

Alfred considered Sonnet for a long minute. If he had another question, it remained unformed. Instead, he reached to nudge her teacup. 'I want to thank you for today, Sonnet. I know you've got a lot on your plate, lass, but you can come here at any time and help yourself to anything you want.'

CHAPTER 11

MORIA FALLS

Late January 1956

The second-last day of summer holidays before the school bell would toll again for Noah Vale students, and Sonnet was all in a dither about Fable heading off to high school. Fable bridled under the fussing. Starting secondary school in Noah meant little more than moving to the opposite side of the quadrangle for classes, with a uniform upgrade from pinafore to blouse and skirt. It was only a big deal for the boys sent away to boarding school at the exclusive St Ronan's.

Nonetheless, Sonnet bossed and fretted. Fable suspected her sister's behaviour arose more from unspoken anxiety at also sending Plum off to community kindergarten. Sonnet was over-attached. It wasn't like she was Plum's real mother – get a grip! But who was Fable to point a single thing out to Sonnet?

The preparations had reached a fever pitch this day, with Sonnet taking it upon herself to re-hem Fable's hand-me-down uniforms to add extra inches to the blue skirts.

Forcibly detained, Fable huddled on the window seat, gnawing on resentment. Something about those lowered skirt lengths piqued a grievance she hadn't known she possessed. Why should *Sonnet* get to decide how long her skirts should be? All the other girls would be gadding about with brand-new, fashionably cut skirts, and here was Fable's not-mother putting her in nun-length skirts with glaring hem bands.

As *if* she needed any more targets on her back.

At the sight of Marco traversing the field towards the cottage, Fable straightened breathlessly. Maybe there was a way out of here, after all! She chanced a glance at Sonnet, who was earnestly cutting the seeds out of lychees for Plummy, thereby ruining all the silken joy of their mouth-popping perfection. Fable sighed. On second thoughts, Sonnet would no doubt take a sharp knife to Fable's pleasure today, too.

She flew from the window seat as Marco peered through the door. Her greeting, uncharacteristically animated, turned his face crimson.

Sonnet came to stand behind Fable with hands on hips.

'Excuse me, Miss Hamilton, but can Fable come tubing down the creek with the gang?'

Fable turned wide eyes on her sister, suspecting a 'please' was in order, but unwilling to produce it.

'No. Sorry. We're getting ready for school, can't spare her.'

'It's our end-of-summer tradition. Raff Hull is catching the train back to Brissie for uni tomorrow, and he always takes us up for a tube before he leaves. When the creek's up after the rains, we can float all the way down from Moria Falls at the top of the gorge. Only takes a couple of hours and Fable can walk home from the bridge. Both Raff and Kate are going, and they're like adults. Adriana sent me to get her and everyone is—'

Sonnet, already shaking her head, paused. 'Who did you say?'

'Adriana. She wants Fable to come. Everyone's at Hulls' waiting for us.'

Sonnet pshawed. 'Well, don't be surprised if they've left by the time you get there.'

The sarcasm was lost on Marco.

Sonnet's eyes narrowed. 'How do I know it's safe? You're not tubing over falls, are you?'

'We paddle in downstream from the falls. Raff drives us up in their truck.'

Sonnet's glare bore him out. He looked at Fable for help.

'Please, Sonnet,' Fable said.

The triumphant flash in Sonnet's eyes signalled acquiescence a dragged-out moment before permission was actually granted.

'Did she?' Fable asked as she and Marco cut a hasty path across the paddock. Around them, the mountains steamed.

'Who, what?'

'Adriana. Did she send you? Or did you say that to convince my sister?'

'Nah. She did.'

'Did someone make her?'

Marco laughed. 'You could put it that way.'

'But who?' Fable was starting to lag behind.

'Mrs Hull, in the end. But it was kind of a big deal before that.'

'What do you mean?' Fable stopped now, forcing Marco back to her.

'I don't want to go broadcasting family dramas. It was awkward. And I don't want to hurt your feelings. Take it from me, in the *end* Adriana said you should come.'

He moved to go. Fable folded her arms.

Marco was faintly exasperated. 'Okay, look. When we met at Hulls' today, I asked if you were coming and Adriana just made some comments about how you didn't belong in the gang or in Noah, plus ... some other things. Raff heard it. He tore strips off Adriana in front of everyone, had a bit to say to Mrs Hull, too. Mrs Hull *was* siding with

Adriana, to be honest, and they went inside to discuss it privately. But we could pretty much hear it. Anyway, Raff put his foot down – said he wouldn't be taking *anyone* up the gorge today unless they cut their rot out. Told them it would be more embarrassing sending everyone home than admitting they were wrong to exclude you.'

Fable exhaled in dismay. 'So, the *only* reason Adriana asked me to come was so tubing wouldn't be cancelled?'

'You have to come – it's your first time. Never mind Adriana. Raff runs this thing anyway.'

Fable wavered, but only for a moment. Adriana could get stuffed. *No one* would stand in the way of her seeing Raff Hull today.

The circle of kids sheltering from the blazing sun beneath the mango trees grew quiet as Marco and Fable approached. By the idling truck, toes scuffed in dirt, girls giggled behind hands, and several boys scuttled away to assist with the last-minute loading of tyre inner tubes. Adriana marched straight up to the newcomers. Fable flinched.

'Hi, Fable. Thanks so much for coming,' Adriana said sweetly, eyes telling a different story.

Fable had the obscene urge to laugh. 'Thank you for asking me,' she replied, with equal sugariness.

The truck grumbled impatiently. Fable's eyes searched reflexively for Raff. He was already in the driver's seat, proud tautness in his back. As Fable shimmied onto the tray of the truck, Raff's face appeared in the side-view mirror.

Fable stared back, deer in the headlights. He nodded at her – a movement so subtle she might have invented it. Fable countered it with a tiny bow, and, heart thumping at her audacity, settled down with a tube.

Diesel fumes rose in an enveloping fug as the truck rattled up the steep, narrow gorge road towards Moria Falls. Fable clutched her tube tightly among the crush of black rubber and sweaty young bodies. It was only when her legs began to cramp that she realised her every muscle was tensed against the precarious rock and clatter of the journey. She closed her eyes, pressed her forehead against the tyre and watched the dance of dappled light across her eyelids. Within minutes, the deep roar of cascades eclipsed the motor's rumble.

The road opened into a car park, dotted with caravans and Volkswagens. Fable marvelled at the sheer cliff face towering above. Moria Falls was a precisely vertical flume, over one hundred and fifty feet high, set against a ragged spill of ferny rocks and ledges. The waterfall tumbled into a large lagoon, peppered with swimmers. Moisture misted from the falls, casting tiny rainbows in the spray. Bordering the pool were picnic tables, hedged garden areas, and a long teahouse proudly proclaiming it had been 'Serving Devonshire Tea since 1920'. Peacocks wandered regally by the water's lapping edge.

'Peacocks live here?' Fable asked. But no one paid her any heed.

Kids dived out in a tangle of tubes and limbs. Arms reached to help the younger girls and Fable took a hand, leaping into the press. She stumbled on landing, and the assisting hand slipped to her swimmer-clad bottom, delving in deeply. Fable yelped, jumping clear. Eamon Hull moved away from her, smirking.

Fable faltered, looking for someone to share her outrage. The group, however, was already peeling off towards a stone staircase. Eamon, at the lead, was surrounded by laughter.

She must have imagined it.

He didn't. Did he?

Tubes were flung down and the grand cast-off began. Fable sidled up to Kate Hardy. As the oldest girl among them – practically a grown-up – surely she wouldn't regard Fable's ignorance with contempt?

'There aren't any more waterfalls after this?'

Kate grinned. 'Nope, next one is ours at the Glade and we get out before that!'

'What should I . . . do? I've never tubed.'

'It's pretty self-explanatory hey, just hop on and float! Paddle away from branches or rocks. If you get stuck, wait, one of the older kids will give you a heave-ho. But if you fall off, hold on to the tube because it's a pain in the bum trying to catch a runaway.'

Fable nodded, drawing herself together in readiness. She followed Kate into the water and their tubes were quickly taken up by the current. Across the pool they sailed, a flotilla of black doughnuts. The banks narrowed, funnelling them into the creek flow. Tubes jostled for position.

Fable felt a bubble of cheer rising in her chest, though she dared not release it.

Look at me, Mama, I'm tubing!

The creek coursed on and the armada began to separate. For now, Fable was sticking doggedly close to Kate, who was oblivious to everything else but the slow kicking of her toes in water.

Overreaching trees sheltered them from the sun and riverbanks offered boundless wonder, changing at every turn: here, a sandy shore; there, choked with buttress tree roots; now a steep cliff, covered in ferns. Turtles fled logs at their approach and eels rippled beneath. An iridescent dragonfly descended upon Fable's tyre like a tiny, glittering helicopter. Oh, she could paint a whole book of Serpentine Creek imagery!

Maybe one day, she would – for Mama.

Fable squinted at a logodile basking on the bank, waiting for it to slide into the water with sly ease. Were there crocodiles in the creek? She hadn't even thought to ask – stupid! She drew her legs up, scanning through Gav's tales for waterway safety tips.

That's right; Uncle Gav said freshwater creeks were home to the small, harmless crocs called freshies. Only estuarine creeks contained the gargantuan salties. The first would give a nip at best; the latter would, after some underwater stalking, take her whole, thrash her in a monstrous death roll, then store her rotting remains underwater like a refrigerated delicacy. Serpentine Creek was home to neither species.

Kate was drifting ahead. Impulsively, Fable reached for a nearby rock. She clung for a minute, allowing Kate to bump out of sight. Alone now, Fable sank more comfortably into the tube. How was it she felt more herself floating in Serpentine Creek than she had for years? Her heart was as light as the air upon which she sailed. She *flowed*.

It occurred to Fable, at idle length, that she hadn't asked where or how to disembark. She'd been sailing for ages now without sighting another tuber. She imagined herself floating right on out to sea, cast adrift on the Great Barrier Reef, and thought with perverse pleasure how that would frustrate Sonnet's back-to-school agenda.

Fable sensed they were nearing Heartwood, flashes of farmland glimpsed through the forest wall. She sagged, loath for her journey to end.

As if a prayer's answer, Fable hit her first snag of the day, marooning on a midstream island of rocks and branches. Water rippled brashly past her on either side, but she was stuck fast. And so *what*? There were other tubers trailing behind. One would arrive eventually – all she could do was wait.

How are you going to make me come home now, Sonnet?

Fable luxuriated in her predicament. Raising arms, she threw back her face to the canopy and released a cry of long-restrained euphoria – swept away, even as she floundered upon the rocks.

'Well, I'm glad you're getting your money's worth,' came a laughing voice.

Fable whipped her head forward, spinning wildly.

It was Raff, sailing towards her. His tube *thunk*ed into hers, a hand shooting out to dock.

'Sorry!' she said, sitting up straight.

'Don't apologise for enjoying yourself. I can't stand it when I bring these kids up here and they think they're too cool to crack a smile all day.'

Fable tried to remember how many smiles she'd cracked.

'Geez, you've really washed up here,' he said, tugging at her tube. 'How'd you manage *this*?'

'I got one of your bodgy tubes. Didn't even come with a steering wheel, much less brakes.'

He laughed. Fable sat back, overawed by this nearness; the nudging press of his tyre, fair-haired arms barely missing hers as he worked to dislodge her. Seen up close, Raff was even more handsome – eyes bluer, face larger, lips fuller, brow darker. Probably best if she stopped breathing altogether now.

He had her freed within moments. Next time, she'd have to get stuck better. Maybe bring a pin.

'There you go!' he said, as their conjoined tubes entered a channel of rapids. 'Now you can go back to your yodelling.'

A vivid blue kingfisher swept low across their course.

'Might even crack a smile,' she said; amber eyes caught, wide and limpid, in a net of dappled light.

He looked at her as one might a puppy. For a second, she thought he might even ruffle her hair.

'Your bridge is just ahead. Want me to wait?'

'No, I've got the hang of it now. Got to watch out for icebergs . . .'

They both laughed.

'Righto then!' he said, tube spinning away in a gliding circle. 'See you next year, kiddo!'

Fable watched Raff's back unblinkingly as he sailed off into the distance. A tight bulge ached in her throat. A whole long *year* until she saw him again – might as well be an eternity. And he thought she was a *kid*.

Raff disappeared around the bend. Fable closed her eyes and let the foolish tears roll hot and large over her cheeks.

CHAPTER 12
AN UNPERFECT ACTOR

December 1956

S onnet could not comprehend how they were marking their second Christmas in the valley. Where was time going? Down the gurgler, with the best of her hopes and ambitions.

It was Sunday morning, which for Sonnet meant a few rare hours of solitude while the girls were at church with their aunt and uncle. Sonnet sat on the cottage stoop, perspiring profusely, lacing her sandshoes to go running.

Running, Olive had intimated recently, was a *man's* sport, and there could be no benefit to it over the much more ladylike option of walking.

Sonnet had tallied an extra benefit there and then: shocking Olive.

But today's run was going to *hurt* – it didn't get any easier to move in the insufferable tropics. The saturated air was a thick blanket under which she moved in a torpid haze. Sweat stuck her heavy ponytail against her neck, moustached her lip, pooled in her cleavage, and ran in great rivulets down her back and limbs. The previous summer, everyone swore she'd be 'acclimatised' by the next, but she was in the same seething mood as last summer. Gav said she'd 'gone troppo'. Sonnet suspected she was just born that way.

Sure, the tropics were stunning in summer: indecent exposure of green; rumbling cumulonimbus cloud formations piling up; mango trees hung in baubled glory; festive flame-tree blooms floating on the creek; red and pink and yellow poinciana trees blinking on like beacons across the vale. Yet who could enjoy *any* of it with the humidity-induced rage?

But today, even if it made her spontaneously combust, Sonnet would *run*! She watched Fable tramp off into the rainforest daily, while she was left holding the fort. Now it was Sonnet's turn.

Sonnet began to run – with vexation hot on her heels. Ahead, the rainforest was an electric fence, humming.

Nineteen fifty-six had been a humbling year for this sister-mother. Full-time guardianship was so much harder than she had anticipated. After the child-rearing and housekeeping responsibilities she'd borne from such a young age, Sonnet had assumed she, of all people, had been equipped for the job.

Oh sweet hubris!

What was the grimmest testament to her incompetence? The sister with the cordoned-off heart and unnerving passivity; or the one with more issues than you could poke a stick at?

The obvious answer was Plum, what with her pants soiling, screaming nightmares, sporadic periods of muteness, and that humiliating fiasco with kindergarten at the beginning of the year. Honestly, who gets expelled from *kindergarten*?

She'd come so close this year to crying defeat over that troubled, stubborn girl. It was only the unspoken tug-of-war with Olive which had spurred her on. She couldn't deny Plum's loyalties were transferring evermore quickly to Olive and Gav now. In lieu of kindergarten, she spent several days a week with Olive, and asked nightly to sleep over at Heartwood. Allowing Plum set days with Olive and Gav had been the first, Sonnet suspected, of many grudging concessions. Olive now had a bedroom permanently prepared for Plum, replete with every luxury of her heart's desire.

That Olive wanted it so badly only made Sonnet more ungenerous.

Olive, for her part, was a model of such persistent charity, Sonnet could hardly stomach it. Take the church thing. Olive got it in her head, months ago, that Plummy wanted to join them at church, and she'd been wearing Sonnet down, drip by persevering drip, ever since. Sonnet wasn't dead set against the idea; the structure and routine of the Sunday School program Olive described actually sounded good for Plummy. She might have wormed her way out of kindergarten, but she couldn't evade Olive's God! Still, Sonnet had made her objections clearly known. She didn't want any of the girls copping damnation and judgement! The Hamilton girls had *never* stepped foot in a church – come to think of it, they might burst into flames if they tried.

Olive had listened quietly, but answered with surprising firmness: 'I wouldn't ask if I didn't think Plummy would feel loved and accepted there. It's a different world to what it was twenty years ago, and besides, wasn't *I* the one who insisted on pulling Plummy out of kindergarten when she was so unhappy?'

Sonnet finally had agreed, with a rigid caveat: 'Your church cronies only get *one* chance. If Plummy comes home talking hellfire, if someone mentions Mama, if anyone as much as *looks* at her wrong, we're done!'

Unexpectedly, Fable had volunteered herself for church, too. Olive merely had rattled off a list of neighbours who attended, and Fable had leapt at the opportunity. Sonnet could discern why – Fable, still yearning to fit in, didn't want to be the only kid in the valley left out of church. And fair enough, the safety of group identification was important for adolescent girls.

111

The next Sunday morning, Sonnet brought Plum up to Heartwood dressed in the sweetest pink seersucker smock and patent leather Mary Janes – proud as if she'd made the girl herself! Fable, will wonders never cease, readied herself willingly, prettily and on time for once. Then Sonnet knew she'd pegged Fable's motives correctly.

And any victory over Fable's barricades, no matter how small, was one to celebrate. Acting as Fable's guardian was an infuriating exercise in futility. Fable was attached to no one, and unknowable to all. She drifted untethered through the days; if not traipsing through the forest, disappearing into daydreams and scribbles. And the more Sonnet grabbed at her, the further and faster away Fable slipped. Maybe it was just being fourteen, and Sonnet had never experienced a normal adolescence herself, so what would she know? Fable had every excuse to embrace angst, especially in *this* town with *their* family background.

In the space of a year, Fable had become a long-limbed, lissom young lady, though she would not reach Sonnet's statuesque height. The commencement of puberty had only strengthened Fable's quiet poise. And by poise, Sonnet meant obliviousness. The girl didn't even seem to care about her changing body. Sonnet rushed out and bought several training bras for Fable once her development became apparent. Looser blouses were hastily sewn up next. Fable had taken both with nary a word, perhaps the faintest smile – then left them in her drawers. Sonnet was flummoxed. Did this constitute rebellion? A sign that Fable didn't want to leave her childhood behind? Was she grieving for her real mother's influence?

Sonnet had agonised over how to broach talk of puberty and sexuality with Fable. Enflamed with poetry, giggling confession and graphic themes as Mama had with her? No, that had been an overstep. Esther had teased Sonnet for being the 'puritan daughter of a floozy' when Sonnet had demurred from such talk – but it wasn't that, not at all.

Sonnet simply wanted a mother, not a girlfriend. Better to be plain, factual with this Hamilton daughter – including discussion of female agency.

But Fable had closed away, indeed *run* away, the moment Sonnet began her spiel. Sonnet couldn't seem to clear that first hurdle. She refused to think of herself as either unqualified, or a novice; though both were true.

Olive disagreed that it was rebellion, reticence *or* grief. 'She's doing fine. She just doesn't want to talk about it. Maybe you're coming on too forcefully. I can chat to her.'

Over my dead body, Sonnet thought.

Nevertheless, Olive arrived home one day with a hardcover book and pressed it into Sonnet's hands: '*Essential Facts for Young Women*. Written by a doctor, with lots of diagrams.'

Sonnet perused the book judiciously first. Well, Olive wasn't exactly fibbing. The book *was* penned by a doctor, and all the relevant facts were certainly there, with beautifully scientific diagrams. Yet, Sonnet's gut twisted at the book's prescriptions for female modesty and its stern coaxing against premarital sex, and the 'monstrous problem' of babies born out of wedlock. *What poppycock!* The book had been sponsored by a church – Olive had neglected to mention *that*, hadn't she?

Moralising aside, the book did offer solid medical information plus some helpful info on deportment and dating, and might have to do until Sonnet could source another one – the market for puberty books in Australia was thin. She had no intention of passing it on, however, until she'd annotated it thoroughly.

One night, Sonnet sat down with a notepad and did just that, hectoring the doctor, throughout his tome. As Sonnet inserted her modern knowledge in between the pages of the book, she imagined the discussions her efforts might finally open up between the sisters. They could jeer the doctor's archaic opinions together! They would be united by a common enemy: traditionalists.

Fable, however, immediately tossed the book, and all Sonnet's accrued wisdom with it, onto her pile of 'Things I'll Never Use Because Sonnet Provided Them'. There all hope of discussion had ended. Being a proxy mother stank!

Sonnet doubled over now to catch her breath. She was going to give herself a heart attack at this rate. She drew in a deep mouthful of pungent rainforest rot, lifting her face to a cooling breeze. *Psithurism*, she told herself, *whisper of wind in the trees*. A smile, only small, tugged at her cheeks. At least she still had her own aptitudes.

In fact, the only area of Sonnet's life at which she excelled anymore *was* her work. She was now doing three days a week with Alfred in his bookstore, and loving every minute. She had, Alfred said, 'the book-seller's touch'. She still helped Olive out with a full day in Emerson's Fashion and Fabrics, leaving the rest of the week for Delia Bloody Hull to pick up her quilting fabrics without the indignity of being served by *that* Hamilton.

By all accounts, Sonnet's alterations were the finest in town. A few customers had even suggested Sonnet should branch out into her own dressmaking business. She was getting a big head with all the feedback, but thank goodness she still had those outlets in her life for success and accolades. It offset the near constant urge to *scream*.

Speaking of which, right now was as good a time as any. And in the humming forest basilica, lungs burning with the worshipful joy of running, Sonnet raised her arms to the canopied heavens and let an almighty bellow go.

CHAPTER 13
THE CATHEDRAL

January 1957

Fable shifted on her rock perch, allowing herself just one glance at the Glade stairway entrance, before returning to her sketchbook, the pencil's staccato beat the only hint of her inner turmoil.

The Sunday train, bearing precious cargo, came in before Christmas, though Fable had yet to clap eyes upon him. Raff's arrival had been trumpeted to the heavens by Adriana, who bragged daily of the board games they'd played, the horse rides he had taken them on, the fashionable families they'd had around for dinner, and the new cubby house he was finishing in a mango tree. The waiting Fable had borne for twelve patient months was now agonising indeed.

Every afternoon she'd been lurking at the Glade and each Sunday at church – hair brushed out in strawberry waves, gaze sliding to the Hulls' front-row pew despite herself, and his absence. Adriana had been incensed by Fable's sudden appearance at *her* church. Fable had almost expected Adriana to chase her back down the aisle; screeching incantations, splashing holy water.

But even that would be no impediment to Fable. Adriana was the sister of her heart's desire – she must be kept in constant eyesight. To that end, Fable would sit at the Glade all day in Adriana's peacocking company, pretending not to notice the girl's every move was a challenge issued to her greatest rising rival.

Fable had coasted aloofly through Grade Eight, an illusion carefully contrived, and posing direct competition to Adriana's status. Though she made no friend her particular, Fable was sought out by misfits and social-ladder climbers alike. Even Adriana circled slyly near. Given half a chance, or a whit of know-how, Adriana would have wrung out every drop of Fable's inexplicable haughtiness.

Fable chanced another glance up, and sighed. She narrowed her eyes on her watercolour – a waterfall, surrounded by naked rainforest faeries, their arms outstretched in an ecstatic worship. It was a recurring theme, one that had scandalised her fellow eighth graders when the nubile nymphs were revealed by the class boofheads, who had tossed the sketchbook between them, whooping over the 'dirty' drawings they had found.

Fable cursed herself for having shoved the sketchbook in her port that morning with the intention of heading on to the Green Woman's Grove after school. It was bad enough she had to conceal the book from Sonnet's prying eyes, much less those buffoons, and it was her own fault for not staying guarded, at all times.

The accusation that Fable was the creator of 'French postcards' – mere titillation for smelly *boys* – had been a crushing shame. But it was only the mocking laughter that had caused her shame. Fable could be no more ashamed of her art than she could of breathing. She was beholden to the creative energy coursing through her veins. She must create as inspiration compelled.

Still, it hadn't hurt to start clothing her faeries.

Fable would never be so daft as to take her sketchbook to school again. She counted herself lucky the boys had been so taken with the nude pictures; scant attention was given to the blue eyes repeated on every other page.

If her suspicions were right, however, and Adriana and company had been the ones to thieve the book from her port, then perhaps Fable's deepest fear was realised. To imagine Adriana sighting those sketches brought waves of dread – a sister would surely recognise her brother's eyes.

And yet, she waited now at the Glade, only a few feet from Adriana, with the very evidence of her obsession held in ink-stained hands. Fable thrilled at her own daring. Now and then, when Adriana was annoying her sufficiently, Fable flipped back to a sketch of blue eyes; smug in furtive victory.

You don't own Raff!

Some days she wanted to throw her book at the back of Adriana's raven head. Even a river rock would do, at a pinch.

On the following Saturday, the gang bypassed the Glade, trekking further downstream to a place they called the Cathedral. Fable knew she'd only been included because Marco swung past the Hamilton cottage on his way through. To be honest, Fable wasn't really in the mood to go – she'd been nursing a tummy ache all morning – but Marco looked woebegone at her initial refusal.

The Cathedral was only accessible via a mile-long trek through thick vegetation. Marco, stampeding ahead, was undaunted even when the path became a funnel of jungle grass higher than their heads, humming with insects. Fable tried not to think of overlarge pythons, and felt thankful they'd moved on from the thicket of tar trees, which, Marco had been at pains to point out, could cause blindness. She had taken him at his earnest word. One could never quite tell what was or wasn't urban legend in this part of Australia; so many otherworldly animals and plants seeking to maim the uninitiated.

Only yesterday, Fable found a new treasure for her diverse collection of rainforest flora: a lurid blue fruit as big as her hand – and yet Uncle Gav had scolded her for it! Cassowary plums, he lectured, were *poisonous* to all except the giant, flightless cassowary birds after which they were coloured and named. Fable was marched off to the bathroom to wash her hands by an officiously smirking Sonnet, and Plum was close on their heels with her hands held out, pleading to know: was she a *poisonous* Plum, too?

Fable decided she would just keep the next exotic fruit she discovered to herself.

Ahead now, a banyan tree rose majestically out of the canopy, with branches spanning absurdly wide, tentacles falling as a thick curtain around the broad, multi-trunked cavern.

They emerged from the grass into dwarfing shade. On the branches, even at dizzying heights, kids lounged like jungle cats, tossing insults or flirtatious banter. Two main groups had formed, allegiances drawn between the returned St Ronan's boys and Noah Vale kids.

Fable was still scanning their gum-popping ranks for Adriana's dark ponytail, when a tall figure dropped from a branch above, to land beside them.

'Hey, Marco,' the man-boy said.

He nodded at Fable, blond hair tumbling over his brow, and she felt herself staggering backwards, though she hadn't moved an inch.

Rafferty was here.

And the blue eyes she had laboured over, from precious memory alone, were alive and blinking upon her once more.

Did the other kids see how she *flamed* sitting on this upper bough? Would she set the whole tree alight as she burned for that boy? Fable had taken refuge here from her own impetuosity, feeling like an unexploded firecracker. The urge to reach out and touch Raff had competed with the terror that he might, merely, look at her. All year she had waited; all month long she had planned for first sight of him, and yet still Raff dropped back into her world with the manner and effect of a falling bomb.

Look at him down there: taller and handsomer than she remembered, arms crossed in his thoughtful manner, nodding at Marco as they chatted; now and then breaking out his gentle smile with no idea of its potency.

She wiped sticky hands against her shirt and gripped tighter at her branch.

Caustic laughter rang out and automatically Fable's awareness moved to assess the threat. No barbs at her spine, so it probably wasn't the cunning slide of Eamon's regard. Casting further afield, she saw Adriana, Jessica, Megan and Isabella crouched in the lower branches with heads together, all eyes on Fable, and laughter leaking out . . .

'Go and tell her now, so we can watch. It'll be hilarious.'

'*You* tell her.'

'No one tell her! The bitch deserves it.'

'She *really* does.'

Fable reassessed her outfit choice for the day – boat-neck summer top tucked into belted white shorts; nothing controversial – and scanned back over her behaviour since she'd arrived. How had she sinned *today*? It had to be the way she was staring at Raff. She mustn't look his way again, even if it killed her.

Fable forced herself to follow the Tree Tiggy game getting started in the cavernous bosom of the tree.

'Same rules as normal Tiggy,' Vince Lagorio was saying, 'but when you're tagged, drop out of the tree. Last man standing picks who's in next round.'

Good old Kate was calling for her to join in, and Fable clambered down her branch towards salvation. Activity would provide release for her pounding anxiety. Or her heart might actually stop, in which case she'd still be better off than she was right now.

Raff remained on the ground, while Marco climbed up to play, aligning himself with Fable. It was no surprise Adriana positioned herself on the limb with the St Ronan's boys, leaning coquettishly over the shoulder of the one who referred to *himself* as 'Van the Man'. What did concern Fable, however, was the way Adriana drew the boys into a ring, indicating Fable with a whisper. Laughing scorn was lobbed around. Fable heard her name on Eamon's lips, then a braying laugh.

Tree Tiggy began. Children swooped and screeched: a tree come alive with clothed primates. Fable was caught and tagged in a matter of moments by Van the Man – to much laughter from higher branches. She slipped from the tree; mortified to hit the ground first and find Raff smiling in commiseration. Fable rubbed her wrists meaningfully, as if some weird wrist condition or pre-existing injury explained her tagging. This juvenile pantomime humiliated more than actually losing.

Over two more Tree Tiggy rounds, Fable was the first one returned each time to the ground. Anyone could see Fable was being specifically targeted by the St Ronan's boys – to wide hilarity. By her third first-one-out tagging, Fable was enraged. She met Raff's sympathetic smile with a scowl.

He held up both hands. 'Hey, I'm Switzerland!'

Fable kicked away, fuming. It was Raff's fault, anyway; refusing to play like some kind of grown-up, making her so uncoordinated and hopelessly in love with him.

For the fourth round, she would change tactics. If she couldn't out-manoeuvre the bullies, she'd outwit them. Wishing she wasn't wearing white on a day when camouflage was essential, Fable eased off quietly at the side of the Cathedral. Behind her, she heard Raff call, in a low voice. 'Fable, you've got—' She closed her ears.

Watch this, Switzerland.

She wove into the Cathedral's underbelly, where hanging roots enclosed her like the tentacles of a prehistoric jellyfish. Light penetrated only weakly into the pungent miasma of swollen fertility.

Fable faded deeper into the lightless, dripping underworld. Now here was something she knew herself the master of: hidden worlds. She grinned as she heard the first person – *not* her – drop to the ground with a dismayed cry, and Raff's muted tones responding. A succession of dropping children followed. Not only was she surviving, she still hadn't been sighted at all. She just had to hold tight here, a few moments longer.

Smile pityingly at me now, Rafferty Hull!

Adriana and Van the Man's crows sounded overhead. 'Four straight wins – new record!'

Fable recognised her cue to emerge as the true victor. Oh gosh, but what about little old *me*, she would ask. Adriana would hiss in defeat as Fable fastened her eyes on Raff's beaming, upturned face.

'Here I come, suckers,' she whispered, not moving an inch.

The darkness held her. Breath softened and flowed. Dreamily detached moments passed, measured out by the slow metronomic dripping of entombed raindrops.

Fable sensed she was alone now in the tree, forgotten in an unheard departure. Fear was only a tiny flicker, easily extinguished. She could not even rouse herself enough to care.

At slumberous length, Fable became mindful of stickiness in her undergarments, akin to having wet her pants. She went to reach inside her shorts, and stopped. From an unseen vantage point, twenty pairs of eyes were probably aimed to catch Fable with her hands down her crotch.

Fable slid from her perch, enfolding herself deeper in the tree. She thrust two fingers under the hemline of her shorts, swiping. Even in the gloom, she could make out a dark gloop on her fingers. She sniffed tentatively and recoiled from the metallic odour. Automatically, she wiped it on her thighs before remembering, with a dismayed breath, the whiteness of her shorts. She scrubbed her fingers desperately on the roots hanging by, until they came away smelling of earth, and something more ageless still.

Understanding surfaced from the murk.

She pushed back through the Cathedral folds to find a beam of filtered light. She spun wildly, and found it: wide red smear, right up the back of her white shorts. All morning, she'd been bleeding for all to see – even Raff!

Fable, you've got . . .

. . . blood, all over yourself.

She could just die. Right here, right now. The ache in her lower belly gripped like a reptilian claw, as the moisture in her pants spread further out.

Beyond her sanctuary, Fable heard voices calling her name. So, she had not been forgotten in the exodus, after all. Fable steeled herself against a trunk, and discovery. She would stay quiet, hide out until night, then run for home. She pictured herself stumbling through the dark forest, straight into a stinging tree, getting strung up in wait-a-while barbs, going blind from a tar tree, tripping into a nest of feral pigs – or a spreading python's maw.

She heard a sing-song voice, close by. In her desperation, she fancied it the Green Woman, come once more to lead her out of trouble.

'Fa-ble,' cajoled the silhouette against the light. Fable recognised that shape as Kate, and realised she knew exactly where Fable was hiding. Pinioned against the tree, Fable watched the older girl ease herself into the darkness.

'Are you there, sweetie?'

Aw, hell.

'I'm here.'

Kate squinted, eyes adjusting. 'Are you *okay*?'

'I'm just . . . exploring.'

'Oh, fun.'

This was what Fable liked most about Kate compared with her cousin Adriana – with most people, in fact – that she bumped happily alongside others, like a leaf in a stream.

'Are you ready to come home? Raffy and I are going now, if you want to come with us.'

'*Rafferty* is out there?'

'He was the only one who saw where you went. The others figured you'd taken off home sooking about losing. Everyone else has gone on for lunch at Summerlinn, want to come?'

Fable's mind ran in panicked circles: she would sprint out of the tree – streaming blood – so fast he didn't have time to see a thing; *no*, she would stay here and demand they go on without her; *wait*, what if she lagged along behind them, barking, 'Don't look at me!' each time they turned her way?

Kate, however, had taken Fable's arm in comradely fashion and was leading her out of this sanctuary.

They came, blinking, into searing-green light. Fable shielded her eyes from a thousand exploding flashlight bulbs trained on her alone.

And yet: no more gloating laughter, just Kate's chatter and an empty clearing. For a second or two, Fable hoped Raff had already left.

But no, there he was, waiting at the grassy jungle, scuffing at the ground with one foot. He glanced up, and Fable saw raw concern. Kate did not speak or let go of Fable's arm, but in the exchange of glances between the older pair, there was an interaction that explicitly related to Fable.

Raff nodded, turning quickly towards home. 'I'm off. See you later, Katy, Fable.'

Fable quivered until his back had disappeared from sight, thankful for the soft arm linked in hers, and for Kate's blithe nattering, which ceased not, the entire way home.

CHAPTER 14

BEHIND THE CURTAIN DRAWN

January 1957

Sonnet jerked awake, gasping. She shuddered there, waiting for fear to take coherent shape. The darkness behind the lace curtains flapping at the window told her it was the dead of night. Torrential rain battered the cottage. A choir filled the attic room with ecstatic, swelling frog song. She might have stepped into an auditorium, a roaring football field, a holy cathedral. Profound, aching sadness beset her.

Something's gone.

She scrounged around the bed for Plum's curled shape before remembering, with mingled relief and disappointment, that she was spending her regular weekend night with Olive and Gav.

Fable!

Sonnet flung herself from bed, racing for the stairs. During the last year and a half, she had come to dread these night wakings, terrified of discovering Fable vanished into the wilderness again. Even the front door deadbolts Gav had installed had failed to reassure. She knew, ultimately, there *was* no true mechanism for keeping her sister restrained, or safe, much less happy. And lately, Fable seemed to be retreating further. She'd barely mumbled a word for days. It was exactly the kind of 'Fable Mood' which most frightened Sonnet.

What if she'd gone chasing ghosts again?

Sonnet charged into Fable's sleep-out. The French doors were widely ajar, curtains billowing in the gusting rain. Sonnet shivered, tripping over her own feet. For a stricken second, she couldn't make out Fable's figure in the darkness. Her hands ran in panicked circles in the bedclothes. At last her fingers found an ankle, and Sonnet could breathe again. She pulled the sheet high over thin limbs, gently stroking tendrils from Fable's brow.

The curtains ballooned and flapped. Fable mumbled and folded away from the damp incursion. Sonnet turned her attention to the open window, kneeling on the seat to tug at the pane. Beneath her knees, the wooden board of the seat jiggled and lifted. She jumped off, fearing she'd broken it, and realised it was a removable lid. How had she failed to find it during her compulsive cleaning sessions?

Clearly, Fable had not been so ignorant. Inside, she discovered secret artefacts – rainforest seeds, iridescent emerald feathers, two halves of a thunder egg, and a pile of linen shoved on top. Fable had appropriated it as a laundry hamper.

Sonnet shuddered at the rank odour of soiled clothing. Just what she needed, *more* washing when the outside line couldn't be used and the clothing draped everywhere inside was refusing to dry in constant wet-season damp. She hauled out the pile, letting the window seat fall back with a clunk. If Fable woke right now, Sonnet had a few pertinent things she intended to say about such stinking, filthy habits!

She'd get started on the soaking immediately. The grip of anxiety was not abating, and her hands needed something to do. Cane toads scattered as she descended the rickety back stairs to the outdoor laundry.

She drew a pail of hot water and reached for the soap flakes, then stopped short. In the light of the swinging light globe, she was sure some of Fable's clothes were bloodied. She squinted, sniffed, and drew back in shock. There was blood all *over* these garments, the odour of stale menstrual blood at once familiar and repellent. Fable had started her periods and said nothing! There was at least a week's worth of clothing and linen shoved in that secret hole.

Sonnet wanted to shake Fable from sleep and squeeze her for both excitement and frustration. But Fable had already greeted this momentous occasion with fear and shame, and, with that knowledge, tears came. Her sister had no mother to usher her lovingly into womanhood, and the fake mother she *did* have was clearly failing. For a week she had battled through her first period, with no sanitary products, no comfort. Goodness knows what she'd been trying to use to stem the flow. Knowing Fable, probably fig leaves knitted together.

The image should have made Sonnet laugh, but tears coursed down her cheeks. *Now* she understood why Fable had refused to leave the house for days, why she'd rebuffed invites to church and, more worryingly, gatherings at the creek with wistfulness now tragic in Sonnet's memory rather than confounding, as it had been at the time. Fable had not a true friend in the world. And even when her distress had been staring Sonnet brokenly in the face, she'd been blind to it.

Sonnet leant over the washing tub now, and joined her tears to the rainstorm.

It was a long time before she lifted her face from the altar of her regret. She stomped upstairs to the attic room, flaming with resolve. She would be a better mother-substitute! Turn over a new leaf. First thing in the morning, she'd race to Hadley's store and buy the poor kid some Kotex. But for once she wouldn't lecture; just let Fable know she was there for her. That she'd *always* be there for her. From now on, she was going to be kinder and more patient; less intrusive but present, too. She'd stop pushing but keep asking. She just would be ... *better!*

When Sonnet settled back into bed, however, the dread upon her heart had not eased a mite. Where normally goals and resolutions soothed her worries, this time they allayed nothing. She flipped and kicked under clinging sheets, unable to throw off the pressing sorrow.

Threnody, she mouthed, without knowing why.

Hours passed. The rain intensified, eased again and returned with a roar; and, through it all, Sonnet rolled from side to side, anguished and afraid.

Fable was still asleep when Sonnet rushed to Heartwood for Plum. She held her sister tightly to herself, exhaling. Plum buckled against the cleaving, as Sonnet's eyes bored into Olive's.

'Was everything all right here last night?'

'Absolutely fine! She woke once and climbed into our bed. But she slept the night through after that.'

'Nothing unusual at all?'

'Not a thing!' After a pause, 'Are *you* okay?'

'I didn't sleep well last night, I'm skittish with overtiredness. Can I borrow the Holden this morning to grab some groceries?'

'You know it's yours to use whenever you need it. I don't know why you punish yourself riding all those hills!'

Plum nattered brightly all the way into Hadley's General Store and Sonnet, shaky with hyper-vigilance, listened for red flags. Plum was spilling over with important news: she'd eaten two bowls of Milo-topped ice cream, won several rounds of Old Maid against Aunty Ov, and kicked obliging Gav out of bed when she made her regular pilgrimage from hers to theirs in the wee hours.

See? Everyone's all right.

No, something's wrong.

They shopped the aisles at Hadley's in companionable bickering over what went into the basket. Plum would eat nothing but sweets if Sonnet didn't keep a close eye on her – and Olive.

They reached Jeannie Hadley at the counter with a hoard of sanitary products, including six different styles of Kotex belts. Sonnet knew she was overcompensating, but once she'd started piling the basket, she couldn't stop. Jeannie eyed the basket shrewdly, but directed her questions towards Plum, taking shelter in her sister's skirt. It was a tactic Sonnet knew well by now: address the smallest Hamilton in the hope of eliciting information about the supercilious older Hamilton girl. Sonnet knew she was intimidating – it was the way she fixed her green eyes upon folks, just daring them to judge her, or tell her another of their damned stories. It was no way to win friends or influence people, but it felt like power.

As Sonnet was grinding her teeth at Jeannie's probing, her awareness piqued at a woman's strident voice, carrying from a few aisles over. She'd know that voice anywhere, but in case she'd forgotten, her spine crawled. She glanced behind and spotted a coiffured roll of dark hair bobbing by the cornflakes: Delia Bloody Hull, gasbagging.

It felt somehow right to have one particular nemesis in this town upon which to project her more general frustrations with the penetrating undertones which dogged her every step down Main Street. Delia was made for the role and seemed eager to fill it. She looked at Sonnet like a boil that needed lancing. The expression was reciprocated.

As Country Women's Association president, Church Ladies Fellowship convenor, Noah Patchwork Club organiser, and matriarch of the most influential founding family in Noah Vale, Delia held the ears and loyalty of most. No doubt she gloried in Sonnet's self-imposed exclusion from various social circles – probably took the damn credit! In the eighteen months since their now-infamous altercation at Summerlinn, Delia had not once deigned to speak to Sonnet, though they skirted one another often enough on Main Street. Delia purposefully avoided Emerson's Fashion and Fabrics on Sonnet's day, and never stepped a heeled foot into Shearer's Books.

The nuclear winter, Sonnet supposed, was here to stay.

Right now, Delia was making no attempt to hush her tone. In fact, Sonnet had the distinct sense Delia was speaking directly *to* her from five aisles over, and not Mrs Hickey and Mrs Johnstone at all. She waited to hear her name, or Fable's, but was taken aback to hear Alfred Shearer's, instead. Her hand stilled on the pads she was unloading, heart churning out a few too many beats.

'Dead?!' came a scandalised cry.

'As a doornail! Found this morning by his cleaner, Glenda Harrison. She's been cleaning Alfred's shop for years now. Not that you can tell from the state of that cluttered bookshop, the *dust* for heaven's sake, she must just push it from one corner to another. Well, anyway, there he was when she let herself in: face down on his study desk. Up and died in the middle of reading correspondence. Must have been some-thing *pretty* shocking . . .'

'Oh, bet I can guess!'

The group snickered.

Delia's voice went up another notch. 'I think we *all* can. Poor man, finding out her *true* colours like that . . .'

The women clucked consensus.

'Anyway, Derrick Windsor was up there this morning, that's how we heard. Maybe it was Alfred's heart, he's always had issues with his ticker, but word is he'd caught a second bout of dengue fever. It's deadly if you get bitten again, you know.'

'Wasn't only a mozzie he was twice bitten by . . .'

Sonnet dropped her basket and hurtled out of the shop with Plum, leaving bewildered Jeannie Hadley holding the sanitary pads towards the still-shuddering door.

Down Main Street Sonnet sprinted, Plum's legs jangling against her thighs, heart pounding in her ears.

Not true, not true, not true, not true!

She collapsed against the railing with a gasp that drew no air. Plum slid down her leg and stood in the white glare, wailing.

Slowly, Sonnet raised her eyes to the shopfront, praying she would see Alfred's face peering through the window, beckoning her inside for a cuppa – ready to dispel Delia Hull's putrid lies.

But the shop was dark and locked with the shutters drawn, as Alfred was never wont to do. A handwritten page was taped to the inside of the front-door window . . .

Closed until further notice, by order of Senior Constable Windsor.

Sonnet fell to her knees, hands sliding down the locked door, head bowing against the wood. Her one friend in the valley, and her mother's only ally, had left her.

Sonnet had slammed through the cottage door this humid morning with a wordless ferocity which sent Fable scuttling away to her latest hidey-hole. Recently, Sonnet had sewn up curtains to hang at the front bay window. The curtains, when pulled, transformed the window seat into another secret sanctuary for Fable. In slanting afternoon light, the old crystal wind chime on the porch spun magical rainbows throughout the alcove. Fable loved to chase the tiny bows across the page as she read and sketched, gratefully concealed from Sonnet.

Today Fable had brought a pile of favourite books to her window nook. They lay untouched, absorbed as she was in trying to capture the post-deluge clarity she so adored.

Sonnet had thundered upstairs for an hour then returned to the kitchen, hauling pots out of a back cupboard to thrash around in a sink full of suds. Fable had inched the curtains tightly closed, hoping Sonnet couldn't hear her breathe, or think. Plum too was strangely morose this morning, not even pestering for food.

Fable stole a peek through the curtains. Pain rolled off her swollen-eyed sister. She winced, letting the curtain fall back, focusing instead on the brush at her command.

A flash of colour made Fable glance up: Olive, flying down the hill with a large paper bag. Fable grimaced. Quite possibly, Olive and Sonnet had already had one of their famous standoffs this morning, in which case their aunt would coast in with 'One more thing I need to say to you, Sonnet!'

These one-more-things inevitably ended with fifty things Sonnet had to say back.

The garden gate squealed. Fable slipped her notebook under her bum, taking refuge in her latest Georgette Heyer romance.

Olive bustled into the cottage without even knocking, throwing herself across the room at Sonnet as though she expected, strangely, no resistance today.

'Oh, Sonnet, I'm *so* sorry.'

Fable's mouth sagged in horror to hear the indomitable Sonnet Hamilton break into a guttural wail.

'He's gone! Just – gone!'

Sonnet's violent crying caused tears to push painfully against Fable's tightly squeezing eyes. Her chest constricted. That *sound*! It was losing Mama. It was every tear she had left to shed, and more.

'Alfred was a good man, Sonnet. One of the best.'

At torturous length, Sonnet spoke. 'He's gone, and I've lost my chance to know him now. I hardly asked him a thing about his own life. I was so selfish, always begging for his stories of Mama – same ones, over and over. All I'd ever known was Mama's brokenness and disenchantment, and Alfred gave me back young Esther Hamilton; full of spirit and ambition. I was gluttonous for it—'

Another breaking cry.

Olive's voice came, soothing. 'And you gave Alfred what he wanted at the end of his days: a daughter, a friend. We're grateful he was with us long enough to finally meet you. I always imagined that dear man was holding on for Esther to return. And instead, it was you who came home to Alfred.'

Sonnet's weeping resumed. Fable massaged her pencil against the headache building between her eyes. She didn't want to be hearing any of this. There was no escape from it, except to go deep within.

Fable was recalled by the rustling of Olive's paper bag. There was no one like Olive for treats and sweets. Hopefully, Olive thought they deserved plenty of sugar in recompense for Old Mr Shearer's passing.

'I'm sorry that you had to find out that way,' Olive was saying. 'Delia must have been in her element announcing her terrible news. Jean told me you dumped your groceries on her counter and ran out of the store. It was quite the scene by her retelling. I can only imagine how shocked you must have been. Wrong place at the wrong time!'

'I bet that woman was lying in wait for me.'

'Jean came to my shop in quite a state herself, dreadfully worried for you. Said to tell you she's sorry for your loss, and that your groceries today were on her. So, here they are.'

'That was generous of Jean, but I certainly am going to pay her back.'

'Nonsense. She *insisted*. So do I.'

'You didn't have to rush them over, though.'

'But when I saw all these pads, I thought you must be in desperate need, better shut up shop and bring them straight over!'

Sonnet laughed. 'You're a woman's hero, but they're not for me.' Her voice hushed – not enough, though. 'Actually, Fable got her first period. But she didn't ask for help, so she's been bleeding everywhere. It was like an abattoir in her room!'

'Oh, the poor girl. Do you need soaker? I've got plenty. How about you give me a pile of dirties to wash?'

'No, I can manage. It's not your job. But I wish the little grot had come to me about it.'

'Perhaps if I talk to her—'

'No. I'll handle it my way.'

'Sonnet, you need more help than you ask for. Oh now, don't start getting all defensive, you've got enough to worry about today. Let's strip her bed and I'll take them to Heartwood to soak. My line's bigger than yours.'

'I can't subject you to that.'

'I cared for my father in his dying days – you think I'm squeamish at my age? Come on, quickly! We'll get it done before she gets home.'

The creak of their determined stride into the sunroom masked the front door's quiet click. The slip of a girl streaking across the field towards the creek, with journal clutched to her chest, went unseen. Her frantic flight did not stop until she'd reached her grove of comfort.

'Oh, Mama, Mama, Mama!' she sobbed.

The Green Woman opened ancient pleats, and gathered her in.

CHAPTER 15

PARAGON

January 1957

Paragon Cafe, enjoying its lunch-hour rush, was thrumming with teens savouring the last of the summer holidays. The milkshake frother bubbled on a continuous loop; ceiling fans whirred at full speed; arcade games competed with the jukebox.

Sonnet rearranged her egg-salad sandwich, and sighed. She regretted not taking her lunch to the shade of Raintree Park, but she hadn't been able to face either the sight of Alfred's store, or the legion of black cockatoos that had taken up a haunting residence along Main Street, two or three birds to each light pole, puffing their dark crests. All birds, but especially black ones, piqued an unearthly terror in Sonnet.

She was venturing forth for the first time in a fortnight, and only because she owed Olive a day in the shop. Sonnet certainly wasn't going to have Olive picking up the slack for *her* self-indulgence. Life went on, and she had no right to mourn Alfred like a father or grandfather, when he was neither.

Another wave of kids shoved through the art-deco doors, and Sonnet hunkered further in her booth, wishing she was safely shielded behind a shuttered shopfront. One of those Lagorio twins thumping at an arcade game hollered at the tall, young man entering, and Sonnet peeped up shrewdly as she recognised Rafferty Hull's name.

She'd seen Rafferty only from a distance, crossing Main Street or the canefields on his way to visit other farms. This was her first chance to evaluate, close up, both his alleged good looks and, from the way Gav spoke of him, the shining halo that must encircle his damned head!

He was indeed handsome – in an obvious way, and *obviously* knew it; carrying himself with Delia's tall, haughty posture.

Not my type, though!

Immediately, Sonnet upbraided herself for having stooped to evaluate him against her standards. But it was the way Rafferty bore himself which so instantly irked her – a strong, quiet confidence bespeaking an idyllic childhood and a boy beloved of all who knew him.

How must it have felt for you to have grown up the darling of an entire community, with never a moment to doubt your own God-given magnificence?

His life was the antonym of the one she had known. She disliked him instantly, and entirely. A Hull was a Hull.

Kids all over the shop were clamouring for his attention. *Who did he think he was, king of Noah Vale?* As his eyes swept curiously over her lonely booth, Sonnet dived into her sandwich. She had a sudden fear Mister Popularity would come and introduce himself. Never had a sandwich been swallowed with such focus, and distaste.

When a male shadow fell over her minutes later, Sonnet looked up, already crabby, expecting a politician's smarmy smile and winning handshake. But it was a portly and much older man who stood grinning at her table.

'Sonnet Hamilton!' he cried. 'You're a hard woman to track down.' He slid into the booth opposite, pushing his meal and milkshake onto the table. 'Harry Payne!' he pronounced, biting heartily into his asparagus-laden toast. 'Solicitor.'

Sonnet braced herself behind a quickly raised teacup. 'I imagine you must be the Harry who's been calling my aunt and uncle constantly?'

'That's me, all right. You girls still don't have a telephone in the old Hamilton cottage?'

'We don't have a need for one. I haven't returned your calls, Harry, because I've had other concerns.'

'Well, I'm glad we bumped into each other like this. I was going to drive out to the farm this week and hunt you down, so you've saved me a trip.'

Sonnet frowned. 'How can I help you, Harry?'

'No, actually, I'm about to help you, Miss Hamilton!' he declared, slurping with great satisfaction. 'Let's lunch; then I'm going to need you to come back to my office with me. We have a will to read, young lady . . .'

'Alfred left you everything?!' Olive cried in the afternoon heat of her orchard. 'The whole shop *and* his unit above?' Garden secateurs waved wildly in the air as she spoke. Sonnet followed their movement, unable to meet Olive's eyes.

'Everything.' It was more an expulsion of air than affirmation. She sank to the earth before Olive's half-pruned star fruit tree.

Olive knelt to the ground beside her, tossing her garden gloves aside. 'My word, Sonnet. My *word*!'

Both women turned to follow Plum's squeals as she navigated the exotic fruit trees with Mama's cane perambulator, filled with porcelain dolls.

After a time, Sonnet said, sotto voce: 'So now I own a bookstore.'

'Yes, you certainly do.'

'But he never said *anything* about leaving it to me. The whole town's going to think I insinuated myself into his life for this windfall.' Sonnet gave a sour laugh. 'Worse: they'll probably say I poisoned him for it!'

'Nonsense!' Olive clucked. 'Well, maybe some of them will *think* that. But you know how minds work in this town.'

'Why would he leave it to me, though? He must have family who will come contesting this kind of lavish generosity.'

Olive considered this. 'Nope, I don't think Alfred has anyone left at all now. You're going to be home and hosed. I think he must have been mighty relieved to finally have someone to leave his beloved store to, actually.'

'I didn't spend all that time helping him out for anything like this.'

'Of course you didn't.'

'I just wanted to be near her memory, and his admiration for her. I didn't earn this.'

'Now, don't get caught up thinking you're undeserving. I'd wager he had your mother's name on his will for the past twenty years, hoping she'd come home.'

Sonnet imagined Mama flitting around a busy bookstore; saw herself banging through the front door in school uniform, with a sweetly smiling Fable trailing after.

Tears pricked. She coughed forcefully, pushing off the ground.

Olive stood alongside her, brushing off her knees. 'I was going to offer you some of my carambolas, Sonnet, but I think life has handed you a gold star far sweeter today.'

Sonnet shook her head. 'Bookstore *and* a cottage both thrust upon me in the space of two years!'

'Got to say, someone up there's looking out for you Hamilton girls!'

'Actually, all my windfalls have come from six feet under . . .'

CHAPTER 16
WHAT'S PAST IS PROLOGUE

October 1957

The knock rattled Sonnet as much as it did Alfred's old front door. She crept from his overcrowded study to the head of the staircase, eyes fastened on the drawn blinds of the shop windows. Noonday light seeped through the slats, filtering weakly across the silent lower level. Colour flashed on the front stoop, and the knock sounded again.

Sonnet took a few steps down, before hesitating. She had no desire to see another townsperson, much less listen to any more of their infernal *bloviating*! She was not working at Emerson's Fashion and Fabrics today, Plum and Fable were at school and the shop was her one private sanctuary where she could pretend not to be an orphaned guardian with a small business thrust upon her.

Moreover, no one ought to know Sonnet was inside; she always snuck in the back entrance. And the now-faded CLOSED UNTIL FURTHER NOTICE sign on the front door was usually enough to ward off busybodies.

A voice came through the crack at the door. 'Knock-knock! I *know* you're in there, Sonnet! Just want a second! Yoo-hoo!'

Sonnet harrumphed down the stairs. She wrestled with the deadlock and flung open the door, scowling. If the waiting middle-aged woman, vaguely familiar in that way peculiar to small towns, was offended, she didn't show it.

'Oh finally, you've appeared. I'm Marg Johnstone, Ned's wife, nice to meet you. Can I come in for a jiffy?'

Sonnet stood back, racking her brain for a Ned Johnstone. Nearly two years in, she still struggled daily with the all-important who's who of small-town life.

Marg's eyes raked the cluttered gloom. Sonnet's arms crept across her chest.

'What can I do for you, Mrs Johnstone?'

'I can see you're not burning books for firewood. Goodness knows what you *have* been doing, squatting in here all this time. Some were afraid you might have gutted Alfred's precious shop.'

Sonnet gritted her teeth, thinking of Olive's honey analogy. It wasn't coming easily though. This woman was almost certainly another ladies-fellowship-slash-quilting-club-friend of Delia's. Probably sent to spy, because wouldn't it be driving Delia nuts not being able to keep tabs on Sonnet behind the closed shutters. Well, now she'd have all the gossip: Alfred's bookshop was in chaos and Sonnet had been hiding out for months, letting it fall apart around her.

'What is it you're looking for?'

Having finished with the lower level, Marg homed in on the second floor. Sonnet pictured the secret pandemonium of Alfred's office, and squared her shoulders.

'Listen,' Marg said, 'I know exactly what I'm after: a large box, heavy, marked in red, addressed care of the CWA. I'm the vice-president, you know. Have you come across anything like that?'

Sonnet wanted to run from the intensity of Marg's look. She was like a dentist drilling for a nerve. 'No,' she answered, hands rising to her hips.

An oddly weighted silence ensued.

'You haven't,' Marg mused. 'I see. Well, it's probably best if I pop upstairs then and have a gander in his office for you.'

'No thanks!' Sonnet spluttered. 'I know where everything is!'

'Not everything, by the state of it.'

'If there's something particular you want, I'll help you with it.'

Marg stared at Sonnet's red bun; the turning cogs in her brain almost visible.

Sonnet tapered indignation, with effort.

Finally, Marg spoke. 'Just before Alfred passed on, I put in a book order. Some hard-covered classics for my son, Dane. Have you met Dane? He's coming up for Dux of St Ronan's. Seventeen, and the world at his feet!'

Sonnet smiled tightly. 'Great, we've got our classics over here—'

'No, Alfred was ordering them for our Dane *specially*. First class, gilt-edged and all. Have you seen any books in a box like *that*?'

There Marg went again with the penetrating look. Sonnet's fists clenched at her waist. 'I already told you, no. But I'm sure I have something that will please Dane.'

'I'd like to get my box before anything is thrown out.'

'Mrs Johnstone, I have no intention of throwing books out.' *I might throw them at you, though.*

'Let me just check. I'll know the box when I see it. Then we can go through it together, and see what we find.'

Sonnet, pre-empting Marg's start towards the staircase, shifted boldly in her way.

Marg was immovable. 'I can wait here while *you* look, then. I only come into town from the farm once a week, you see.'

'A week? Perfect. That will give me plenty of time to go through my orders. Now let me see you out.'

Marg allowed herself to be led only as far as the old counter. She stopped and looked Sonnet dead in the eye. 'I only want to help you.'

'I can handle it myself, thank you.'

Marg's eyes ran over her face and hair, before sliding to the second floor. 'You say that now, Sonnet,' she said significantly. 'But call me when you're ready to talk about it.'

'The hide of that woman!' Sonnet cried as she paced back and forth. 'What the hell was she even on about?'

'You're going to wear my carpet out,' Olive noted from behind her counter.

'I'm sorry, but that woman! Accusing me of burning books and squatting in Alfred's shop! What *box* was she harping on about, and why would I want *her* help? She certainly did not order books. It's a big, fat lie; a cunning ploy to stick her interfering nose in my business and report back to all her cronies. She's as obnoxious as Delia Hull. How do you bear this town with all these awful women?'

'Oh, Marg's not too bad on her own, but when the ladies of the CWA get a bee in their collective bonnet about something, she takes her role as Vice President very seriously.'

'But that's just it! What on earth does *my* shop have to do with the CWA or Marg Johnstone?!'

Olive suppressed a smile. '*Your* shop now?'

Sonnet whirled off on another circuit. 'It *is* my shop, and they're going to have to get used to it! I'm not babysitting a shop for a dead man. I'm the owner now and they'd better start treating me like it!'

Olive came out from behind the counter, moving to embrace her. Sonnet stepped quickly out of reach, but her breath was held for Olive's response.

'Gav and I had been hoping for this. I can't tell you how glad I am to finally hear it. There's been plenty of conjecture floating around town about what you're planning. Even some suggestions you're going to deny townsfolk the bookstore they routinely neglected but now consider indispensable to Main Street.'

Sonnet exhaled forcefully.

'I didn't mention it before, because I knew you were taking your time to grieve and consider the responsibility left to you. But I can see you're ready now.'

'Hell yes, I am! Alfred left *me* the bookstore because I loved it as much as he did and he knew I'd modernise it the way he couldn't.'

'You bring that old shop right back to life, and show them all!'

Sonnet harrumphed. 'First, I've got to burn a few boxes, but after that I have some renovations to plan . . .'

Sonnet slammed the back of Gav's Ford coupé utility and motioned for her uncle to pull away from the shop with yet another load of books – bound for storage at Heartwood. If the town had been worried Sonnet was gutting Alfred's store before, they were *convinced* of it now.

For weeks, folks had been watching Sonnet empty out the old shop, with no clue as to her plans. The Emersons had remained as tight-lipped as Sonnet herself. The newspapered windows spoke more of paranoia than privacy, perhaps. But Sonnet wasn't giving anyone a look-in!

A full makeover was under way. It was far more than she could have achieved on her own, and Gav had pushed his resources upon her with more knowledge and expertise than she would ever have asked for herself. Gav had even brought in some painters and chippies from Innisfail – tradesmen happy enough to walk in and out as needed, without sharing progress reports with every nosy parker circling for gossip.

When Sonnet's moniker finally hung on Main Street, announcing *her* claimed ownership, then, and only then, would the locals be invited back into her domain.

CHAPTER 17

WHIMSY

Autumn 1958

Winter was Fable's middle name but her least favourite season, shipwrecked halfway as it was between Raff Going and Raff Coming. And the winter of fifteen and three-quarters was proving interminable. The summer of fifteen had been full of Raff sightings and even, remarkably, close encounters. The latter being the only thing sustaining her now through the months of Raff gossip laid on thickly by Adriana. Had Adriana known how famished Fable was for any word of Raff's faraway uni adventures, or how much her gloating reportage of Raff's latest model-beautiful, college-sophisticated girlfriend hurt, she couldn't have wielded more power. Enduring Adriana all through autumn, winter and spring just for the summertime boon was tough going.

A sigh escaped Fable. She reached automatically to cover her mouth, but there was no one awake for miles – the splendorous dawn hour was hers alone. Orchard Hill, here overlooking Heartwood, was her favourite place to watch as morning light limned the valley with gold. It wasn't a perfect vantage point. Enclosed within their steep mountain basin, Fable could only invent the full, theatrical colour of the coastal dawn from the spilling crescendo which lipped the ranges. She might one day come to begrudge these restricted horizons, to resent being left behind in the small antechamber of regional life. But here and now, on Orchard Hill, Fable felt herself an enchantress, conjuring forth the day. Magic quivered in every atom. The future was a green bud, perfect and complete, already curled within her.

This was Fable's morning pilgrimage: escaping secretly through her bay window, from behind her now lockable sunroom doors.

Following Sonnet's degrading announcement of her menarche to all and sundry, Fable had gone privately to Gav to petition for a lock on her doors – which he had done without question, and without consulting Sonnet. Sometimes, when especially irritated with her sister, Fable enjoyed a revenge daydream of the door-rattling moment Sonnet tried to sneak into her sunroom, and met unyielding physical resistance.

Fable kept her door locked at all times.

Some mornings, Fable slipped out of her window bare of foot and hand, threading between the giant golden orb webs built in the garden overnight, tiptoeing past the grass spiders' faerie handkerchiefs. Other times, she carted watercolours, pencils and notebooks along with her. She had not yet mastered either the description or depiction of the valley sunrises and despaired of her skills, which failed her dreaming heart, time and time again.

Every morning so far, she'd managed to sneak back in through her window before breakfast, with no lectures from a bossy sister. But Fable's hackles rose when she even thought of Sonnet having the nerve to criticise *her* for secretiveness, when the whole town knew Sonnet had been hiding out in Old Man Shearer's bookstore for over a *year*.

What Sonnet was doing in there behind the newspapered windows was anyone's guess, and Fable heard people make plenty of guesses: pawing through his undies drawer, maybe sniffing his pillow, burning books, spying on passing townsfolk, or playing some imaginary game of bookstore owner; serving make-believe customers and giggling with the ghost of Alfred Shearer.

Fable snorted. Thank goodness Sonnet's shop renovations were almost finished. The Hamilton girls should not provide any more cause for ridicule. The bullseye on Fable's back was already big enough without Sonnet making a spectacle. After the shop's grand reveal next month, they could finally put this whole strange chapter behind them.

Fable reached for the sugarcane flower rescued earlier. She held it before the sunrise, squinting so that light flared through the silvery-lilac feather duster. *Inflorescence*: the name of the flower faerie she was currently working on, though her sun-speared sugarcane skirts were coming out all wrong in sketches. She needed more time for practice.

If she could evade Sonnet late this afternoon, she'd come out again, armed with her sketchbook. The golden hour, as the sun slipped towards the western ranges, suffusing the valley with light, was Fable's second favourite. Sunset was best enjoyed at the creek: sunlight glittering on the water even as darkness slid up from valley floor to looming peak, swallowing mountains whole. '*Darkrise*', Sonnet had coined it, and though it nearly choked Fable to use her word – Sonnet was right.

It was much harder to get out for a sunset. Sonnet was always in a mad flap – hurrying them into baths, hushing Plum's pre-dinner whingeing with both exaggeration and ineffectualness, packing lunches with one hand and ironing uniforms with the other, while stirring saucepans with her foot. Sonnet's amplified stress made Fable's own heart beat faster, her breath come shorter. Sonnet called it the 'witching time', referring, Fable supposed, to the way she turned into an unbearable witch. Evenings were calmer when lucky Plum had escaped to Heartwood for a sleepover. If only Fable were permitted the same freedom.

Fable's coping strategy had been to hide down the creek at dinner time, until her aunt had put a stop to it with a distinctively Olive lecture about Sonnet's job being hard enough and how Fable's help could make such a difference. Blah, blah, blah. Fable couldn't understand how her casual flinging of knives and forks onto the table made one iota of difference to Sonnet – nevertheless, she had reined in her sunset forays.

Well, mostly . . .

She'd made stubborn exceptions for herself during Raff's last homecoming, after the serendipitous discovery that she was not the only one who enjoyed meditative time alone in the rainforest. Close to dusk, Raff could be found scything quietly along the creek in his kayak, arms moving confidently at the paddle. Or, he might be encountered walking home again, strong, tan arms holding aloft the kayak as he negotiated the narrow pathway. And though her face froze up and all words were sucked into a gormless whirlpool, just raising wide eyes to Raff's as he passed by with a chummy greeting, was *everything*.

One afternoon, Zephyr had followed her to the creek, and Raff's grin as the dog bounded up to him with a bark of long familiarity was heart's elixir. When he gently stroked Zephyr's tawny pelt, it was her skin which shivered with pleasure; her hair that stood on end. From that afternoon on, she made a point of whistling for Zeph every day as she set off on her meanderings. That Olive and Gav were soon singing her praises daily as diligent dog-walking niece did not cause Fable a moment's guilt. In the realm of contrived coincidences, she was comfortably innocent.

If Raff thought it odd that Fable was always at the creek at the precise time of his solitary kayak, he didn't let it show. In her most regularly played fantasies, he actually slowed his pace to ensure they caught each other.

On Raff's last day in Noah for another long year, a miracle had occurred. Standing aside for Fable on the cane bridge, Raff handed her a treasure: one solitary Ulysses butterfly wing cast asunder, and found glistening on a rock.

'Got any use in your scrapbook for this, kiddo?'

Fable received the iridescent blue wing in her cupped hands with the reverence of one taking communion. And, looking up at him, finally found her words. 'So, you're still pulling wings off bugs, then . . .'

He chuckled, and his serious lips stayed curved to one wry side long after she had passed by.

For days, Fable petted that delicate wing like a lucky charm capable of bringing Raff home again, or speeding up the endless months of school ahead. Eventually, the wing had disintegrated in her hands; turquoise glitter falling through her fingers. In a fit of fancy, she smeared the last iridescent shimmer on her forehead, behind which she guarded his image.

Sonnet, predictably, had ruined it with one swipe of pungent tea towel.

So now, Fable was waiting the long way. How long? Still *five* dry months to go!

Fable sighed again, and blew hard at the cane arrow; scattering the shiny motes into the golden light.

CHAPTER 18

SONNET'S BOOKS

September 1958

Main Street on a Sunday morning held a reverent, sleepy stillness, but for the hymns that swelled across Raintree Park, spilled over the long lines of cars baking in the heat, and swept past the respectfully shuttered shopfronts, hushing all.

Sonnet felt like the only heathen in town. And, thankful as she was to be free of the sanctimony and superstition which drove *them* to church, there was an indefinable sense of being . . . left out. The satisfied placidity with which they returned only magnified her irritation.

While Olive and Gav were at church with the girls, Sonnet had slipped into the bookshop to make the last preparations before her grand opening on the morrow, well over a year since Alfred's passing. A respectful period of mourning, Sonnet liked to think of it, though in truth it had been cowardice, and conviction of unworthiness.

Sunshine splashing through the bay window – which now featured a satire book display, her favourite genre – cast a flattering light over her hard work: gleaming whitewashed shelves and front counter; newly polished wood floors and book ladder; freshly papered walls; dark window blinds replaced with light muslin curtains; and, most importantly, every book dusted to within an inch of its life, and slotted neatly back into position. It had been a labour of love removing every last one of Alfred's books to Heartwood and back again, without damaging or misplacing a single one. Her modernised front counter was now sparse and neat. She hadn't changed the old cash register, its vintage bells and whistles evoking the many happy hours working under Alfred's tutelage. Gav had built Sonnet a high bar extension off the counter, which she'd coined her 'Story Bar'. On the bar waited mismatched vintage teacups, plates and teapots, collated from Grandmother Lois's collection, ready to serve Devonshire tea with every purchase. Her hand-lettered sandwich board, footpath bound, promised as much.

Hanging above all her handiwork was an unexpected gift from Gav, a majestic crystal chandelier. He had brought it to her, shrouded in dust and cobwebs, with the bearing of a boy presenting a hand-plucked flower.

'Think you could find a use for this? It was originally your great-grandmother's, and it's been languishing amongst tractors and hoes in the Heartwood shed.'

'Are you *kidding* me?' Sonnet cried, throwing her arms around him. 'I love it!'

The chandelier had, like the bookshop itself, scrubbed up magnificently. In the afternoon light, it sent dazzling crystal-cast rainbows spinning through the shop.

The final touch to her bookshop had been the hand-painted sign hung last night and now receiving its first morning sun kiss on Main Street.

She'd entrusted the typesetting and graphic illustration entirely to Fable, and each time Sonnet gazed on her sister's scrupulously rendered artwork, her shoulders drew back. The sign embodied everything this shop meant to Sonnet: an image of her yellow bike, with a stack of best-loved books in its basket (*Persuasion* atop the pile), and her name in Fable's elegant calligraphy – *Sonnet's Books*.

And look, there was the artist herself coming across Raintree Park now, with Olive striding alongside and Plum leaping excitedly before them – all eager to see Fable and Sonnet's sign triumphantly hung.

'It's simply beautiful!' declared Olive. 'Well done, Fable.'

Fable assessed the signboard, head crooked. 'But the perspective's a tad off, though, see how the—'

'Nonsense,' said Sonnet. 'Olive, I had to drag it out of Fable's paint-stained hands. She could have spent another year on it and still wouldn't have been ready to hand it over. You're just a perfectionist, Fabes.'

Fable hurled a withering look. 'If I were a perfectionist, it would be perfect, wouldn't it?' She flounced into the shop.

'Oww,' Sonnet said, clutching at her chest. 'The scathing tone I can live with; it's the constant eye rolls that do me in.'

Olive smiled. 'I wish you knew how much like your mother Fable is. That eye-roll-flounce combo is pure Essie. But remember, she's frightened about her artwork being on public display.'

Sonnet harrumphed. 'She's got to start sharing it sooner or later. I'm going to push her to make something of her gift, like Mama should have with her writing!'

She looked to Olive for agreement, but Olive was staring at Sonnet's dress, reaching to finger the fabric.

'Are you wearing one of my mother's dresses?'

'Maybe.'

'I *knew* I recognised that blue rose print.'

'Found a whole wardrobe of old frocks in my bedroom. They're . . . sweet, but hopelessly out of date, stinking of mothballs. Thought I could get some use of out them, with a few nips and tucks.' Sonnet braked in sudden guilt. 'I hope you don't mind?'

'Mind?! I'm delighted. Those ancient dresses never dreamed they'd see the light of day again. I can't believe you've managed to make it work on your figure, though. Mother was six inches shorter and three dress sizes larger!'

Oh yes, Sonnet knew Lois Hamilton's dimensions by heart now after the many hours she'd spent bent over her grandmother's floral *sacks*, altering them to swing-skirted, whippet-waisted tea dresses. The 1930s gowns, which had so obviously belonged to her mother, were a welcome surprise among the shabbier florals. Those gowns, however, Sonnet had left alone, unwilling to bring the shapely spectre of Esther Hamilton back to life.

'Believe me,' Sonnet said, 'this one took quite some alteration.' She twirled, and the rose garden flared.

The cut accentuated Sonnet's toned hourglass figure usually lost in slacks and shirts, and her hair was, uncharacteristically, unpinned. The combined effect was disconcerting; vulnerability revealed, perhaps even a desire to be found beautiful.

'You're such a clever girl,' Olive said. 'I miss you in my shop now that you've stepped into your own. You brought a youthful air I can't replicate.'

'Flatterer. You know I'm available to help you out with alterations, only have to ask. Anyway, I might be just twiddling my thumbs here, probably won't get any customers . . .'

Initially, her prediction seemed to come eerily true. Sonnet did not see a customer for three torturous days after her launch.

Just when you want all the local busybodies keeping you busy, they're nowhere to be found!

It was a conspiracy. Those bloody cows from the CWA probably handed out defamatory pamphlets on the next corner about Sonnet's store, revenge for Marg Johnstone's imaginary lost box.

Sonnet outlined her theory of townsfolk collusion to Gav when he popped down for his now regular afternoon tea break; rather, long hour of yarns over the Story Bar.

'How's that chip on your shoulder going there?' Gav asked, over a gigantic jam-laden, cream-topped scone.

'How else do you explain it? *Sure* you haven't seen a posse of peeved women shooing book lovers away?'

'Only peeved woman I've met on this street today is you.'

He ducked as she swatted at him with a tea towel.

'Tell you what, though, these are the best flamin' scones I've ever eaten. If the bookshop doesn't work out, pet, you start selling these things, instead. You'd give ye olde famous teahouse at Moria Falls a run for its money.'

Only Gav could get away with calling Sonnet Hamilton 'pet'.

'Come off it. You've probably eaten these scones a hundred times before. I filched the recipe from Grandmother Lois's old book.'

'Must be your jam, then.'

'The jam recipe, also Lois's, uses Davidson plums from your *wife's* orchard.'

'Alfred's stove is working some kind of magic, then. As I recall it, Lois's scones were rock hard, and her jam bitter . . .'

Sonnet turned away, squeezing a smile flat between tight lips. She'd never truly known a man, until Gav. The nearest thing to a father she'd ever had. The thought always stopped her cold. *Imagine* how life might have been if she'd skipped over one recklessly fertile Hamilton womb for the other Hamilton womb, which had waited and wanted forever.

Sonnet pinched the traitorous thought away and swung her sign back to OPEN.

'Best be off, Gav. Can't keep the store closed just for you, got customers beating down my door.'

Gav heaved himself off the stool with a reluctant wheeze. 'Well, if you want that smile fixed back on, I know a bloke who sells hardware up the road—'

'Oh, shoo!' Sonnet said, smiling at his departing bulk.

Gav, her only patron. So be it. She'd take Gav's stories of Noah any day over a hundred big spenders.

On the fifth day, at mid-morning, the shop bell clamoured noisily. Sonnet, having a nap upstairs on Alfred's office settee, jerked guiltily to her feet.

Fine look for a new proprietor, can't even keep my eyes open!

She hadn't meant to fall asleep when she'd started poking, reluctantly, through Alfred's office-cum-storage-room earlier. The mere sight of his disarray, decades in the making, had been soporific. One day, Sonnet planned to disembowel Alfred's office, too. But the dust, and her sense of unworthiness, needed to settle a little longer.

Hearing a voice below, Sonnet squeezed out of the study, sticky and flustered. She descended the stairs in twos, swiping at her rumpled dress.

The dark-haired young woman loitering at the bay window display turned with a warm grin. Sonnet checked the corners of her mouth and eyes for evidence of her geriatric behaviour.

'Hullo!' sang the woman. 'Sorry, didn't mean to drag you out of bed there!'

'I wasn't!' Sonnet cried, taken aback. 'I was just sorting things. I mean I was asleep, but I wasn't in bed—'

Her visitor shook with laughter. 'It's all right,' she said. 'I won't tell. I've been known to sleep-ride home after work, practically topple straight off my horse into bed. I'm Kate Hardy, anyway.'

Sonnet's interest was piqued at the surname. She tried to mentally map the Hardy clan as she accepted Kate's hand.

'Sonnet.'

'So, these are all your books, huh?' Kate said, with ironic brows.

'Yes . . . these are my books.'

'That's a shame, because I wanted one, but if they're all *your* books . . .'

Sonnet shrugged helplessly. 'I'm sorry, I don't follow.'

Kate laughed again; an open, easy sound that made Sonnet's cheeks feel imprisoned.

'The new sign out front – *Sonnet's Books*?'

Sonnet nodded, frowning.

'OK, sorry. I'll stop teasing. Let's start again. Hi, I'm Kate. I manage the trail riding for tourists up at Moria Falls. Horses are my thing, not humour.'

'Hi, Kate, I'm Sonnet.'

'So, these are all your books, then?' Kate replied in a rush, before hooting with laughter.

Weary now, Sonnet retreated behind the front counter. 'Can I help you with anything in particular today?' She hated herself for the cold professionalism of her tone.

Kate wandered, hands tracing the book spines. 'Tell you the truth; I'm not a serious reader. Unless we're talking about romances, those I devour. But last I checked, you weren't stocking much new stuff. In fact, Old Mr Shearer used to tease me mercilessly for having read his entire collection of "frothy rubbish", as he called it.'

Sonnet latched on to a constructive task. 'I'm proud to say, I've been expanding the romance section since taking over from Alfred.' Sonnet headed for an impeccably organised row. 'I know he didn't think much of lighter women's fiction, but I'll be catering to all tastes. This is a *modern* shop.'

Kate followed, grinning.

'I can make a few recommendations, too, if you might like to try something a little more daring?' Sonnet's voice dropped to a conspiratorial murmur. 'Have you ever heard of *Forever Amber* by Kathleen Winsor?'

Kate leaned in, shaking her head.

Sonnet handed her a chunky hardcover book. 'This novel was banned in Australia for "sex obsession" by men who think *they* know better than female readers. The censors deemed it obscenity. It was only just taken off the list of prohibited imports this very year.'

'*Sex obsession*,' Kate breathed, turning the novel over twice, studying the beautiful woman in the cover illustration.

'In truth,' Sonnet said, with what she hoped was a proficient tone, 'it's an epic historical romance.'

Kate flipped through the pages dubiously. 'It looks *long* though . . .'

Sonnet laughed. 'You're right, more than nine hundred pages. But if you want to try something meatier than your usual fare, a romance you can . . . get your teeth into?'

'Exactly!' Kate cried. 'Okay good, I'll take this indecent book of yours.'

Hurrah! Sonnet had won her first official sale as bookstore owner. Nevertheless; she winced all the way to the counter. It had been far more nerve-racking than anticipated. What if she'd misjudged her customer's pluck and open-mindedness? She'd have every book burner in town pounding on her door come the morrow!

Kate gazed around the shop, eyes alighting on the grand chandelier. 'I, for one, love what you've done with Mr Shearer's old digs. It doesn't look showy at all to *me*.'

'Excuse me?' Sonnet's hand stilled at the till.

'You've gotten rid of the old fuddy-duddy vibe, and I think that's fine. Haven't ruined the shop as far as I can see.'

'*Ruined?*'

'A few people, don't want to name names, think you've gone over the top repainting it all, see.'

'Think I can guess who.'

'Yeah well, I wouldn't worry yourself too much with what Aunt Delia says.'

'Believe me, I don't.'

'Besides, how were you to know it was Daintree silky oak before you painted it over? "Desecration" is a horrible word to use – it's not like you vandalised his grave. It is *your* shop now.'

Sonnet clenched a shilling coin deep into her palm. 'You don't like my repaint, Kate?'

'No, *I* like it. But some people say it's a *sin* to paint over vintage rainforest timber.'

'Lucky this is a bookshop, not a church.'

'You know Noah; folks get their knickers in a twist when anyone changes anything. Can't move a fence post without someone accusing you of spoiling the heritage vibe!'

'Funny, because you're the only person to step foot in here since I reopened, so it sounds like *they've* had their noses pressed against my glass just looking for something to judge.'

'You wouldn't be far wrong there.'

Sonnet slammed the cash drawer closed. 'I see. Would you like a bag with that?'

'Yes please, have to ride home.'

Sonnet slid a paper bag across the counter. 'Thanks for coming by.'

'That's my Misty out there – see?' Kate tipped her head towards the white mare tethered to a post in Raintree Park. 'I was going to park her out front, but your bike hogs the horse post these days.'

'I'm sorry,' Sonnet said, without a note of regret. 'Didn't know a bookshop needed a horse-parking bay. Chalk it up to another thing I ruined. Have a good day!'

Kate made no move to leave. 'This has been awkward, hasn't it?'

Sonnet considered Kate for a flummoxed moment. She discarded cold indifference and thought better of sarcasm, before settling on honesty. 'I don't know quite how to take you.'

'I can tell you don't like me, which doesn't bode well for future book advice.'

'It's not that I don't like you.'

'But you didn't offer me a Devonshire tea, even though your sign promised me one, and you keep taking that snooty tone with me. You're treating me like a spy for the CWA!'

'Are you?'

'Never! Look, I love my Aunt Delia, but, frankly, those cliquey old cows have had this place stitched up the way they like it for decades. It's about time we had someone new in town to liven things up.'

'It's just a bookshop.'

'Not the way they're nattering about it in the CWA tea rooms. Here you are, marching into town with your liberal paint can, changing time-honoured shop names, hanging flashy crystals, and, worst of all, pushing your free tea service in direct competition with the old guard. Apparently, you need to be brought down a notch or two.'

Sonnet slumped against her counter. 'So, I poured my heart into a shop that's being embargoed.'

'Chin up! Didn't say it will last forever. But you need help getting the word out on how fabulous your tea service is. How about a complimentary sample for me to test?'

Sonnet snorted. 'After all that, you're hitting me up for free scones?'

'Wouldn't call them *free*. I shelled out my precious wages on this grim-looking novel. And do you know how many dopey tourists I had to drag through the wilds of Noah to afford your naughty book, with no guarantee it's going to stoke my fire?'

Sonnet's mouth fell open.

'So, let's have it!' Kate said, claiming a bar stool. 'White with three and don't go easy on the jam or cream!'

Sonnet would have to shut her own fly-catching mouth by hand. She reached for the kettle, impelled by curiosity.

Who *was* this girl?

CHAPTER 19

IRIS

December 1958

Thank God for Old Mr Shearer, Fable thought on a daily basis. So obsessed was Sonnet with her shop, her other obsession with curtailing Fable's freedom had slackened somewhat. And the bookstore couldn't have come at a better time; the summer of sixteen was proving to be Fable's favourite yet.

She was riding an unsolicited wave of popularity, buoyed by her recent advancement to the top of the 'Knock-outs' ranking at Noah Vale High; her name and associated virtues now scrawled on the senior boys' toilet wall in permanent marker. A fact Adriana had verified for the other girls by striding in to see the legendary listings in the middle of lunch hour.

It had been a dare by Christy, and Adriana had readily accepted. No one wanted to be thought lacking in boldness these days, especially not in comparison to the growing legend of Fable Hamilton.

The newly acquired 'jugs', which had elevated Fable above the urinals, might have been the physical drawcard, but it was her inscrutability which conferred greater pull.

Fable Hamilton was so quiet and such a loner, she wasn't worth noticing – yet all eyes were on her. Where other girls demurred to tread, Fable went with a rambler's grace. Bound to no clique, she drifted where and when she pleased; including, shockingly, with the local farm boys. But she didn't agree to go steady with any of them, so why did she bother? Fable didn't fit the most obvious labels – Tomboy or Easy – and how else were they to pigeonhole a girl who'd never had a date, yet spent the majority of her time hanging out with guys?

The boys themselves were largely intimidated by Fable, and feigned comradely indifference, even though she was the cause of more missing tissue boxes in Noah homes than any other 'well-stacked' girl in town.

In the spring holidays, a story circulated that Fable had been out at night with the Lagorio twins riding the cane trains and jumping off at bridge crossings for the pure thrill of it! On the first day back at school, the rumour became legend – confirmed by Vince Lagorio, after Marco refused to be drawn.

No one could remember another Noah girl doing such a thing.

That was the problem with Fable Hamilton. She just wasn't . . . normal. She hardly seemed a threat at all. Nonetheless, most girls were determined to despise Fable for so successfully shirking the mould, and for her ostentatious strawberry beauty.

Fable thought all the fuss about train-riding and creek-jumping was, frankly, dangerous. Someone's mother was bound to mention it to Sonnet or Olive down the street, and then all bets were off. There was even a story doing the rounds that she'd been out 'pigging' with the Ravelli kids, which was rubbish. Fable never wanted to see a wild pig slaughtered! She'd only snuck out of her window that full-moon night – with an under-blanket pillow effigy left guarding her sunroom – to hunt moonbows at the Glade. It wasn't her fault the Ravellis' pig dogs had hunted her, instead.

Fable wasn't trying to draw any attention at all. But hanging out with the boys, she had access to all the wilds of Noah Vale. Were she to trail the local girls, none of whom had invited her *anyway*, she'd be loitering at Noah Vale Public Baths, hoping one of the lifeguards would notice her in a halter-neck swimsuit. She didn't even own one!

Fable could spend all day with the boys, or avoid them for a week, and none of them seemed to begrudge her either way. They didn't expect gossip or forced gaiety; simply grabbed their towels or fishing lines, and went. It suited Fable to a tee.

Every day so far this summer, there'd been a new adventure. And the best was yet to come; Raff Hull would soon be home, and then the Glade Gang would re-form.

Fable had positioned herself perfectly for his arrival.

The week of Christmas brought with it news of Raff's homecoming, and hot on his heels, a tropical storm wheeling in from the Coral Sea: Cyclone Iris. The postmaster had hung out the red warning pennant, sending Sonnet into a predictable flap and flurry.

Sonnet dragged the girls with her into the General Store to assemble cyclone essentials – along with everyone else in Noah. Hadley's was chockers! Fable wandered, overwhelmed, through the crammed aisles, past bare shelves and barely contained excitement. With only hours to spare, the whole town was prepping!

Having lost Sonnet and Plum in the madding crowd, Fable absconded for the exit. First, though, she had to get through all the chinwaggers blocking up the narrow shop door. Hot anxiety crawled up her back.

Get. Me. Out. Of. Here!

Spying the door held open from the outside, Fable saw her chance. She took a breath, tucked in her head and dived into the stream of townsfolk, shouldering her way towards the rectangle of light. Humid air and extravagant sunshine hit her face as Fable looked up to thank the door's holder – who was already smiling down upon her.

'G'day . . .' blurted her traitorous lips, having never uttered the broad colloquialism in her life.

'Mate,' Raff finished, with amused inflection.

'Glad to see you're finally making yourself useful around here,' Fable said.

He laughed, but the crowd carried her out before he could make his rejoinder. Not until Fable was kerbside at the Holden could she turn back, heart hammering, for another glimpse.

He was still there, holding open the door, embroiled in conversation. *Rafferty, Rafferty, Rafferty, Rafferty.*

Her eyes drank their fill of him for five heady minutes. Three times he looked directly her way. The first two glances swept past with a smiling familiarity, but the third look stalled on her person; lingering much, much longer, before a flush of male awareness made him turn carefully away.

It was a reaction Fable recognised well by now in the grown men who passed her on the street, though never before had she comprehended that look so clearly.

Heat, not of high summer, threw her face into full colour.

Fable was not the same as she had been.

At home, a drill sergeant was barking out cyclone-preparation orders: Fill the bathtub with water! Mattresses off beds for the shelter! All windows taped! Prepare the candles! Double-check the first-aid kit! Stack the cans of food! Ports packed, in case we need to flee rising floodwaters! Clear the garden of possible projectiles!

Who Sonnet was trying to prove her cyclone-preparing prowess to was obvious. Earlier, Plum had protested tearfully at being hauled away from Aunty Ov and Gav for the duration of the storm. Olive had deferred to the jurisdiction of her niece with a tight chin.

Fable pressed her forehead against a window criss-crossed with adhesive tape. The weather was fast deteriorating – the bright, burning day, doused by rain, smouldered now in eerie, restless embers. Darkening clouds were sucked to the canvas edge by the approaching tempest. Marauding gales whipped palm fronds about like ribbons. The dark jungle wall swayed and reared, a beast, sensing danger.

Protected as their valley was by steep mountain sentinels, it hardly seemed possible that the storm would find them here. And yet, their hand-drawn tracking map, meticulously updated at each new emergency broadcast, showed Iris circling ever closer; Noah Vale marked as prey in an open field.

A terse voice issued from the radio. Fable listened, without turning, to the Weather Bureau's three-hourly advice on the cyclone's latest position. 'Forewarned is forearmed,' the voice said gravely. '*This* will be a powerful blow.'

Fable imagined the deep gorge at the top of the valley rippling with anticipation. The rains would fill the ravine, flood the creek, and spread, irresistibly, towards their cottage. She shivered with pleasure.

Sonnet was engrossed in the construction of a makeshift shelter – dragging the dining table to the bathroom, lining it with mattresses and pillows. The thought of being stuck in such intimate quarters all night with Sonnet was untenable. Fable had built herself a nest in the claw-foot bath, but Bossy Britches was having none of that. She didn't even seem to *care* that Fable would rather *die* than jam herself in beside the loo, and worse, Sonnet.

A gale-driven splatter of rain against the windowpane made Fable push harder against the glass. For there, charging down the hill, with an agitation rarely witnessed, was Cyclone Olive. By the time Fable had opened the door, however, Olive was perfectly calm; manner befitting a fine lady out for a gentle stroll. Only the tight tremble at her chin hinted at anything else. Fable masked a smile.

'Oh, Son-net, Olive's here!'

Plum flew up the hallway to greet her aunt. Sonnet appeared a moment too late, forehead tight, towels hoisted under her arm.

'Just checking in,' Olive breezed, Plum already clasped possessively to her side. 'Making sure you don't need help with anything.'

'All good. Finishing up now.'

'Must be something I can do. Such a big thing facing your first cyclone *all alone*! And you don't even have stay-cables on here, or extra nails in your roof. Sure you wouldn't feel more secure at Heartwood?'

'You and Gav have spent enough time drilling cyclone preparedness into me, I'm sure we can handle it. Anyway, Gav said this cottage has withstood more than its fair share of crossings – "a seasoned survivor" were his words.'

'Yes, Gav did say that.' Olive buried a kiss in Plum's curls. 'Naughty Uncle Gav, such a boaster. Any problems getting the old crystal wind chime down off the porch?' Olive asked, nodding towards the discordant clangour.

Sonnet launched, but Olive was already making her break for the door, Plum securely in hand.

'Not yet!' Sonnet said, tailgating Olive. 'It's next on my list.'

The chimes shuddered and peeled in another gust.

'Should've taken this old thing down years ago,' Olive tutted. 'It'll be a missile through your window, and once you've lost a window, the house is in a world of trouble.'

'Yep, taking it down in a jiffy,' Sonnet said, hands extended for Plum.

'I want to stay with Aunty Olive!' Plum cried, arms circling Olive's waist

'She can go with me. One less worry on your mind tonight.'

But Sonnet was in her own domain this stormy eve. 'Come, Plum, we have to finish making your dolly's hidey-hole!' She levered her sister's hands off Olive with smiling force, hustling away.

Olive mirrored Plum's mournful expression.

'You're going to have trouble getting that chime down. I don't want you wobbling up on a chair.'

'Thanks for checking on us! All under control here!'

The screen door squealed shut.

No sooner was Olive out of sight than the clouds opened thunderously.

Sonnet's victory lasted a half-hour. As premature darkness fell over the wind-lashed valley, Gav stomped onto the porch in gumboots.

'Now, let's see about this blinkin' wind chime.'

Sonnet prevaricated at the door as Plum throttled into her uncle's sodden embrace.

The chime was down in moments and jammed away in a cupboard. This time, however, Plum refused Sonnet's reaching hands 'No! I want to go to Aunty Olive's!'

'Oh, Plum-pie, 'course you can. Aunty Olive sent a raincoat,' he said, fishing out a tartan mackintosh and hood. To his credit, the glance he gave Sonnet was abashed.

Gav looked expectantly Fable's way next. Sonnet flinched and withdrew, without looking at Fable.

'You coming?' Gav asked, large hands struggling with Plum's small belt.

Fable listened for the sound of Sonnet kicking walls inside – something not *un*heard of in such instances – and imagined herself nestled luxuriously in the bosom of Heartwood, waited upon by their aunt, feeling more a child than she ever could beneath her sister's watchful eye.

From inside, a furious screech of adhesive tape made Fable start.

She sighed. 'Thanks, Uncle Gav, but think I might see it out here.'

Gav winked, pushing himself to a stand. 'Listen to Sonnet, 'kay? She's got a smart head on her shoulders.'

In the privacy of her room, Fable opened her art journal to a blank page. She smoothed the paper, considering the nib of her pencil. How then to draw Iris, training malevolent eye upon their lonely cottage?

Within the hour, they'd lost power. The lights browned, flickered and died; the pedestal fan whirred to a halt. The sudden, humid silence in the midst of the tumult was stifling. Sonnet appeared at Fable's side in a jostling glow of light. She set a candle on Fable's window-sill, and leaned to inspect the drawing covered by an indignant hand. A crash in the garden made both sisters peer into the dark-ness, though only their reflections – awed, avoiding each other's – could be seen.

'We're getting trashed out there,' Sonnet said, too loudly for their airless proximity. 'There'll be a hell of a clean-up once it blows over.'

How inordinately pleased Sonnet was at the prospect! It made Fable's own delight in the storm feel childish. Fable shrugged and adjusted her candle's position so that Sonnet fell into shadow.

Another emergency broadcast brought the sisters together at the kitchen bench. Fable tracked the advice coordinates. 'But it looks like she's turning more south-west – we'll miss the direct hit.'

Sonnet snapped the page out of her hand and studied it herself. Their shared disappointment was palpable.

'You never know with these things,' Sonnet said. 'We should bunker down in the bathroom, just in case.'

Fable sighed, following after her.

In the bathroom, Fable planted herself in the claw-foot tub, ignoring the surfeit of padded space under Sonnet's dining table. She pulled the shower curtain across to form a partition.

Rain battered the cottage in waves. In their muggy epicentre, a perspiring sheen formed thickly over Fable's skin. She peeled clothing off, swished her hair into a top knot, and settled back against the bath. Sonnet tossed Fable a pillow around the curtain.

'Know what we should call this, instead of a bunker?' Sonnet asked.

Fable knew her sister wasn't going to shut up until she obliged. She pulled the curtain aside, with impatient brows.

'*Stormoon*,' Sonnet said, in theatrical tone. 'As in: storm cocoon.'

The curtain didn't close quite quickly enough to cover Fable's eye roll, though it managed to conceal the silent movement of her lips trying out Sonnet's word for herself.

After a long silence, Sonnet spoke again. 'Thank you, Fabes.'

Behind her curtain, Fable stiffened, wishing she'd thought to fake sleep more quickly.

'Whatever else we face in life, Fabes, whoever tries to come between us, we'll stick together. We're Mama's daughters. We're sisters—' Sonnet's voice broke.

Fable felt the great ache opening again. She teetered on the edge of that vast canyon, felt the edges crumbling at her feet. On a stricken breath, she turned away to face her lambent porcelain silhouette.

Abruptly, tears drying before they'd had a chance to fall, she was furious at Sonnet. For all of it – the storm, being forced to choose between aunt and sister, the intimacy of this sequestering; even Cyclone Iris itself, which now felt like nothing more than a pantomime of sisterly manipulation.

In that spirit of throbbing resentment, the last of the storm passed over them.

Early morning brought two haggard-faced girls to the front window, where they surveyed the cyclone damage through the veil of heavy rain. No major structural damage, but it was a bedraggled vale. Trees stood unclothed, and cowering. Hill slides and waterfalls sprang from exposed peaks. The creek had engulfed its banks and rampaged through the flood plains, within yards of the cottage. In the dark of night, and their blessed ignorance, it had come terrifyingly close; there were catfish beached in the cottage shrubbery.

'Malcolm built our cottage *just* above the flood line,' marvelled Sonnet.

For three more days, the heavens wept.

'Wouldn't want to have *ombrophobia* in this valley,' Sonnet said, flicking a glance at Fable for the answering eye roll.

Power remained resolutely out. Each day, Gav clomped onto the porch, shaking off leaves and rain, to deliver barbecued meals from Olive. Plum stayed out of sight, at their aunt's side. The use of candles and flashlights had quickly lost its romantic novelty, and the humidity sucked them dry.

Hour by vigilant hour, Fable awaited the serpent's retreat. *A watched flood never recedes*, she thought glumly, fogging up the windows with hissing impatience.

CHAPTER 20

VINELANDS

O n the fourth day, they woke to find the creek, thirst slaked, withdrawing to the forest line. Bright mist swirled and roiled off the mountainsides. Trees dripped and glistened.

At noon, the door knocker thudded. Fable skidded to answer it, thankful Sonnet was up at the main house, gathering Plum back to herself.

Waiting on the front stoop was not Marco, as Fable had expected, rather his brother, Vince, and Eamon Hull. Behind them, hanging over the picket fence, was a clutch of St Ronan's boys. Fable observed them only in the periphery, overcome by the thought of Raff being among them.

'Coming up to see the Falls in flood?' asked Eamon, with the lifting inflection Fable always found so arrogant. 'Gang's going.'

Fable nodded assent and grabbed her rucksack. She scrawled a note for Sonnet, and flew out of the door.

Two St Ronan's boys exchanged sniggering comments as she joined the group, and Fable lowered her face to hide disappointment. Raff was not with them. Even with her eyes on the ground, she would have recognised his large feet anywhere.

Never mind; they were heading to Summerlinn – and like a tracker on the scent, Fable locked her eyes on Eamon's back. Where Eamon went, Raff would surely be found, too. Perhaps he had waited in the truck, watching for her in the rear-vision mirror.

The flood had subsided just enough to make the crossing. The bridge seemed to float on the surface of the water, which churned beneath. Fable crossed with leaden feet – a single misstep, and she'd be swept away.

At Summerlinn, however, there was no truck, and no Raff. Only a panel van, which Derek Parker boasted was his. Fable hesitated for only a moment. Obviously the truck, with Raff at the helm, had already left. She must be in the second wave. Never mind, the important thing was she had been remembered, and at Eamon's specific invitation, no less.

They piled into the van, and Fable's nose wrinkled at the heavy male odour in the close confines. She wondered if there would be a tube waiting for her at the falls. She could have asked one of these guys, but baulked from the opening niceties. Most importantly, she was aboard and en route to Raff: this was simply a means to an end.

She averted her eyes from the unfamiliar chauffeur's mirror reflection.

Moments before they set off, Vince Lagorio made an abrupt, muttering exit from the vehicle, promising to catch them later. The heckling laughter which followed his departure made Fable clutch her rucksack tightly. She wished Marco had waited for her today, and felt queasy, off-centre.

The coarse laughter continued as they wound up the gorge road. No one acknowledged Fable directly; though she couldn't shake the sense that they were acutely conscious of her.

Within cooee of Moria Falls, the panel van made an unexpected right into a narrow road. Fable strained to see. The van jolted over ruts and roots, the canopy darkening all the while. The jungle encroached – foliage slapping the sides and windshield of the van as they pushed deeply in – there was no way the truck could have come this way before them. The anticipatory hush made Fable think her fellow occupants already knew about the detour.

Finally, the van turned into a cliff-side clearing, densely overhung. The back doors flung open to a spattering of raindrops and the creek's swollen roar. The hairs on Fable's limbs leapt straight up. It was a behemoth thundering by.

To their left, stood the crumbling ruins of an art deco mansion, strangled by the vines thickly festooning the clearing. The great, dark maw of the grand entranceway was overgrown with moss and vegetation, dark with mouldering. The smell of rot was everywhere; putridly thick. The front terrace, which once might have hosted garden parties and moonlit rainforest balls, spilled in broken stone relics out to the cliff edge.

Fable stumbled on a creeping vine. 'What is this place?'

Her question sank, unanswered. Beer bottles clinked, and cigarettes were lit.

'Where *are* we?'

'Vinelands,' said a St Ronan's boy as he passed by, with a long coil of rope.

Fable wandered to the terraced cliff edge, finding a gap in the heavy curtain of vines. Clutching the disintegrating balustrade, she peered down at the brown torrent. Her heart cantered over itself. The wonder that would normally have greeted such power, those vertiginous depths, was absent this day. Fable tried to summon it, but the ache in her gut intensified.

She wandered back into the clearing. Discarded beer tops fell like pennies. Laughter and a sweet, earthy smoke drifted from within the mansion's gloom.

Fable scrutinised the dispersed boys, carefully blank-faced. She noted a ring of overturned milk crates surrounding a makeshift camp-fire. Litter lay, half submerged, in mud. Initials and crudely intertwined stick-figure drawings were engraved in the thickest vines.

Now Fable understood. This was a party. She'd heard bragging about such forest gatherings, but had never imagined herself cool enough for an invite, especially from a *Hull*. Fable had the dawning sense that she might even be the guest of honour today.

Wait until Raff heard how popular she was becoming! Adriana had always seemed the most direct route into Raff's notice, but maybe becoming a favourite among Eamon and his mates was a more dramatic way of earning Raff's attention.

Here was her chance to show him she was not a kid anymore.

Her hand was already reaching for the bottle offered her, when the most important thought occurred: Raff was probably on the way to the party himself. And she'd better damn well be acting like a grown-up girl when he arrived!

Her first taste of yeasty-sour alcohol made her cough and shudder uncontrollably. The laughter of the surrounding semicircle affronted her. She was Fable Hamilton, she'd been invited to Vinelands over all other girls, and she could sure as heck *drink beer* as well as any boy.

The next swig went down quickly – with neck-bracing willpower – and a warm smoulder began to overtake the clamping in her tummy.

The earth kept dropping away from her feet – silly planet! Fable supposed she was drunk. It was akin to spinning manically on the spot to get dizzy, like having misplaced a part of herself, and though she cast around, she couldn't remember what she even wanted. Her words caught at her tongue like wool on sharp edges. Or else, they spilled out like a dribbling decrepitude. She wanted to laugh at herself for every moment of her life gone before. It had all been so serious, hadn't it? If only she'd glimpsed the world from this tilting, anaesthetised vantage point sooner.

Fable lurched towards the ruins, in search of Eamon's orange shirt: her homing beacon. As long as she could locate that orange shirt, she would not slip away from reality, and her only objective. She swayed at the dark entrance, peering.

Tiny moving lights glinted within, like eyes; low laughter seeped out.

Fable staggered back from the threshold with a sudden, unnerving sense of peril. She skidded on the roots creeping forth, felt her heart thud out of time. She caught sight of Eamon over on the crumbling terrace, in a huddle of boys, and stumbled towards them with the aggravating slowness of a dream; convinced now something was at her back, in pursuit.

Fable pitched into their midst. Her arm, landing on Eamon's orange shirt – safety – and pulled him heavily towards her.

'Hey, *baby*! Let's get it going!' Dane Johnstone said.

Eamon straightened them both. Dully, she registered his disgust before he turned away, beer raised. She felt someone pinch her bum, a finger hooking inside her shorts. She spun to catch the culprit, even as Dane's hyena laugh gave it away. Another beer was pressed into her grasp as a different hand now slid past her bum.

Fable swigged.

The boys were brewing bravado at the cliff edge. Legend had it you could swing right across to the opposite bank on a long vine. No one could qualify which vine might reach, and none would volunteer to test the theory.

'But in a flood?' Fable asked.

'Nah, mate,' a St Ronan's boy said. Not the one who kept rubbing his crotch against her back. 'It's a death trap. You pick a vine too short, you're gonna be left dangling in the middle, then soon as your arms give out, you'll be swept away.'

'Raff Hull crossed it once, in the flood of forty-nine,' Dane offered. 'Took him another five hours to hike home from the other side, though. Ain't no return vines.'

Eamon harrumphed. 'He missed a whole day of slashing! Came home bug-bitten, sunburned, torn up by wait-a-while, then he got welts from Pa's belt to top it off.'

The crotch pressed against Fable's back again. She felt it at a benumbed distance, riveted by the image of Raff, wearing only a loincloth, sailing across the creek, and from tree to tree, all the way down the valley. A puckish giggle rose.

'I want to see you do it, Eamon!' Fable said, nudging him.

He pushed back. 'I'm not stupid.'

'Go on! Your brother did it.' She could not say Raff's name aloud in this circle, even with yeasty courage flowing through her veins. 'If you go, I'll do it, too.'

The group erupted into bawdry laughter. 'Go on, Hull; make her do it.'

Eamon tossed his bottle over the balustrade. They watched it disappear into the maelstrom.

'Get stuffed,' he said, turning on Fable with an expression of such loathing she staggered backwards.

Without warning, she was hoisted onto the stone balustrade. Fable screamed, fighting to get down, but there were too many of them pushing back. A rousing cheer erupted.

Fable seized at the vines, feet seeking purchase on the mossy stone. She was hemmed in, yet bared to the flood.

Someone squeezed her bottom.

The boys jostled for better position around her, and in their unloosening Fable stumbled, stone breaking away beneath her feet. She clutched the vines tighter, trying to shake off her spinning head, their jeering.

But Raff crossed it.

With that, brazen mettle supplanted fear. 'Let go of me!' she shouted, attaching her body to a single vine. She tested its strength – once, twice – gazing up along the great, falling length.

The boys thought her act was a great lark. Mocking laughter rang out.

'Bloody girl thinks she can do it.'

'I'm not chicken, like the rest of *you*,' she cried.

Still they held on; groping tentacles tethering her to safety. She was between a flood and a hard place.

Fable grunted explosively now: '*Get off me!*'

The joke grew old, their laughter hollowed. One set of arms released her, followed by another, and another. Laughter fell away completely.

Fable tugged on the vine, letting it take her weight off the balustrade for a moment. It held, and immediately she felt the vine yearning towards the creek. A single, skittish catcall issued from her audience.

She did not yet swing – the vine was still moored to the balustrade by the pressing boys.

'Let go of me!'

The boys tittered uneasily, then one by one, they released the vine.

'Oh, stuff this! What a joke. I'm not being a part of it,' Eamon said, disappearing into the clearing.

But Fable had been released. And without another conscious thought, she flung herself over the roiling abyss.

For one wild moment, she simply fell.

The wind rushed, the forest screeched – or was it her? – the flood roared and rose to claim her, then her vine reached its ultimate, rippling length, and she was yanked quickly back again towards the cliff edge.

She crash-landed in a stunned heap on a lower outcrop. Someone above was shouting at her, or for her, or about her. The vine escaped her, drifting out to hang, suspended, above the torrent. The cliff tilted away under her, threatening to yield her into the water.

Fable sagged. She was about to vomit – oh look at that, she already had.

Voices roused her from imminent collapse, and she lurched once more to her feet, nails dug deep in earth as she clambered back to the balustrade. Limbs scraped on stone as she dragged herself over. The face she lifted to her spectators was blanched white, stained with mud and stomach matter; and triumphant.

Fable raised her arms in victory, stumbling.

A rousing cry went up.

'You're *crazy*!' Dane said.

Two unfamiliar faces, grown men, had emerged from the mansion gloom and stood watching their group now. Eamon was nowhere to be seen.

A tepid beer appeared in her hold.

Fable was alone with the St Ronan's boys, and the hands were back on her once more.

The reeling fugue seemed to drain away all at once and the world, growing dim at day's end, snapped back into murky focus. Fable found herself seated on a milk crate before a wetted-out campfire pit, with arms heavy on her shoulders from both directions, hands resting on her upper thigh.

She was afraid.

How did she get from the vines to here, and how long ago? When had she consented to all these hands and how did she now remove herself from them?

Fat plops of rain on her face and shoulders brought some semblance of awareness back – she was soaked through, and longed to pull her clinging blouse away from her body. Instinct, however, told her not to draw attention, or invite any comment.

She was holding yet another beer, half finished, judging by the weight of it. How many had it been now? And why did she have the distinct impression the boys surrounding her, their mouths running off with vulgar jokes, were waiting with barely concealed impatience for Fable to finish *this* particular beer?

It was because she'd agreed to something, wasn't it? Only now she couldn't recall what, exactly, only that groping back for the answer made her feel sick, and cold.

Coarse laughter issued from the ruins on a coil of acrid smoke, and Fable remembered.

She was supposed to join the boys inside the mansion, to try the marijuana they'd all been darting in and out to smoke. Their insistence had sounded playful when she'd agreed. But now, she intuited the sobering truth: she must not go into that dark lair.

Fable shivered, raising the bottle to her lips as though to sip. The liquid briefly infiltrated her mouth before washing straight back into the bottle. Her eyes scoured the thick wall of vegetation, inscrutable in the gathering darkness, for Eamon's orange shirt.

Any moment now, Eamon would have to return. He'd been missing so long, but the boys kept saying, laughingly, Eamon had only gone to find the powder room. Maybe he'd wandered to the toilets at

Moria Falls? Even *Eamon Hull* wouldn't just abandon a Glade Gang friend.

For now, she would swallow this beer in careful, diminutive sips, suffering the proprietorial arms, until Eamon came back. Then she could go *home*.

CHAPTER 21

STARS, HIDE YOUR FIRES

Blunted as her senses were, leaden as her thoughts felt, Fable didn't at first notice the new arrival at the glade. He emerged from the overgrown road on foot and stood for a long moment, watching.

It was one of the boys who sighted the intruder.

'Heeeey! It's Raff!'

'Raaaaaaff. Maaaaate!'

'Fellows,' said Raff. 'This is some gathering you're having here.'

He stood at confident albeit unsmiling ease – hands in pockets, brow rutted. Boys rose to greet him with hands outstretched to shake and were rebuffed; Raff's hands remained pocketed. The boys at her side did not budge, however, their arms weighing unbearably upon her now.

Raff stepped no further into the clearing, and seemed indifferent to her presence. She wanted to rise and say something, *anything*, but the bravado with which she'd swung across a flooded gorge deserted Fable now in Raff's presence.

'Wanna beer, Raff?'

'No thanks.'

'Come on, get it into you! Have a cigarette.'

'Got the truck waiting out on the road, can't stay.'

'Ah, come on, Raaaaaaff. You gotta cut loose one time.'

'Not for me, Dane. I'll keep going.'

Dread made Fable shrink beneath those heavy limbs. Would Raff turn now, as quickly as he'd materialised, and leave her to them?

Laughter issued from the ruins and Raff's gaze shot to the mansion. He stepped closer. 'Who else is here?'

Dane listed boys according to their larrikin nicknames. Raff's brow did not soften. 'This isn't your usual gang, is it, Fable?'

He'd finally addressed her, but his eyes traversed only the boys. Fable shook her head, a lump forming in her throat.

'Don't matter,' came one boy's cocky reply. 'We're all firm friends here now.'

'Yeah, Fable's having the time of her life with us,' Johnny Fletcher said from the milk crate adjacent. 'She's been swinging on the vines, right over the creek!'

'She's even taken your title,' bragged one heavy arm's owner. 'And *she* managed it as a rebound.'

'Brave girl,' Raff said, his eyes still not moving to Fable.

Dane made a noise like a primate. 'Nah, not a girl – if you know what I mean?' Beer sloshed as he mimed breasts. '*Coconuts!* Ay, fellas?'

Laughter spread around the fire.

Raff alone remained serious. 'And which one of you is driving back tonight?'

'We'll draw straws.'

'Don't think so, Johnstone,' Raff said, patience now disappearing. He stepped closer to the fire pit. 'I'm going to offer Fable a ride home now. And anyone else who thinks it might be time to leave . . . seeing as I've got the truck ready and all.'

'Fable wants to stay with us,' Dane said, tightening his moist grip on Fable's leg. 'It's her first time going to Vinelands.'

'Yeah, she's here for a good time.'

Someone moaned in a long falsetto, and the group exploded.

Raff straightened to his full height, with a look that could fell a tree. 'It's getting dark, and Fable's people are going to be looking for her.'

One of the men had resurfaced from the mansion gloom. 'Don't be such a bloody party-pooper, Hull,' he said, a cigarette hanging limply from his lips.

Fable swung a breathless glance at Raff.

Raff's serious lips twitched. 'These kids are a bit young for your company, aren't they, Furse?'

The man called Furse crushed his fag beneath his foot and slouched back against the stone, languid resistance in every line of his body. 'Fable's enjoyin' herself. Let her be.'

The other man's voice echoed from the dark innards, 'Go home, Hull.'

Raff's face remained emotionless, but, at his quiet persistence, courage flared at last in Fable. She began to struggle free. The arms clung, even in their unravelling.

'I am ready to go home.'

Raff's eyes shifted to Fable, with a single, emphatic nod. He motioned with one arm. A cry of disgust encircled Fable as she picked her way free, evading reaching hands. She stumbled over a large root, into Raff's grip.

'Well, we're off, fellows,' he said, guiding Fable away from the fire circle with a firm hand at her elbow.

The clearing was in an uproar as Fable and Raff disappeared up the track. His grasp was unrelenting. All thoughts flew from Fable's head at both his nearness and the fear besieging her. Raff walked at a full pace, penlight scything the blackness before them. Fable had to jog to stay abreast of him.

She'd thought herself sobering up at the campfire, but now they were in motion she felt the world spinning beneath her.

'Hang on, I need—' Fable doubled over to vomit.

Raff waited, his eyes focused over her head at the dark pathway behind, the ruins beyond.

Fable wiped her mouth and reached for Raff again. The compassion on his face withdrew behind brusqueness.

'You're too young to be drinking, Fable Hamilton.'

She tried to roll her eyes, but the resulting head spin only made her turn and puke violently. When she staggered upright, it was to Raff's unnerving seriousness.

'Fable, you've got something on the back of your legs.'

She spun to see, achieving only a wheeling lurch. 'What?!'

'Nothing, forget it,' he said, moving on again.

'Please! What is it?'

At her pleading tone, he stopped. 'Stay still.' He retrieved a scrap of cloth from his pocket, stooped and swiped gently up the back of her leg. At his touch, Fable swayed widely. She reached for his shoulder to steady herself, but Raff had moved clear.

He lifted an inky-black shape, glisteningly engorged, for her perusal.

'Only a leech,' he said, sounding more relieved than she felt. 'It's been having an absolute feast. Check yourself at home for more.'

In his hand lay a white handkerchief embroidered with a blue R – and covered with her blood. Fable stared. A rude thing to have done, bleeding over a man's pretty handkerchief like that.

'*Out*, damned leech,' she said with a weak smile.

Wryness tugged at his lips. He placed the handkerchief in her hand. 'All right, Lady Macbeth, I'm taking you home.'

They pressed on. As they neared the road, Fable remembered Eamon. 'Wait! Your brother's back there, too!'

'Eamon isn't there.'

'But he is! He brought me here. You can't leave him—'

'He's not. Let's go!'

Fable stumbled after Raff, confused by his tone. Moments later, the truck came into view. A hunched shadow in the cab moved away from the window at their approach. Raff banged on the door.

'Get in the back!'

The door opened and Eamon swung down. Even in the weak light seeping from the doused pools of headlight, even in the haze of inebriation, Fable saw the dark bruise that stained one side of Eamon's face. He glowered at Fable in passing.

She climbed into the cab, lost for words, or indeed thought. The situation was bigger than she could presently muddle out. For now, she wanted to rest her head against the window, just for a wee while.

Raff leaned over Fable, placing a balled-up jacket between her head and the door. The truck shuddered into life and Fable closed her eyes. Raff's steely silence and the rocking motion of their descent tipped her into sleep.

Fable stirred with the engine's cessation at Summerlinn. Eamon leapt off the truck and disappeared into the dark drizzle.

Raff turned to Fable. 'Hang on a sec, I'll be right back.'

He crossed the manicured lawn and bounded onto the front stoop. Figures waited in a frame of spilling light: Mrs Hull and someone else Fable couldn't distinguish through the rain-rippled glass and her drunkenness. It could only be Adriana, awaiting the gossip she would disperse, methodically, like a spring back-burn. The same rumour Mrs

Hull would spin up and down Main Street in hushed, yet no-less-flammable tones.

Raff conferred with the pair, using explosive arm motions, pointing in her direction several times. The smaller figure turned to peer. Yes, Adriana. With a theatrical display of pity, Adriana's darkly fringed face began to shake slowly at the truck. Her lips moved in silent chastisement: 'Fable, Fable, Fable . . .'

The mimed words hit Fable with the force of a shout.

Raff's voice was audible now even over the distance and rain. He was furious. At Fable, obviously: the inconvenience of bringing her home, not to mention the scandalous position in which he'd found her, surrounded by groping boys, on the cusp of something irrevocable.

But *what*? Fable couldn't get it all straight in her head. She only knew she could not bear another moment of Adriana's scorn, and Raff's ire.

She slipped out of the cab, fleeing for the forest.

The distended serpent rolled beneath Fable's feet as she skirted the bridge unsteadily towards home. How many times must she cross this flood today?

Dead centre of the bridge she slipped on a sleeper, and for one terrified moment felt the creek opening to swallow her. At the last second she managed to right herself, giggling with the terror of it. She planted her feet, and raised her face and arms to the few stars which shone against the cloud-strung sky, her body absorbing the power surging against the bridge.

Raff arrived on the bridge with a panting stealth that was somehow reassuring.

'Fable . . . ?'

'I don't need you to rescue me, Rafferty Hull!'

'Of course you don't.'

'I'm going home!'

She whirled to leave, only to sway wildly again. Beside her, she heard a pronounced intake of breath.

Once she'd regained her balance, he spoke in a slow, placating tone. 'I know this bridge better than you – at least let me see you across.' He advanced carefully, hands ushering her forward.

'I don't need you *or* your stupid brother.'

'*Nobody* needs *my* stupid brother.'

Raff was so close now she felt rather than saw his grin. Her urge to return the smile was unexpected. She fixed her feet, indignantly.

'Come on, couple more steps and you're there.'

'You always treat me like a child!'

Raff paused now. 'No, not a child. Like a newcomer to Noah Vale – which you are.'

'You mean an outsider! Or, worse, a Hamilton!'

'The Hamilton name is as old as the hills, and us Hulls. But I grew up here, and you did not. There are things you only learn by long immersion – things that nobody is apparently going to let you in on.'

'In other words, I'm only pretending to belong here.'

'In other words, if no one else here is watching out for you, I will.'

His words stung. 'I don't need a babysitter! Nobody asked you to drag me home. Matter of fact, I was having fun until you showed up.'

'Oh sure, it's all fun and games until someone's hanging dead from a vine.'

'What does that even mean? Is this the kind of interfering Adriana has to deal with whenever *she* goes off without her party-pooper of a brother?'

His brow tightened at her words.

Fable hurried beyond him. Crossing the last sleeper, she contemplated sprinting straight on for home without another word – then let

Sonnet do what she did best with Hulls, should he dare come after her. But beer was a boldness she'd never known before. Fable swung back, outrage on her tongue.

His quiet wrath, however, stopped the words at her lips.

'Adriana would *never* go to Vinelands because she knows what Vinelands *is*. What no one else has cared to tell you. And those boys specifically took you there today, *without* saying anything, because they were pinning all their sordid hopes on your reputation.'

'What reputation!'

'You're the daughter of Esther Hamilton. In this town, stories, true or false, circulate for generations. You're climbing a mountain other girls, especially *my* sister, have never had to face. And let me tell you, every one of those boys there tonight was betting on you being as . . . "easy" as the town legends claim your mother was.'

Fable's bottom lip was no longer obeying her.

'Do you have any idea what they had in *store* for you today?'

'I went because Eamon invited me! And Vince, too . . . but they both disappeared.'

'And Eamon will *never* ask you anywhere again; neither will Vince after I get to him.'

Fable held her head, voice small. 'Would you just tell me?'

Raff dragged a handful of hair back from his own forehead, looking away. He sighed but began to speak – in quick, stilted phrases.

'The Vinelands ruins are the . . . sexual initiation spot for the St Ronan's boys. Each summer there are girls they take up there. Or maybe lure there. Get them drunk. Then share them around. Like animals. Who can go the furthest? How many turns can you have? They always say the girls are willing. But they only take the . . . vulnerable ones. It's drunken, macho one-upmanship. They brag among themselves for years to come. It's a tradition for the seniors. Usually, a couple of guys from the old boys' club rock up, too, reliving their own hazing rituals. Every year there's a girl, sometimes two together.'

On he went, sparing her nothing. 'There was one girl, the year I graduated, lovely person, but she "went to Vinelands". *They* swore willingly. She said it was a bit of fun. It was a . . . big year. None of it bears repeating. And it's only because she fled town that it didn't go to the sergeant. It never does, though! Vinelands is only ever talked about as silly kids' play. Everyone getting what they asked for, especially the girls. But only a few months later, that poor girl came back to hang herself at Vinelands. On the vines you were swinging from today.'

Fable gagged, tasting bile.

'I hate that I'm the one telling you this. It should have been my sister, or yours. But now you *know*. You can do whatever you want, but in future they'll never have the advantage of your not knowing again.'

Fable tried to shake her head, but it was too heavy for her control.

'When I found my godforsaken brother stumbling down the gorge road this afternoon, drunk as a skunk, and he said *you* were at Vinelands...' His jaw jumped. 'I couldn't just leave you there, could I?'

He seemed to think she might answer this.

'Fable?'

Her thoughts were a slow turmoil in a whirling world. She bent and heaved repeatedly. He moved to help, then stopped short.

Understanding finally punctured Fable's stupefaction. Raff had expected to find her in the worst predicament imaginable, and he'd come for her, anyway. What had Fable ever been to Raff but his sister's pitiable friend? What did it matter to *him* what she chose to do with boys, how many of them there were, or where she chose to do it?

Yet he'd come for *her*.

It was too much to process. With a guttural cry, Fable turned and sprinted for the rain-enfeebled glow of the cottage. Behind she heard, or thought she heard, Raff call: 'Take care, Fable.'

Fable dropped into the cottage with the impact of a pebble into a pool, absorbed without fuss or notice. There were no inquisitions to greet her, no need even to feign sobriety. Sonnet wasn't home. In her stead, only a mildly defensive note propped on the kitchen bench in answer to Fable's earlier message: Sonnet was staying late at the bookshop to attend rain damage, it had to be done, Fable should make dinner from leftovers and not worry about Plum, who was *still* at Heartwood. She too could duck up the hill if she really wanted company.

The words swam as relief and dismay jostled for position. There was no one in the world Fable wanted to see or touch or be comforted by more than her big sister, but thank God she wasn't home. Moments later, Fable was tumbling down the long, spinning slope into grateful oblivion.

CHAPTER 22

ECHIDNA

Spring 1959

Sonnet's daily bookseller routine unfolded precisely so: soaring down Main Street on Freya at eight o'clock, disobedient red strands already escaping her bun; a pot of tea straight up, with the quiet unpacking of orders, followed by dusting, rearranging and a fresh batch of scones out of the oven. She turned her sign to OPEN and put out the Story Bar placard promptly at nine, then her customers came, in a slow and steady drip until, at 3 p.m., Sonnet twirled the sign to CLOSED and marched proudly up the street to do her banking, mailing and groceries. Along her route, familiar faces smiled and nodded, and fewer people mentioned Esther Hamilton than ever before.

Which made Sonnet think: perhaps there *was* a position on Main Street – and in Noah Vale – for a Hamilton girl, after all. Far be it from Sonnet to suggest Olive had been right, though. Now marking her first anniversary of proprietorship, these were quietly fulfilling days, and Sonnet wondered if she was content, perhaps even happy, for the first time since arriving in Noah.

She had a business *and* a best friend, now.

Sonnet acknowledged she had softened in unexpected ways under Kate Hardy's influence. For starters, she had marked Plum's ever-increasing presence at Heartwood with fewer plates shattered for cathartic relief than she might have expected. Kate's counsel – 'Let Olive have the weekdays, then you get to enjoy the weekends. Quality not quantity, Son' – had proved, ultimately, true. Sonnet would have preferred quality *and* quantity, but Plummy seemed to love the arrangement.

Kate was tonic for the soul. And at four o'clock every Thursday afternoon, she also ushered in Gin and Tonic Hour. Sonnet pulled out her largest teacups to hide their tipples, and served up a stack of romance novels, while Kate dished out juicy town twaddle. It was a puerile diversion, and Sonnet knew she was no better than her worst gossiping enemies. She didn't care! Their cackling chatter enriched Sonnet's life more than a constantly ringing till could ever have done.

Not that Sonnet had relinquished the dream of a booming business. Time would prove her mettle as a bookseller, and her loyal stable of readers was being built with patience and aplomb, one cuppa and book recommendation at a time.

The Story Bar was proving her biggest drawcard. Sonnet had never rated herself much of a listener before, but in the cosseted quietness of her shop, people sure liked to talk. Her patrons peddled tales over the counter as much as she sold stories back. And with such a slow trickle of customers, Sonnet had time to listen. It was remarkable what you could learn about a person when you kept them talking about themselves, instead of others; when their impetus to appear perfect was less appealing than the longing to be heard, and seen.

In this way, Sonnet had met inveterate womanisers, hypochondriacs, unpublished authors, avid birdwatchers (filthy habit), barely literate literature lovers, reformed shoplifters (she hoped), divorcees, veterans, hoarders, gamblers, loners, losers – even the odd lush, loitering on Thursday afternoons.

Her Story Bar had become a kind of confessional, though Sonnet thought of it as a sanctuary for bibliophiles. She'd always liked people who read best – but she was falling in love with narrators, too. And, as it turned out, everyone had a tale to tell.

Initially, it felt like a leap going from dressmaker to bookseller, but Sonnet had come to realise how similar they were.

Stories garbed the soul.

Scent of molasses hung in the spring air as Sonnet strode up Main Street towards the post office. She always hurried past Canecutter's Hotel – the central pub, known colloquially as Cutters – with floral dress flapping determinedly, and head tucked low. The male laughter rolling out on a swell of yeast and cigarette smoke opened a pit of loneliness in her belly she could neither explain, nor quell. Worse were the crude laughter and catcalls. Sonnet was outraged by the nerve of them, though she would never give them the pleasure of knowing it. And though she loathed their attention, she refused to concede defeat by crossing Main Street to avoid them.

Sonnet coursed along the fig-lined pub veranda, bracing for the stench and yowls, fixing her eyes above on the freshly watered ferns, dripping lightly on her shoulders. Distracted thus, she failed to spot the man sweeping fig leaves until the last moment. She pulled up with an almost audible screech, careening into a wooden pole.

He was at her side in an instant. 'You right there, darl?' Cologne was a full-frontal attack.

Sonnet dusted off her dress, and pride, hastily regaining her full height. 'Fine. Didn't see you there.'

'Saw *you* coming a long way back, Sonnet.'

Her eyes snapped to his face. Before her gaze skimmed away, she registered dark handsomeness and an indolently vulpine smile.

Something prickled in her stomach. 'Have a good day,' she said, dashing away.

'Will *now*.' A few steps past, he called after her. 'I'll be here tomorrow, sweeping off your red carpet . . .'

Sonnet turned. He leaned on the broom, insouciantly, brows lifted.

Her hands rose to her hips. 'Well I won't be repeating *that* performance.'

His smile spread, like a languid wave. 'No, we can't have you going bottoms up, can we?'

Sonnet choked on a retort, spinning to leave. Her face glowed all the way to the bank, stayed hot throughout her dealings at the post office, and veritably burned on the return journey. Only once back in her shop, did the ball drop.

He'd used her name without introduction.

True to his word, he was out sweeping off the veranda the next day, with one-liners primed, and then every day for the rest of the week. Cutters' corner had never been so tidy before.

By the fourth day, he'd pressed a name upon her: Brenton Furse, hotel proprietor. The publican *himself* pestering her. She'd supposed a general maintenance man, but it made no difference; she was no more intimidated by his flirtations than the ogling Cutters' catcalls, which had only intensified now that he'd made such a spectacle of her passage.

'Can't you quiet your rabble?' Sonnet asked after one particularly noisome volley of wolf whistles and lewd comments.

'Boys, eh,' he said, with a shrug. 'We can't help but admire beauty when we see it!'

It was hardly 'beauty' they were proclaiming appreciation for, the filthy old men! Never before, in all Sonnet's years of running, had her heart rate hammered quite as it did when she rounded the corner of Cutters each afternoon readying her caustic rejoinders to Brenton Furse's overtures. She felt like a crazed schoolgirl, though it was unlike any attraction she'd relished or acted on before. Sonnet struck out on her quotidian errands with as much trepidation he would be waiting for her, as that he wouldn't.

There was something else, too – a visceral feeling, uninterpretable. She had no lived experience of it, only the nostalgic recollection of her mother's counsel . . .

'Listen to your tummy,' Mama had told her during senior year. 'It's the seat of intuition, and will always tell you what you need to know. Don't trust your heart, don't let your head overthink it; your *gut* knows.'

Sonnet couldn't work out why she'd retained that advice, given her adolescent propensity for filtering out her mother's every word on relationships as the regretful mutterings of one who'd failed innumerable times to keep a man. But still, stick with her it had. Not that Mama's teachings made any sense right now. There was an echidna in *her* belly, quilled and cowering, and how was she meant to interpret that?

The following Friday, Sonnet sashayed up Main Street towards the man waiting in the literal hopes of sweeping her off her feet, only to be distracted instead by a flash of movement in a Ford Mainline, parked at Cutters' verge. Sonnet diverted, peering through rolled-down windows. There were two sweat-matted children in the back seat: a boy Plum's age in a filthy school uniform, and a girl, perhaps a year younger.

'Hey!' Sonnet cried, rapping on the car.

Both faces turned dully on her. Sonnet leant into the window. 'You kids waiting on your parents? Do you think they'll be much longer?'

The boy shrugged.

'What's your name, young man?'

'Jim.'

'And your sister?'

'Jackie.'

'Listen, I've got errands to run. But I'm going to check back on you, all right?'

Having lost interest in her afternoon tête-à-tête with Brenton Furse, she crossed the street away from the pub, frowning.

Sonnet's return was delayed by a long line at the General Store, twenty questions from Smithy over the newsagent counter, and footpath hijackings by loquacious townsfolk. By the time she was rushing back down Main Street, she'd forgotten the two children. With much dismay, she sighted the Ford still there; blond heads bobbing in the back seat, and the afternoon sun beating upon it.

She hesitated. If she put her head down and kept going, she would be back at her shop in a minute, maybe less.

Stay out of it.

But of course she wasn't going to. She crossed the street, hand diving into her string bag to locate the banana bread she had been anticipating all day, and the rare treat of a bottled soda.

The kids were kicking at the seats, sweat streaming down their backs. Tired eyes slid away from Sonnet.

'Still here, huh?'

Jim shrugged.

'That sucks. Bet it won't be long now. You guys hungry? I've got some banana bread, want to polish it off for me?'

The boy darted to take the bread and soda, dripping with condensation.

Sonnet straightened from the window to find Brenton lounging against an adjacent pole. Not a broom in sight.

'You know anything about these kids left in the car? Their names are Jackie and Jim.'

'Yeah, they'd be Joe Taylor's kids, I reckon.'

'He's a patron of yours?' she asked, more impertinently than intended.

Brenton's grin returned, easily as that. The ruder she was, the faster he smiled. Sonnet couldn't understand it.

'Too right,' he said, 'Joe's one of my best. After a hard day, a man needs refreshment.'

'Does he often leave his children unattended out here?'

Brenton laughed. 'He's certainly not bringing them into my pub. No kids allowed.'

'No, I suppose not, considering you publicans won't even allow *women* at your bars.'

'I'll sneak a door open for a fine woman like you any day.'

Sonnet flushed. 'You'd better remind Joe Taylor he's got small children sweltering in a hot car out here. Next time he orders *himself* another nice cold beer in there . . .' She moved briskly around him.

'I'll do better than that for *you*, Sonnet!' he called after her. 'I'll send them kids out a cold schooner, too!'

Sonnet didn't acknowledge his words, other than to raise a trembling hand to her burning cheek.

It perturbed Sonnet that she couldn't bring herself to even mention Brenton to Kate. Instead, she broached the infuriating subject of Jackie and Jim Taylor, found languishing in the Ford most afternoons. She had taken to carrying a basket filled with books and scones on her daily errand run for the children.

'Those kids are parked out there, day after day. It's wilful neglect!'

'Believe me,' Kate said, 'an afternoon in a quiet car is probably the better option for Joseph Taylor's kids. Joe's a tobacco farmer outside Noah, and it's a hard life for his little blighters. Sorry old bastard, that one. I'd say Joe brings them in so they can all have a breather.'

'So, you already knew about his kids out there?' Sonnet couldn't keep the disappointment from her voice.

Kate shrugged. 'Most people would have noticed. But they're not the first kids sitting in a car at the local watering hole, and sure as heck won't be the last.'

Sonnet blew a sigh through her nostrils. 'Why doesn't anyone tip off the constable? Surely you don't all turn a blind eye to a damned drunk getting behind the wheel of a car, with kids in the back?'

'Actually, I don't think he—' Kate stopped, choosing a different route. 'Why does it bother you so much?'

Sonnet watched a jolting image reel: tiny Hillman Minx crushed around a power pole, with unimaginable carnage within; two rain-washed police officers hunched together in the apartment doorway, blocking out the cold night beyond; the bereft, foetal curl of a tiny girl, clinging to her mother's pillow.

Nope. She wasn't going to touch that conversation, even with Kate. *Especially* with Kate.

'It just does! And the *nerve* of Brenton Furse serving that man beer after beer, knowing he's got kids sweltering out there alone and he's going to drive off, sozzled, at the end of it.'

Her face had flared hotly into colour as his name left her lips. The effect did not escape Kate's notice.

'Brenton Furse, you say?'

'Think that's his name. The publican. Dark-haired man?'

A tongue had appeared, rather prominently, in the side of Kate's cheek. 'Hmm. I'm actually not sure if that's Brenton Furse. What colour would you say his eyes are?'

'Not sure. Greyish, probably.'

'So it's like *that*, is it?'

Sonnet's eyes slunk by Kate's scrutiny.

'Sonnet and Brenton Furse!'

'Sonnet and nobody!'

Kate stroked an imaginary beard, eyes narrow. 'Brenton's always been a catch, even more so since he came into the pub inheritance this year. He's an old St Ronan's boy, graduated the same year as Raffy and I did. He's good-looking, I'll give you that. Brenton's always been wildly popular with the girls. Hung like a donkey, *he* reckons. Can't say I would have called the match myself . . . but you'll be the talk of town if you pull it off, Son.'

'Kate, if you've learned anything about me by now, you'll know the last thing I'm keen on is becoming the talk of this hellhole!'

In any case, Sonnet's name was soon linked with Brenton's across town: at Hadley's store, volleyed over the nets at the Ladies Tennis Club, hollered from the pub windows as she passed, ladled out in the CWA tea rooms and, eventually, even mentioned over the Heartwood Sunday dinner table.

'So, Sonnet, I hear you've taken up hard drinking lately,' Olive said. 'Word in Noah is that they can't keep you *away* from Cutters these days.'

Gav added the salt: 'Listen, pet, you'll have to beat off all the other girls in town if you've got designs on making the publican's wife.'

'I've got no such thing! What a load of hogwash.'

Olive and Gav exchanged a long glance, and Sonnet exited stage right with a screech of chair on deck. There couldn't be two people in the world she wanted to discuss Brenton Furse with *less* than Olive and Gav – with their indulgent smiles, and cautioning eyes.

Brenton appeared in her shop on Friday afternoon. The barbed creature in her belly, awakened from slumber, rolled irascibly.

His eyes travelled the length of her body. Her hands flew to her hips.

'Thought I'd better pop in and see about some belongings you carried off from one of my patrons.' His voice was officious, but his smirk sensual.

Sonnet recoiled. How *dare* he? It was an excruciating few seconds before she realised he meant the two kids quietly colouring with Plum in 'Esther's Corner' beneath the stairs.

'I think you'll find those *belongings* followed me home – not unlike strays, actually.' She glanced at Jim and Jackie to ensure they weren't following the conversation. Only Plum's eyes were fixed on the pair.

'Dunno about that,' Brenton said, 'I saw the kidnapping with my own eyes.'

Sonnet frowned. He'd been nowhere in sight when she had made her usual Ford drop-by. 'Well, if you *were* spying on me,' she said, voice dropping low, 'then you would have seen them climbing out of the window of their own volition, and trailing me back here.'

'And are you returning them anytime soon?'

'There's no need for those kids to go back in that stinking hot car anytime soon. I'll bet said owner hasn't even realised they're gone. I'll shoo them out of my door at closing time, they'll scoot back into their cage, and no one will be the wiser.'

'What *is* your closing time?' he asked, stepping closer.

'Five o'clock, like the sign says.'

'That's good to know. 'Cause I'm going to swing by here at closing, and take you out.'

'Take me out?!' Her face must have registered indignation, for his smirk deepened.

'Yep, I'm takin' you out to dinner. Once you return those children, that is. Big-kids date only.'

'I'm sorry, I'm not free tonight. I have my sister Plum with me.'

'Leave her with the Emersons.'

Sonnet straightened her shoulders. 'No, I can't do that.'

'Ah, come on now, don't play hard to get.'

'No, I can't spring it on my aunt and uncle. They already have Plum tomorrow.'

'All right, so Saturday night it is, then.'

Sonnet laughed, startling herself. 'All right.'

'All right?'

'Yes. You can take me out to dinner tomorrow night.'

'Atta girl!' he said, as though she were an obstreperous child. 'Pick you up at Heartwood at seven.'

He didn't wait for her assent, barrelling out in a jaunty rush.

Plum appeared at her side, slipping a chubby, freckled hand into hers. 'Who was that?'

'Just my friend,' Sonnet lied. There were many things Brenton Furse might be, but friend wasn't yet one of them.

'I don't like him,' Plum said.

Sonnet snorted. 'Oh, Plummy, you don't even know him.'

'I don't *like* him,' Plum insisted.

'You don't have to like him.' She tousled magenta curls. *I'm not sure how I feel about him, either.*

CHAPTER 23

THE PUBLICAN

How she felt now, waiting for the long sweep of headlights up the drive to Heartwood, quite frankly, was *petrified*. And fear wasn't a becoming look for Sonnet. She blotted ineffectually at her face in the bathroom mirror, rechecked for sweat stains.

'It's the pits being a nervous sweater,' Sonnet told her reflection, then grimaced. 'I know; that one was terrible.'

She took one last look: at the powder sliding further off her skin with every passing second, knowing full well it had no business being dabbed on a face like hers; at the chiffon cocktail dress cinched in two whole notches this evening; at her mother's pearls nestled above the sweetheart neckline; and, with the most misgiving, at the hair she'd allowed Fable to pin in a soft Grecian pile before she'd left the cottage.

She wished she'd worn pants. Couldn't even remember right now why she'd started wearing these stupid dresses in the first place.

The rush of Plum's feet up the hallway truncated her spiralling angst. 'He's here! He's *here*!'

Sonnet gulped a breath, grabbed the drawstring purse she'd sewn up just for the occasion, and thrust the bathroom door open with what she hoped was a confident smile.

'So, what do you feel like for dinner?' Brenton asked as the car roared through the rainforest towards town. The smell of cologne, shaving cream and polished car interior was a warm, masculine fog. 'The world is your oyster tonight!'

'Actually . . .' Sonnet began, pressing her skirt over her knees, hotly conscious of his side glances, and her body's response.

'Just kidding!' he said. 'There are no oysters tonight. You've only got two choices in Noah: Gino's restaurant or the Greek café! Don't know what we'd even eat in this town if it wasn't for all the wogs invading us.'

'I'm happy either way,' Sonnet replied, with a terse edge.

'Happy with *either* way . . . well then, I think we're in for good night, Sonnet.'

Her belly echidna ruffled. Sonnet turned to check her reflection in the car window. In the final seconds before greeting Brenton, holding his bouquet of carnations, Sonnet had whipped her hair up into a bun – it was much messier than she preferred.

Sonnet returned her attention, not without effort, to her date.

He was re-screwing the cap on a discreet silver flask. Seeing her looking, he offered. 'Rum?'

She began to refuse, and found the flask pressed into her hand, anyway. She ought to say she didn't like rum – not the smell of it, not the effect of it, and especially not taste of it – but nerves *were* nerves.

She had a tiny sip.

'Bottoms up!' he said.

Sonnet gave a subdued cough, handing back the flask.

'Tell you what, though,' Brenton said. 'We could skip the restaurant altogether and I'll show you round my pub, instead. We'll sneak upstairs, I'll scrounge us up some food, and we can find a quiet corner to get to know each other.'

'You want to walk a *woman* through your pub on a Saturday night? That's bound to set off the bush telegraph!'

Brenton lifted the flask to his lips again. 'She'll be right. But I gotta say, Sonnet, I wouldn't mind ending up in a rumour with you, anyway . . .'

Sonnet managed a non-committal shrug. 'How about we try Gino's new restaurant, and that famous spaghetti bolognese they're all talking about?'

Brenton laughed. 'I get it. Have to win a girl's heart with a nice dinner first.'

'You won't win it with a horrid dinner.'

Their shared laughter soothed. Sonnet sank back against her seat with a slow outbreath.

Look at me, Sonnet wanted to cry, to an offstage audience. *I'm on a date. I'm dating!*

She hoped no one else could tell it was the first time Sonnet Hamilton had attempted such a basic life skill. At the old-maid age of twenty-four, no less. She knew just enough to fake it. How to allow Brenton to lead her through the busy restaurant, to pull out her chair, order for her, and pour her a glass of wine. There was no doubt *he* knew all the moves.

Sonnet was under no illusions here. Their table, hidden inadequately behind a rhapis palm, was the central topic of conversation across the restaurant. From the familiar faces at neighbouring tables smirking at one another, to the clanging, hissing din of camaraderie between Mr and Mrs Rossi in the kitchen, Sonnet and Brenton's date was the hottest news story of the evening. Every time Mrs Rossi swished, grinning, through the kitchen door, Sonnet was reminded again this was not so much a date as a declaration.

Sonnet felt not unlike the goldfish swimming in the bowl at the restaurant counter; with nowhere to hide, only maddeningly polite circles to make.

The outrageous flirtation, which normally bamboozled her defences, was nowhere to be seen. Brenton was the perfect date – smooth as silk and so perfectly proper it was a downright yawn. The languidly grinning man who'd picked her up earlier with an unapologetic ogle at her chest, had been supplanted by this chivalrous gentleman feted by all the townsfolk around, eagerly tipping their hats to him.

They meandered out of the restaurant at meal's laboured end into a warm October breeze, carrying with it the scent of countless rainforest trees coming into bloom.

Sonnet took Brenton's arm as it was offered and let him lead her, inevitably, towards his pub. He'd done his legwork getting the elusive Sonnet Hamilton out, had executed the textbook dinner date, now he schemed to be seen with her in his own realm. And fair enough. Sonnet didn't know if it was the copious glasses of wine thrust upon her or simply relief at having escaped the awkward small talk, but she was feeling uncharacteristically charitable.

'Back to mine?' Brenton asked with a bowing flourish, motioning towards the open door, blazing with light and music beyond it. 'For a tour of my fine establishment,' he said, noting her dubious pursing.

'A tour?'

'Quick one,' he promised. 'I'll show you mine, then you show me yours.'

Sonnet laughed, but stayed rooted to the spot. Brenton's face faltered briefly in its confident expectation. Behind him: the clank and scatter of the billiard table, a tumble of glasses.

'Do you have a staff entrance?'

'Slinking in the back – I like your style!'

They skirted the leering comments already ricocheting through the open windows for a rear staircase.

'After you, m'lady.'

Sonnet ascended the staircase with steps as nonchalant as she could manage under the circumstances; those being the appreciative whistles of the man behind her.

'You've got *some* legs! Must be all that riding you do.'

'Not a very professional tour guide, are you, Mr Furse?'

'Hey, what kind of tour guide would I be if I didn't point out the local attractions when they're looking their best?'

'I don't just ride. I run.'

'Long as you're not running away from me, I don't mind what you do to get pins like that.'

'I wasn't asking your permission.'

'So, these are my rooms, then,' Brenton said with a sweeping gesture up a long hallway of numbered rooms. Painted images of Noah Vale hung askew in ornate metal frames, and silk flowers dangled from dusty sconces. The smell of alcohol and cigarette smoke was all-pervasive here, competing with well-used linen and tropical mildew. A hollow ache, triggered by the cocktail of smells, had opened up in her throat.

Ignoring the guest room door he'd swung open for her inspection, Sonnet paused to examine one of the oil paintings. It was a familiar sweep of banana plantation near the school, stately old Queenslander sitting atop a rise, the whole scene scythed by long, golden sunrays.

'*Crepuscular*,' she breathed.

'What?'

'Nothing. Just saying how pretty this is.'

'Not too bad for pub art, you reckon?'

'Who painted all these?'

'An artist,' he said, nodding encouragingly towards the open room.

She turned back to the painting, ignoring both his persistence and her baulking belly. 'I'd love to know. I want to feature something local in my shop.'

'Sorry, can't tell you. They were already here. I'll ask round, though.'

'Maybe there's a name on the back?' she mused, unable to tear her eyes from the picture.

'Let me show you my big one in here,' Brenton said.

Sonnet held back a ribald retort, following.

It wasn't innuendo. The large painting above the bed was magnificent: a shining waterfall in full flow, tiny rainbows dancing before the curtain.

'Now that *has* to be Moria Falls,' she said, drawing close.

'Like it?'

'It's beautiful. Why on earth do you keep this hidden away in a . . . guest room?' She'd almost said dingy, and censured herself for her automatic fault-finding.

Sonnet glanced at the bed over which she leaned. 'I see; a hoax to lure unsuspecting young women in. How do you plan on wrangling me into this next?'

Her frank manner seemed to throw him. He considered Sonnet for a sluggish moment. 'Another drink?'

Sonnet burst into laughter, stopping short when answering humour failed to materialise on his face.

'A drink would be fine, Brenton.'

'I'll nip down to my bar. Stay right here.'

He disappeared, not unlike a small boy running to locate and show off his favourite toy. She squinted critically at her muted reflection in the picture glass. Her bun was a mess. She tried, in vain, to tame the unruly red.

'What a tangle!' She didn't mean the hairdo. She held her hands to her cheeks and blew a long, steadying breath.

It's my choice, I'm a grown woman, I brought my own protection, and I'm attracted to him. So, if I want to have sex tonight, I can.

She sat on the bed, to wait.

Sonnet held the empty spirit glass in her hand, stifling the urge to yawn, while her date mauled her neck. That last, heavily spiked drink had dampened any desire she'd harboured this evening. On Brenton, however, their nightcap had worked a wonder. He was panting with inebriated enthusiasm now, all trace of languor vanished. She suspected, from the fumes coming off the mouth toiling near her ear, he'd shored himself up with multiple shots, and several cigarettes with the blokes downstairs.

She sighed to cover an escaping yawn, and Brenton drew back with a grin. 'Yeah, you like that? Oh, baby, I can do more of that . . .'

He pushed her back, and she acquiesced with an awkward crumpling that did nothing to improve the emerging feeling of pointlessness.

His hands began an insistent groping of her layers, and she amended her objective for the evening: *As long as I stay in my garments, this is just necking. He hasn't even bothered to kiss my mouth . . .*

In experiment, she nudged her lips towards his and was rewarded with a kiss, which, though failing still to ignite any fire, sent a minor crackle of excitement skittering down her spine. She wriggled, trying to unpin herself, and Brenton used the moment to press himself heavily between her legs. His jeans generated a mild abrasion against her bare legs as his hips rocked rhythmically against her pelvis. Brenton was already at a gallop, puffing hotly at her throat, while she hadn't yet quickened her pace. She turned her head away, and immediately two hands rose to paw at her breasts.

'You Hamilton chicks have got enormous knockers,' he said, pulling roughly at her dress, sending one delicate button flying across the bed.

It might have been that sentence alone.

Perhaps it was the frantic, churning plight of her little belly echidna. Or maybe it was merely the waste of the delicate button. In any case, Sonnet became very, very still.

Her eyes flew open – long enough to take in the antediluvian gaze of a giant blue bird, fixed upon her.

Sonnet wriggled beneath him for a better glimpse. It was a luridly hued dinosaur in close-up portraiture: large, grey helmet, two holes bored in a scythe-like beak, and blood-red wattles hanging from a cobalt-blue face. Amber eyes fixed upon her with an unblinking stare so recriminatory, Sonnet gasped.

Brenton fumbled roughly at their compressed groins, shoving layers aside.

'What's *that*?' she cried.

'Yeah, that's me, baby.'

She strained around him, exasperated. 'No, that picture, the . . . bird thing. Look!'

'It's a bloody cassowary painting.'

Cassowary.

Instantly, the word invoked Gav's gristly after-dinner tales of feisty, flightless rainforest birds – taller than humans, with talons like cutlasses, which could garrotte a jugular in a single kick. Elusive as they were dangerous.

Who got so close to a cassowary they could paint such a marvellous image?

The shock of cool denim against her innermost folds was galvanising. Sonnet came back to herself.

'Brenton – no, wait!'

He grunted, struggling free of his fly.

'Hang on!'

He pushed back against her with a growl, releasing himself fully.

For a split second, Sonnet heard her own voice commenting from a patronising height: *Like ripping off a bandage. Real quick, then it'll be over.*

But she wasn't a bandage, and nothing was getting ripped tonight. She fought the crushing weight.

'Geez, you like it a bit rough,' he said, lining himself up.

'Brenton, stop!' It was a sob.

He was deaf to her entreaty. His engorged flesh pressed, solidly, into her dry lips. Sonnet had a brief image of a broom handle; a sword.

'No!'

He pushed harder still for admittance. She felt the first stinging ring of his ingress.

'Get off of me, you sonofabitch!'

She pummelled at him now, but he was a tree fallen upon her, impervious.

'*Stop!*'

He fell from her with a yowl, halted only by the searing rake of nails on his neck.

'What the hell?'

His shocked disgust curdled her terror instantly into shame. 'I'm sorry!' she cried, scrambling away – scrabbling together her dress, her underpants; herself.

They panted at each other from opposite corners of the room now.

He clutched at a scarlet clawing on his throat. 'What's *wrong* with you?'

'I told you to stop!'

'You want it one second, and next thing you're tearing at me like an alley cat.'

'I wanted to stop!'

'You're just being a prick-teaser! Come here . . .'

'I don't want you, Brenton.'

His lips curled. 'You don't know *what* you want. Leading me on! What are you doing up here, if you're such a frigid prude?'

'You brought me up here for a *tour*! Can't you be alone with a woman without assaulting her?'

'You knew what we were coming here for.'

Sonnet trembled to her feet, chin thrusting. 'I am taking myself home.'

'You're a lesbian with that heifer of a Hardy chick, anyway. Everybody knows it.'

Sonnet picked up her empty glass and held it high in the air, fingers trembling, until he began to smirk.

She let go.

Brenton winced as the glass exploded on his wood floor.

'Useless cow,' he spat. 'You don't even deserve to be screwed out of pity.'

Sonnet put one heeled toe on the last, thinning cube at her feet, and crushed it. 'Don't ever come near me again, Brenton Furse.'

The door slammed behind her as Sonnet dashed for the rear stairwell.

The back entrance was now shut and deadlocked. Acid rage rose in Sonnet's throat to comprehend a man who would wheedle her into bed, but lock her escape route, just to be sure.

The erupting roar as she descended the grand pub staircase in pursuit of freedom was only confirmation that every cad in town knew Brenton Furse was upstairs bedding Sonnet Hamilton.

She faltered on the final step, wondering if he'd sold bloody tickets. The pressing crowd and vulgar catcalls were, altogether, a fray she could not conceive of breaching.

Just put your head down and run for it, idiot!

Then, she perceived another, gentler voice . . .

Hold your head high, my Sonny girl.

Her mother's voice, her mother's saying – the first she'd heard of it in years. And just in time.

Sonnet lifted her chin, fastened her eyes on the doorway, and pushed forward. She was a bull bar, ramming through lowing cattle, towards home.

CHAPTER 24

PEARLS AND SWINE

The face peering through the cottage door was strained with worry. Sonnet plodded up the sunlit hallway, eyes enflamed, nerves jangling at the hurried rapping. Just Olive, returning the girls after church.

Breathe.

Sonnet could hear Plum leaping up and down on the porch, eager to show off her Sunday school craft. She slid the double bolt aside.

'Good morning, sleepyhead!' Olive said, scrutinising her face. How anomalous to find Sonnet, of all people, still in a nightgown at midday.

'Are you okay?' Olive asked, ushering the girls through.

For a second, Sonnet thought Olive could smell the rank odour of fear leftover from her long run home in the wee hours, wearing a damned cocktail dress. But she couldn't possibly. Sonnet had scrubbed that man, and her humiliation, right out of her body.

No, more likely Olive wanted Sonnet to confirm the gossip she'd already heard in the church pews this morning.

Sonnet's inflection was tight. 'I'm fine.'

'Are you sure?'

'*Why?*'

'I was worried when you didn't come home last night.'

'Obviously, I came home. I'm here, aren't I?'

'I didn't hear Brenton drop you back. I was . . . concerned.'

'He didn't.' Sonnet received Plum's proffered Garden of Eden mural with a mimed wow. 'I brought myself home.'

Olive was open-mouthed. 'He let you walk home in the *middle of the night*? That was inviting trouble for a young woman like you, Sonnet!'

'No woman *invites* trouble,' Sonnet said coldly, turning away to thumbtack Plum's garden to the pantry door.

'But anything could have happened to you!'

Like what, getting raped? That was only if I stayed.

Plum whined that Sonnet had bent her picture, she'd covered over the serpent; she was ruining it! Sonnet threw her hands up, and left her to the rearranging.

Olive studied Sonnet. 'You're definitely okay?'

Sonnet's urge to cry was unexpected. 'You can *see* I'm fine! Unless you've heard otherwise from that ruddy pulpit and your morning-tea gossipers.'

Immediately, she regretted her tone. Her conscience throbbed.

Olive laid an alfoil-covered plate on the kitchen bench. 'Just some lunch I saved for you. I'm glad you're safe. I'll leave you in peace now.'

Sonnet shrugged coldly, hating herself for it. 'No thanks, I'm not hungry.'

When Olive appeared in near-identical fashion the following morning, rubbing one foot along the opposite calf in that irritating habit of hers, Sonnet's first reaction was sheer peevishness, born of guilt. Another tiff with Olive was *exactly* what she didn't want on a Monday morning while trying to hustle two contrary sisters through breakfasts and into uniforms.

Plum, throwing herself around Olive's waist, was extricated with uncharacteristic brusqueness. 'Plummy, I need to talk to Sonnet. Fable dear, best you pop up to the bus, too.'

Fable's ensuing eye roll, as she shepherded a complaining Plum from the cottage, expressed Sonnet's feelings precisely.

'What's with the secrecy?' Sonnet asked, nipping at her toast.

'Oh, Sonnet,' Olive cried, forehead puckering with anguish, 'I'm so sorry! I was wrong!'

A sour wave rose in Sonnet's throat. She couldn't seem to swallow her mouthful.

'I misjudged this town. I promised you the furore about you girls would die down. I said *you* had to be patient and *they'd* eventually come to accept you as individuals in your own right.'

'I know what you said then – what are you saying *now*?!'

'It's your shop—'

Sonnet launched to her feet. 'What have they done to my shop?!'

'Your beautiful sign. Someone's ... defaced it with something ... awful!'

'*What?!*'

Olive shook her head, backing away. 'I *can't* repeat it. I won't! Gav's already there. He was in early this morning, saw it before almost anyone. Leave your bike, come with me.'

Arriving at the bookstore, they found Gav atop a ladder, Sonnet's sign already covered in a drop cloth. Gav's assistant, David, was on the other end of the sign. Both men nodded briefly at the women as Sonnet flung her way out of the car, but nobody spoke.

A running commentary on the sign's removal, however, was being provided by curmudgeonly Edward Fletcher, who walked Main

Street early each morning with his blue terrier, minding everyone else's business, except his dog's.

'Ah,' he cried, as Sonnet appeared. 'Here's the "lady" in question now. Raking up all kinds of trouble round here, aren't you? Just like your mother.'

Sonnet stumbled at the gutter, blinded by ballooning rage.

Edward turned back to the sign, summarily dismissing Sonnet. 'That's it now, fellas. Lift her up to the left and unsnag her there.'

Sonnet whirled on the man, spittle at her lips. 'I saw some of your dog's trademark defecation up the street there, Mr Fletcher. Go take care of your *own* mess!'

Finally, the sign was down, and carried into the shop on their shoulders with the sombre, stilted manner of pallbearers. David headed back to Emerson's Hardware. He would not meet Sonnet's eyes as he left.

The front door jangled closed. Sonnet wheeled on the Emersons.

'*Show me!*'

Gav stooped, grimacing, to sweep the cloth aside. It was a sickening do-over of Fable's grand reveal: her whimsical artwork ravaged by violent, slashing strokes of red paint. The only part of the sign untarnished was Sonnet's name, which had been worked into the staining curse, twisting her sign into a foul palimpsest ...

Sonnet'*sucks*
old mens dongs for free
Book*stores*
HAMILTON WHORES!

Sonnet staggered back from the sign. '*Sonofabitch!*' she roared, sweeping a stack of books off the Story Bar.

Gav moved quickly to cover it over.

'No!' Sonnet cried. 'Don't you dare! If the whole town's talking about this sign, there's no use trying to protect me now.'

'Whole town didn't see it,' Gav soothed, 'I was one of the first in this morning, had it covered as fast as I could.'

'And yet it only takes *one* loudmouth in this town, doesn't it? They'll talk of nothing else for *years*! Another town legend they'll all agree to never forget!' Sonnet smacked another pile of books onto the floor for good measure. Olive rushed upstairs, stifling sobs.

Sonnet thought then of Lowe's school bus, shuddering its way into town, about to deliver two girls into a furious green ants' nest of biting hearsay. Her blood boiled. Fable must never, ever see the artwork she had laboured over so cruelly corrupted.

'Get me some paint, Gav.'

'How much and what colour?'

'Don't care, just get it for me! Please.'

'On my way!'

Olive, descending the staircase some minutes later with eyes wiped clean, and aspirin dissolving in a glass of water, was taken aback to find her niece kneeling before the sign, tracing letters in the air.

'Can we please cover it up now? Haven't you seen enough?'

'Not on your life, Olive! I'm staying shut today, and I'm going to repaint this damned sign myself. I'll be back in business under my own banner by tomorrow!'

'You're just going to paint right over Fable's lovely work?'

'I'm not quite the dab hand Fable is, but I did all right myself in art – well enough to string a few letters together. Don't care about aesthetics anymore. It's about ownership and pride now.'

And war.

Olive nodded, foot worrying at her calf. 'What can I do to help?'

'Cups of tea, Olive. Lots of tea.'

It was back-breaking work, requiring multiple coats to cover the scarlet letters. Not until her sign was redeemed, could Sonnet breathe easily.

She worked until late into the night, with Gav keeping a dogged, silent watch over the process, and later, Kate propping her up with irreverent humour. Kate had arrived unexpectedly after her own day's work – slipping in quietly to kneel beside Sonnet and take over the hair-drying of stubborn wet patches, without being asked.

Kate's presence, salve though it was, only confirmed Sonnet's dread. These hateful words could never be obliterated, neither by time nor paint, and indeed already had seeped forth, like fetid swamp waters, into every home in Noah.

When the hairdryer finally gave out in a smoky puff, Kate sat back on her haunches to muse, 'Sticks and stones may break my bones, they *reckon*, but words will never hurt me. Always thought that saying was bulldust, but frankly this proves it.'

Sonnet saw an image of Fable's face, shuttered by blank despair. Her heart hurt.

She'd sent Olive home to care for the girls with strict instructions to defer any discussion of the sign until Sonnet could talk them through it. She had an epic rant scheduled for later. The sign defacement provided the perfect illustration for two young girls who needed to learn how the world generally, and Noah Vale specifically, treated women. Olive's case for sweeping it under the carpet as quickly as possible – for the girls' sake – had met searing rebuttal.

'Half this town is already draped in carpets! It's my sign, and my story to tell!'

How quickly Olive's horror had been overridden by reluctance to make a fuss, much less a scene.

At last the sign was finished. Sonnet stood between Gav and Kate, face tipped critically, assessing her finished product.

'That'll show 'em!' said Gav.

'But why *Hamilton's* Books?' asked Kate. 'My "Sonnet's Books" joke wasn't that bad!'

Sonnet knelt to dab at a suspicious wet patch. 'I'm taking back our rightful place on this street. Now, let's get her up!'

Rumbling home in Gav's utility at midnight, Sonnet's mind turned determinedly to her imminent reopening. Olive had insisted she should take a few days off to let things 'cool down', but Sonnet was already raring to go.

She *wanted* to show her face in town tomorrow, and it would be on a head held high!

I hear you, Mama.

Sonnet prowled her book aisles the next day in a barely tempered fury, fists buried deep in the pockets of her faithful old capri pants. Her homily over breakfast on misogyny hadn't gone quite as impressively as planned. For starters, Plum was absent, having been spirited away by Olive. And Fable, for whom the lecture was designed to serve the most benefit, closed up the moment Sonnet started in on all the injustices of being a woman. She hadn't even shed a single tear at her sign's deface-ment – though Sonnet *had* laboured that point excessively.

There was no opening of the Story Bar today. The few loyal cus-tomers stopping by were escorted out of the store sans long chat. She would not be justifying her new sign to anyone – friend or foe, full stop – and the surprised comments which inevitably came bounced right off Sonnet. She had one objective today, and one alone: to make her customary errand up Main Street at three o'clock.

She'd show them. Sonnet Hamilton would not be cowed, and was not beaten!

When the appointed hour rolled round, Sonnet set off to the accompaniment of a bass drum's beating. It felt like a marching band. Certainly, the roar erupting from Cutters at the sight of Sonnet's approach was more befitting a parade, than one woman, austerely dressed and fierce of face, merely navigating a footpath.

Only job these bludgers have, Sonnet thought, as the familiar tide of alcohol and profanity surged forth, *is killing their livers every damn day!*

Sonnet had wondered if Brenton might be perverse enough to appear at her regular passing. She was relieved to see his veranda littered with leaves, a broom languishing against the wall. Her breath constricted to a pant as she neared the open doorway, crude insults washing right over her. Hardening her jaw, locking her eyes on the Paragon Cafe ahead, Sonnet took her last few strides towards victory.

Who could say which vulgar cry finally punched through her steely facade? Perhaps it was the one about Sonnet 'sucking wrinkly cocks'.

She lurched to a stop. 'Shove your useless honeypot, Olive!' she hissed, rounding on the pub door so contemptuously even the rollicking drunks at the entrance were taken aback. She marched into Cutters, incandescent with rage.

Brenton was at the bar and the visible blanching of his face, smirk notwithstanding, was worth each step into his lair.

He laid down a glass and swung a red-checked tea towel over his shoulder, leaning forward expectantly. Sonnet's gaze blistered right over him as she turned to address the rabble.

Her tone scorched, like pavement on a summer's day. 'Who's the coward that illegally defaced my business sign?'

The leers and knowing glances passed one to another, offering no answer.

Sonnet harrumphed. 'Like I said – *coward*! Skulking in the dark with a paintbrush, trying to pretend you're tough. But you're just a *weasel*!'

Individual faces blurred into an amorphous blob of bulging eyes and hanging mouths.

'You want to besmirch my reputation and a good man's legacy? You want to try to shame my family? You don't have the chops to insult any of us!'

Brenton smirked, saying nothing.

Sonnet had a flashing desire for another glass to smash, not on the ground this time, but right into his face.

She was *done* here.

Sonnet strode out of Cutters on a white-hot upwelling of wrath, which had no other outlet now but her eyes.

She did not halt until she was three blocks clear, shaking under the awning of a boarded-up shopfront. Her pressing fingers failed to stem her flowing eyes for several minutes.

A voice at her side made her jump.

'Didn't yer father teach you not to cast yer pearls before swine?'

Turning, Sonnet took in the dishevelled bulk of a middle-aged man. He was odorous with tobacco.

'I never had a father.'

'I'll tell yer, then. Don't cast yer pearls before them swine.'

Sonnet was utterly depleted. The whole town could *go to hell*, starting with this guy.

His brow rutted. 'Don't get me wrong. I see yer walkin' stubbornly past every day and I think to meself: that girl's got guts like this town ain't never seen! Just like yer lovely little mum. But they're swine! Yer

221

don't need to hear it, best walk up the other side of the street. Don't yer go castin' yer pearls there no more.'

I'm not jewellery!

'And listen, I want to thank yer for the books yer been sending home with me kids all the time. They love those books like nothin' else. Sleep with 'em under their little heads, turn the pages till they're nearly fallin' out. I keep telling 'em they're gotta give 'em back. Just, they've never had any books before.'

'Oh, *you're* Joe Taylor.' All the indignant lectures she had prepared for this man, and now there were no scolding words, only a kind of enfeebled gratitude for his presence with her on this friendless street corner.

'I'm sorry if them kids have been pestering yer down there,' he said. 'Just haul 'em back any time they're bothering yer.'

'I would rather Jim and Jackie be in my shop than roasting away in your parked car, Mr Taylor.' She was unexpectedly gentle where she had always intended to flay.

'They just like comin' in with their dad.'

Sonnet frowned. 'I wouldn't think any kid wants to be left in a car all afternoon only for a drunk to drive them home.'

There was no injury in his reply. 'Gave that up years ago. Don't touch a drop now. But there's not many places an old farmin' man like me can go find some solace in the company of other fellas. I just like to sit and 'ave a yarn.'

Sonnet sagged now. 'Well, your children are always welcome at my shop. My sister Plum looks forward to seeing them every day. And the books are my pleasure.'

Joe nodded, something like a smile pressing on the corner of his mouth.

'It wasn't any of them blokes in there.'

'What wasn't?'

'Yer lovely sign. It was a bunch of young bucks the other night. The Johnstone kid, a Logan, that Hull boy. Off their faces on somethin' and causin' all sorts of trouble round town. Don't you let it get to yer, but. Just remember yer pearls.'

Of course it was a Hull! Wouldn't be surprised if Delia Hull herself bought the paint!

Three days later, a large cardboard box appeared on her shop's front stoop. A note was taped to the top:

> *Wish our date would have gone better. Maybe we can give it another shot one day. These are for you. Come have a chat, you know where to find me.*
> *Brenton.*

Inside, haphazardly wrapped in newspaper, was over a dozen framed paintings from Brenton's hotel. Sonnet sank, bewildered, to the step, thumbing gently through the frames. Her first instinct was to wound with further rejection – smash them to smithereens and dump them, post-haste, on *his* front step.

If he thinks he can make it up to me, much less woo me back again with these paintings, he's even stupider than I thought!

The final painting at the bottom of the box, however, was her cassowary. And it *was* her cassowary. That primordial gaze had haunted her dreams for night after tossing night. It stared out at her from the darkening rainforest as she pedalled home in the gloaming. Swathed in mist, it stalked outside the cottage in the morning gloom as she bustled about the breakfast table.

She lifted the painting clear of the box, so that she might behold that scrutiny boldly in kind. The sense of knowing or being known, of both prescience and presence, struck her as keenly as it had the first time. Only now there wasn't a bloodsucker to scrape off her neck. She regarded the painting in a long silence, eyes poring over the oil strokes, unable to break the creature's stare.

Finally, she pushed to her feet and carried the cassowary into her shop. Taking a hammer, with nail pressed determinedly between her lips, Sonnet located a spot on the wall opposite her shop counter and Story Bar. In a trice, the cassowary was hung. Against her white walls and shelves, beneath the chandelier's grandeur, the black sheen and cobalt blue of the bird was unearthly. His follow-you-round-the-room gaze would no doubt provide a talking point with patrons.

Sonnet blazed with embarrassment as she bound the box of paintings to the back rack of her bike. It felt like stealing; worse, like accepting a whore's pittance.

The cassowary *was* hers, but what about the others? She'd probably just shove them in the back of her bedroom armoire, already filled as it was with her mother's moth-eaten dresses.

The overloaded ride home was slow and strenuous. At every bump or wobble, Sonnet considered spinning back to return – no, *throw* – the paintings at Brenton forthwith!

It was almost a relief the next morning, to discover the box empty. Almost as if she'd dreamed the paintings into life, and had carted a hollow box home, instead. She gawked uncomprehendingly.

The slam of the bathroom door brought Sonnet back to her senses. *That thieving little mongrel!* Who else would have robbed her box but Fable Hamilton?

Sonnet grabbed her not-so-secret copy of Fable's bedroom key from the top of the fridge, and headed for the sunroom.

Enraging as it was to find the paintings in her younger sister's brazen possession, there was a sense of . . . rightness to the scene that greeted her. For not only had Fable stolen every last painting from the box, she'd already affixed them to all available wall space. This wasn't mere pilfering; it was a flagrant assumption of ownership.

The sunroom had become an art shrine to Noah Vale: mist-roped mountains, noble rain trees, blood vine snaking up stone ruins, a pair of paradise kingfishers, secret waterfall grotto, a fire rainbow daubed over the valley, glittering sugarcane arrows, and Moria Falls, above the window seat, in pride of place.

Sonnet's indignation dissipated. She couldn't name another person who would revere and cherish these artworks as Fable could. They should be in an art gallery, or up for sale. But perhaps there was serendipitous justice in this, after all. If Fable had lost anything in her sign's defacement, she had gained infinitely more in return. Sonnet eased the door closed on Fable's reliquary with a quiet click.

CHAPTER 25

THE BUTTERFLY PATCH

November 1960

F able was on her belly in the luxuriant tangle of her garden, ministering to a sketchbook – oblivious to both the spring sunshine overhead and the barefoot visitors approaching the gate, towels slung over shoulders.

Around her, bloomed the pentas and ixora flowers she'd taken as cuttings from gardens all over the valley. Her foraged flowers thrived like weeds, attracting her two favourite butterflies to the garden: the peridot Birdwing, and cerulean Ulysses. Hidden inside the flowers, slept Fable's faerie garden; rather, Olive's tiny tombstones.

Fable hated how weird Sonnet got whenever the graves were mentioned. Even after all these years, the adults maintained the pretence that they were faerie houses. So, faerie houses Fable had defiantly made them, weaving Olive's river stones into her drawings of ferny glens and linns. Long had she laboured over this theme, adapting it from her water nymphs of earlier years.

In the last two years, as Fable's garden had sprung into glorious, fertile life, so too had her journals burgeoned. Between the pages lived a bevy of faerie folk, with butterfly wings draped around whimsical figures, and clothes spun from rainforest blooms or fruits.

Today she was filling in the iridescent peridot wings of a faerie frolicking on a bird of paradise flower. *Absinthe*, she had named this, her favourite heroine. She had resolved at day's beginning, not to get sidetracked by yet another rendering of blue eyes.

Two young men leant over the fence to watch Fable, her face hidden by a long fall of red-gold, feet kicking together. Their convivial chatter dwindled into silence.

The first young man smiled at his friend as one might an endearing toddler. The playful urge to ruffle Fable's hair, however, had melted into distant memory. Marco never touched Fable these days, except inadvertently, and each time it nearly stopped his heart with fear she'd think it deliberate, and incongruous with his loyally platonic presence. Always lurking, was his terror she might withdraw from him, as she had every other male of the old Glade Gang.

Ever since that hullabaloo with her sister's bookshop sign – no, earlier than that, ever since the hurriedly stamped-out controversy with Vinelands – Fable had removed herself entirely from their group.

Marco knew just enough about Fable's near-miss at Vinelands to guess why. But only because he'd been there the night Raff came over to the Lagorios' and ripped shreds off Vince about his involvement in it. If not for overhearing that, Marco wouldn't have had a clue why Fable went so cold, so quickly on the Gang. The Hulls, after all, had put a self-serving embargo on the whole topic. Marco had never pressed Fable directly to explain herself, though Fable, guardedly, and only once, had offered this: 'Boys have changed.'

And sure, boys had. Although Marco, loath to contradict Fable, might have pointed out that girls had changed first, and with few exceptions for the better. Gone was the easy mateship of the Glade

Gang days. Now it was impossible to find a girl without a head filled with dating wars, movie-star fixations, and trends changing so fast they could give a bloke whiplash. Marco preferred girls without all the artificial gloss, and unknowable motives. In truth, Marco didn't prefer girls at all.

Fable was his only exception. He wasn't stupid; he could tell Fable put on her airs, too – like all that makeup she wore lately. He wished she wouldn't because it ruined her wholesome naturalness. But at least Fable showed little interest in that incomprehensible female triad of gossip, fashion and flirtation, and was immune to the wild romantic vicissitudes of their peers. When all the other seniors gathered in Raintree Park after the Friday-night movie at the Royale, with nicked bottles to imbibe, Fable was never in attendance.

Marco was secretly glad his friend shunned the popular crowds – even if it *was* only around the farms she would abide Marco's company too.

At school or down the street, Fable drew right back. She spent her school lunches with the motley misfits and oddballs who congregated loosely near the art demountable. Fable hung out a lot with Sally Hobson, an Aboriginal artist whose traditional techniques so contrasted with Fable's whimsical watercolours. Marco supposed Fable was glad to have found someone whose love and knowledge of the rainforest surpassed even hers. In a reversal of her alliance with Marco, Fable's relationship with Sally was mostly confined to the schoolyard and raucous Paragon booths. Outside hours, they went to much different sides of Noah Vale.

Somehow, despite surrounding herself with social pariahs, Fable couldn't escape the aura of small-town celebrity. All eyes, ears and tongues were always on her.

For the boys, it seemed it was all about her long hair and big norks. The girls' ongoing obsession with Fable was harder to understand. When they gathered behind the toilet block to have a mild Virginia, Fable was their number-one topic. Did they hate everything about her, as they readily professed, or did they envy her allure? Other kids weren't sure how to pigeonhole *or* neutralise Fable. She acted like a tomboy, dressed like a charity-shop raider, drew weird pictures, had that crazy harlot mother, hung with D Block Losers, yet outshone them all. Fable Hamilton was the most hateable thing of all – an impervious girl, who thought she was too good for everyone else.

Marco whistled tunelessly over the fence now and grinned as the strawberry head lifted slightly, and an arm flew into the air, one finger raised.

Marco spoke in an aside. 'That means she—'

'Needs one more minute, I get it. Never interrupt an artist.'

Fable rose to her feet, brushing grass from her sundress, kicking pencils into a pile. She turned to Marco with a warm smile.

Discovering he was not alone, however, her smile vanished.

Marco lambasted himself. He thought he was bringing along one of Fable's few remaining allies from the old Glade Gang days, but evidently not, from that panicked look on her face. He should have known better than to bring a Hull over!

For a protracted second, he thought she might even run away. But she came towards them after all, and Marco released a breath, as much in relief, as admiration.

Fable Hamilton, just gone eighteen, was a vision to behold: hair aglow in the sunshine; mint sundress, a relic of earlier years, too small on high curving bust and womanly hips; and those large eyes, fixed wide upon the pair.

'Hey, Fabes! Whatcha doing?'

Fable smiled at Marco, but it was to his companion she turned to speak.

'Hello, Rafferty.'

'Fable.'

They just seemed to stare at each other then. It went on way too long. Marco shrank, wondering if Fable might actually tell Raff off for stepping foot on her soil. You never did quite know with Hulls or Hamiltons.

Instead she said: 'You're late home.' There was the smallest furrow between her brows.

'Early, rather. I'm here for Adriana's graduation.'

'*Our* grad!' Marco interjected. 'About time, too. This last week of school is going to draaaag. Can't wait for next weekend! We're going to have the biggest party this town has ever seen, hey, Fabes?'

Fable ignored him. 'Are you staying on till Christmas?'

'No, I've got to get home before then.'

'*Home?*'

'Back to work. I'm with a firm in London now.'

'You're a bona fide Londoner?'

'I wouldn't say that, yet. I still feel like a tourist most of the time. Though I'm grateful for the expat community in London; keeps the homesickness at bay.'

'So, you do miss Noah.'

'Noah will always be home. I'd be lying if I said I miss the cane-growing life, though. Still, my old man reminds me constantly he's just waiting for me to step into his shoes and take my "rightful position" over Summerlinn.'

'Do you have plans to?'

'None.'

'None?'

Raff's answer was akin to a sigh. 'I've well and truly outgrown my boyhood dreams, confined as naively as they once were to the valley. Real life and most careers are out in the world. You guys will find that out soon enough now.'

Fable disregarded this. 'There's nothing worth coming back for?'

Raff smiled. 'Since I don't have any other baby sisters graduating . . . not likely.'

Fable busied herself picking at stray foliage in her hair, a corner of her mouth gathering.

Marco, unnerved by Fable's uncharacteristic boldness, lunged in. 'What's it been anyway, two years since you were last home? You'll hardly recognise Noah now, so many new shops going in on Main, they're even talking about a department store coming! John Belden's finally subdivided, and there's a brand-new crew at the Paragon, too.'

Raff laughed. 'I think I'll manage to find my way around. Most things change pretty slowly in good old Noah.'

Fable snorted. 'Yes, we're just a primitive backwater here.'

Raff went to speak, but seemed to think better of it. Fable moved to gather her art roll, back placed firmly to them.

Marco pushed through the gate after Fable. 'You want to come with us to the creek, for old times' sake?'

'No thanks,' she said – too quickly.

'You sure?'

'I'm *sure*.'

Marco found himself blathering. 'I was telling Raff about your paintings, you should show him the one of the Glade!'

The look Fable turned was incredulous. Too well Marco knew her fierce predilection for privacy to have suggested a thing in forgetfulness.

'She's way too shy,' Marco told Raff, 'I keep telling her she's got to get her stuff in a gallery. People would go nuts for it.'

Fable's packing up had quickened to a flurry. Perhaps it was her modesty, then, which finally pushed Marco over the line. He swooped on her art journal, opening it to Raff.

'Seriously, you *have* to see these. She's amazing!'

Marco was flipping pages as Fable dived towards them. Raff stepped back from the fence, hands up. 'No advance previews unless the artist permits!'

Marco's hurried page turning halted with a triumphant cry. He shoved it across the fence, into Raff's face.

'Recognise these?!'

Fable stopped short, too late to intervene.

'Undoubtedly,' Raff said, after a tremendous pause.

'Give it to me,' Fable hissed through her teeth.

Raff pushed the journal, still in Marco's hands, back towards Fable.

Fable clutched her image of the faerie-filled Glade against her chest, glaring at Marco.

But Marco had come too far now for remorse. 'No one will know how good she is as long as she keeps pretending she's mucking about, she's got to get it out there—'

Raff cut through. 'Were you inspired by Faerie Falls?'

'What's Faerie Falls?'

'You haven't discovered them yet? Honestly, it's something straight out of your drawings.'

'Is it nearby?'

Raff nodded at Marco. 'Yep, get this lad to take you up for the day. There's no pathway, so you'll need the guide. It's accessed off the top of Moria Falls, fair climb.'

'I don't know how to get there, Fabes,' Marco muttered. 'Wouldn't have a clue.'

Raff grinned. 'You young fellas these days spend too much time haunting the public baths on weekends, you're letting the old valley secrets fade away.'

'Sounds more like the old guard hogging the valley secrets,' Marco flashed.

Fable turned to Raff then, raising eyes wide and gold and luminous. 'Would *you* take me to see it?' she asked.

For a moment, less than a second really, an expression crossed Raff's face that Marco had never before glimpsed there. Almost instantly, it was covered by amiable agreement.

'Sure, I can probably make time for that. You guys get the crew together, I'll take you for a look.'

There was no hesitation from Fable. 'Tomorrow!'

'I can't, Fabes!' Marco cried. 'I'm working at Perroti's all day.'

'Can't you change your shift?' she asked, not looking in his direction.

'I'll try,' he said miserably.

'What time do you want to head up?' she asked Raff.

Raff looked between the younger pair. 'So long as my old man doesn't rope me into anything on Summerlinn, we could set off at eight. I'll have the truck ready to go. It's a long, steep hike. Bring food, water and so on.'

'Righto,' Fable said, with a pat on Marco's shoulder. 'See you bright and early.'

'I'll try to talk Vince into working for me,' Marco said, without expectation.

'OK, do that!' Fable chirped, already flitting away.

Marco kicked at a fence paling, no longer in the mood to swim with Raff Hull at all.

CHAPTER 26

FAERIE FALLS

If she slept a wink that night, Fable didn't note it; as every fibre of her being strained, in suffering impatience, towards the dawn. Countless times she threw herself from bed to window, double-checking the sun had not, as she feared, forgotten to rise.

Would morning never come again? And if it did, would she discover Raff's materialisation had been only a lucid dream born of the achingly long years she had watched for his overdue homecoming? Only deafening rain on the cottage roof served to reassure her fears. It might be a month too early, but Raff Hull *was* here.

He'd once again brought the rain.

By the time dawn filtered through the bay window in a hushed glow, Fable was already at her dresser: massaging blemished cheeks with the unguent appropriated from Olive's bathroom cabinet; struggling to mask her acne with none of the usual deft steadiness of her artist's hand; knocking her precious makeup pots off the dresser in her shaking rush. It was no use; she was making a *mess* of it!

She took a washer, wiped her face clean again, and looked critically. Her flaws were exposed, but her bare eyes shone with hope and

234

wonder; those violet shadows and amber pools brighter than she'd ever seen. And that, today, would have to do.

She rose from the table.

Discarding thirteen outfits of varying levels of earnestness, Fable settled finally on a halter-neck playsuit with her brand new high-waisted bikini underneath, something she'd never had the courage to wear publicly. Why was obvious – she *spilled*.

Fable flew out of the door at 7.45, high pony swinging, hasty note left for Sonnet with no mention of the day's company. She had fruit shoved haphazardly in her rucksack, but not a bite to eat in her tummy.

The valley was resplendent after the first spring rainstorm, draped in mist and tented by a white canvas, beneath which white cockatoos dived and squawked.

Her heart battered wildly against its moorings as she crossed the bridge towards the Hulls', and the dream she had nurtured so fervently, so foolishly, for so long: Rafferty.

Her eyes fastened on the truck idling beneath the mango trees, as promised. Her breath tightened to a pinhole as she remembered the last time she'd stepped foot on Summerlinn. She squinted for a glimpse of Raff's fair head in the driver's seat.

No need to pinch herself, for there he was – already waiting.

Fable was within a few feet of the truck, when, before her disbelieving eyes, the tray of the truck filled with kids – Adriana's dark head instantly recognisable.

An icy hand grasped her heart, squeezing.

To the watching eye, and blue eyes were certainly watching her approach, Fable glided serenely up to the truck without a ruffle of dismay. She tendered an offhand greeting and swung on-board, neglecting to address the driver himself, or his co-pilot, Eamon.

Raff leaned out of the window. 'We waiting for Marco?'

'Not coming!' Fable sang, squeezing in beside her tray mates with the nonchalance of one slipping into a peak-hour train.

The truck rumbled into answering life.

'Ooh, look whose boyfriend stood her up,' came a nearby snigger, to tittering response.

It was Christy *Logan*. Of course it was. Fable's wretched disappointment would not have been complete without Christy in attendance today.

Fable knew better than to react. Nevertheless, 'Where's *yours*?' she asked sweetly.

Christy, so recently humiliated by the loss of hard-won and even-harder-kept Van the Man to a younger, prettier, less inhibited version of herself, made no attempt to curb her loathing lip. 'Least I don't go round sucking dago dicks.'

That Christy had gone too far was evident in the group's hollow laughter.

Adriana, rarely one to address Fable directly, spoke quickly to redress the balance in Christy's favour. 'Why are you here anyway, Hamilton? No one even invited *you*!'

On they all piled now. Isabella, Jessica, Megan, Christy again ...

'And what are you wearing? We can see *everything* in that suit.'

'You're always *desperate* to make yourself the centre of attention. Runs in the family.'

'No wonder you wear so much makeup to cover *that* complexion.'

'Look out, Mount *Vesuvius* is erupting!'

Satisfied to have exposed their ugliness, Fable settled back against the rattling tray. A salty plum from her bag provided relief in the cat's-bum-sneer elicited. She'd suck salty plums all day, if she had to.

Fable turned lash-hooded attention to her remaining travelling mates – two new guys from St Ronan's plus Adriana's latest crush, fellow school captain, Greg Hadley. The group's objectives were clear. Escape from the drudgery of Sunday-morning services and lifeless Main Street for the consumption of contraband: alcohol, and a *Playboy* magazine, over which boys and girls alike would huddle – the boys, with explicit comparisons against their classmates; the girls, with offended huffs, and studying eyes.

It didn't take long for deeper motives to reveal themselves in breathless tones. There were several ardent admirers of Raff Hull present and vying for the attention of Noah's Most Eligible Bachelor today. Adriana, usually fanatically possessive of her brother, was strangely certain Raff was not only enamoured with at least two of her friends, but had always harboured a specific type: green-eyed brunettes of Isabella's exact dimensions. He had literally *begged* her to bring along her girlfriends today, even though they had *better things to do*.

The girls were all a-twitter.

Oh, the lengths Raff Hull would go just to avoid being alone with her. Fable had misjudged the tone of today's adventure entirely – *she* was the postscript. Well, she still had the option of throwing herself head first from the truck, and this doomed mission, into the dizzying depths of the gorge.

Thankfully, before she had to, Moria Falls rose thunderously out of the forest. Fable leapt into the car park, braced rucksack straps and nerves alike, affected blasé indifference to Eamon's sly breast-nudge as he squeezed by, and took up the rear.

A chorus of laughter broke out in the assembling group as one of the boys sent a brush-turkey squawking off with an imitated footy kick.

The stream of hikers, under Raff's lead, was absorbed through an unsigned slit in the forest wall. Had Fable's eyes not been locked on that tall, broad back – with its throng of giggling admirers and trailing deputy, Eamon – she might have overlooked the path altogether. Dallying behind, Fable considered turning around in her see-everything suit and not-covered-enough skin, and fleeing. She wouldn't even be missed. It was only refusal to look childish in Raff's eyes that drove her on.

Her reward was instantaneous: cool, pungent cloak of rainforest; her familiar, draping solace. She inhaled slowly.

The trail, deep with mud, climbed abruptly, and Fable smirked at the rising complaints from the girls clamouring at the fore. The quiet burn of her thighs was a wicked pleasure. After years of tagging along up mountains with the boys, here was something Fable knew how to do well. When Raff finally decided to look back, he'd be sure to see only one girl belonged here today.

Squeal on, dimwits!

They were following a goat track up beside Moria Falls. The roar was a colossal, chest-filling presence. Fable wanted to fling her arms wide and allow it to engulf her. A break in thick vegetation afforded a momentary view and Fable's heart thudded from both the pleasure of exertion and the plummeting heights they were attaining above the sheer drop of Moria Falls. The altitude of their expedition had revealed itself to all, thanks to the large rock Eamon decided, in typical wisdom, to unhinge and push over the cliff face. The sound was of a landslide setting off. Back-thumping cheers from the boys only fuelled the sense of precariousness invading the party.

Isabella started into a panic attack, feigned or otherwise, and fear became a palpable cord running back along the party. Raff was saying something to soothe beautiful Isabella's angst, but his words were lost to Fable at line's end.

Deep in the cloud forest now, any pretence of a pathway gave way to a steep, root-choked tumble of boulders. Progress was slow – they might have been climbing a giant's marble toss. It was arduous, dirty, and a satisfying challenge.

Or at least Fable thought so. Perfectly competent hikers had somehow disintegrated into a gasping flock losing shoes, sunglasses; their strength. Girls insisted on being hoisted between rocks, predictably by no less than their handsome, intrepid leader, though Eamon leapt forward with a hand under a pert bum or three. The affectations of female helplessness rendered Fable white with rage.

Isabella was trailing Raff so closely she was practically being piggy-backed. Fable wondered if she might actually faint into his arms next. And, if so, whether a good face slapping might help?

The ache in Fable's clenched teeth increased.

They had entered a natural nave, formed of stone and sheer cliff face, roofed by canopy. Here, their path was ruptured by a crevice so black it might have been bottomless.

There was no way forward now, but over the breach.

Surprising no one, Isabella consented to continue only after cajoling inducement, and the promise of male arms to guide her over. What else did she need, Fable fumed, a marriage proposal on the other side?

Clutching her rescuer's hand, Isabella flung herself across the cavity in a screaming spectacle.

Fable wished they'd all topple through the crack, straight to Hades, with Rafferty Hull leading the damned way! Unwilling to watch Raff hold the hand of every shrieking girl, Fable lifted her eyes to the immense bird's-nest fern in the bower overhead. Nature's chandelier, she thought, dreaming up a faerie ballroom.

A falling hush alerted Fable to her position at the front of the queue. Waiting on the opposite side of the breach and looking directly at her for the first time all morning, was Raff. A strong hand was already extended patiently. Behind him, every face fixed expectantly on Fable.

Raff searched her face; finding in Fable's eyes both refusal and a warning. Almost imperceptible, but the message was received. He stepped back a few paces. Raff bore no small amount of concern, and his expression sent a frisson of fear into her belly.

Without giving herself time to overthink it, or in fact think about it at all, Fable took a breath, and flew over the chasm.

She landed well clear of the hollow, but stumbled for purchase on the slippery rock. Raff's hand shot out to support her, even as hers went up to fend off assistance. Their hands met in a tight grasp, which released as quickly as it had formed.

'Nearly there now,' Raff said, cutting through the murmuring. Flirtatious mirth resumed around Raff at the column's head, and on they journeyed.

Only then did Fable's heartbeat take off on a renegade gallop. Her hand burned and shook. It required all her gumption to trail sedately on.

Soon, they ascended a crudely hewn pathway between giant fan palms, and into a faerie linn . . .

Every expanse of rock was bedecked with bright green moss and tiny, waving ferns. A long, slender flume plunged into a hidden grotto pool, rushing out of the rock in rivulets, to coalesce in a deep pool. Above the falls, trees were garlanded in silvery epiphytes stirring like seaweed in a current. The diffused light here conjured up a hundred faeries at play: dancing in tiny rainbows; twinkling between mossy streams; flashing in puddles of sunlight formed by snaking roots. The beauty struck Fable as a physical ache. She was ensorcelled.

Kids fanned out into the scene, shattering the serenity. Fable hung back, unable to invade it herself. Bitterness surged at the injustice of witnessing this magical realm trampled by a stampeding herd.

Her stalling sourness must have disappointed their escort, for he appeared quietly at her side.

'You don't like it?'

Fable turned a disbelieving look upon him. 'I like it *too* much.'

His relief, plain to see, sank the hilt of aching wonderment deeper still.

'It's straight out of your paintings, hey?'

'Like I dreamed it.'

He smiled.

'Thank you, for – this.'

'You're welcome.'

'I wish I didn't have to share it with anyone else . . .' A high-pitched melee broke out as Eamon dragged a girl under the spray. 'Hopefully they'll all drown, and I'll have the place to myself.'

Raff laughed. 'Well, I know you're being genuine.'

They smiled together, standing at a distance not quite apart, neither together. A waiting silence hung over them like a net.

Raff nodded coaxingly at the rucksack she clutched, the bound edge of her favourite journal clearly visible at its opening. Fable shook her head, drawing it tighter still to camouflage the beating of her journal's heart, its yearning for release. Nothing on earth could induce her to open her book here today, before those vultures. Not even Raff Hull.

Screeches from the nearby pool made the pair turn. Eamon had found a stinkhorn mushroom – an outrageously phallic fungus with a lacy white net falling from its head like semen. Predictably, he was hollering after the girls with the phallus held at his thrusting groin.

'Who likes *mushrooms*?'

'Get away, it stinks!' Megan screamed.

As he passed Fable, the vulgarity went louder still, the stinkhorn stabbing towards her shorts.

'Pull your head in, Eamon,' Raff said with quiet deadliness.

Eamon paused. His eyes flicked between Raff and Fable, narrowing. 'Oh, that's right,' he muttered, 'can't offend *Fayyyyble*, can we?' He thrust the stinkhorn once more at Fable with a dramatically expulsive motion, and fled his brother's expression for the higher falls.

Fable was avoiding Raff's face herself.

The girls, at Adriana's direction, were assembling for a group photograph: limbs draped over one another, hair perfectly flipped out, legs crooked just so. Christy and Adriana, front and centre of the loose pyramid, gazed into the camera with matching head tilts and aggressively confident smiles. Eamon, leaning precipitously from a rock ledge, waved his stinkhorn at them. A strident cheer went up, and the shutter clicked.

That Fable was so casually excluded from 'the girls' made her wilt. She fidgeted with a loose thread on her bag. It was one thing to live daily as the outsider from across the creek, but another indignity entirely to have it demonstrated to Raff.

Raff inclined his head towards Fable. 'You know, the falls actually got their name because of the fireflies you can see glowing here at night. They look exactly like faeries. Or, at least how I'd always imagined faeries.'

'You're *kidding*.'

'Not even a little bit. I used to sneak up here at night when I was a kid to try to catch them in a jar. It was one of my favourite spots in all of Noah. I wanted to see for myself if they were actually faeries.'

'And did you ever manage it?'

'No, sadly I—'

His answer was interrupted by Isabella, sliding between them. She pressed a bottle of tanning lotion into his hands. 'Would you do me, Raff?'

Fable averted her dismay.

'I'm sure one of the girls can help you with that,' he said, returning it.

'Here, let me,' Fable said, reaching for the lotion with a beatific smile.

Isabella snatched it back with sibilant haste. 'As *if* I would!'

The slowly mouthed word as Isabella spun away – *h-a-r-l-o-t* – set Fable's face afire. She felt, rather than saw, the tension jumping in Raff's jaw.

'Well,' she said, regaining her composure, 'if you routinely decline offers like that, no wonder you failed to catch any pretty faeries.'

'Alas.'

They shared a wry smile, which lasted some time after each had looked away.

'Fire flies but water falls,' Fable murmured, mostly to herself, but Raff tipped his head to better hear her. Though he hadn't moved an inch closer, the distance shortened intimately.

Quiet lay between them, full and soft.

Fable patted her rucksack, wondering what she was dreading most – the moment Raff should move away, or the day's curtailing before she'd had a moment to sketch.

At length, reluctantly, Raff roused himself. 'Hey, tell you what, I was actually going to get the rest of them moving on now – you should stay behind and get some drawing done.'

He left her.

Promising them another lookout, an hour ahead, offering a panoramic view of the gorge, Raff spirited the group away. They fell in without a backward glance at Fable. In all the clamouring to be near or outdoing Raff, she was forgotten.

Only as the last braying note of laughter died away did Fable exhale and let loose her grip on the journal. She was alone, and Raff's gift of Faerie Falls was finally hers to unwrap.

A shudder of immense happiness ran through her as she scaled the rocks, unfastening her rucksack.

Feverishly she worked: pages turning frantically, hands throbbing with urgency, gathering as many details as possible. She had roughly two hours before Raff and his groupies returned, and did not pause for a moment. Fable was alone in a candy store, gorging herself sick.

At the hour of their expected return, Fable concealed herself down inside the sunlit grotto, to watch the slender cascade spin dazzling light as it dropped into the pool beside her. She sagged back, exhausted, with the journal splayed open on her lap. Vision and breath softened into a languorous daze

She drifted into dreaming.

It was into this beguiling image of girlish repose that Raff blundered a half-hour later. Arriving back ahead of the others and finding the falls uninhabited, he assumed Fable had gone back down the mountain. He whipped off a sweat-soaked shirt and was leaning out beneath the flume to shower when he was startled to spot Fable slumbering in the grotto below; light caught in her strawberry tresses, the pages of her journal glowing blindingly.

Raff jerked back and, overcorrecting his balance, toppled forward into the faerie pool.

Fable roused to find a man falling bodily through the air towards her, as though in a most fanciful dream. His drenching splash was bracing reality.

When Raff surfaced, Fable uttered the first thing that came into her mouth. 'Look who's fallen head over heels.'

Laughter broke Raff's face wide open.

The last dreamlike vestiges drained away as Fable watched Raff pulling himself out of the water onto the ledge. This bare-chested man, raking hair back from his forehead, was most certainly flesh and blood.

'Oh geez, your book!' he cried. 'All your drawings!'

Fable stared dumbly at the lines of sodden colour leaking across her page.

'Here,' he said. 'Let's put it in the sun to dry.'

She climbed out of the grotto after Raff.

He turned to her, stoop-shouldered. 'I've wrecked it for you.'

She *should* have been dismayed at the ruination of her day's zealous work, much less the many months before that, but all she perceived was the surging heat, low in her belly, at the sight of Raff, saturated and shirtless, holding *her* book in his large hands.

Vulnerability was a throbbing bruise, seeping in revelatory colours across her countenance. Raff stepped mutely forward and placed the journal back into her hands.

Dropping her gaze, Fable peeled pages apart. Most of it was indeed ruined – drawings leeching one into the other, bleeding from the page.

None of that mattered like his current proximity. She'd have thrown every journal she owned into the falls just for this breathing closeness to last longer.

'Don't worry,' she said. 'It's just a rough journal. I wouldn't have brought my best one up here, would I?'

His exhalation proved it one of the sweetest fibs she'd ever told.

'See,' she said, turning sodden leaves. 'Nothing important.'

'I beg to differ, Fable,' he said. 'You're ... gifted.'

An ache crept up her throat. She shrugged.

It was Raff's curious expression that made her glance down then at the open journal. A thunderbolt seemed to run through her. A disembodied pair of eyes, rendered finely in graphite, had caught Raff's interest.

They were his own.

If a long-extinct volcano had opened, right then, beneath that gorge of stone wonder and faerie falls, to swallow Fable in one belching, magma gulp, she might have felt marginally better than she did at that moment.

Raff studied the drawing, brow gathering, tilting his head.

Did he note the way her hands shook in bilious terror?

For nearly six years, she'd sketched Raff's eyes compulsively. That motif had captivated her more than any other. If she had any skills, *any* at all, they were encapsulated in those eyes.

She hovered, surely, on an abyss. *How can he fail to see?*

And yet, she saw not the dawning repulsion most feared, but open admiration. With the artlessness of a child, she blurted, lie of all lies: 'They're mine.'

Raff looked up to consider her true eyes. Fable's heartbeat had overtaken her body. She throbbed.

'It still needs colour,' she squeaked out.

'Let's see, then. Amber – no, more like a glowing caramel – and shades of violet, too. You have the most unusual eyes, Fable. They remind me—'

He went silent.

Fable's lashes lowered to shield her eyes. She pressed the journal firmly closed.

His sentence, when finally he finished it, was almost – but not quite – a casual addendum. 'Your eyes are the same colour as the water in the Glade. You could call this piece "Fable of the Glade".'

He moved away then in search of his shirt, leaving Fable to shiver uncontrollably where she stood, heedless of the warm rays on her shoulders, the sunshine in her heart.

For the first time in her life, Fable was thankful for the sight of Adriana and friends trooping into the clearing, reeking of cigarette smoke and teeming with complaints over the cloud-impaired view, inadequacy of their snacks, the ancient Aboriginal rock art Raff refused to let them pose in front of, and the speed at which their no-longer-loyal guide had pressed ahead of them.

CHAPTER 27

FRANGIPANI CORONATION

Late November 1960

F our faces at the Heartwood dinner table were trained on the long hallway down which a fully arrayed, adorned and accessorised high school graduate would sashay at any moment.

'We're ready for you!' sang Olive.

'We don't want to be late,' Sonnet added. 'It's going to be hell finding a parking space at the school.'

'*Sonny*,' whined Plum. 'Why is she taking so looong?'

Gav said nothing, as though even his droll humour was held back by the formal suit constraining his hulking shape.

Sonnet had been oddly touched by Gav's insistence on wearing a suit – something he didn't even do for Sunday services, and a feat which hadn't been achieved, Olive declared, in the thirty years since they'd been married.

Olive hadn't scrubbed up too badly herself, Sonnet thought, glancing at her aunt in her specially tailored dress.

This was a historic moment for them all: the first Hamilton to finish Grade Twelve at Noah Vale School! Sonnet felt a secret flash of affection for Olive. It had been an unlikely partnership, fraught with conflict, but together she and Olive had propelled that exasperating, talented girl through her high school years. They'd made it to her graduation and, as far as Sonnet was concerned, Fable's springboard right out of Noah Vale's suffocating limits.

The hesitant creak of the bathroom door cast an expectant hush over the table. A few seconds of anticipation followed before Fable stepped, eyes downcast, into the hallway.

Oh she's a bride, was Sonnet's first thought. And truly, she could have been. She was sylph-like in a white dress that flowed from delicate spaghetti straps, through sweetheart neckline and along perfect hourglass curves to puddle daintily at her feet. It was not a tiara or veil she wore, rather a simple, shining coronet braid, pinned thrice with white frangipani flowers. Strawberry-gold waves tumbled below her breasts.

As she came towards them, the sconced lights set every crystal on her bodice twinkling and turned her hair to spun gold. Sonnet corrected herself: no, not a bride – a faerie queen en route to her coronation.

It was Gav who first found words to speak. 'You little *beauty*.'

Olive was speechless, and Sonnet wondered why the old girl wasn't patting herself on the back right now for a job well done. This gown *had* been Olive's idea, after all.

When the graduation ball invites had arrived, weeks back, Fable had desperately wanted to wear one of Mama's mothballed gowns from the cottage wardrobe. Sonnet had acquiesced readily, glad both to save money and play her own small part with the alteration of Fable's dress. When she'd mentioned the idea to Olive, however, she had been vehemently opposed.

The green dress Fable selected with such dreamy reverence was *unsuitable*, Olive said. Too grown-up, not a fashionable colour, impractical for climbing the steps to the graduation stage or celebrating wildly at the after-grad party, not to mention the fine crystal beading would make alteration a difficult if not impossible task for a seamstress of Sonnet's ability.

None of which Sonnet had actually believed. It didn't take a genius to figure out Olive's waffling refusal had less to do with fashion and practicality than it did some mawkishness relating to that *particular* dress. Fable's dismay and Sonnet's suspicions had been allayed by the speed at which Olive swooped to order *and* pay for a brand-new gown for Fable from her favourite supplier. Sonnet's initial scepticism of the colour choice, or lack thereof, was quashed by Olive's insistence that no other girl in town had come into Emerson's to order anything white, everyone else would be wearing long lace sleeves, and this simple dress was a nostalgic nod, instead, to the Noah balls of yesteryear, held in a grand riverside mansion called *Vinelands*.

Noting Olive's pensive pinch now, Sonnet intuited the white dress had not quite produced the picture of virginal innocence she'd engineered. On the contrary, the girl who stood before them now was utterly desirable. The white dress hid nothing of her figure, only highlighted her magnificent colouring, and the pinned frangipanis, with their fragrant yellow hearts, conjured up sultry, far-flung isles.

Fable looked exactly like she was too good for this damned town, and wouldn't be stuck here much longer! Sonnet *heartily* approved.

Aloud, though, she said, 'You look fine. Now let's go!'

'Wait!' cried Olive. 'I want to get a photo with our dear girl.'

It was only later, as they settled into their school-hall pew, the reality of where they were finally struck Sonnet.

She turned to Olive in mute distress and was just in time to glimpse Olive swallowing a telltale aspirin from her purse.

It was true then! *This* was the infamous school hall in which the Hamiltons had been stripped of their pride, their reputation, and all their hopes for their gifted younger daughter. *This* was where Pandora's box had been opened.

Sonnet's panicked gape settled on the heavy curtains still drawn on the stage. Had those curtains hung there these past twenty-six years? On which pew had Lois and Malcolm Hamilton sat when their daughter's transgressions had been exposed for all to know; worse, to see?

'*On the school stage, in flagrante delicto*,' Sonnet imagined she could hear, not in distant memory on Alfred's lips, but like a viper's hiss at her shoulder. Sonnet spun accusingly, and found plenty of closely tipped, murmuring faces fixed on the Hamilton-Emerson clan. Sonnet's eyes dropped quickly to the programme quaking in her hands. Her stomach fell faster.

Bloody hell, I might have been conceived on that very stage!

And how many people here were thinking the exact same thing, with the spitting image of Esther Hamilton about to cross that stage this very evening.

From the studious way Olive was avoiding her niece's eyes, she was most certainly thinking of nothing else. Poor Olive, her unflappable belief in the fundamental kindness and mercy of Noah residents had taken a severe hit since 'The Sign Episode'. Sonnet was sorry to have witnessed the taint of Esther Hamilton's misfortune seep back into Olive's cheerfully respectable life, but there it was.

Still without looking in Sonnet's direction, Olive took another aspirin from her purse and slipped it across into her hand. Touched, Sonnet forced herself back against the wooden seat, gripping the medicine in her lap as though it were the last cyanide pill out of captivity.

OK, breathe.

She just had to grit her way through a few inevitably verbose speeches, definitely roll her eyes through Adriana's valedictorian address, cheer Fable across that stage to accept her certificate – digging nails into her palms as every jaw in the audience dropped – then wave Fable off to the after-graduation celebrations at Moria Falls.

She could handle this.

The Hamilton girls were making history here tonight, not repeating it.

The clock was about to strike midnight on the after-grad party and Fable, sober and sombre, was ready to go home. She was sick of the leering lot of them! Skirting yet another crowd of revellers in various states of frottage, she slipped through the teahouse doors, and sucked in a breath of balmy air.

She'd survived. *All* of it: not only six years of school, and the shame and fame that had preceded her each step of the way, but also the terror of ascending that stage tonight in front of the whole town, and somewhere out there in that huge audience, a pair of cerulean eyes.

But it was done. She would never again spend time around her school peers, with two exceptions: Sal, when she might come back to visit Noah from her job at the newly opened Aboriginal cultural centre up north; and good old Marco, whose dad was giving their retinue a lift back to Heartwood tonight. No sign of Mr Lagorio yet, though – the car park was dark and empty.

And that gave Fable precious time alone to explore.

Ebullient now, Fable veered off between floundering flame-lit torches into the hedged tea gardens.

CHAPTER 28

TORRID TORRENTS

The tea gardens provided still, shadowy respite from the spilling laughter and music. The roar of the falls drew her ever closer until she was descending stepping stones to the lapping edge of the pool, where a line of rowboats languished under the full, bright moon.

She was leaning to unbuckle her preposterous heels, yearning to have her toes in earth, when a male greeting arose. She yelped and half toppled into the closest boat, just catching herself on the edge.

It was Raff Hull, supine on the boat before her, as though moonbathing beneath the myriad stars.

'Well, if it isn't Fable of the Glade,' he said.

'You *startled* me.'

'Now we're even, then.'

'At least *I* made it look elegant, though . . .'

'I just had further to fall.'

Fable laughed – a great bubble of warmth releasing. 'What are you doing at a high school party, anyway?'

He sat up with a mock start. 'Oh, am I in the wrong place? I thought this was *my* misspent youth.'

'Clearly not – where are your groupies?'

Raff circled his arms around imaginary passengers, nodding, and Fable rolled her eyes.

'Actually, my mother sent me to bring Adriana and her friends home tonight.'

'I see, so there *will* be groupies, after all. The ball doesn't officially let out until one o'clock, though, looks like you'll have to keep the pumpkin running.'

'How was your graduation?'

'Like a successful parole hearing after many botched escape attempts.'

It was Raff's turn to laugh.

Fable held up her rolled certificate. 'But at least I have this now. Rumour has it this is the Scroll of Power! Did you see me graduating tonight?'

'It's hard to miss you these days, Fable.'

Fable braced against the shiver that ran down her spine at the familiar gentleness returning to his tone.

When she didn't reply, he said, 'And how was your after-party?'

'Tolerable, until I ran out of tolerance. We've reached the pairing-off stage. A wallflower can't even find a corner to hide in now that everyone's making out.'

'No one I know, I hope.'

'The two school captains *were* trying to rub their last remnants of prestige together earlier.'

'That doesn't sound like *my* sister, I'm sure you mean the vice-captains.'

'I'd better say yes, since I know you're not opposed to dragging girls out of compromising situations.'

He paused. 'Only the ones unwittingly led into that predicament in the first place.' There was no apology in his tone.

After a long pause, she said, almost inaudibly, 'I never thanked you. I'm sorry. I was too young to understand . . .'

'I was only looking out for you, Fable.'

He never used her sobriquet. From his lips, her full name felt like a caress.

'What are you *really* doing out here?' she asked with forced lightness.

'Same thing as you, I imagine – soaking up moonlit falls. Life doesn't get much better than this.'

They turned together to the waterfall. After a minute of silence, Raff shuffled over on his seat. 'Do you want to sit?'

'Depends,' Fable said, hands on her hips. 'How much is a gondola ride these days?'

Raff laughed. 'The Bridge of Sighs is far too expensive for the likes of you, but I can do a special deal on a waterfall circuit for a newly graduated girl.'

'I can only pay you with a Scroll of Power,' she said, holding out her certificate.

'OK, but if the Paragon rejects this currency, I'm coming after you.'

'I'm willing to take the chance,' she said, climbing into the boat without airs.

Raff leapt out to push. Fable settled the puddling folds of her dress. Within moments, they were afloat. The quiet lapping of the oars took them further from the seeping flames and laughter, towards the tremendous roar of the falls.

Lulled into silence, Fable cast a lash-sweeping glance at Raff: he was still wearing a starched shirt from earlier in the evening, tie long since discarded. With his sleeves rolled to the elbow, strength rippled in his rowing forearms. He was an entirely different creature to the boys she had left behind on that shore. She was in this tiny rowboat with a *man*.

'So, what are your plans for next year?' he asked, distracting Fable from the warm building throb, low in her belly.

'Do you want the answer I give to fend off my controlling sister, or the truth?'

'I bet the truth is far more exciting.'

'Honestly – I'm going to trek into the wilds each day to paint, and I'll only come home for sustenance and sleep ... and even that part's debatable.'

'I would expect nothing less from a struggling artist. And humour me; what do you tell your sister?'

'She's determined I'm getting out of Noah Vale as soon as possible, and she's prepared to drag me out by my hair if it comes to that ...'

'If she manages it, my folks should hire her to bring *me* back again.'

'So, I promised her I'm only trying to decide on the right college, having a break from the demands of high school education. I can't bring myself to tell her I had an interview with Smith's the other day for a shop assistant.'

'It's not called Smith's Newsagency for nothing. I'm sorry to tell you, she'll already know.'

'Yep, she's probably been down to talk Smithy out of hiring me. All for the greater cause of booting me out of town.'

'We need to swap problems, Fable.'

They shared a smile.

'And what is it you need to paint so badly in Noah Vale that you can't in the comfort and freedom of a college dorm?'

Fable tilted her head towards the nearing falls.

'OK, you've got me there,' he said, smiling.

'You want to know the truest truth? It's actually *your* fault, Raff.'

His smile faltered for a fraction of a second, but she saw it.

'How so?'

Her mind whirled with possible answers – all the ways in which every beat of her heart was his fault, and his alone.

She said instead, 'Faerie Falls,' and did not miss the way his brow loosened. 'If you hadn't shared that enchanted place with me, I might have been on the next train out of here, headed for some mundane, thoroughly useful secretarial course.'

'The local business college is going to have my scalp for this.'

'Plus, *you* ruined my sketchbook, so now I have to start over.'

'OK, I'll admit to that.'

'But it all works out the way it was meant to, because when I was interviewing at Smith's, I found myself a brand-*new* journal, leather bound, plus supplies – working in a stationery shop is going to have some career advantages, you see – and now, I'm going to illustrate my own book.'

'Of course you are.'

'About Faerie Falls.'

'A whole book about Faerie Falls!'

'Not just Faerie Falls – *every* magical place and creature in this valley. It's why I *can't* live anywhere else. As a favourite heroine once said, "there's so much scope for the imagination" in Noah.'

'Well, I've never found anywhere like it.'

'Only last week, I found my first waterfall frog. Everyone says they're extinct now, and yet there he was, hiding under the Glade waterfall. You should *see* his colours!'

'Cute little fella, isn't he?'

Fable stared at Raff, torn between a frown and a laugh. After a pause, she said, 'If I had to kiss a frog, it'd be that one.'

A whisper of a smile played across his lips.

'I'm determined to do him justice in my book.'

'A book about faeries and frogs! Fictional?' He grinned.

'Growing up,' she replied, all seriousness, 'I pictured my book as a kind of illustrated guide to rainforest faeries – a children's collection. But I don't have it in me anymore to paint the perfect faeries of my girlhood. In fact, faeries were never perfect.'

'Weren't they?'

'Not real ones. How could they be anything but flawed and vulnerable, like the rest of us? Or at least that's how it struck me at Faerie Falls the other day. See, when I first started creating my faeries, they were already their . . . bare selves. Then, I don't know, I copped some flak at school for my "dirty pictures"—'

'No one understands an artist.'

'No one,' she said tragically. 'After that, it felt like my faeries weren't good enough anymore. Guess I thought I had to cover them up, and make them decent. "Clothes maketh the faerie" . . . so to speak. But I think I need to unclothe them again. Not literally make them naked, though some of them might be, but I mean: exposed. Really themselves . . .' She trailed off, heat swamping her face.

The oars stilled. Raff sat back; unreadable.

'I'm rambling,' she said, fiddling with a frangipani bloom to cover her face. What was *with* her effusion tonight? She'd never uttered her idea aloud, not even once, and now she'd blurted it out to Rafferty Hull – of all people!

Time to swim back to shore! No, sink to the creek bed and die.

'It's just an idea,' she muttered. 'Probably *should* pack up for college, it's not like I'm—'

'Fable,' he interrupted. 'I didn't think I'd ever tell a talented young person not to pursue tertiary education, but listening to you – the valley is clearly in your blood. If Noah is where your inspiration lives, you have to be here.'

Fable looked away. *And what about you, what's in* your *veins, Raff?*

'It's funny,' he said, without a skerrick of humour, 'I used to see you tramping along the creek with your sketchbook under your arm, and I always wondered what you were keeping in it. You reminded me of when I was a kid; I used to get around Noah with a notebook in my pocket. Fancied myself a newsman, back then.'

'A *hack*?' She didn't mean to sound amused, but Raff smiled back.

'Most unbecoming dream for a farm kid – probably lucky it didn't pan out. These days, the only writing I do is letters to clients. Very dry, not like my *Noah Vale Post* used to be. I'd keep tabs on forest and farm happenings. I was always over-invested, though. Interfering little blighter, actually. At one point, I was the self-appointed president of the first Noah—'

'Valiant Society for the Protection of Valley Beasts,' finished Fable.

Raff's head fell back on a laugh. 'I can't believe you know about that.'

'I was always interested in stories about Noah Vale's most notorious chicken snatcher.'

'I think you have me confused with the whopping scrub python that terrorised local farms for a while. No one ever caught him, though.'

Fable laughed, and they sat in a gently rocking camaraderie. A light flurry of raindrops sprinkled over. They looked at the thinly wreathed sky together. Fable stretched a hand to collect errant drops.

It was with regret he next spoke. 'I wish I had more time here, I could show you all of my secret childhood haunts. Give you enough material to keep you churning out books for years.'

'Moonlighting as my muse?'

'First spot I'd take you would be my grove of rainbow trees.'

'Your *what*?'

'When I was much younger, I planted a grove of rainbow eucalyptus trees on the lower farm flats my old man used to promise would be mine one day. Promises that have become outright blackmail in recent years,

I might add. When I was a kid, though, I didn't think there would be anywhere else in the world I'd rather live. Had my heart set on a farmhouse beneath my rainbow trees. Rainbow gums are these incredible trees with—'

'Coloured bark,' Fable interrupted, 'in hues of blue, purple, orange, maroon and green. *Eucalyptus deglupta*, native to New Guinea, actually. They need copious rain, perfect for Noah Vale.'

Raff shook his head in slow wonder.

She went on quickly. 'I read about them in a rainforest book old Mr Shearer gave me. Sounded like a myth! I drew my own, but, without the real thing to study, not very well. I can't believe there are some only a few miles away from my own home. You've been holding out on me, Raff Hull.'

Her teasing smile sputtered away under the intensity of his admiration. She didn't trust herself to speak.

'Well,' he said, after a pause, 'they didn't look anything special for the longest time. Sometimes I wondered if I had the wrong trees altogether. I had to wait years for the colour to show.'

'I want to see them,' Fable interjected, surprised by the boldness of her own asking.

'One day.'

'*When?*'

Raff's eyes slipped away. Seeing they'd floated far from their course, he began to pull at the oars again.

'Beats me,' Fable muttered, 'why anyone would want to live in stupid smoggy England rather than a grove of rainbow gums, anyway.'

But Raff had drifted into unsmiling thought.

Fable plucked at moonlight caught in a crystal of her gown. A sob, unsummoned, built in her throat.

Raff started, an idea coming to him. 'I can give you rainbow *fish*, though!' He was rowing in earnest now. 'There's a spot near, where rainbow fish often gather. I don't usually tell anyone, because they're a favourite for home aquariums. But for our artist in residence . . .'

They'd reached the opposite bank, where thick buttress roots snaked into moonlit ripples. Flames glimmered across the pool, distant notes wafted on the balmy breeze; the falls tumbled on.

Raff fastened their boat on a thick root. 'Now, if you're quiet . . .' he said, peering over the boat, motioning her to his side.

Fable drew nearer – so near her knees were now within his opened thighs.

Raff sat back, allowing her to lean forward, right over his lap, to stare into the moonlit water. Her own reflection – faint wraith – rippled before her.

'See anything?' he asked in a low voice.

Fable saw nothing. She was conscious only of the breath stirring her hair, and her drumming heartbeat – surely reverberating in the high cliff basin surrounding them, louder than the falls.

A single frangipani dropped from her hair into the moon-washed water. Fable observed it, helplessly.

Raff reached for the bloom and Fable sat back, watching him wipe the water gently from the petals. It might have been her own skin, so hotly did her flesh colour.

He looked up, extending the flower, as though to hand it back to her. At the last moment he raised it higher, to her left ear, tucking it gently behind. His hand drifted lower, lightly picking up a tendril of burning gold, eyes lingering upon it. When he lifted his gaze once more to her face, it was to discover a countenance so profoundly altered, his trailing hand froze.

Every tumultuous undercurrent was finally revealed.

Their eyes locked. The star-scattered, rain-bejewelled night swirled around Fable. A squawking bat flapped off.

Raff's hand slid up, unhurriedly, to rest right where her fine chin adjoined her neck, her rose-gold hair. Flames danced in her peripheral vision; a melody lilted afar.

Still their gaze held.

Fable's neck elongated yearningly. Raff bent his head and raindrops spangled like diamonds in his hair as that long-beloved face, those blue eyes came towards her.

Warm lips pressed gently against hers. Her mouth parted instinctively, welcoming in Raff's breath as his other hand flew to cradle her face. Fable's tongue ventured tremulously forth, and his mouth crushed upon hers. Two strong hands now enveloped her face.

At last, at last, at last, she sang, drinking in the first and most wanted kiss of her whole life.

His hands loosened around her jaw – a low, regretful groan beginning in the back of his throat, even as his body leaned closer still. He broke from the kiss, his breathing uneven against her cheek.

'Fable . . . I need to stop.'

'But I love you,' she whispered against the side of his face.

He stiffened, eyes squeezing shut.

'Ever since the first time . . . at the Glade . . . when I saw you . . .'

He drew gently away.

Fable fell silent.

Their anchoring rope began to unspool.

'You're the same age as my baby sister,' he said, voice heavy. 'I'm way too old for you.'

'I'm *eighteen*! My birthday was in August.'

'Nevertheless, you're still a girl – with your big future ahead of you.'

The boat, loosened from its moorings, began to drift.

'Wait for me, then. Wait for me to grow up.'

His eyes blazed with tenderness.

'Some days,' she said, 'it feels like I'm growing up just for you, and it's taking so long.'

He looked away, raking a hand through his hair. 'I'm sorry, Fable. I can't. Of all people, you deserve better than—' He broke off, reaching blindly for the oars.

'Raff...'

'I've been seeing a woman in London,' he said abruptly, without returning his gaze to hers.

An afterthought.

'Wait for *me*,' she said.

He gripped the oars in his lap, knuckles white. 'I feel ... protective of you, Fable. I always have, right from the first time you appeared at the Glade that day.'

The hope flaring in her eyes at hearing this seemed, perversely, only to harden something in him.

'But ... like a kid sister.'

She shook her head, tears welling.

On he went. 'And my life and career are now in London. While yours is just beginning, *here*.'

When she didn't reply, he sank the oars into the pool. 'I'm going to take you back, Fable. You'll forget about this.'

'I won't,' she said, staring at the clenching of his jaw.

He began to row, looking over her shoulder to the tea house. 'I won't be coming home to remind you. And you'll find the creative world out beyond Noah has been looking for a talent just like you. There's nothing in this valley that should ever get in your way – especially not me.'

She wanted to wail and cry and plead. But she knew that no daughter of Esther Hamilton should ever beg, for any man.

Turning away, she pulled up her knees and, setting her eyes on the shore, hardened her back against him.

Each stroke took them closer to the flames, and further from the fire. A cold, dark terror crept into Fable's heart. This night, the first of her emancipated life, was the end of every romantic reverie she had nurtured for over six years. When she reached that shore, the dream of Rafferty Hull would be gone forever. She pressed a fist into her silent scream.

Perhaps she'd always believed sheer desire alone would be enough to surmount every other obstacle to her dream. But now Fable knew: she would never be worthy in Raff's eyes. Always she would be his kid sister's foe. Worse: a Hamilton.

Their gentle bump against the rocks stirred Fable into action. She was out of the boat in a trice, before he could even think of helping, much less speak to her again.

She was six steps up the shoreline when, driven by one last hopeful impulse, she spun to face him.

They stared at each other.

'*Wait* for me, Raff.'

'Write your book, Fable of the Glade.'

She glowered, and in a bitter, white whirl was gone.

The man left alone in the tiny boat dipped his head between his hands. His long groan was swallowed by the roar of the falls, and the flood of Noah Vale's latest graduates into the balmy night.

CHAPTER 29

UNBOUND

March 1962

S onnet had been in a stare-off with her cassowary when the idea, nay the *compulsion*, seized her. Afterwards, when the manic urge had been fulfilled, Sonnet would wonder if the cassowary had planted the idea there *himself.*

It didn't seem so far-fetched a thing for that cassowary to do. He and Sonnet were always getting into eye-wateringly intense staring competitions over the Story Bar when shop traffic lulled. She was convinced he'd have tried anything to win. And this particular tactic had worked extraordinarily well . . .

With the glazed eyes of one under a hypnotic spell, Sonnet departed the Story Bar, spun round her WELCOME sign, ascended the staircase, and flung wide the door to Alfred Shearer's private office.

It was exactly as he'd left it, five years ago. Great half-bombed sky-scrapers of books, papers, boxes and files rose in the unbreathed air – scale model of a crumbling city. His disorder; her: secret hoarder.

Sonnet clenched her hands into fists and squeezed hard: once, twice, a third time. Only on their release was she ready, at long last, to begin her excavation.

She proceeded to gut the room entirely. But first, every box of books and leaf of paper and sheaf of files was meticulously combed through, and consigned either to her shop below, or the skip she'd hired before she lost her nerve. Then, the dark drapes were flung out, Alfred's heavy furniture and pictures were sold to the local antiques dealer, the fusty rugs were rolled up for good, and even the walls were repainted.

All the while she harangued herself: she should never have let her morbid memorial go this long! It was so unlike her to cling on like this. And how had entombing her guilt in this room, ever served that lovely man?

Sonnet did not return to her counter for another seven days. Hamilton's Books remained resolutely shut until the last sunlit dust mote was sent scurrying, and the enchantment wore off.

Alfred's office was purged clean.

Sonnet smiled now at the room gleaming white in the sunshine splashing through uncurtained windows. Her Shrine of Unworthiness had been dismantled.

What to do, however, with the last three boxes left in the middle of her newly minimalist office? One box was chock-full with Alfred's favourite books – those she could not bear to toss or sell. They would go home to her personal bookshelves.

The second box was crammed with local memorabilia she had gathered together, certain it would be of interest to the Noah Vale Historical Society, conducted out of the CWA tea rooms. This box she intended to dump on their doorstep in a late-night drive-by, with headlights dimmed.

The final box was an enigma. Already opened and missing its original addressee, Sonnet's name had been appended to the top in Alfred's spidery handwriting: 'For Sonnet, from Vera'.

But who was Vera?

She wasn't a contact, and the box hadn't come from one of their regular suppliers. No familiar publisher's logo adorned the side. Based on the post stamp, the box had been mailed only days before Alfred's death. Alfred must have received and opened it at some point himself, but had, unaccountably, not got around to mentioning it.

The box contained a strange hodgepodge of items: faded show tickets, black feathers (disgusting!), a jar of earth, fountain pen, silver barrette, a cone shell, fabric scraps, violet pebbles, tarnished letter opener, and a pile of hardcover books from antiquated authors: Keats, Shakespeare, Wordsworth, Tennyson, Lord Byron, Elizabeth Barrett Browning, Coleridge, Blake, Shelley, Hardy – even an Austen or two.

What on earth had Alfred been doing sourcing *these* books? No one read the romantics in these parts anymore. Sonnet couldn't even remember the last time she'd waved a bag of stuffy Victorian literature out her front door, much less pre-loved, musty stuff like this.

She turned a fine, grey-spined edition of *Persuasion* over in her hands, holding it against her forehead. What had Alfred expected her to do with this order? Well, she hadn't come this far, with such ruthless, purging pleasure, to go soft now. She'd give these books a chance; make a decent effort to sell them. Maybe a vintage-themed display in the window would draw in some old literate types. Perhaps a markdown table, or a two-for-one deal, would do the trick.

But the rest of this box?

Sorry, Vera.

Without further thought, Sonnet tipped the bric-a-brac into her garbage bag, and stamped the box down beneath her feet.

That Sonnet had just completed the last task Alfred had ever given her did not, for a moment, twig consciously.

It was her office now, and it was good.

The spirit of mercilessness that had driven Sonnet to discharge years of physical and emotional weight could not, yet, seem to find rest. Home she charged to do more!

She'd only intended to reorganise her lounge-room bookshelf – making room for Alfred's favourites. Then it occurred to her that she could take out all Plummy's Blytons and schlepp them up to Heartwood, where her youngest sister seemed to hang out near-constantly these days. If Olive wanted to hog Plum so much, she should have the kiddy clutter, too.

While she was hauling out dusty childhood classics, Sonnet decided to free her lounge-room shelves of all Fable's L. M. Montgomery books, too. All those Annes and Emilys and Pats had never been to Sonnet's taste; too dreamy and fanciful. At nearly twenty, Fable was surely beyond them now. Not to mention the saccharine Heyers, melodramatic Brontës. They all must go!

'A job worth doing is worth doing well!' Sonnet said, rolling up her sleeves. She was about to attribute the idiom to her mother, but realised Mama would never have said it.

'Sneaking into my head, aren't you, Olive?' Sonnet chuckled, as she pushed Fable's door open with a hip, balancing a high book stack.

She had free rein to poke around the sunroom today. Saturday was Fable's longest and busiest shift at the newsagency.

Not that Fable and Sonnet seemed to cross paths much these days. What with Sonnet's workaholic tendencies and Fable's ... well, who knew *what* she did on her time off? Roamed the forest, wasting her talents away.

These days, Sonnet and Fable were no more than flatmates – one of whom didn't cook, clean or pay her own way, if it must be said. (It must.) They all but lived separately.

It wasn't for lack of trying on Sonnet's part. She set the table for two each evening, clanged the breakfast dishes with sufficient invitation each morning. But late-wandering and even later-sleeping Fable was impervious to sighs, suggestions and passive-aggressive digs. In Fable's defence, Sonnet knew she sucked at the passive part. All her notes blew off mirrors, benches and doors.

Even Olive's gentle attempts failed spectacularly. Secretly, Sonnet was gratified – imagine the alternative! Fable had stopped going to church altogether with the Emersons, and shied away from Sunday family dinners. The girl couldn't even walk in a front door like a normal person – she still insisted on sneaking in through her window like a fifteen-year-old.

Under such circumstances, who could blame Sonnet for having to snoop like this, now and then? It was for Fable's own good. Thanks to such spying, Sonnet was confident Fable didn't have a penchant for drugs, didn't seem afflicted by Mama's writing demons, and wasn't keeping a menagerie of cats. Even a secret boyfriend couldn't be blamed, since the only boy who called persistently for Fable was so proper as to be nauseating. Sweet a friend as Marco was – who could stand those puppy-dog eyes?

Fable certainly wasn't painting her way out of this damned valley, though.

For a while there, Sonnet had been excited. She'd spied the magnificent leather-bound journal Fable had purchased during her first few weeks at the newsagency, even dared to hope Fable had a serious plan in mind! But the journal had disappeared too. Sonnet had stopped nagging Fable to pursue her creative dreams after the first year, and had taken up less direct persuasion. But the art-course pamphlets she left lying out were binned. Prearranged conversations with Olive about correspondence courses, or a distant relative in Brisbane with a room to spare, or a job going in a Cairns art gallery:

269

all were frozen out. If Sonnet pushed, Fable recoiled. It had always been this way. But *now* was Fable's best chance to make something of her life – to escape small-town obscurity and rural mentality. They couldn't afford to play this childish, circular game anymore! They still did though.

Sonnet discovered the loose board almost immediately after emptying Fable's window seat. It fairly popped up into her hand – almost as though it wanted to be discovered; yearned for Fable to be found out, after all these years.

Out of the secret hole, Sonnet pulled something heavy and calico-wrapped. The ivory cloth fell aside to reveal a hardcover book, bound with a leather braid. She recognised it immediately as the journal that had made its brief appearance two years earlier.

That Fable didn't want it found wasn't nearly as outrageous as the realisation that she specifically didn't want *Sonnet* to read it. There was no one else to hide it from in this cottage.

Must be worth seeing, then!

Urgent hands cast aside the braid and opened the book.

The title page, in font tangled with vines, read:

Faerie Falls
by Fable Hamilton

The dedication on the following page was baffling: '*It was and is and will always be – all for you.*'

Mama? She must mean Mama.

Carefully now, Sonnet turned the first page.

For several pages, she hardly knew what she was seeing. She sank to the bed, flipping pages slowly. When she reached the end, Sonnet turned the book over and began once more, trying to browbeat her mind into comprehension ...

Fable was an illustrator, a writer, and this ... *book* was a work of art.

'Oh, Fabes,' Sonnet breathed, 'you brilliant girl.'

For many minutes she sat, trying to come to grips with what she had uncovered. It was a book, but unlike any she had seen or sold before. And boy had she seen some books these last few years!

Fable had created a sensual, eviscerating fairy tale. A love story between two faeries – *Absinthe* and *Ulysses* – set in the enchanted rainforest. Each faerie had been crafted from a tropical bloom, berry or butterfly, in the familiar mode, along with anthropomorphised animal characters – waterfall frogs, sugar gliders, forest dragons, rainbow bee-eaters. Even Sonnet's cassowary had made an appearance, reimagined.

However, this was no children's world of storybook perfection. Fable had taken a scalpel to the underbelly of faerie life, slitting it gullet to groin. Each page of this fractured fairy tale bore intimate vignettes, accompanied by sardonic commentary. Sonnet imagined those clever words narrated in dulcet tones, and shivered.

All the shame and vulnerability of faerie life – *no*, human life – had been revealed as ordinary, utter beauty

It was astounding; disturbing. This was May Gibbs without the gum leaves to protect their privacy, and true motives. Cicely Mary Barker overrun by fungi and faeries screwing.

Yes, *screwing*.

Sonnet had not been able to spend long on *those* pages at all, before an ache in her groin made her flip by. Even thinking about what she'd seen made her want to ... straddle something.

How had Fable understood any of this? Innocent little flower Fable!

Sonnet went hunting for the most erotic image again now, breath shortening in expectation.

There it was, on the final page, Absinthe and Ulysses finally consummating the love story that had flamed throughout Fable's book: a roaring waterfall, and on the jutting ledge above it, peridot-winged Absinthe, with head flung back in ecstasy, hair falling rope-like into the abyss, and bare-chested Ulysses labouring over her in earnest, cerulean wings straining from a furrowed back. Beneath it, the shortest caption in the whole book, only a single line: *Come home*.

Sonnet snapped the book shut again. How on earth had Fable managed to create this masterpiece without giving Sonnet the slightest clue that she was working on anything?

More importantly, what was Sonnet going to do with this book?

'What do you mean, what are you going to *do* with it?' Kate demanded across the Story Bar, unable to drag her eyes from the journal in her hands. 'Put it right back where you found it, obviously.'

When Sonnet didn't reply, Kate glanced up, amplifying: 'I mean *obviously*, Son. You're going to put it back – *right*?'

Sonnet shrugged, dabbing at spilt sugar.

'Sonny!'

The front door rattled open to admit Hetty Warren. Kate slammed Fable's book closed.

'It's her diary!' Kate said, between clenched teeth. 'What on earth are you thinking? You can't "do" anything with it.'

Sonnet offered to assist Hetty, though she knew Hetty only ever came in to write down the titles she intended to purchase more cheaply in Cairns.

Once Hetty was busy scribbling her booklist at the back of the store, Sonnet leaned close to Kate. 'Well, if I leave it to Fabes, it will languish

272

in her secret window seat until the next once-in-a-century flood washes the whole cottage away.'

Kate shook her head. 'It's. Her. *Diary!* That's kind of the whole purpose of them. Most people burn or toss their diaries well before her age. I sent mine sailing down Serpentine Creek when I was fourteen.'

'It's not a *diary*, I keep telling you. Do you recognise anyone in it? Can you imagine sweet, innocent Fable having seen anything of this?'

Kate bore the oddest expression.

'It's *not* a diary,' Sonnet said, louder, ignoring Kate's disturbing look. 'It's a story, her first book, and it needs to be published and loved and critiqued and to make her famous.'

'Published? Famous? Critiqued?! I can't imagine anyone in the world who would want to be critiqued less than Fable.'

'Nonsense, no one's going to say anything bad about *Faerie Falls*, other than how amazing *she* is for creating it.'

'Wouldn't be surprised if some people called it smutty, actually,' Kate said. 'Have you looked at page twenty-seven? That's not two branches getting all twisted together in that grove of trees there!' She pretended to fan herself. 'I mean, you know I like my romance, but that got me *all* hot and bothered!'

Sonnet harrumphed. 'It's art. There's supposed to be nudity. Otherwise it would be a children's book.'

'Definitely not a children's book . . . it's a girl's *diary*.'

'Fable just doesn't believe in herself,' Sonnet said. 'And she'd never have enough courage to launch this herself. She's such an ingénue—'

'Sonny!' Kate cried, pausing as Hetty exited the store without a goodbye.

'There goes my best customer,' Sonnet said in mock lament.

They laughed, but Kate had not forgotten her indignation.

'What exactly are you planning?'

'Nothing yet, I'm still thinking . . .'

'About the quickest way to return her diary and forget you've ever seen it?'

'About how Fable needs a ticket out of Noah Vale, because she's too talented to be stuck in this festering hellhole like the rest of us.'

'Seems to me, the valley she's painted here is anything but a hellhole.'

'Seems to me you're a fraud, given you've now got a first-class ticket out of here for yourself, Mrs *Willard*.'

'Ha! I'm still Hardy for life, though.'

Sonnet busied herself at her till, her dismay hidden. She would forever curse the day Brett Willard had ridden into Noah Vale on his . . . wait, *driven* into the valley to take a horse-riding tour, and had pounced on the best thing in Sonnet's life. Rockhampton was too far away, the wedding date was too close, and once Kate was tied down to the family she desperately wanted, let's face it: Sonnet would never see her again!

Kate was escaping where Sonnet suspected she never would. For years, they had joked how they'd be dried-up old spinsters left on the shelf together.

Now Sonnet was the joke.

As ever reading her mind, Kate added: 'Son, don't conflate your ambitions with hers. You don't have to push her out into the big, wide world first before you get permission to go do that fancy language degree you want.'

'You think this is about me wanting to live vicariously through my sister? You can't see the stupidity of Fable hiding her talents under a window seat?'

Kate was unrelenting. 'I keep telling you, we'll have a spare room at our home in Rocky – you can stay as long as you like.'

Tears sprang unexpectedly. Sonnet jutted her chin, reaching for the journal. 'No way I'm crashing a newlywed couple's love nest. Especially not when the wife's as randy as you.'

'Speaking of which,' Kate said, 'how's your business going to survive when your entire local market for breathless romance drives out of town next month with tin cans on her bumper?'

'Ah, you underestimate the sexual boredom and frustration of Noah Vale housewives. But you'll find out for yourself soon enough.'

Their shared laughter curtailed the conversation, though not the plans steadily brewing into hot water.

CHAPTER 30

EXPOSÉ

July 1962

S onnet stood before the red pillar box on Main Street, parcel at the ready, shoulders sizzling under the midday sun, summoning up the courage of her convictions. What was the *worst* that could happen?

Most likely: a returned parcel with a rejection slip, to tear into a thousand fragments. Fable would never even have to know.

The parcel, containing a forged letter of introduction, was heavy in her hands but had weighed heavier on her heart for many fraught weeks now.

With no one else to bounce ideas off now her best friend had married and, moreover, *escaped* Noah Vale, Sonnet had been left alone with this decision.

Well, except for the author-illustrator, if one wanted to quibble with details. But Fable had negated involvement of her own free will. Sonnet had tried every imaginable tactic to induce Fable into confessing the manuscript's existence or admitting she secretly dreamed of an artistic career outside the mountainous borders of Noah. But Fable continued to act for all the world as though the journal didn't exist, and she had never painted a damn thing in her life.

276

This much was now obvious: Fable had either forgotten about, or given up on her book.

Sonnet had even gone so far as to set a snare in Fable's window seat to ascertain how often, if at all, Fable looked at the journal. She didn't. Not even *once* in eight weeks! How much more proof did one need of artistic dreams rotting away?

Sonnet was confident then she could carry this off without detection.

Before sealing the parcel that morning, Sonnet had made one last executive decision. From the book, Sonnet had torn the most amatory pages: the copulating couple among those improbable rainbow trees; the frangipani faerie astride the man in the leafy gondola, her spine arching, his head buried; and that final, toe-curlingly erotic page. Sonnet was just being a shrewd editor. She might be a dilettante when it came to art, but she was an expert on small-town minds. No need to scandalise Noah unnecessarily. The book worked as well *without* the dirty pictures.

Sonnet smoothed the sticky-taped seal again, and turned the parcel over to check the address one last time: Margaret Mathers at Golden Apple Press, Brisbane, Queensland. Her contact was at an independent publishing house, with a keen interest in Queensland fiction featuring an evocative, environmental flair. They were currently scouting, albeit quietly. Sonnet had been given the tip-off only after hounding every publishing connection she'd forged over the last few years. Securing this editor's contact details was a hard-won prize.

No way Fable would have had the temerity to do so herself. This would be Sonnet's all-important contribution to the success of *Faerie Falls*.

Her sidewalk reverie was disturbed by the shudder of sixth sense which always preceded Delia Hull's presence.

Sonnet cast a glance up Main Street through the side of her sunnies. Sure enough, there was Delia, as proudly straight-backed as ever, leaving Dr Herbert's surgery with her husband. William Hull was a hunched figure at her side, walking slowly, with a gripping reliance on her thin arm as they moved towards their gleaming Chrysler Royal.

Sonnet turned her back against them, clenching her parcel tighter.

Some of us get stuck here in this valley thinking we're the Queen Almighty of the Universe, but some of us are going to get the hell out of here!

Aloud, she said: 'You're too good for this town, and for all of them, Fabes.'

With that, she pushed her parcel into the mouth of the pillar box, and let it tip from her trembling hand into the darkness below.

Away from the Hulls Sonnet skedaddled, balling her hands to stop their tremor.

Summer 1962

Sonnet's bookshop was crackling with excitement this steamy Friday afternoon – the last before Christmas. All her family was crowded into Hamilton's Books, perched on stools and benches, egging her on impatiently as she rang up the till and tidied her accounts. The pressure of their enthusiasm was too much – she kept making mistakes, shushing them sternly.

Tonight, as soon as Sonnet was finished, they were heading up to the brand-new drive-in at Cairns, for a Christmas double feature. For weeks they'd been planning it, and Sonnet didn't know who was more thrilled. Plum, whom Olive claimed hadn't slept in a week, what with visions of Fantales dancing in her head, or herself, after Fable had actually *acquiesced* to a family outing. The biggest child this evening had to be her big uncle, though. She looked at Gav bouncing up and down on his bar stool, hiding coins in Plum's ears, tapping Olive's shoulders when she wasn't looking, and wanted to laugh herself.

'Oh, go make yourself useful, Gav,' she said. 'See if you can sort my mail pile for me. I haven't had a chance.'

'Righty-oh,' he said. 'Let's see, then . . . well, this one can wait till tomorra, this one, too, this one can definitely wait, another one here is going to have to wait . . .'

Sonnet slammed her till closed, gathered her cash tin and headed for the stairs.

'And this one's gonna have to wait, nope not opening this one until tomorrow . . . Oh look, here's one for you, Beauty.'

'For *me*?' Fable said in surprise.

'Got your name on it, my girl.'

'That's bizarre. May I?'

'Here you go, don't forget it's gotta wait till tomorra, though.'

Fable was laughing as she began tearing the large envelope open. 'What could be more important than Christmas flicks?'

Sonnet was nine steps up and already at the turn, when comprehension finally crashed in on her amusement. She lurched to a stop, hand gripping the railing.

In the same instant, behind her, she heard Fable's voice – inflection rising more steeply than the stairs themselves. 'Sonnet? Son? Sonny? *What is this?!*'

Silence dropped over the group.

Sonnet turned, slowly, to face her sister.

Fable, however, was focused on the thick sleeve of papers, lips murmuring quickly, her index finger on a shaking journey across the page.

'Fable, please,' Sonnet said, rushing down the staircase, crossing the floor, reaching for the papers.

Fable spoke again, no longer with incredulity, rather revulsion. '*No!* You stop right there!' She threw a hand up, halting Sonnet in her tracks. Fable skirted away, placing a row of bookshelves between them. She scanned frenziedly on.

'Fabes, let me explain.'

'Just shut up! Shut up right now!'

'Girls?' Olive said, stepping between them, face stricken. 'Sonnet? Fable! What's going on?'

Sonnet could only shake her head. 'Stay out of this, Olive.'

'Stay out of *what*?'

Fable was still flipping pages, mouthing words, her countenance paling. When she looked up, it was with so cold and callous a fury, both Sonnet and Olive recoiled. Sonnet's hands flew up, as if to cover herself.

'I didn't want you to find out like this, Fabes. I was only trying—'

'You're a *thief*!'

'—to help you.'

'No! You helped *yourself* – to my private possessions, for your own fame.'

'Not my fame, *yours*.'

'I don't want fame! I want my privacy. It's all I've *ever* wanted! Give me my book back – you lying, interfering, controlling *bitch*.'

'Hey now!' Gav said, jumping up. 'That's enough.'

But Fable was out of the door in a furious jangle before anyone could intercede. They watched her disappear down the road, running at full pelt, before Olive turned, wilting, to Sonnet.

'What have you *done*?!'

It was with sheer relief that Sonnet slipped from the taut silence of the Holden at Heartwood, and fanged it for the cottage. Fable would surely be there, and already beginning to see sense. Sonnet would explain to her all the ways in which this was a good thing, a silver lining, the pot of gold at the end of a rainbow.

'Come and get us straightaway if she's not there,' Olive called after her, as Gav steered a weeping Plum inside. 'We'll drive around all night, if we have to. *Poor*, dear girl . . .'

The cottage was ablaze with light, doors and windows and cupboards flung open. The place had been ransacked. And Fable wasn't there. Her room had been torn apart, as if she'd hastily packed. There was food pilfered from the kitchen, too.

Fable had run away.

Sonnet collapsed on the couch, buried her face in a pillow and let loose an almighty scream.

Tomorrow she'd sort it out. Fable needed to sweat on it a little, before she came to her senses.

Fable stayed sweating it, not coming to her senses, for more than five days. Olive was a mess. Sergeant Windsor was almost called, but for Olive's dread of making another spectacle of the Emerson–Hamilton clan. In the end, it was the pile of dirty clothes left on Olive's back stoop for laundering – like a cat's mordant offering – which had convinced Olive not to call in the cavalry.

Fable had also presented for her Saturday-morning and Monday-afternoon shifts in town. Thanks be to Smithy, for keeping them in the loop. The glaring fact was Fable hadn't fled her whole life – only Sonnet. And soon enough, Sonnet told a distraught Olive, Fable was going to run out of purloined food.

'Unless she's learned any bush tucker skills?' Sonnet mused, eyes on the distant creek line. 'Perhaps she's living off sugarcane juice?'

Olive clucked her disapproval at the droll undertone Sonnet was taking throughout the whole affair.

'Oh, come on!' Sonnet snapped. 'You've got to admit; this is like a seven-year-old running away. She's a grown-up now! If she doesn't want her book published, she can come back here and say so, instead of sooking out there in the forest like a bloody child.'

'*Language!*'

It was Gav who ended the impasse. Tired of Sonnet's heckling and Olive's huffing, he strode out one afternoon and brought Fable home. As it turned out, he knew exactly where to find her. And when Gav's hulking silhouette had appeared at her feeble encampment in the Green Woman's Grove, Fable had seemed neither dismayed nor surprised to see him. What Gav actually said to Fable between the rippling roots of that tree, though, no one else would ever know. Clearly, it had been just the right combination of gentle empathy and subtle empowerment (a mix Sonnet admitted she hadn't yet perfected) to induce Fable not only to return to the fold, but even to be reconciled, grudgingly, to her older sister.

It was with quiet pride Fable stood before Sonnet at the Heartwood dinner table, to propose the terms of their reconciliation.

Fable protruded her chin, Sonnet had to admit, with as much majestic stubbornness as she'd ever hoped to inspire in her sister and began thus so: 'I can't undo your green-eyed thievery . . .'

Sonnet stayed her laughter.

'. . . but since you've already set in motion this train, I am taking over the reins before you derail my dreams.'

'Wheel,' said Sonnet.

'What?'

'You're mixing your metaphors. You started with trains but then you went to horses and back again.'

Rage glittered in Fable's eyes.

Sonnet quieted, sitting back. Fable's hands went to her hips. Up she rose; poised to strike.

'As,' Fable hissed, 'has been wisely pointed out to me, this book, and the book deal itself, is mine and not in fact, nor ever *was* yours, Sonnet Hamilton. It has only been pitifully covetous thinking on your part.'

Sonnet's mouth twitched.

'So, you should stop playing pretend now and go back to your day job. I am the author and artist. This is my book and my . . . message to Noah Vale.'

Sonnet finally released the smile clenched between her lips – it spread widely, wildly across her face. 'Heck *yes*, my little authoress!'

CHAPTER 31

LIT

Late March 1964

'Night of all nights,' Fable sighed, watching the scurrying hub-bub of garden-party preparation from her sunroom window. On this night, she would be launched into the world as authoress and artist! Well, launched into the small sphere of Noah Vale – the only world that had ever mattered to her. And tomorrow afternoon, Fable would board the Sunday train for a six-month adventure: first, a round-the-country tour of media interviews, bookstore signings, library appearances and writers' festivals, followed by a three-month stint working with her publisher, a thousand miles away in Brisbane, on her next book.

Next book, at only twenty-one!

It was unfathomable, yet coming true before her eyes. No matter how steadfastly Fable clung to the familiarity of Noah, and her unre-quited romantic dream, the great tide was sweeping her out, anyway.

And it was all thanks to Sonnet – or *all her fault*, depending on Fable's mood. She watched her older sister rushing around the garden commanding her league of helpers – her new bookseller assis-tant, Hayley; ever alacritous Olive and Gav; even heavily pregnant Kate, who'd driven twelve hours north, all by herself, to support the

Hamilton girls – as they converted the cottage gardens into Fable's unofficial book launch. Or rather: her 'Enchanted Garden Soiree'.

Her publisher's official book launch was still slated for a week's time, in the Brisbane Botanic Gardens. But no one Fable knew or cared about would be there – by then, she'd be entirely in the hands of her new publicist, Sarah Timmons. Sarah herself was in attendance at tonight's party. She'd arrived yesterday, accompanying a large box of first editions for Fable to share with her friends and family, and for Sonnet to proudly display in her bay window; the first bookseller in the country to stock *Faerie Falls* – by special arrangement.

It was the least Fable could do for her sister-agent. Ultimately, Fable was only at this preposterous juncture in her young life *because* of her sister riding roughshod over all her plans, or lack thereof. In ways Fable had never expressed to another living soul, *Faerie Falls* was more the realisation of Sonnet's greatest dreams than her own. Some days, it felt like she was merely going through the motions, for her sister's sake.

And look at Sonnet out there, in her element, bossing everyone like some big budget Hollywood director: setting up long trestle tables; wrapping all the trees in faerie lights; overseeing the assemblage of a low stage; assigning places for the jazz band, the wood-hewn bar, the dance floor.

Tonight was Sonnet's big night. Fable could see the gloating pride in nearly every step her sister took: *Look how Esther Hamilton's daughter turned out!* To such end, Sonnet had fought long and hard to host the book launch in town, specifically at the CWA hall. It had been one of many heated arguments between the sisters which Fable had won by simple virtue of holding the trump card: her talent. As it turned out, being the mother to Sonnet's vicarious book-baby had subverted a decade-old power struggle more expediently than Fable could ever have hoped. Sonnet's ulterior motive in submitting so was patently obvious:

whatever it takes to appease Fable, do it; just get her the hell out of town, and into the bookish life a Hamilton girl deserves! Correction: Sonnet coveted.

Fable won the battle of location, but she'd relinquished invitation rights – had to give Sonnet something to stake her revenge on. Goodness knew who'd be turning up tonight, or what Sonnet intended to say in her speech. Fable wouldn't put it past her to thrust a copy of *Faerie Falls* in the air with a champion's cry: 'Stick *that* in your judgemental traps, you bloody no-hoper blabbermouths stuck in this godforsaken town!'

Fable grinned. It didn't matter who Sonnet had or hadn't invited. The most important people in Fable's life would be here.

All but one.

Instantly, the haunted longing was back in her eyes. It never went away, but she'd learned to mask it as vigilantly as anything else.

Fable gave herself a shake. *Not tonight, heart.* Tonight, she'd be surrounded by people who would distract and console her – though they could never know it – her glory-bathing eldest sister, indefatigable aunt, the uncle who'd embarrass her with paternal pride, and younger sister to whom she'd promised the first signed copy.

Out in the garden, Sonnet was arranging garden lanterns – in long rows on the tables, hanging from the arching branches, lining the bar. This bewitching evening would be, most fittingly, a faerie-lit celebration under the stars, and Fable had only a few hours left to become her own faerie godmother!

First and foremost: get into town and rescue her gown before closing time, from her dressmaker. *Dream*-maker, Fable thought, smiling.

The door of Emerson's Fashion and Fabrics jingled closed behind Fable. On the front step, she hugged the dress bag to her chest, sighing. Joanna Ellis, Olive's new seamstress, had done a marvellous job with the alterations to the old gown Fable had nabbed from the mildewing cupboard in Sonnet's room. A peridot gown, colour of both her Green Woman and Birdwing faeries, which had surely waited there all these years, just for her.

And who cared what Olive had to say about it?

Well, actually, Fable did. Hence, sneaking behind Olive's back and getting Joanna to do last-second adjustments. Joanna had practically sewn Fable into the dress this afternoon, so perfect was the fit. And now Fable had just enough time to race home, do her hair and makeup – then let the grandest party of her life begin!

Draping the bag over her arms to prevent creases, Fable danced up the street to the Holden. It was the 'Golden Hour' and autumnal sunshine flared beneath the shop eaves, suffusing her vision. With her hands trapped beneath her gown, Fable was unable to shield her eyes. She bent her head against the light, and continued blindly on.

The pedestrian striding tall around the corner towards Fable, obfuscated by the glare, was upon her before she had corrected her drifting path. They collided abruptly: Fable, with a yelp; he, with a dazed cry.

'*Fable—*'

Her head snapped up to take in the face forming out of the sun. Her hand, free of the dress, flew too late to stifle her shocked utterance.

'Oh, *Raff*!' Emotion broke its banks, flooding her eyes.

'I've hurt you.'

'No,' she answered, blinking hard. 'I wasn't watching out for you.'

They stood for a mutually searching moment; stretching long. His face held none of its usual good-naturedness.

She ventured first to speak. 'Why are you back in Noah?'

He gave a mirthless laugh. 'Believe me, I asked myself the same thing for the whole three days it took to get home.'

She frowned.

'It's my father,' he said, and the thickness of his voice told her everything.

'I'm so sorry.'

'Yeah, he's only got a couple of weeks – if that. Prostate cancer, highly aggressive.'

Fable's eyes swam anew.

'He and Mum have been keeping it secret from everyone, even us kids. I suspect my stoic father thought it would be mind over matter, like everything else. And now it's too late for anything, they haul us back together for last-minute farewells. I've come home to watch my old man die . . .'

Fable let the dress bag fall away, laying a slim hand on his forearm – an arm more densely roped with muscle than she remembered it being.

They both stared at her hand. She withdrew it, and Raff seemed to lose some of his height with the sigh that followed. Fable felt an intense urge to draw his head against her breasts, run her fingers through his hair.

'He's decided he can't go until he's put all his affairs *and* ours in order. So this morning, we all had to gather round his deathbed for a premature will reading. Apparently, he wants to spend his final days watching his children bickering over property. It's a kick in the teeth.'

'*You're* squabbling over the property?'

'No, *I'm* not – because he's gone and left the lot to me as eldest son. All these years I've been fighting off the old bastard, not wanting to take up his reins, and then he tries to foist the whole farm on me – by dying.'

She winced, eyes soft.

'It's archaic, Fable. I won't take it!'

'Of course you won't. What do Adriana and Eamon say?'

Raff raked a hand back through the hair she so longed to touch. 'Don't get me started – nightmare! No one's listening to me when I swear I'm not stealing it off them, that we'll sort it out fairly. I've appealed for Mum to intervene, but she's had more of a hand in it than anyone. I know she wants me back, and they probably think this is the way: force me into Dad's shoes, then I have to take care of them all—' He stopped, pinching his brow hard.

Fable stayed her hand against another forearm touch.

'I *had* to get out of there, couldn't stand another minute of it. Came charging down the street with no idea where the hell I was going, and then I run smack bang into you.'

'Listen to you hogging the credit,' Fable said, 'I did a pretty admirable job of running into *you*, actually.'

He smiled, tension easing. 'Either way, I'm glad. I needed to see a friendly face.'

The warmth of his tone and expression both made Fable stiffen. It was *too* warm; a brother's easy familiarity. The last thing Fable wanted to remember was how Raff Hull thought of her as nothing but a pestering kid sister – one to protect, and reject.

'Look,' she said, manner cooled, 'I don't mean to be rude in the face of your terrible news, but I do have to get going. I actually have a thing on tonight and I don't have two minutes to spare.'

'Your book launch!' he said, recalling himself. 'I've seen your invites all over town. It's a marvellous achievement, Fable – though I can't say I anticipated anything less for you. And *I'm* sorry, here I am taking up your time with Hull drama, and you've got the most exciting night of your life ahead of you.'

'No, I'm grateful you told me about your dad. Would you give my best wishes to Adriana?'

The hoarseness returned to his voice. 'Thank you. Good luck tonight – you deserve every success.'

'Okay, then.' she murmured, moving past him. 'I'll see you later.'

'Take care, Fable.'

But she went on only a few paces, before stopping. It was the *take care* that did it – and the twigging memory of her flight across a storm-ravaged field from the man who'd come for her, anyway.

She turned again, and found Raff standing exactly where she'd left him, following her leave-taking.

'Oh hey, listen,' she said, as casually as she could; fighting screaming resistance. 'Probably the last thing you're up for tonight . . . but if you felt like dropping by my launch? It's nothing too fancy, don't worry. But I'd like to give you a copy of my book.'

CHAPTER 32

GARDEN OF EARTHLY DELIGHTS

Fable stood inside the cottage doorway, beckoning small breaths past constricted throat. From the garden swelled music and laughter, chinking glasses, high heels clipping on stone pathways. The soiree was well underway, but the guest of honour had yet to make her appearance. Fable pressed her hand against her belly, then higher at her shallow-breathing chest. She told herself it was the too-perfect fit of her green gown having a corseting effect – though it hadn't in the store.

It was indeed the faerie-tale gown of her dreams. The shimmering peridot, encrusted with Swarovski, skimmed every supple curve – from lacy cap sleeves at narrow shoulders, curving over generous bosom, nipping in at diminutive waist, flaring over graceful hips, tucking under the pert shelf of her bottom, and falling away in long, gossamer folds.

She was an effulgent faerie lichen glowing in the forest.

Fable spotted the blaze of Sonnet's hair through the stained glass, hovering on the front stoop. It was *her* reaction Fable wanted to see first and foremost. Sucking in an inadequate breath, Fable swung open the door, and stepped into her shining future.

Her next breath was a gasp. The garden was no longer a garden at all, rather a faerie wonderland: every tree branch outlined in twinkling lights; mason-jar candles lining the winding pathways; hurricane lanterns set along the tables and dance floor, and upon the bar. Her heart throbbed with the resplendence of it all.

Sonnet's exultant face was the first Fable brought into focus as she gazed from the lighted garden to the swarming circle of her loved ones. Plummy was already pulling at her arm to come see the wishing well lit up, and the dance floor beneath the faerie stars, and everything, quickly! Uncle Gav looked as though he might roughhouse with her. But Olive, now *there* was a face Fable hadn't expected. Tears streamed down Olive's cheeks, and it wasn't for joy alone.

'Are you angry, Aunty?'

Olive shook her head, crushing Fable into her arms. 'Oh, bless you, dear girl, you're the very image of her,' Olive said in her ear. 'This was her most favourite gown – no matter what. It's only right you should wear it on *your* big night.'

Sonnet swooped in. 'Come now, Olive. No one's being maudlin tonight!' She pulled Fable into a hug, or as much of a hug as Sonnet was wont to give. 'It's time for you to get out there and start mingling!'

Sonnet pressed a glass of sparkling wine into Fable's hand, and pulled her from the intimate family clutch into a wider circle of well-wishers: Kate, lavishing compliments, Sarah Timmons calling her a 'publicist's dream', Smithy complaining he was about to lose the newsagency's biggest drawcard; and Marco, beaming proud.

Fable noted the blood-red wild hibiscus spinning in her champagne glass a dazed second before she raised it to her lips. She wiped Olive's tears from her ear lobes, recomposed her countenance, and let herself be gathered up by the teeming crowd.

'Everyone's here to celebrate *you*, Fable Hamilton,' she heard Sonnet proclaim as she was carried away.

Well, as it turned out, no, not *everyone*.

Fable had been twirled around the garden, across the dance floor, over to the bar, and by the box of books – in pride of place on its own table – by nearly every familiar face in Noah Vale.

But no Hulls.

Not one!

Somehow they'd come to the speeches, and Fable sat poker-faced atop the stage, with her uncle's arm heavy about her shoulders, as her book was duly introduced.

Sarah proudly officiated – Fable wondered how she'd managed to get *that* past Sonnet – speaking of her 'favourite' new writer/illustrator in glowing terms, compelling Fable to centre stage for at least a bow, after she'd squirmed out of a speech.

Olive had spoken, eloquently, of how proud she and Gav were to see their niece achieving the dream her talented mother had always cherished. At this, Fable had buried her face in her uncle's shoulder. She felt the shudder in his body, too, and dared not look at him. It was uncharacteristically vulnerable, yet unflinching of Olive to have said such a thing, in front of so many townsfolk. Again, Fable marvelled at how these speeches had slipped past Sonnet's censoring net. What on earth would *Sonnet* bring to her speech, then?

Fable was delayed from finding out, however, by the young man who leapt, unprompted, to the stage, stealing the mic from Olive's hands as it was passing to Sonnet, already bristling for her turn.

'I can't let this night go by,' Marco began, in grand tones, 'without something I have to say too.'

A warning prickle ran the length of Fable's spine.

'Fabes,' he said, 'I've known this day was coming ever since I used to sit next to you in art class. While I was drawing my dopey stick figures, there you were creating absolute masterpieces, and I told myself, "This girl is going to be *famous* one day!"'

Fable glanced at Sonnet, jigging at the stage edge. Beside her: Sarah Timmons stood with one elegantly pencilled eyebrow arching.

'And look, she's done it!' Fable saw the red bleariness of his eyes and sway of his posture. Well, he'd *over*done it tonight. Her smile fell from polite to enduring. She felt her uncle shift impatiently beside her.

'Now if I may be so bold tonight . . . I've got some stories about our Fabes to share too!'

A loud whistle went up from the rear of the crowd, followed by a stir of laughter.

Fable flashed a wide-eyed, desperate plea at her friend. *What was he thinking?!*

Sonnet was an assassin, about to take down her target. Luckily for Marco, it was Gav who moved swiftly to jostle for the mic: 'All right, my turn now, young fellow!' And Olive, who directed Marco off stage, with a freshly opened bottle of beer proffered enticingly.

No public speaker, Gav was doing an admirable job of redirecting the audience's attention with impromptu anecdotes. By the time Gav's performance had come to an end, Fable's queasiness was abating.

She squeezed Gav's hand gratefully as he resumed his guard at her side.

Sonnet, final speaker, and prouder sister than ever known before, spoke of Fable at extravagant length and in such glowing terms, Fable had to wonder quite how many glasses of sparkling wine her sister had imbibed.

Who knew Sonnet could muster such princely praise?

'Fable Winter,' Sonnet declared, raising her glass, 'you are capable of more magic than most people could ever dream of. And as Mama would surely have quoted, could she have been here tonight: you must *always* make a "wild dedication" of yourself to "unpathed waters" and "undreamed shores" . . .' Sonnet choked on the words.

Fable's throat swelled in turn.

In a voice controlled by effort, Sonnet proclaimed: 'So, here's to Noah Vale's very own success story!'

The crowd turned, with glasses raised, towards Fable.

'To Fable!'

Fable dipped her head to her chest, and Uncle Gav deposited a kiss on her crown. She looked up again, lips fighting to maintain tranquillity, and across the crowd, watched a tall figure step through the cottage gate, blue gaze already set upon her.

Wine flowed, music ebbed and swelled, dance floor whirled, lights twinkled; all her senses reeled with the unbearable pleasure of waiting until he finally came to her. For hours now, he'd been circling on the periphery of her vision, never out of her awareness for a moment; moving, ever so slowly, through the throbbing crowd. Everyone wanted a portion of Rafferty Hull tonight – he was surely the guest of honour now. Was there a person in Noah Vale who didn't love Raff like a son, cousin, former student or playmate, who didn't have a decade of news to impart? Fable's cheeks ached from the blush withheld, the mild smile sustained.

When Raff reached her aunt and uncle, the restrained delight in their reunion made her heart beat double.

'Raffy, my boy!' cried her uncle as he enveloped him in a hug, though his 'boy' towered a foot above him. Olive reached to hold Raff's face between two hands and murmured something Fable would have given every cent of her book advance to have heard. When was it ever to be her turn?

The night grew long, the crowd thinned, and those left were flushed full and mellow by alcohol, music and food. It was not unlike a wedding reception. Only, at the end of this eve, she would be carried off by a career, rather than the mate of her soul.

The way Gav held her now on the dance floor and how his eyes crinkled as he looked at her, was every bit the father of a bride.

'I'm so proud of you, Beauty.'

'You keep saying that, cut it out!' She laughed, with an admonishing smack.

'It's an uncle's job.'

'No,' she said, growing meaningful. 'It's the role of a father, and you're the closest thing I ever had. I'm so thankful you're my uncle-dad.'

'Oh, Beauty—'

Gav pulled her into the heartiest of bear hugs – she sensed to hide his tears as much as her own. As they drew apart, the notes of a slow song began. Gav, wiping his eyes roughly on his sleeve, reached for his wife dancing nearby.

'Come on, my love,' he said, 'this one's for you and me.'

The exchange of partners was so quick Fable had no time to smooth her features. The face she raised to her new partner, shone already with raw emotion.

Rafferty.

Her feet baulked at the transition, but he was already catching her up in arms, moving her lightly away from her aunt and uncle.

'You came,' she breathed, lowering her face to stare at the pulse in his throat, struggling to control a full body shiver. If only he knew how his touch scorched, perhaps he would be more careful with those large hands.

'Well, it *was* awfully nice of you to put on this massive Noah Vale welcoming party for me.'

'Yes, you don't seem to mind stealing my thunder tonight, do you?'

There was careful pause before he answered. 'All eyes are on you tonight, Fable.'

She blew out a tiny breath, without confidence another would be coming along after it.

Raff's arms on her waist were warm and confident, and burning a hole through her middle. Hers, strung about his neck, began to tremble.

They had fallen into a silence familiar in its weight, and waiting. Every heartbeat was a treacherous hammering; each inhalation, a victory. Would this song last forever, if she willed it so? Only the dread of leaving his arms stirred courage in her breast. She looked up, to speak.

At the meeting of their eyes, she stumbled. He held her, strong and sure. The faerie lights around Raff's face were outshone by the lustre of his contemplation.

He spoke gently, the words meant for her alone. 'So you're finally all grown up, Fable Hamilton.'

Her gaze dipped hurriedly away. But there had been a question in his measured tone. And if she had any doubt, the insistent tightening at her waist, urged her reply.

Once more she lifted her face, her every hope. Fable had not mistaken the question. It was there, in his eyes, wholly undisguised.

Before her throat could close over, she must answer. 'Yes.'

Raff's expression did not outwardly change, but Fable felt the quickening of his breath, the tightening of his embrace.

To be sure, she spoke again. 'I've never felt more grown up in my whole life. I'm only sorry that it might be too late . . .'

Raff unfolded her favourite expression in the world; his smile. A hot wave hit her eyes.

'Not too late,' Raff began, 'I was—'

'Oi, there you are!' came a cry at her side. It was Marco – buoyant, inebriated pup. 'Who says *what's* too late?'

'Marco!' Fable started, flushing.

Marco was holding out his hands expectantly for her. 'Nah, it's not too late, Fabes. I reckon we can keep this party going all night and halfway into tomorrow, too! Look how much fun everyone's having!'

Marco reached for her, as Raff's hands slid gently from her waist. Before she could even excuse herself, Marco was already whirling her away.

Just like that, the song was over.

The empty garden, littered with glasses and chairs, still glowed with unextinguished lights. Sonnet had sent home the last stragglers offering to disassemble the faerie realm for her.

'It can wait until the morning, go home!' she cried, wanting nothing more than to topple off her heels into bed.

Home they all went, clutching their copies of *Faerie Falls*, personally handed out at the gate by Fable – more radiant at party's end than she had been at its beginning.

'Success suits her,' Olive said to Gav, as they ascended the hill to Heartwood, her arm linked in his, her shoes in his hands. 'Have you ever seen her look so happy, in all your days?'

Sonnet stumbled up to bed and, having imbibed far more wine than planned, watched the ceiling spin dizzyingly above her for a moment, before she tumbled into a dreamless slumber.

Plum, sleeping the night on the cottage couch after having made the mistake of closing her eyes for just one second while the party whirled around her, now blundered her way, disoriented, to the bathroom. Through the frosted glass, she squinted at a slim shadow sliding past.

Back at the lounge-room window she rubbed her eyes, watching Fable stand on bare tiptoes to detach a lantern from a branch, before slinking out of the front gate, with a book tucked under her arm.

Across the field the slender green figure streaked then – the leaping flame of her lantern growing smaller and smaller, until it was subsumed by the rainforest.

In the lambent light, the long, buttress roots rippled like unearthly tentacles. The green woman knelt to lay her book in the heart of the deepest groove.

'*This* is my book, Mama,' she said, leaning forward to rest her head, as if she sought to kiss ageless feet, hidden within an undulating forest gown.

'There were some pages missing for a while. But they're all here now. I want *you* to have the whole book. You'll hold them for me.'

Tears, hidden by the spill of rose gold, wet the ground; the book.

'I have to go away tomorrow – just for a while. But I'm not leaving you, I promise. Keep my book safe, Mama.'

Fable rose, sniffling, to thread out between the roots.

Behind her, pages stirred, and turned.

The lantern flame danced as Fable floated back along the creek-side path. Closer to the cane bridge, a violent flap of wings in the canopy sent her heart rate rocketing skywards.

Only a bat, frightened away, taking all her courage along with it.

Darkness seemed to press in on her circle of light now, shapes leapt forward, and shadows loomed.

A moment later, she heard the crack of branches underfoot, followed by a muttered cursing. Fable stilled, peering breathlessly into the creek gloom. A carried light on the opposite bank bounced into view, travelling parallel to her path. At the bridge, the light turned towards her, and began to cross the tracks.

Fable's lantern trembled wildly as she raised it to her face, straining to make out the advancing figure.

'Hello?!' she called.

Closer, relentlessly closer, came the light.

'Oh, it's *you* . . .'

CHAPTER 33

ROOTS AND WINGS

S onnet juddered awake in the light-saturated attic. She lurched up and fell back against her pillow in one hastily aborted motion.

'Urrrrrgh.' Her throbbing head, roiling stomach, the stink of her skin, the fur on her teeth.

Outside in the garden: murmuring and light laughter, rustling garbage bags, a broom screeching across the pavers.

Sonnet fumbled for her watch, staring at it disbelievingly.

An hour past midday?

To the dormer window, she pitched. Gav and Olive were outside, cleaning the mess from *her* party in *her* garden, while *she* slept the day away. *Malingerer* . . .

Downstairs she slanted, a foul-smelling hunchback, to take cleansing refuge in the bathroom.

It was a freshly scrubbed, though no-less-rotten-feeling Sonnet who emerged weakly into the sunshine sometime later.

'Hello, sleepyhead!' Olive trilled.

Bloody teetotallers, Sonnet thought.

'Just getting a head start here, hope we didn't wake you.'

'Leave it, I'll do it.'

Olive's dry grin swept her from head to toe.

Sonnet grimaced, plonking into a chair. 'Maybe not, then. I can cheer you on.'

'There's bacon and eggs on the stovetop,' Olive said 'It's probably cold by now. Just heat it up to share with Fable.'

Fable! Leaving! The afternoon train!

'Holy hell,' Sonnet said, staggering back to her feet so quickly, she felt her brain rattle.

'Language,' Olive said mildly, turning back to her tray of glasses as Sonnet flew, holding her head, for the stairs. 'And there's aspirin above the fridge!'

Sonnet hammered on the sunroom door. 'Fable? *Fable*!'

'Chill out, Sonny,' came a voice, from behind her.

Fable: returning from the bathroom, with towel-wrapped hair, face and limbs pink, eyes inflamed from a dearth of sleep, or a surfeit of decadence, or could she have even been . . . crying?

In any case, she looked exactly how Sonnet felt.

'Are you okay?' she asked, as Fable swept by on a draught of soap fragrance.

'Fine. Why wouldn't I be.' It wasn't a question, rhetorical or otherwise.

Sonnet dallied for a moment, unable to justify her sense of unease, eyes boring into the slim back turned against her.

'We're late now,' she said. 'Train leaves at three. I need your bags out front in half an hour.'

'I'm not going,' Fable said quietly.

Sonnet was neither surprised nor alarmed by this attempt on Fable's part. She realised now: she'd been anticipating it all along.

'Nonsense! That's only last-minute nerves. Nothing stands between you and that train today.'

'I mean it, I'm not going. I need to stay here.'

'Under no circumstances,' Sonnet replied. 'If I have to tie you to the carriage and drive the train out of Noah myself, I will.'

'Sonny, I *can't* go, I—'

A knock at the front door made both women jump – Fable, perhaps more so. A male voice was heard conversing with Olive and Gav outside.

'No, you've got to be ready!' Sonnet said, intercepting her sister's improbable move to answer the door still half naked. 'I'll go. You get dressed.'

'Marco,' Sonnet said, opening the door to a bloodshot, nonetheless grinning young man.

'Morning!' he sang.

Sonnet had a rankling memory of his unendorsed, though mercifully thwarted speech, and hardened. 'I'm sorry, Marco, we're quite late.'

'I'll keep out of your way then, I'm only here to say goodbye to Fabes. Did you guys hear the news from Hulls yet? I ran into Raff on my way over and he told me first hand.'

Fable emerged from the sunroom, with clothes thrown on, blinking warily.

'Hear *what*?'

'Eamon went missing last night!' Marco answered. 'He was drinking heavily at Summerlinn, got violent – you know how he does – and disappeared near the creek. He still hasn't come home! The Hulls are all going out of their minds about it. Apparently, Eamon's been beside himself over old man William; they're afraid he could do anything in the state he's in. They convened a search party before lunch. I was gonna go help look, right after I saw you off.'

Will the Hull-led melodramas in this bloody town never end? Can't you see *what you're escaping from, Fable!?*

'Guess you better get going then, Marco,' Sonnet said, not bothering to affect neighbourly concern. 'We're leaving momentarily.'

Sonnet clapped her hands. 'Right, come on, Fable! We've got thirty minutes to get you Brisbane-ready.'

They skidded into the train station at five to three. Sarah's pinched face in the rear-view mirror – perturbed by either the speed at which Sonnet had swerved kerbside at Canecutter's Hotel to pick her up, or the haste at which she was taking the tight mountain corners – relaxed only as the car boot clunked and handbrake screeched in one victorious declaration of arrival.

Fable was inscrutable as ever, not uttering a word the whole way to the station. Which was fine by Sonnet, *she* had copious pearls of wisdom to impart before releasing her charge into the big, wide world. In any case, Fable seemed grateful for the coverage Sonnet's lecturing provided. Sonnet had not missed the way Fable's hands roamed from cheeks, to heart, to mouth, to belly – as though to hold herself together.

Olive and Gav, already waiting responsibly at the station, and having by now procured the travel passes and dinner menus, in addition to locating the correct carriage, seats and nearest bathroom, were already assuming the mantle of calm, parental farewelling. It was into their words of comfort and courage Fable leant now, in a three-way cuddle. Sonnet did not push forward in competition, neither did she interrupt their progress towards the carriage, nor did she push herself to the forefront of the party. She'd been forgotten in the rush, and this time, she didn't object.

Sonnet could feel it already: the final yielding in a long line of concessions to their competency, signalling her cue to step back into her true role, as sister.

She'd given her all as guardian and substitute mother. Now Fable was free of this damned town. Sonnet had nothing left to do.

And look; Fable hadn't even missed her sister's part, or marked the transition. It was Olive and Gav handing her off now to climb the ladder, Plum begging for souvenirs through the window, her publicist settling in beside her as seatmate and new journey's companion.

Tears came, stinging, to Sonnet's eyes as the sleek, silver carriages wound around the verdant bend, a plume of smoke in their wake. It was Olive, drawing near to squeeze her shoulder, who triggered the waterfall. Olive was to blame, entirely.

'Remember,' Olive said, as the last carriage was swallowed up. 'We gave her roots, and now she finds her wings – or draws them, same thing.'

Sonnet smiled, despite her misery, and stepped out of Olive's touchy-feely reach.

Her brain clobbered at her skull. She wanted to hurl. Most of all, she needed to see Kate, pronto, and have a bloody good gasbag about all of this.

CHAPTER 34

PRODIGAL DAUGHTER

Late October 1964

F or the first time in her life, for over seven wondrous months, Sonnet lived the life of an unfettered woman. She had expected to miss Fable exceedingly, and stress every second she was out of her reach. To her surprise, however, Sonnet mellowed out. Freedom was having the cottage all to herself, and only the demands of her own work to consume her. Cutting the apron strings turned out to be as liberating as a haircut – another invigorating experience she'd had lately.

Shoulder-length locks swished, loose and glossy, around her face now. Most people said the haircut suited her – though they meant 'softened' – and Sonnet was inclined to agree. The loss of her high bun was akin to dropping years. Sonnet didn't feel almost-thirty anymore, more like the fancy-free young woman she'd never got to be.

She knew folks in Noah said Sonnet Hamilton had a 'big head' now her sister was gallivanting about Australia calling herself an 'author-illustrator' – and the new city haircut, new bookstore furniture and new spring in her step were proof of her increasing pretentiousness. Not to mention her scandalous *Brave New World*-themed window book display!

But this time? Sonnet didn't even care. Freedom was its own reward.

When Fable had rung Heartwood from Brisbane after her book tour ended to confirm she would be staying close to her publisher for another six months to collaborate on several children's books, Sonnet nearly leapt in the air to click her heels together. She wasn't even envious of her sister's exodus from the valley. Though by all rights, she should have been. Fable, living in a flourishing city, an author-illustrator already earning real dosh and creating her own reputation, while Sonnet was stuck in a tropical backwater – in years gone by, it would have been enough to make her *scream*!

But Fable's triumph felt like her own. Almost the moment Fable steamed out of town, Sonnet noticed the effect on her own disposition. She just . . . stopped thrashing. It was like the expectant lull between the agitation of a wash cycle and the rattling spin dry. Suddenly, she found inconsequential all manner of small-town idiosyncrasies and injustices, which might once have nettled. She even seemed to detach from matters closer to her heart.

Take, for instance, the Marco Lagorio rumours arising after the book launch. Sonnet had weathered the incessant blabber-mouthing down the street about Marco and Fable with uncharacteristic restraint. She could easily have flown into a corrective rage at every busybody to bring it up: *They're only mates! Never been a spark of attraction between them!* Instead, she simply shook her head. What did it matter? There was no way Fable would be coming home to this staid old existence after her taste of glamorous city life.

Marco seemed to know it, too. He'd frequented the cottage for weeks after Fable's departure, hunting news of his friend. Sonnet had been gently fobbing him off, until the day he asked for Fable's book-tour itinerary, or an address to write her. No way she'd let *anyone* in

Noah have contact with Fable at such a pivotal time. Sterner words of advice had been necessary then.

Marco had left Noah in recent months too, apparently after non-farming work. It looked like he went as far abroad as London, based on the fat airmail letter that had arrived at the cottage not long afterwards. Fable never even had to know about that. Sonnet had unceremoniously trashed it, unopened.

And that was that: small town rumour forestalled, and successful, independent author-illustrator none the wiser!

The most surprising example of Sonnet's new-found serenity was during the Hull family dramas, which first erupted with a week-long disappearance of Eamon Hull the night of Fable's launch party. They had volunteers out dragging dams, walking the canefields in long lines; even put divers in the creek, before he finally washed up in town at the end of a wild bender. He would have looked better as a bloated water carcass, actually.

Two or three weeks after Fable left, William Hull died and then the whole town seemed to fall into a fit of depressive, nostalgic pandering, promptly followed by opportunistic scandal-raking.

First, there was the grand funeral cortege down Main Street with an informal public holiday declared for all, whether or not shop owners gave two hoots about attending the Hull funeral. Strangely, even that didn't seem to faze Sonnet. She just went home and enjoyed some therapeutic cleaning.

Following that, the CWA windbags organised an enormous shindig for the Hulls over at Summerlinn. Olive and Gav insisted the Emerson–Hamilton clan should be in attendance. Sonnet squirmed successfully out of that one (she was mellow, not stupid), but for the rest of the day, she had such an unsettling feeling of something strangely like . . . guilt?

Then there was all the salacious speculation about conflict over the Summerlinn distribution of property, which had preoccupied the town for months on end. Normally, Sonnet would have gloated over the Hull discord, at Delia's perfect world torn asunder. Or, at least revealed for the fallible family it was. Instead, Sonnet moved right on by the Main Street broadcasters and bank-line rumourmongers.

One day, Sonnet happened to spot Delia and her golden boy outside the General Store. Delia was standing uselessly by their car, staring off into the distance with what, if Sonnet didn't know better, might have been construed as normal human vulnerability, while her son packed bags into the car for her. After slamming the boot, Rafferty moved to take her in his arms – and stood there holding her for the longest time, while cars streamed slowly past, faces peering. It looked like Delia was crying, genuinely shaking with grief, and for a moment Sonnet wanted to cross the road and extend condolences to her worst enemy. It was only the fact that Mr Bloody Perfect himself, sighting Sonnet, looked to be coming over to try to speak to *her* that sent her streaking away on the pretence of anything else than converse with a *Hull*.

Dodged a bullet there.

The Hulls finally were pulling themselves back together again, anyway. Rafferty went back overseas after the harvest, Eamon's transgressions were neatly forgiven and forgotten, and Adriana continued to think she was Lady Muck. Delia had even brushed past Sonnet in the post office the other day with a magisterial sneer, which was a great relief. Imagine if Delia had known how close they'd come to *rapprochement*?

Sonnet would never forgive the way those Hulls had treated Fable, so soon after Mama's passing. Sonnet had many reasons to relish this calm new phase of life, but paramount among them was Fable having transcended the bitter friends and strictures of her childhood.

Never would Sonnet forget, but thankfully never again would she have to bear the sight of that stooped and tragic strawberry-gold figure trudging down the hill, towards home.

Until, one ordinary October afternoon, she was.

At first sight and from afar, Sonnet thought it was a traveller having lost their way to Moria Falls. The young woman descending the hill was heavily laden with bags. Her face was obscured by a baseball hat as she seemed to watch her every footfall home.

Reality crashed in like a tree through the roof in a cyclone. Sonnet had to grab a wall against collapse. That was *her* lost, laden sister limping home.

Sonnet flew across the paddock to meet Fable.

They'd never spent so much time apart in all their lives, and Sonnet imagined they might fall upon each other now in tearful reunion. But Fable stopped at her approach, keeping a stiff distance. Sonnet, for her part, felt an intense desire to slap Fable.

'What are you doing here? You've got another six months in Brisbane still! How the hell did you get home? What happened to your new books?'

Fable hoisted a bag higher on her shoulder, grimacing. 'Well, nice to see you, too. Mind if I put these down first before we start with the Sonnet Inquisition?'

Once inside, Sonnet sat, stupefied, across the table from her travel-worn sister, watching her throw back another glass of ice-water. Sonnet's body twanged with curiosity.

Would Fable ever open her mouth?

And she looked terrible. (Sorry, but that was the truth.) If freedom from guardianship had loosened Sonnet's hair and temperament, liberation clearly had the opposite effect on Fable. Her mane, lank and oily, was tightly coiled beneath that bizarre hat. She was ashen and rumpled; bloom of youth replaced by a weary strain only another adult could empathise with. A bath was the first thing Fable needed, squeeze her out of those awful pants and flannel shirt; spray her down with deodorant . . .

'Would you stop staring at me like that?'

Sonnet choked down a sigh. How quickly it came flooding back, the barely tempered rage at Fable's smooth evasiveness. Well, she wasn't going to beg for info this time. She sat back, crossing her arms.

'I like your hair,' Fable said.

'Thanks.'

'Can see you've been changing things up in the cottage, too.'

'Yep.' Sonnet refused to make small talk. Refused!

Fable resumed an ice-cube-swirling contemplation of her empty glass.

Sonnet checked an offer to refill the cup.

'Hope you left my room the same.'

A retort here was inevitable. 'Oh, is it your room again? No one let the concierge know.'

The flash of hurt – dorsal fin quickly submerging – was not missed by Sonnet. Fable's reply, however, was petulant. 'Didn't know you needed a personal copy of my itinerary.'

'A simple phone call would have been enough.'

'I wanted to come home, Sonny. That's all. I *needed* to.'

Sonnet swallowed the lump of empathy which had risen unbidden. 'Zephyr's gone,' she blurted. 'We think snakebite. Plum hasn't stopped sooking about it.'

Fable just stared at her – whether in disbelief or dismay, Sonnet couldn't discern.

'I have to go to the toilet,' Fable said, rising abruptly.

Sonnet remained at the table, stewing, as she listened to the toilet flush, faucet squeal, a shower curtain rip closed and, at length, familiar footsteps creaking up the hallway to the sunroom for the first time in more than six months.

Sonnet straightened in her chair.

Wait for it . . .

A turning handle, then the gasp: 'For God's sake, Sonnet! What have you done to my *room*?!'

'Fable's home? You're joking!'

'Wish I was. She's home, and adamant she's not going back.'

Olive came out from behind her shop counter to stand before Sonnet, lowering her voice so the rotating radar ears over by the large floral prints had to readjust, in vain, their position.

'But how did she even get home?'

'Best as I could get out of her over breakfast, she caught the coach to Cairns, then thumbed a lift with perfect strangers in a Kombi.'

'Fable, hitchhiking? The poor girl. Is she *all right*?'

'She's fine. Everything's fine. It's all going to be fine.'

Olive clucked. 'I don't believe it. What happened with her work?'

'She was "homesick". Brisbane apparently wasn't for her . . .'

'Bless her soul.'

'No blessing her *anything*!' Sonnet whispered fiercely. 'She has to go back, and I won't rest until she does!'

'Oh, Sonnet. You haven't been hounding her again already, have you?'

'I'm not a monster. She got the first night off. But I'm shutting shop early today so I can get right back into it. I'll have her packed and on the next train out of here.'

'Don't you dare!'

'I will so.'

'You're terrible. I won't let you.'

'If Fable didn't want to be nagged, she shouldn't have come home.'

'She wouldn't have come home if she didn't feel safe here.'

'Safe from what – adulthood? Responsibility? *Success?*'

'Balderdash. She must have good reason for limping quietly home. I'm going to knock off early myself today. I can't wait to give our Fable a big cuddle.'

Well, Sonnet would just cut her off at the pass. She had a few stern lectures on resilience and *never, never giving up* to impart before blasted Olive got there oozing grace and welcoming.

Sonnet was home by three, but Fable was not in the cottage, or at Heartwood. A snoop through the already trashed sunroom only elevated Sonnet's ire – it was like she'd never even left! If Madam Backtrack thought this was going to work, she was sorely mistaken.

Stuck in a time warp and needing to alleviate her Fable-wrought frustration the only way she knew how, Sonnet donned her sandshoes and hurtled off along the creek-side path.

Darkrise was on the move and the forest was steeped in shadow, all the bright gold of the spring day sliding down the riverbank, to gild the creek. The effect was of racing alongside molten lava as it coursed through verdant jungle.

Sonnet ran hard over roots and rocks, ridges and ruts, hard as ever she had, halted only by her stomach's revolt against her pounding legs, and a stitch in her side; like a reopened wound. She came to a reluctant, heaving rest against a giant blue quandong tree. Sweat flooded from Sonnet's pores as she stomped the berries underfoot with an inexhaustible fury.

The rush of a nearby waterfall promised hydration, drawing her closer. Someone was already swimming below, Sonnet realised too late, as she came out onto a rotting, cantilevered cubby platform. She panted quietly, waiting for the swimmer to emerge beneath her.

Aha! Found you, Sonnet thought as a strawberry mane fanned out behind the figure stroking across the golden pool. She should have known Fable would be hiding in the creek. And what serendipity! Now Sonnet would block Fable's exit, and they'd thrash it out here, once and for all. Sonnet melted back into the cubby gloom, heart rate slowing, to wait.

You've got no idea what's coming for you, Fabes.

Her sister was bathed in light, the amber glow seeming to emanate from the depths below. Back still turned, Fable rose out of the pool to squeegee water from her hair. Her white shirt floated about her sylph-like form, refracted light surrounding her like wings. How long Fable's hair had grown – it tumbled down her back, dissolving into liquefied light. Even Sonnet's unromantic heart could not help being moved. Fable was a waterborne faerie, straight out of her book.

Sonnet felt a covetous ache – not for Fable's beauty, but her talent. Oh for the skills to capture such loveliness as this. How could anyone let it go to waste? Sonnet wouldn't *let* her!

Her resolution was interrupted by Fable's submergence. In a single, gleaming streak, she crossed the bottom of the pool in Sonnet's direction. Propping her elbows on the rocky edge, Fable drew a shuddering breath. Sonnet took one of her own. In another second, Fable would look up, spy her lurking sister, and then the haranguing, from both sides, would begin . . .

But Fable rose from the water with eyes still cast down. Eyes fixed upon her own wet form, explicitly outlined, and revealing all: her full, heavy breasts, and the high, protuberant curvature of her belly.

Fable Hamilton was lush with child.

PART THREE

'She hoped to be wise and reasonable in time; but alas! Alas!
She must confess to herself that she was not wise yet.'

Jane Austen, *Persuasion*

CHAPTER 35

GRAVID

Sonnet couldn't remember how she got back to the cottage. Her last cognisant action, before abandoning rational thought, had been to hide. She'd crouched down in that cubbyhouse, waiting for Fable to finish drying her unfathomably changed body, and leave. And after that – who knew which path she'd traversed home?

She ascended the cottage steps as a gaping sleepwalker. Fable was already inside, the shower running. Sonnet sank to the couch, shaking her head to cast off the nightmare.

It was Fable's humming while she bathed, which finally shattered Sonnet's trance. *Humming*, like she had no concept of her own predicament! Humming like a child, not as one illegitimately *with* child!

Up the hallway Sonnet stormed, banging open the bathroom door without knocking.

Fable screamed, clutching the shower curtain to her body. '*What are you doing? Get out!*'

The clinging plastic curtain was no protection. The dark areolae of her nipples, thatch of pubic hair and prominent belly were starkly visible.

'*Shut the door!*'

'What the hell, Fable!'

Fable clambered from the claw-foot to fly at her – a tribal fertility statue springing to combative life. For a moment, Sonnet thought she might tear her face off. It was the door she was after, though. Screaming an illegible curse, Fable flung it shut. Sonnet offered no counter-resistance as the lock turned in her face.

From the other side of the door came sobbing.

Sonnet pummelled the wood. 'How could you be so *bloody stupid*, Fable! What were you thinking?!'

'*Sonnet!*'

Olive, aghast, came charging through the front door, with Gav and Plum on her heels. 'What's all this screaming? Leave her alone!'

'Like hell I will!' Sonnet hollered, spinning on Olive. 'Do you want to know what she's done?'

'Sonnet Hamilton, get a grip of yourself – this instant!' It was more commanding a tone than Olive had ever taken with her. 'You've got no right: she's her own person!'

Sonnet laughed; a harsh bark. 'Oh, she's more than one person now!'

Sobs intensified in the bathroom.

Olive, green eyes glistening, stepped as a buffer between the girls. 'You're out of line! Move away!'

'You can't lock yourself in there forever, Fable!' Sonnet called over Olive's shoulder. 'You're going to have to come out here and tell them, too.'

Olive hustled her towards the lounge. 'How could you be so cruel? I told you this was not the way to talk to that little girl.'

'She's not so *little* anymore,' Sonnet remonstrated. 'But, by all means, keep lecturing me. You'll see for yourself!'

Plum's tear-stained cheeks caught Sonnet's eye. 'Actually, on second thoughts, Gav, you should take Plummy back to Heartwood. This is no place for her right now.'

Gav had ears only for his wife. 'What's going on here, Olive?'

'It's only a sisters' tiff, my love. One I tried to warn Sonnet off—'

'It's much bigger than a childish fight, but you're not listening to me.'

'For pity's sake! Would you—'

Olive's crossness, Gav's consternation, Plum's frightened tremble, none of it mattered now. At the end of the hallway, the bathroom door scraped open.

Four heads swivelled to watch as Fable appeared, wrapped in a green towel. Along the hallway she came towards them, eyes not leaving her feet. The towel, tucked into her bosom, too short on her thighs, still managed from the front to conceal the shelf of her belly. Gav cleared his throat uncomfortably and moved to leave.

When she was yet a few feet away, Fable paused. She lifted her eyes, and Sonnet grimaced at the fear laid bare on her face.

Fable turned to stand side on. Where her waist, whippet thin, should have been, was the blatant protrusion of advancing pregnancy.

'Oh my dear girl,' Olive said, moving to envelop a sobbing Fable in her arms. 'My dear girl.' She motioned over Fable's head for Gav, who joined her in two quick steps. Around wife and niece, swept his big arms.

'You're safe,' Olive crooned. 'You're safe here. It's all going to be okay.'

The front door thumped closed as Plum disappeared into the garden.

'Is she asleep?' asked Sonnet, looking up from her untouched plate as Olive slumped wearily into her seat at the Heartwood table. Gav's plate wasn't much emptier.

'Yes. Finally. She's all cried out. I had to pat her back to help her go to sleep.'

'Like a baby,' Sonnet said.

Gav clucked and pushed his chair away to stand on the veranda, his back to the women. Moonshine lay over the newly sprouted canefields, and on the train tracks. A dog howled distantly. Giant jungle moths butted at the light.

'Sonnet, you have to go gently on her. We won't make it through another day like today. You've got to lay off!'

Sonnet snorted.

Unexpectedly, Olive burst into tears, dropping her head onto the table. Gav came quickly to her side, big hands diving into the gaps between shoulder and neck, steadying her.

Sonnet looked away, teeth fastening on her tongue.

'I'm sorry,' Olive said, after an achingly full moment. She leaned back, airing her eyes. 'I don't mean to be melodramatic. But she's the spitting image of Esther. She's even carrying the same way!'

'She's not Esther,' Gav said gravely.

'No, she's not,' Olive agreed. 'She's an adult, for a start.'

'Barely,' Sonnet interjected.

'And they have proper support for unmarried mothers these days,' Olive said, ignoring her. 'Fable won't have to scrape by, like Es had to. And she's got us. This time, she's got us.'

'And she's got choices,' Sonnet said, meeting their eyes straight on.

'What's *that* supposed to mean?'

'It means don't go counting chickens before they hatch.'

Olive's eyes narrowed. 'In the eyes of God, every life is unique and precious.'

'Oh sure,' Sonnet replied. 'Until said unique, precious life refuses to follow the script, then He prefers fire and brimstone, actually!'

Gav cocked his head. 'There will be no reproach here for Fable.'

'Doesn't mean she doesn't have choices.'

'You're not making any sense,' Olive said. 'And you won't lay another unkind word on that girl. Not under my roof.'

She's still got to come and get all her rubbish from under my *roof, though.*

'Did she tell you anything?' Sonnet asked.

Olive pursed her lips.

'Come on, Olive. She's withholding enough for all of us. Don't you start!'

'I got out of her that she's just over six months along.'

'Six months,' Sonnet mused, calculating quickly. 'So it can't be Marco Lagorio's then.'

'*Marco's*? They're just friends! Why would you think—'

'He's the only boy who ever hung out with her in Noah, but it doesn't work for her dates.'

'In any case, she said it was just something that happened, on her tour. That it didn't . . . mean anything.'

Gav left the table abruptly. The women watched his thumping progress down the stoop, into the cane.

'Dear,' Olive sighed. 'I should go after him.'

'Why? Because he can't bear the idea of his precious Fable being sexually active? That's not the issue here, Olive. The problem is she didn't do it safely and now she's gone and jeopardised everything she's worked so hard for – *everything* she deserves. It was a careless blunder to make.'

Olive lapsed into a lip-chewing silence.

'And what else did she say?'

'That's it. She didn't say much. I mean, it's Fable. To be honest, I think this pregnancy is a little traumatic for her, I'm worried this baby might be the result of . . . coercion.'

'Rape?!' Sonnet's nails raked the table.

'No, no! I didn't say that.'

'I'll kill the sonofabitch!'

Olive tutted. 'Language, please.'

Sonnet drew herself up. 'I mean it. I bloody will!'

'She's plainly not going to tell us who the father is, so you can stop being so dramatic.'

'I'll get it out of her!'

'You'll leave her alone.'

'And it's just one? She looks big enough to be carrying twins.'

'Yes, she's all belly, isn't she. Well, this part will rile you up – she hasn't had any antenatal care!'

'She hasn't even seen a doctor?!'

'No. She's been in denial, obviously. This is what I mean about it being traumatic for her. I suspect she wanted it to stay a secret forever, maybe pretend it wasn't happening.'

'At least she was thinking sensibly on one count. No point telling anyone and risking her career if she's just going to—' Sonnet withheld the rest of her sentence.

'Going to *what*?' Olive's face was as hard as stone.

'Make her own choices, that's all.'

'Not under my roof, Sonnet.'

'Yes, we've already established that.'

Sonnet recalled Plum's disappearance earlier in the afternoon with a start. 'And what about Plum? Is she all right now?'

Olive sighed. 'I think so. It's hard to tell with Plum, she's always so emotional lately. It was overwhelming for her seeing Fable like that, and you girls screaming at each other like banshees didn't help! You've *got* to tone it down. You know how sensitive she is at the moment.'

'You need to explain sex and babies to her now, too.'

322

'Plum already understands how babies are created. I talked to her a while ago.'

Sonnet found herself smiling. 'Seriously? Well done, Olive! I'm proud of you.'

Olive came close to a smile herself. 'I'm trying, my dear. Between us, we'll have to figure this out somehow. We're a team here, I want you to remember that.'

Yes, a team, Sonnet thought. And every team needs a captain . . .

CHAPTER 36

GREAT EXPECTATIONS

The doctor's receptionist, Edna Parker, was glaring at Sonnet around the potted rhapis palms. Hadn't stopped glaring at her since the moment she'd arrived in Dr Herbert's Main Street rooms, as the first patient of the day. Admittedly, Sonnet had all but screamed 'medical emergency!' when she called for an appointment the afternoon previous, while shamelessly refusing to disclose said medical issue to the receptionist herself – cardinal sin in this place.

Frankly, if Edna kept that death stare up, Sonnet might drive north for a doctor anyway. The narky old bat! It was only the memory of Dr Herbert's soothing grandfatherly manner when she'd brought Plummy in for her immunisations that kept her sitting here in this tiny waiting room . . .

Edna stood with obtuse leisureliness and entered Dr Herbert's consultation room. Sonnet focused on the hands gripping each other on her lap, and went over her spiel once more.

Friend – pregnant – unmarried – career – too young – options?

Edna appeared again. 'The doctor will see you now.'

Sonnet sprang to her feet, straightening her pantsuit and cinching her belt. She squeezed by the receptionist monopolising the doorway, with a beatific smile. Far from thawing, Edna only hardened. Sonnet couldn't help herself: she gave Edna a petulant wave, and firmly pulled the door closed in her face.

'Thanks for seeing me on such short notice, Dr Herbert,' Sonnet said, turning to the bulky wood desk.

But it wasn't the black-rimmed glasses, phlegmatic cough and substantial girth of Dr Herbert that greeted her. The man getting to his feet and coming out from behind his desk with hand extended was far too young to be a *real* doctor. Brown hair and eyes, tallness and strength, and a chiselled parenthesis at the lips bespeaking a ready smile; all registered in her baulking mind.

She halted, dismay evident, and his hand fell politely to his side.

'What have you done with Dr Herbert?!'

He turned to his desk with alarm, pretending to shuffle frantically through his papers. 'Now where *did* I put him?'

Sonnet burst into laughter.

His smile was one of eye-curving sincerity, and Sonnet saw now he was older than on first impression. The laughter lines sprayed around his eyes hinted at alacritous amusement, and years numbering to mid- or late-thirties.

'Please have a seat, Miss Hamilton.'

Sonnet perched on the proffered chair, looking uneasily about the room. 'He's really not here?'

'I apologise, no. Dr Herbert has had a family medical emergency arise, and unfortunately, he's had to leave in a hurry, and indefinitely.'

'He just left? How did *that* one slip past the town crier?'

There were those smiling strokes of eyes and lips again. 'Oh, I can assure you, word is getting round. Half the town is already booked in on questionable pretexts just to meet me this week.'

Sonnet smirked. *Poor Edna.*

'You're actually my first patient. I'm Dr Fairley – up from Sydney. Here for a tree change, you might say.'

This time Sonnet accepted the outstretched hand. Heat rose along her neck as her slim hand was taken in his solid grip.

'I don't think,' Sonnet said, 'there are enough trees in the whole valley to justify leaving a big cosmopolitan city for this hole. You will find a lot of deadwood here, though.'

Dr Fairley settled into his chair. 'I'll hazard a guess you're not an agent for the local real estate or tourist bureau, then?'

'Ha! The only appreciation I have for trees, is the books produced from them. I'm Sonnet Hamilton, of Hamilton's Books.'

'What a Shakespearean name.'

'Yes, I was conceived over The Bard. You'll think I mean figuratively, and I mean literally. But that's a story you'll hear about me soon enough.'

The urge to cringe made her temples ache. His expression, however, was one of tempered amusement.

'And have you moved here with a family?' she threw out, desperate to bury her last words.

'No, just a lot of exotic souvenirs, I'm afraid. I've spent most of my working life in far-flung locales. More recently, I was with the Flying Doctor Service.'

'You're going to be bored out of your brains in Noah, then. There's nothing worth seeing here.'

He uncapped his fountain pen, suddenly gone businesslike. 'And how can I help you today, Miss Hamilton?'

She'd quite forgotten herself, or rather her sister. It was with some effort she scrambled for an affectation of anguish.

'There's . . . some trouble, and I need medical advice.'

The sincerity of his eyes was dreadfully off-putting. She lowered her gaze to his primed pen, rapidly reworking her story. She'd come prepared with a few vague falsehoods to probe out conservative old Dr Herbert. But to hell with it, she didn't know this guy, and he didn't know *her*. If Sonnet truly wanted to help Fable, she needed to ascertain exactly what options her sister had left . . .

'You see, I was stupid enough not to use contraception. And now I'm six months pregnant and I would just like to know what my choices are – medically speaking.'

'Six *months*?'

Sonnet's consciousness flew to the belt cinched tight over her waist. 'I don't know, six . . . and a bit maybe.'

'OK. What was the date of your last menstrual period?'

His pen lowered to her card.

'Six months ago.'

Dr Fairley looked up, and Sonnet raised her eyebrows dauntingly. 'Just write that down. Six months.'

He paused. 'I don't see any record of antenatal appointments here, Miss Hamilton. In fact, we haven't seen you, according to my records, for well over a year. Is this your primary medical practice?'

Sonnet shrugged. 'Sure. I've just been in denial about the pregnancy.'

'This is your first presenting appointment?'

'And hopefully my last, once you outline what options we have.'

He frowned at his card, scratching a quick note. After some consideration, he looked up at Sonnet. Brown eyes crinkled with thoughtful warmth. She resisted the urge to grip the table.

'Is this your first pregnancy?'

'Unfortunately.'

'Okay. So, how about we start with a few basics to confirm pregnancy and your well-being. I'll organise a test—'

Sonnet quickly interjected. 'No thanks! I'm not interested in tests. I just want to know more about . . . getting rid of this problem.'

Dr Fairley sat back in his chair, steepling fingers to lips. His eyes were kinder still. Sonnet squirmed under the scrutiny. She jutted her chin, meeting his gaze straight on.

Just when it seemed like he'd never open his mouth again, finally he spoke: 'You said six *months* – right?'

'And a bit.'

'Which places you at approximately twenty-six to twenty-eight weeks' gestation.'

'Sure. Whatever.'

'Miss Hamilton, do you know much about foetal development?'

So, he thought she was a moron. And for Fable's sake, she was just going to have to wear it now . . .

She squared her shoulders. 'I want to make sure I understand *all* my options.'

'Well,' he said carefully, eyes steady on hers, 'having not established gestational age, or having discussed your mental and physical health, and thus going only on the information and dates you have given me so far, I have to say there are no other options for the time being.'

'*None!*'

'However, there are some choices available, for after the birth—'

'It's not *fair*! He gets off with impunity and she has to—' Sonnet's lips compressed to a white line.

The doctor waited her out, with that infuriating frankness of eyes and brow.

'I had my whole life ahead of me,' Sonnet corrected. 'This is not an option right now. I've got to get back to Brisbane!'

'Brisbane?'

Swiftly she was on her feet. 'Yes, *Brisbane*! One slip-up shouldn't have to ruin all my plans. This is *bloody* ridiculous!' She gathered her bag.

'Please, Miss Hamilton.' He opened the desk drawer and rifled through it. 'I actually have a brochure right here on—'

'Making it all go away?' she cried, hands on hips, no longer caring a whit how the action threw her stately hourglass into dramatic relief.

He straightened, dark eyes curving with compassion. 'I want you to know you'll have my full support. I also have a close colleague in Cairns, whom, with your permission, I would like to—'

'Forget it,' she raged. 'I'll just take care of it myself! Nice to meet you, Dr Fairley.'

'Sonnet, would you stop staring at me like that!'

'Sorry. Just thinking.'

Sonnet leaned back in her wicker chair, stretching with feigned nonchalance.

In truth, though her eyes had been fixed on the way Fable was scraping frozen mango out of the cup balanced on her belly, her mind had been six miles away, right where she'd left it that morning: perched in front of Dr Fairley's desk like a vexatious child at the principal's office. With every passing hour, her mortification increased.

He'd seen right through it the moment she'd opened her mouth! Any doctor worth his salt would have. What must he think of her?

In my defence, Sonnet imagined herself telling the doctor, it really does feel like my sister's pregnancy is happening to *me*. It's certainly ruining all my best-laid plans . . .

Sonnet returned her gaze to Fable's fecundity. In mere days, she'd bloomed obscenely larger. It seemed impossible she'd been able to keep the pregnancy hidden for even the first night. Which begged the question – how had Fable covered it up for six months while travelling and working in strange new cities?

There was no way she could ask Fable directly. *Ask me no questions and I'll tell you no lies*, seemed to be the law underscoring their every interaction – with Olive always hovering near, monitoring Sonnet's speech like Big Brother himself.

Big Aunt.

The jibe lifted her out of rumination. 'So, is the frozen mango thing a pregnancy craving or something?'

Fable looked surprised at her interest. 'I've always loved mango.'

'Olive froze an entire box of mangoes last season, and you've already eaten through the lot.'

Olive appeared, clattering plates off the table. 'Everything OK out here, girls?'

Sonnet wasn't going to dignify that with an answer. She waited, smiling tightly, until Olive had gone, and the kitchen tap squealed on. Warily, she began. 'You know you still have options – right, Fabes?'

Her sister said nothing, cleaning her teeth with her tongue.

'It's your life, and your choice.'

'My choice is pretty clear here, isn't it?'

'For now . . . apparently. But you can still make a different choice – after.'

'It's one and the same to me.'

'But it doesn't have to be. You're not beholden to or trapped by one single event. Your life is still your own. I just want you to know that it's okay for you to prioritise your dreams over biology.'

'That's exactly what I'm doing.'

'No, I mean—'

'I know what you mean.'

Sonnet clenched her toes, her teeth. Again she tried. 'I hope you haven't burned your bridges.'

'All but one.'

'Because you don't *have* to give up your artistic ambitions.'

'I'm not.'

'But . . . Brisbane?'

'No, I'm not in Brisbane anymore.'

'What does that mean – have you given up on writing and illustrating?'

'A baby and work are not mutually exclusive, Sonnet – you and I should understand that better than most people.'

'On the contrary, we lived always in the shadow of Mama's broken dreams. She gave up everything for us.'

'She still wrote.'

'Words that never saw the light of day! Her talent squandered away while she ironed and sewed other people's expensive outfits, wiped their crumbs off tables and numbed her own brain to exhaustion in factories. Don't you remember how hard she had to work at menial jobs; how absent she was; how much she suffered; how often we all went without, just to survive?'

'So, her artistic endeavours meant nothing because they weren't paid?'

'Not paid, not seen, and never appreciated. We don't have a single thing left of her writing now! She died, and all her gifts died along with her.'

'They were still *her* talents. She got to be a mother and an artist.'

'How can you play her martyrdom and misery down? Stop kidding yourself. She missed her potential. She got nothing more than secret scribbles in a dark room between bouts of depression. Motherhood drained her dry. Having illegitimate children ruined her plans. *Men* ruined her life.'

'Or, she made a few sacrifices – gave up some things, to have what she most wanted.'

'What on earth was worth giving up the creative success she desired?'

'Love. A family. Us!'

'Hogwash. It didn't have to be either-or. She should have established her life and career and *then* love and children. She should never have had to give up what made her Esther Hamilton – all her aspirations for her *own* self. That just made us a consolation prize. I can't believe you're justifying what he did, what they all did to her! Why would you want to make the same mistake?'

'I'm not making a mistake—'

'Yes, you are! By carrying *his* mistake for him, whoever he bloody well is. He gets off scot-free while you've got to sacrifice *your* life and happiness. It's not fair, just like Mama!'

'I'm not Mama!'

Sonnet sat back, breathing heavily, alert to the dangerous undercurrent of emotion in her sister's features. This was the moment, in any conflict, at which Fable would inevitably flee and hide.

Olive had burst onto the veranda at the moment of impasse. She looked between the sisters in abject horror.

We're here now; might as well score the point before Fable's security detail escorts me out . . .

'You don't have to keep an illegitimate baby, you can *choose*!'

'I am, Sonnet – I'm choosing my baby.'

'It's not a stray kitten you keep because you're lonely!'

'You don't get to control this.'

'It'll be a bastard, just like we were – why would you want that for it?'

'Sonnet!' exclaimed Olive.

But on, Sonnet bludgeoned. 'Haven't you had enough of the shame and the struggle and the hardship? *Your* life can finally be different. *You* don't have to exist that way!'

'*Enough!*' Olive cried, throwing herself into the fray. 'Fable wants to keep her child. And she's got nothing, absolutely *nothing* to be ashamed of.'

Sonnet spun on Olive, rage springing forth unexpectedly. 'You've got a hide to lecture *me* on shame! Your religion has been drowning improper women in shame for aeons! Your bloody father rejected his own daughter for *shame*! Your church excommunicated her! You didn't have anything to say *then* in Mama's defence, did you?'

Olive collapsed into a chair with a guttural cry.

Fable shook her head in a slow lament, hands cradling her belly. 'Why is this so hard for you to accept, Sonny? You're doing the same thing as Grandfather. *You* want me to give up my baby, too – only you're couching it in concern for my "career" and ability to make money, rather than my morality. And it's all the same anyway – a woman's value, determined by others. You're just a hypocrite.'

'No, it's only freedom *I* want for you! Unlike the rest of the bloody do-gooders in this family.'

'Oh, Sonnet, stop!' Olive cried. 'Will you please just *stop*!'

Plum appeared at the door in her nightgown – ablaze, agape. The table collapsed into winded silence.

Still Fable stayed.

'Wait, Fable,' Sonnet said, softening. 'Wait a couple of years to get established and *then* tie yourself down to motherhood! Just, wait.'

'I *am* waiting!' Fable cried, eyes wild with anguish. 'You have no idea! Waiting is all I have left!'

Sonnet turned to Olive. 'I said my piece. She's all yours now.'

It was Sonnet who fled from the table first.

Sonnet was high atop the ladder, when the doorbell tinkled open. 'Be right with you!' she called, stretching precariously to shelve a book. She should have moved the ladder first – never did, though, no time. She was anchored by only a single leg now – capri pants stretching wide, the tightness of her sleeve constricting her arm's reach. The ladder wobbled as she thrust out one last time, grunting.

'Good morning, Miss Hamilton,' came a voice below, and the ladder lurched perilously. She had no time to cry out, before a hand below moored the ladder to the ground.

Sonnet disguised an exhalation of relief and turned to thank her customer.

Dr Fairley was looking up at her, amusement in his eyes. 'In my professional opinion, that's not physical activity I would recommend, all things considered.'

'How very Victorian of you.'

'Just wait till I prescribe leech therapy for your head injury when you hit the floor!'

She wobbled the ladder, deadpan.

'However,' he added, 'in my non-professional opinion, while you're up there, would you mind grabbing me that copy of *Catch-22* by Joseph Heller?'

Sonnet handed the book down. 'Have you read this yet?'

'It's one of my new favourites, actually. And I need a good book or three now – nobody warned me you don't have television yet in Far North Queensland.'

'We entertain ourselves in Noah.' She descended the ladder. 'I hear it keeps the birth rate up, though.'

She stood eye to eye with him now, and felt a hot current run into her tummy. It was rare to meet a man on equal standing, even rarer to feel diminutive, as she did in his nearness.

'What else would you recommend for a fan of *Catch-22*?'

'Let me think,' Sonnet said, not having to think about it at all. It was one of her favourite books. '*One Flew Over the Cuckoo's Nest*?'

'Read it, loved it. More?'

'*Brave New World*?'

'Brilliant book. What next?'

'*Vile Bodies*.'

'Finished it a couple of months ago. Most excellent.'

'You sound like the perfect reader for *Lucky Jim*, then.'

Now she had him.

'I was.'

It wasn't considered good custom for a bookseller to glare at a customer, though that didn't stop her. *Must* he be so well read?

While she mulled further, scanning her shelves, irony crept into his tone. 'Maybe a story about a woman in a catch-22 situation?'

Sonnet turned narrow eyes on him. Blood pounded in her ears. 'If I had permission to give out a story like that,' she said slowly, 'it wouldn't be a catch-22 situation, would it?'

Did she mistake the relief on his face?

'At least,' she appended, 'I don't yet.'

He nodded, in perfect comprehension.

Silence ballooned.

Dr Fairley gazed round her store, nodding to himself. 'You've got it here, too.'

'What?'

'That wistful, achy feeling you feel in bookstores.'

Sonnet raised a brow.

'No, it's a good thing – a longing.'

'You mean *biblioepithumia*.'

'There's a word for it?'

335

'Nope. I squashed that one together myself to mean "intense yearning or desire for books". Or maybe . . . "book lust". One of my favourite creations, though. You may borrow it. Unless your particular brand of bookstore wistfulness is related to the stockpiling of books never read, in which case the Japanese already have a word for that: *tsundoku*.'

'You know your stuff,' he said, eyes crinkling

'I was lucky to have a word-loving mentor.' She took the book from his hands, and marched to the till.

'By the way,' he said, 'I sent a reminder letter to your home address last week. Did that arrive?'

The cassowary over his shoulder caught her eyes. Sonnet bit her tongue, lest she poke it. 'Yes, I got it. You're most thorough, thank you.'

'I hope it will be useful. If not for you, someone else . . .'

Sonnet extended a hand.

He felt for his wallet, sliding out a paper note. 'I actually had to get directions in town to the bookstore. Turns out you can't ask the way to Hamilton's Books without getting a local history lesson first.'

'Didn't take you long to stumble over the deadwood in town, after all.'

'And I'm led to understand you also have two younger sisters.'

Sonnet shook open a bag, harder than necessary. 'Are you looking for new patients, Doctor?'

'Seems I might have lost a patient a few minutes ago – may have to open my books to another.'

She handed over his parcel. 'If I can persuade anyone in particular to see a doctor, you'll be the first one I call, Dr Fairley.'

He smiled, hefting the bag under his arm, relief now plain to see. 'It's Jake, please.'

Jake Fairley.

She nodded tightly. 'Thanks for coming, enjoy your book.'

At the door he turned back, warmth in his smile.

In lieu of returning it, in flagrant defiance of her resolve, she heard herself blurt: 'Jake! Dr Fairley, I mean. Do you . . . Would you happen to do house calls?'

Sonnet was washing her plate and fork after dinner when the knock came. Standing on the dark porch, with a low, sultry moon at her back, was Fable.

'Everything okay?'

'I wanted to come down and thank you.'

'Thank *me*? For what?'

'Dr Fairley came by Heartwood to see me this afternoon.'

'Oh yes.'

'He sure mentions *your* name a lot.'

Sonnet shrugged. 'Man's trying to pick up new patients; I found him one. I'm just glad you didn't throw him out of the door. How did it go?'

'He said everything's progressing fine now. Baby's healthy, I'm healthy. But it's a big baby . . . might even come earlier than my dates.'

'Yikes.'

'He's referring me to the midwives up at Cairns Base Hospital for the birth.'

'Yes, I imagine so. None of the women here give birth in Noah.'

'He's going to do my antenatal appointments, so I don't have to drive all the way up for every appointment. My booking-in appointment at the hospital is in two days.'

'Great.'

'Yeah . . . I guess . . ' Fable regarded her belly, biting her lip. Sonnet stared at the strawberry part of her hair, waiting.

'The thing is,' Fable said, 'I don't want to go up there on my own. But I don't want Olive and Gav to take me, either . . .'

'Yes, I can,' Sonnet volunteered unsmilingly.

Fable's eyes were wide. 'Are you sure?'

'Don't be stupid, 'course I'll take you.'

'Thank you,' Fable said, voice small. 'I'll feel better, if you're there. I know *you'll* make me stand up for myself. Even if you don't agree with me – you'll make me stick up for myself.'

Sonnet laughed, with gusto. 'Sorry,' she said, stilling her mouth, 'but that's pretty funny to hear.'

Fable's face gave nothing away.

'Okay. Yes. I'll make you stick up for yourself – no matter what anyone says about anything. Deal?'

Fable nodded gratefully, but made no move to leave.

Sonnet's hands went to her hips. 'Was there something else?'

Fable stepped aside, and Sonnet saw the pile of bags behind her. 'Are you going somewhere?'

Fable raised doe eyes.

'But you *can't* be serious.'

Fable's eyes widened further, a tremble at her lashes.

'Well,' Sonnet scowled, 'I can see how you landed in your predicament in the first place – using eyes like that. Won't work on *me*, though.'

A smile moved behind Fable's downturned lips.

'*Fine*,' Sonnet sighed. 'Come in, then. But I've already eaten, you can cook your own dinner for two . . .'

CHAPTER 37

ENCIENTE

Summer 1964

But why, Sonnet yearned to ask, as her sister unpacked, humming, in the sunroom, *would you choose querulous me over grovelling Olive*? Olive would probably have anointed Fable's feet with oil each evening if she'd stayed there.

Awkwardly, they danced round Fable's belly when passing in the narrow kitchen and hallway. Sonnet fumed in silence – how could Fable possibly prefer this tiny cottage to *Heartwood's* sprawling rooms?

As Fable fashioned a careful nest for all her paints and brushes, journals and sketchbooks, Sonnet boggled: *Where exactly are you planning to put the damn baby?*

Who is he? Sonnet screamed soundlessly, at Fable's back each time she drifted into one of her window-pressing turns of gripping sadness.

If he hurt you, I swear I'll smash a glass in his bloody face.

She'd never had as many questions or wanted so badly to drag the answers out of Fable. She asked nothing. What was the point? Against Fable's barricaded heart, she'd never prevail.

They drove to Cairns through sweeping banana plantations and canefields as far as the eye could see, and past the sugar mill puffing white plumes into cumulus skies, like a cloud factory.

Still she asked no questions. She sat with Fable in the waiting area at Cairns Base, between blossoming bellies and rotten toddlers, and she didn't attempt to prep her sister on how to act or what to ask. Fable's name was called, and Sonnet stayed resolutely seated. When her sister turned doubtfully back, Sonnet mouthed, 'Good luck!' then looked back at her *New Idea* magazine, flipping a page with feigned ennui.

Afterwards, Sonnet didn't ask how the appointment went; only what Fable might want for lunch. Then she took her shopping at the Bolands department store; an anonymous realm, far from Noah Vale eyes. Fable still looked over her shoulder in the baby aisles, though – and Sonnet pretended not to notice. She trailed after Fable, nodding blankly at the rompers and rattles picked out. Sonnet frothed behind her mild smile as she watched Fable hand wads of her Brisbane-earned notes over at the checkout. *How are you going to afford to raise a child in Noah?*

Sonnet was silent once more on the ride home – no longer from resentful self-restraint, rather exhaustion on her sister's behalf.

They cruised back along Main Street and Fable slipped down in the passenger seat, pulling her baseball hat low, bags across her belly. Sonnet clenched the wheel. Whatever plans Fable had devised for the moment she was finally discovered home, and knocked up, they were not Sonnet's to know, much less interfere with. She heard Fable's violent inhalation at the sight of Delia Hull and Marg Johnstone crossing the road ahead, their coiffured French rolls leaning close. Sonnet let the women and indeed the moment pass without a single snide comment hurled Delia's way.

They were making their ascent to Heartwood when, unexpectedly, Fable spoke.

'You know, Dr Fairley isn't actually the first doctor I've seen.'

Sonnet fought back a scream: *I know nothing – nothing!* 'OK.'

'I saw a doctor once in Sydney. About my bleeding.'

Bleeding?!

'I knew I was pregnant really quickly, because my boobs just wouldn't stop growing. Plus I felt seedy all the time, and tired – *so* tired. But mostly it was these boobs.' Fable ran hands over her chest in wonder. 'It was like being sixteen all over again, as if my body had gone into a second puberty.'

'And then you saw a doctor,' Sonnet said, leaning to tidy her hair in the rear-view mirror, drilling her own reflection with a warning glare.

'No, not for a while. Because then I started bleeding, you see. I thought my period was coming, after all. But it was so heavy! I swear I filled a toilet bowl one day.'

'Oh, Fabes.'

'It wasn't painful, though. And I didn't have cramps. It just . . . didn't stop. Every day, I bled. For days, and weeks, for nearly four months! Every town we visited, each state line we crossed, I was bleeding. Some days were bright red, other days it was old, brown blood. I thought I couldn't possibly stay pregnant after all that bleeding. But I went to see a doctor in Sydney anyway, mainly because of the boobs. They still got bigger, despite my bleeding.

'The doctor was really dismissive, and he talked so fast, right over the top of me, like he wasn't even listening or I didn't know what I was on about. It was so confusing. But he said I was definitely miscarrying, there was no baby anymore; it would stop soon. So I went back to my room, changed my pad, and I waited.'

The plantation house rose regally before them. Olive's new black Staffy, Tess, came scuttling towards the Holden. Olive herself appeared on the grand sweep of the veranda, foot worrying at her calf. Fable fell silent as she started gathering her bags.

'I'll help you with the stuff in the boot,' Sonnet said.

Fable shrugged, her face smoothing over once more.

They stood at the clothesline together, heat trickling down their backs, pegging white terry squares, muslin wraps and yellow singlets.

'The bleeding eventually stopped,' Fable said, words materialising out of nowhere, 'but the fear didn't. Even after my belly button popped out, and I started feeling those fish-like flurries inside – the quickening – still I was convinced it would all be over any moment. I was growing my baby in thin, fruitless soil, and any second it would fall right out of me.'

Sonnet had two pegs between her lips – a useful gag. She flapped another nappy over the line, listening.

'Once the baby started moving, my fear only intensified. It made me cry, and I begged it to stop moving so much. All I could think was: the poor little thing's just trying to hold on, even as the earth is slipping away beneath her.'

'Haa?' Sonnet asked around pegs.

Fable's hands slid from breast to pubic bone. 'I got bigger and bigger. Her kicks became stronger, all the time. She was fighting to stay – even if I just couldn't believe I'd hold on to her.'

Sonnet clucked, eyes filling.

'But I had to give her a chance, Sonny. And the only one I believed she had was coming home. If I could just get her into the waters of Serpentine Creek, I told myself, it would bind us up. Then I could keep her.'

Sonnet reached for Fable's trembling shoulders.

'I knew you'd be angry, Sonnet. I knew the hopes you'd always had for me. But I had to come home. She belongs here, too. If I could save her, I thought it would all be worth it; all the recrimination, all your disappointment in me. I had to come home.'

Sonnet held Fable's head against her throat, closing her eyes over tears hot as the sun above.

'Once I got her into Serpentine Creek, only then did I start to believe it might be all right. See, she's safe here. She grows so strong now – and she kicks harder and happier in the creek than at any other time.'

'Probably just the cold water.'

'No. She's a Hamilton. She's home.'

'What did Kate have?' Fable asked, watching Sonnet paint her toenails for her after a foot scrub and massage.

'A girl.'

'What did she call her?'

'Amber. After a book I sold her once.' Oh, how Sonnet had laughed over that one.

'And how's it going for her?'

'It goes at all times of night, she hardly gets a minute to bathe and her useless husband wants to have another one already.'

'Did she have a christening or anything? With all the Hardys . . . and the cousins and everyone?'

'Don't have the faintest, Fabes – why don't you phone and ask her about all the baby stuff?'

'No! Don't you *dare* tell her about me!'

'It was just an idea. You know Kate – she'd love to talk your ear off.'

Fable frowned at her pearly toes. 'You messed up that toe.'

'Those who can't reach their own feet shouldn't criticise those who can.'

They were washing up together at the sink: melamine weaning bowls and spoons mixed in among their grandmother's ancient crockery.

'Tell me again, why didn't you want any bottles or dummies?' Sonnet asked, turning a tiny fork over in her tea towel.

'Because I'm going to breastfeed and I don't want to confuse the baby with other nipples.'

Sonnet had a flashing image of other women pushing their nipples into her niece's mouth. 'Babies can get confused about that?'

'Are you reading *any* of the passages I've been marking out for you?'

Sonnet glanced at the kitchen table – birth and baby book high-rises under rapid development – and cleared her throat. 'It's only my job to procure the books, isn't it?'

'You are the worst aunt she's ever had.'

'At least *I* know about her.'

Fable surprised Sonnet with genuine laughter. 'Right place, right time, that's all.'

'See, there you go, sweetie,' Sonnet crooned, reaching to pat the belly pushing close to her own. 'Aunty Sonnet is always right.'

Day by day, in this way, the walls were coming down – and a whole new enclosure going up around the sisters, one built with tiny stacks of infant clothing, piles of fresh linen, hospital-stay suitcases mounted by the door; the daily growing amity which confounded their aunt, and younger sister.

They were carting mail-order parcels home from Heartwood together. Sonnet carried the largest, containing a new white wicker bassinet. They'd had to fight off Olive's heirloom Hamilton cot first. 'Hideously old-fashioned!' was the shot with which Sonnet had finally won the battle, as Fable nodded apologetically at her elbow.

'I don't want you to be worried about what I'm spending, Son.'

'I'm not. You have your share of Mama's money. And your own savings. Plus, I'm sure you have . . . other things in the works.'

'Thank you for saying that,' Fable said, stopping.

Sonnet turned, heaving the bassinet up, all ears.

'I am still working. I have books I'll be collaborating on in the near future, and I have my own dreams, still. You need to know I can work from here just as well as I can in faraway Brisbane. This is just like . . . an intermission.'

'Okay.'

'Okay?'

'Yep. Okay.'

Dr Fairley, having been once more to see Fable, was striding back up the hill to Heartwood, leather bag under an arm. Sonnet watched from the bay window, her belly heavy and warm. Having Jake inside her domain – tall and brown and smelling, somehow, of green apples and zinc – had been comforting, intimate. She hadn't wanted the low murmuring voices in Fable's bedroom to cease, or the bedroom door to open, or Jake to ever leave.

'Do you reckon he'll make it home safely?' Fable's voice, at her shoulder. 'Should you follow him, just to be sure?'

The sarcasm startled a blush right out of Sonnet.

'Don't be stupid. He's your *doctor*.'

'Too bad, because I know that look.'

'What look?'

'The one on your face. I've felt it, too.' When Sonnet didn't answer, Fable pinched her waist. 'Actually, I'm beginning to worry there are better doctors in town, but maybe you just picked the dishiest one.'

'I never!' Sonnet cried, turning indignantly. 'We didn't have a choice!'

'Oh boy, do I know that look . . .'

They sat in heat-hampered silence on the lounge each night with matching topknots. Sweat sprang from their graceful Hamilton necks, running long beneath their shirts, gathering under their knees. The rainforest stirred restlessly. Geckos chased each other, clucking noisily, round the walls.

Sonnet was pretending to read one of Fable's books, but was really watching the way Fable's hand stroked her baby unconsciously, unceasingly.

On Fable's lap, below the more important work of her belly, lay a sketch pad. Every time Fable picked up her pen, it went back to the same point – a dark full stop, bleeding into the page.

As was their new pattern, Fable started talking without preamble.

'It's not his fault. It's mine.'

Sonnet strove to fill the gaps, leaping blindly: 'Nonsense! It takes two to tango.'

Fable sighed, and tried again. 'No. This.' She waved a hand around the cottage. 'That I'm here, and your problem.'

'You're not a problem, Fabes. Not to me.'

'You wouldn't have to deal with me crashing back in on your empty nest, asking you to help me go through with it, especially all this secrecy, if it wasn't for my cowardice.'

'Actually, I've never met a braver person.'

Fable sank over her belly. 'I'm not, you have *no* idea.'

Silence reigned for an agonising minute.

Sonnet meted out her words cautiously. 'If he *hurt* you . . . if that's what happened . . . I'll wring his bloody neck.'

'No. He didn't hurt me.'

Sonnet frowned.

Fable drew a sob back into her chest. 'I am hurting, though. More than I ever imagined possible.'

Sonnet pressed her temple against her sister's, summoning the attack dog back on its ever-shortening leash. *Who*, barked that beast of fury, *who, who, who!*

When she glanced once more at Fable's sketch pad, she saw it was not a full stop, but a comma.

CHAPTER 38

BUILD-UP

High summer came on as a grill – blisteringly; all at once. The worst build-up Noah had seen in decades, everyone said down the street, as they panted air so thick with humidity it was like drowning in a sauna. It's going to be a Big Wet, they promised each other. Clouds foamed high and black over the mountains, rumbling impotently; sunsets ran blood red; bats dropped dead from the sky; the rainforest screeched for its due.

The rains did not fall.

'Insufferable!' Sonnet declared, taking her third shower of the morning; perspiration leaching out of her skin before the water had even dried. Her hair never dried.

'And why do you keep shutting these windows, Fabes?' she demanded, pushing open the pane, desperate for air. 'Are you trying to broil us alive?'

'I'm not, I thought it was *you*,' Fable said, coming up the hall in nothing but a breast-wrapping sarong. She parked herself an inch from the pedestal fan, with a vibrating sigh. Sonnet watched, transfixed, as Fable coiled her hair up slowly at her crown; every ripe curve silhouetted against the window light.

'Rain, just rain, bloody Hughie!' Sonnet beseeched the sky. '*You're* the fertility goddess!' she muttered, turning on Fable. 'Get out there and do a naked rain dance for us.'

Yellow sunbirds were building a nest on the crystal wind chime outside the bay window, made of grasses and spider webs – with long strands of red hair wound into the construction. A Hercules moth, with wing-span wider than a book, had taken up residence on the porch. Each night she flapped frantically at the front door.

Sonnet was under *siege*!

On Christmas Night, explosions drew Fable and Sonnet to the porch. They sat on the front stoop in silence, watching fireworks flower over the dark wall of rainforest. Iridescent Christmas beetles flew in a metallic frenzy around the porch light.

'Looks like the rumours in town are true, then,' Sonnet said as they followed a screaming rocket skywards, holding their breath for the pop. 'That Hull boy, whatshisname, must be home for Christmas.'

A star burst overhead.

Sonnet watched the sparks cascade, realising Fable had not exhaled. She turned to look at her sister. Fable was preternaturally still; the tautness of her posture belying the soft curves of her body.

Sonnet stared at her fine profile, frowning. After a strained silence, punctuated only by whistling blasts, she said, 'Word is he's been in a Very Expensive Sober House in Sydney since his dramatic little disappearance. It was around your book launch. Do you remember?'

Fable said nothing.

'If you ask me,' Sonnet sniffed, 'the bloody Hulls orchestrated the whole performance, trying to overshadow your big launch.'

Fable's eyes were fixed unblinkingly on the sky.

Sonnet turned back to watch the next firework bloom – her mind spinning, spinning, spinning; ending up nowhere.

It was the last Friday of the year. Sonnet clattered home through the low, heat-seared cane, old Queenslanders growing farther apart with every mile. Sweat sluiced off her pinking skin, and she hankered for the forest shade. The runner who came alongside her from an adjoining alleyway did so with such beaming pride, she couldn't help but laugh.

'And where are you off to in such a hurry?'

'I would say following *you* home, but looks like I'm going to beat you there.'

Jake took off at a sprint. Sonnet gasped resentfully, pedalling hard after him, and then beyond his long stride.

He was beaten but not slowed. She decelerated, allowing him to stay just within reach, quickening whenever he came too near. By this method, they continued on to the winding creek-side trail.

'Why are you coming out our way?' Sonnet asked, easing off; gratified to observe his pace slow to match hers. 'You only just saw Fabes last Friday.'

'We're down to weekly appointments now.'

'Already! She's only eight months along.'

'Thirty-five weeks, and almost fully engaged.'

'Is that bad?'

'It's not uncommon for a first baby. It's not particularly comfortable, either.'

'Yeah, she's getting around like there's a bowling ball about to roll out between her legs.'

'I think many women are shocked when it doesn't simply drop out. Apparently, feels like the bowling ball has to be blown uphill, instead.'

'And she reckons it's a big baby, too. Poor Fabes!'

'She's a tough cookie, that sister of yours.'

'I know.'

'This humidity!' he exclaimed abruptly. 'How does anyone do anything in it? We need a twenty-four-hour siesta.'

'Southerner!' Sonnet disparaged. She stood out of her saddle and pumped hard beyond him, aware of how well her long thighs and toned glutes looked in a sprint.

When Jake caught her – breathing hard, with a brow-raising smile – it was with a challenge of his own. 'How about no head starts this time?'

'You're on.'

Sonnet dropped her bike, arms akimbo.

They considered each other for a mutually appraising moment. The slight forward tilt of her head acted as starting pistol – they took off. Sonnet dived ahead of him on the narrow trail, scheming to monopolise the middle path. She suspected he'd be too much of a gentleman to push by her, and was not wrong. Hot on her tail, he stayed; panting hard at her back, feet falling in long-legged, near-perfect unison with hers.

'There are no overtaking lanes on my runs!' she puffed.

'I'm happy back here.'

She slowed only when they reached the overarching bridge of a fallen tree. They both came to a stop, panting against the pungent rot of rainforest overpass. Vivid orange fungi sprouted between their leaning hands. She had only to slide her hand over one, maybe two, and her fingers would rest on his.

He turned an admiring smile on her. 'You're pretty fast for . . .'

'A girl?!'

The parenthesis around his lips reached their full potential. 'No, actually, a cyclist.'

She hooted – most unglamorous of all possible laughs, but didn't have time to curb the sound before his honk covered her own.

'Back to the bike . . .' she said, growing wily-eyed.

He rocketed off first, hogging the path for himself. This time it was her turn to admire muscular calves and buttocks in full flight.

The next Friday afternoon, he waited at her shopfront – sandshoes knotted, doctor's knapsack on, sweat already a dark semicircle at his polo collar. They set off in companionable silence. Sonnet did not speak until they were into the forest, well beyond the glare of sun and townsfolk, conversation finally their own.

'What will happen with the birth certificate? I mean, with the space marked "Father"?'

He looked at her oddly. 'That's entirely up to Fable.'

'But if she won't put a father's name down?'

He shrugged. 'It happens.'

Sonnet sighed, without meaning to. 'So, the poor blighter will be no different to any of us Hamilton girls, then, yet another to grow up under the curse of illegitimacy.'

'There are far worse things than not knowing who your father is, Sonnet. Like knowing him better than *any* child should have to, having an actual bastard of a father.'

She heard the child's anguish in his pant, and slowed. 'I'm sorry, Jake.'

He waved it away, ran on watching his feet. 'It drove me into a profession where I thought I might be able *mend* broken bones and hearts.'

Sonnet blinked away a mental image of his hands on her bones.

'And I was fortunate to experience the fierce love of a single mother. Nothing quite like that strength, that devotion.'

'*Yes*,' she said, remembering it with more clarity than she had in years.

They breathed together for several minutes, sweat a not-unpleasant miasma between them.

'Where is she now – your mum?'

'Graveyard,' he said, already smiling before she could be embarrassed. 'Two years now. Part of the reason I came, grieving, to the wilds of Far North Queensland.'

'So we're both orphans.'

'Well, near enough. Some men don't deserve a second, third or fiftieth chance.'

'Some men don't even get their first chance.'

'Do you *wish* you'd known him?'

She rubbed at a patch of rust on her handlebars. 'Only since I came to Noah Vale, and only because the stories of him live so strongly here. I'm tired of being the passive beneficiary. Even my mother lied about him all her life. I'd like to have my own stories.'

'Have you ever tried?'

'How?'

'Make contact with his family? Ask. Then wind those tales into your own story, keeping them as long or short as you please, or not at all.'

She frowned at him. 'I thought you were a doctor, not a shrink.'

The following Friday, Jake didn't show. Sonnet waited, sweating, on her front step, watching his unit above the surgery, until rippling clouds crimsoned across the vale and the bat legions soared over.

'Stupid, desperate idiot,' she castigated herself, pushing off the stoop. Of course she hadn't been stood up. He was her sister's doctor, not *her* dishy date.

Nonetheless, she smarted all the way down Main Street.

Electric hum and muggy gloom pressed in on Sonnet as she pedalled, manically, alongside the creek. Shadows sprang, branches whipped at her face, sticks under wheels snapped up to bite at her ankles. Oh, for a headlamp! She jutted her chin harder still against her thudding cowardice; and the ache of humiliation.

A dark figure loomed in her pathway. Sonnet shrieked, tried to brake, and went flying over the handlebars, crash-landing among roots and rocks.

She lay winded, in a world of pain. Slowly she rolled to half sitting, looking for her accoster.

There he was, still planted unyieldingly on the path. But not a man, worse, a visage straight out of her nightmares: a towering cassowary, with its antediluvian eye fixed upon her.

Never turn your back on a cassowary, she heard Gav say. *Back away slowly. Never run. Do not make yourself appear bigger than you are.*

Sonnet whimpered, unable to move for pain, waiting for the bird to garrotte her, ear to ear. He waited too, with a velociraptor's cold grace and beauty. He tilted his helmeted head to the side, heavily lashed eye boring into hers, red wattles swinging.

Sonnet squeezed her eyes shut, expecting at any moment the leap – talons thrust forward – a scarlet smile opening at her creamy throat.

Terror pounded under her ribcage. A scream gathered at her throat. When she squinted open again, there were three small, striped birds at his feet.

His babies.

The chicks skittered across the pathway, disappearing between the trees. Sonnet bowed her head against the ground, shrouding her eyes from his maddening amber stare.

Please leave me alone.

Leave me alone.

Leave me.

Leave.

At last, the heavy crunch of leaf litter as he moved ponderously away, and silence.

Oppressive blackness had dropped by the time she groaned to her feet and hobbled to her fallen bike. Her limbs were all scraped up; how badly she couldn't tell. Her bike was damaged. Her heart must have beat right through a rib, based on the pain each breath took. The worst was the humiliation of her long, slow limp back into town to her bookshop. She didn't dare go the way of the cassowary on this starless night.

Sonnet dumped her bike unceremoniously on the stoop, wobbled through the door and flipped the lights back on with a stifled sob. She hadn't cried yet; she wouldn't start now.

Sonnet stood boldly before her cassowary, aching all over.

'What do you *want* from me?!'

His implacable stare went unblinkingly on.

'And where's my first-aid kit, you bloody useless bird,' she cursed, scrounging under the counter.

The knock at the door made her yelp. It was, of all people, *Jake*. She felt the sob, still caught in her throat, threatening to dislodge.

She nodded ascent to his mimed request, and the door jangled open.

'Saw your lights on. I was just on my way back from Heartwood.'

'You went without me?'

His brow corrugated. 'I left you a note on your door at lunchtime! Didn't you get it? I wanted to let you know I'd drive out today.'

Sonnet pushed back against the urge to blubber.

'I thought it might be better to meet you there in future. I'm sorry, Son.'

Sonnet shrugged, finally locating the kit.

Jake seemed to take in her condition at the same instant she retrieved the medical kit, emblazoned with serpent-entwined rod.

'What have you done to yourself?' he cried, immediately at her side, lifting her arm gently.

'Nothing. Just went a gutser over the handlebars.'

'Geez, look at the skin you've taken off. Come, sit here.' His hands went around her waist, lifting her effortlessly onto a bar stool. Sonnet tugged a corner of her lip into her teeth as he began his ministrations.

The man kneeling at her feet, unzipping the first-aid kit with cool expertise: that was the last straw.

She broke.

Jake worked quickly and unflinchingly through her shoulder-racking sobs to assess, clean and cover each wound. His professional mantle did not waver – though if Sonnet could have seen through her tears, she might have noted the tremble in his hands, and how he pressed them periodically against his chino pants to still them.

'There we go,' he said, looking up again. 'No major harm. You'll be right as rain in a few days.'

Her gaze remained over his head, unfocused: blue and red and black and amber distorted by tears.

'Are you okay, Son?'

'Fine.'

'Like hell you are.'

She looked at the man still on his haunches before her, head tilted with concern – antithesis of the painted face above him – and smiled fondly. A single pearl of sweat ran from clavicle to belly button. The scent of books mingled with iodine and musk of man.

Jake cleared his throat. 'After Fable delivers, hopefully not too long from now, I was hoping you might be able to find another family doctor.'

'*What?*'

'Maybe one in Cairns, or Innisfail.'

'*Why?*'

He seemed to taste his words carefully before they were ready to leave his lips. He laid a hand on a non-bandaged portion of calf. Sparks leapt along her skin, setting points alight at groin, belly, bosom.

'Sonnet Hamilton, I would very much like to not be your family doctor, so I can kiss you, instead.'

'Seems like an awfully long way for me to have to drive, just to get a kiss.'

'I'm a rather good kisser.'

'You'd better bloody be.'

Alone in her bookshop again, now nursing an unrequited thirst in the pit of her being, Sonnet went to stand once more before her cassowary. So many hours she'd stared him down and yet never before had she noticed that dark shadow within the bird's right eye; in the bottom of the iris. It had only occurred to her this evening, after seeing those eyes in the flesh.

She grabbed a print magnifying glass from her desk and placed it over the amber orb. The shadow shimmered like a mirage, seemed to dance and flicker and leap, before finally differentiating into a circle of text.

A hidden signature . . .

Archer L. Brennan, 1935.

Her father, the year of her birth.

CHAPTER 39

THE SERPENT

January 1965

Plum knew where Fable got the baby. Plum had seen, that night, the lights in the forest: first, just the one – dancing across the field, weaving lightly between the trees – then the second, striding out, converging on the first. They'd whirled sharply into a single light, and disappeared.

Fable had gone away on the train the next day, and nobody mentioned any of the lights Plum saw. She had been relieved, for Fable's sake.

But then Fable came home again, and all hell had broken loose. Because Fable was pregnant, and she wasn't married!

Babies born outside wedlock were a 'monstrous problem' in society – it had said so in Olive's book, the one she had given Plummy some months back, when asked how babies were made.

Plum had stared at Fable across the dinner table, trying to imagine her sister in contortions of monstrous-problem-making until Fable had tossed a bread roll at her and told her to take a picture because it would last longer.

Since then, Plum had watched Fable sitting longingly by the window, all pent up and sputtering, and she'd known Fable was thinking about the forest, and the lights.

Plum wondered if Fable knew just how much trouble she was in now.

When Fable moved to the cottage to be with Sonnet, but really to be closer to the creek, a terrible thought occurred to Plum: perhaps Fable could actually *die* in childbirth, punishment for this abominable thing she'd let happen to her. Women did die, all the time! Plum had seen it in movies, read it in books. Ergo, childbirth could also kill Fable.

It was up to Plum to protect her.

Ever since, Plum had been keeping vigilant guard over the cottage, and over Fable. She closed and locked the cottage windows whenever she found them open, and sealed the front gate with vine. She filched a box of nails from Uncle Gav and dropped them in a perfect perimeter around the cottage fence. Three times a day, compulsively, Plum performed her checks on the cottage – plus once more after she'd been sent to bed. She didn't miss a single check.

Which was how she came, one sweltering morning, to find the serpent.

As she passed the cottage, creek-side, there it was: the iridescent sheen of an amethystine python, coiled beneath the dove orchid. It was thicker than a man's arm, with a waiting maw wide enough for Plum herself.

When Plum flapped onto the veranda at Heartwood, crying alarm, it was already an outpost of urgency. Her shouts were lost in the general commotion. Gav was boarding up windows and Olive was atop a ladder, removing hanging ferns. Sonnet was unpacking bags of canned food, divvying them into piles, distracted thoughts playing across her brow. Fable was nowhere to be seen.

'What's going *on?*' she asked, cross at their indifference.

'The red pennant is out in front of the post office. The Wet's finally coming in, on the front of a monster cyclone.'

Cyclone. Any other day, that word alone would have tipped her into a wretched terror. But today, she had even worse news to break.

'Uncle Gav, there's a giant python at the cottage!'

'Ay?'

'A snake – a horrible, horrible snake. Down the cottage. You've *got* to come!'

'Inside, is he?'

Sonnet and Olive didn't even look up.

'*Uncle Gav!*'

'All right, Plum-pie. Gimme a sec.'

Gav crashed through greenery while Plum shrieked at him from the cottage gate not to go any closer.

'Do you want me to find him or not?' her uncle asked, pitchfork gently pushing aside a prolific shower of white flowers.

'Big rain on the way,' he said. 'The dove orchid hasn't flowered like this in decades.'

'Uncle Gav!' Plum cried, stomping.

'Ah, here he is. Geez he's the biggest one I've ever seen. Might be over twenty feet long, what a *beauty* you've got!'

'He's not *mine*! Uncle Gav, *take it away*!'

'No need. He'll take off himself to find shelter from the storm soon enough.'

'What if he tries to shelter inside? Would you get rid of it!'

Her uncle stood a moment admiring the python. He rapped on Fable's bedroom wall, just above it. 'You in there, Beauty? Seen your visitor out here?'

Gav stepped back from the orchid, its tiny birds falling into place once more. 'Come on, we've got more than enough to keep us busy at Heartwood. And you, little miss, have got chores to start on. Let's go.'

Just before the gate squealed shut behind them, Gav mused: 'It's funny, though, that snake turning up right now.'

'What do you mean?'

'Nothin' really. Just, there used to be an old wives' tale you'd hear in Noah, years ago, 'bout them big pythons turning up on properties, just in time for mother's milk. Apparently, they've got a taste for it. Or maybe it's the smell of a woman full of baby. Anyway, women used to say: if your wee babe's just not thriving, all skin and bones, fadin' away, best you check them rafters above for a big healthy-looking snake.'

'But how would they get a mother's milk . . .' Plum trailed off. 'Oh, I see.'

'Look out,' said Gav, 'here comes breakfast again!'

CHAPTER 40

FLAMES OF THE FOREST

Voices in the garden, just beneath the sunroom window, wrenched Fable out of sleep. She rolled with an unwilling groan, finding herself sticky with sweat, with a heavy discharge at her groin. She didn't want to get up – not now, not ever. She just couldn't seem to escape the heavy lassitude of the last few days. A piquantly sweet odour pervading the sheets made Fable swipe between her thighs: gloopy, blood-streaked yellow jelly came up on her fingers.

Showtime.

Fable dressed in the only thing left to fit her: one of Grandmother Lois's hideous floral dresses. Her faerie-tale green gown was a thousand years ago, another life entirely.

One she must summon forth now.

She slipped out of the garden gate and on towards the creek line; oversaturated green against the blue-black sky fast encroaching. Heat was a wall, pushing back. Her feet burned on the grass. She struggled to even draw breath.

Quickly now, quickly!

Fable guzzled cool air as forest shade fell blessedly upon her. To the bridge she went, hearkening for the river rush. Never had she seen Serpentine Creek so depleted.

Summerlinn, seen across the bridge, glowed vividly – the last vale of sunshine holding out against the storm.

'Come,' Fable whispered. 'Come home.'

She smoothed the floral monstrosity over a bump much lower than the night before. She stared at her belly, past the mothballed flowers, allowing her eyes to lose focus. Slowly the vintage print unravelled, blurred into peridot lichen, morphed back to tiny waist and flat stomach, flowed to her feet, spread with iridescent sparkles.

When she looked up again, a spangled net of darkness had fallen over the bridge. A figure stood on the bridge, in a ring of lamplight, waiting.

She raised her own lamp, peering.

'Oh it's *you*!' she said, taking a step onto the first sleeper.

Raff stopped halfway across the bridge. 'Is the party over?' He raised the copy of *Faerie Falls* in his hand. 'I wanted to come back and see you – I just finished reading your book.'

She took another step.

'It's everything you said it would be.'

'Not everything, Raff. There were a few pages omitted. Editorial decision – I still don't see the sense in it. They were my best ones.'

'Material for your next book?'

She advanced another sleeper; bolder now. 'I hope so. But why did you want to see me?' The buoyancy of her tone belied the tension of her throat.

Raff spoke with equally fragile lightness. 'I think there's something amiss with my copy.' He placed the lantern at his feet and opened the first pages of *Faerie Falls*. 'Here, on your dedication page – the one with the bonus handkerchief? Nice touch, by the way. But, unfortunately, my hanky has already been used.'

She'd traversed several sleepers as he spoke. They were only two apart.

He held up the cloth. 'You see?' Even in lantern glow, the hanky's imperfection was apparent, embroidered R long since unravelled.

'You were the only one who got a hanky, Raff.'

'I was wondering about *that*.'

Fable stepped onto the final rung before him. She stooped to place her lantern on the bridge. His eyes followed her every move.

When she straightened again, there was a wobble in her chin and voice. 'You're wrong, though. It's not used – just pre-loved.'

Her words hung in the shifting night air.

Raff grappled with his response. 'And so . . . the dedication . . . was for . . . ?'

Fable contemplated her answer. Her dedication was still true, and it wasn't. She understood this now. *Faerie Falls* had been for Mama and Raff equally – and the vital force sliding beneath them this very moment.

'Yes,' she said, 'for you.'

'But I thought it was just a schoolgirl crush,' he said, shaking his head.

'What part, exactly, didn't you understand at Moria Falls?'

'Adolescent passions are strong, but they rarely last. You were my kid sister's age. It wasn't the first time I'd seen that happen.'

'When did you see?'

His eyes were gentle. 'Your drawing, at Faerie Falls . . .'

Fable flushed but did not retreat.

'I thought you'd outgrow it,' he said, 'if I gave you half a chance.'

She shook tears away.

'I'm sorry I hurt you that night, Fable. It's tormented me since.'

She kept her eyes from him, watching the dark sheen of water coursing beneath.

'It felt like the lesser of two wrongs. For years I'd had you on a ... pedestal. I tried to look out for you. I *couldn't* take advantage of you, or expose you to hurt from my family.'

'Yet you were willing to hurt me, all the same.'

Fable's eyes fixed on the quickening rise and fall of his chest. Her own breath had long since shortened.

'You must understand: for a long time, I thought myself a grown man infatuated with a girl.'

'How long?' she asked, holding him to the point.

'You'd always had this sort of ... poise. A quiet strength and depth to you, different to anyone else. Then the year Iris hit us, you hit me. But you were only sixteen, and it made *me* no different to anyone else. So, I tried to stay away from Noah. I couldn't do that of all things, to you of all people.'

'Because of the brotherly protectiveness,' she said. *There* was the sting, still.

'No. There hasn't been anything brotherly in my heart of hearts – for a long time.'

Fable took one last step forward, to share his sleeper, trembling in his proximity, and under his ragged breath.

'It was a lover's protectiveness.'

She lifted eyes ashimmer. Raff's hands rose to her elbows. He held her for a long, steadying moment, then up along her bare arms his hands slid, unbearably slowly, raising goosebumps in their wake. She drew a breath, lips parting, and he lifted her chin near to his.

'It was because you're Fable of the Glade.'

She gave a little sigh and his mouth flew down upon hers. Her arms sprang to his neck, as much to possess him as to stop herself from falling. His kiss opened her, entered her, and went deeper still.

Along her skin his lips moved, to her ear. 'I was always waiting for you to grow up.'

She whimpered, and his mouth sought to cover the sound. Water rushed beneath their feet; eternal flow seeking ever a path of least resistance. One hand buried itself in her long tresses, the other slid to her lower back, pulling her firmly against him. Aching heat and moisture filled her groin. She moaned into his mouth, pressing nearer still, every curve lush against him. He groaned back, steadying her against the need threatening now to sweep them away.

She broke away. 'Raff, we have to get off the bridge.'

Together they went – half dancing, half stumbling – across the sleepers. On solid ground he rounded on her again. Her breasts arched high against him, pressing; her hands slid under his shirt to clutch at his back, pulling. His lips burned along her neck, her décolletage. She threw back her head. 'Please, Raff, please . . .'

'Where?' he gasped, capturing her face between his hands.

'Where else?' she said, enchanted.

Yes, where else could this night have led them, if not their starlit waterfall?

Raff's lantern was already hidden in the cave, transforming the waterfall into a flowing stream of gold.

He was treading water below her, waiting. Fable stood on the jutting ledge, as the canopy undulated in the balmy breeze. Soon, the first ribbons of dawn would ripple across the starry night, and birdsong begin. She would not make it home before the world awakened.

Their gaze held across the Glade – across the Cathedral, the ruins, crowd, boat, bridge – for this asking now, and her assent. Moonshine and lamplight glimmered in long waves of rose. Fable bent to place the lantern at her feet. Shadows danced up around the high rock basin as she twisted to unzip herself. Her gown fell: a silken slide from curve to aching curve, into a shimmering green puddle at her feet.

His desire was a flame leaping across the water, skimming her hardening nipples, to flare, hot, in her belly. Wordlessly, she stepped out of her faerie ring and descended the stone staircase into the pool.

Raff waited in the deep. What was one minute more, or two?

She stroked out to meet him and face to face they circled, panting as though they'd swum the length of the valley just to find one another. Behind him, the flame-lit falls tumbled into inky darkness. They could not stay treading water here, not when the weight of wanting might sink them both.

Side by side, they paddled over to find foothold before the waterfall. Only there did he give hesitant pause, turning back to her. She smiled at the boyish diffidence casting their roles in a sudden reversal, erasing the years between them.

'I'll be gentle,' he said, 'but it still might—'

'Nothing could hurt so much as *waiting* has.'

In a single, answering sweep she was cradled in his arms – cool and wet and hungering against him. She felt the shake in his grasp, and placed a steadying hand on his bare chest, over his thudding heart. 'Don't worry. It'll be just like—'

'Coming home,' he finished, stepping through into the hidden chamber.

The rushing curtain of light closed behind them, and the glade was still.

The cascade absorbed the forest song, the dipping bats and dripping leaves, and Raff's roar as he took Fable.

The long walk home, with her gown tucked up at her hips and hand cradled in his, for the most part, silent; every footstep another too close to home. Her body was tender and soft – a mango in fullest summer bloom, sticky with sap. She stole glances at Raff in quiet, marvelling memory of his face, contorted with the pleasure of being inside her. So there *was* an expression she loved more than his smile, after all.

'I'm coming home with you,' Raff said, without preamble. 'I should be there when you tell your family.'

She shrank to a stop. Concern creased his face at the sheer terror of hers.

'I can't, Raff. I don't want to tell anyone! It's just – too soon, and Sonnet will be . . . she'll say . . . *please* don't make me do that today!'

He gathered her to him. 'It's your secret to keep as long as you want. You let me know when you're ready.'

She breathed in his scent. 'I think I'd prefer to phone the news in from Brisbane, actually.'

He laughed. 'Can you at least give me warning before you do, so I can be prepared for Sonnet to turn up on our doorstep?'

She drew back, searching his face. 'Will you stay *on* in Noah then?'

'I'm still on compassionate leave here until . . . Dad . . .'

She raised a hand to his cheek, and he held it there, closing his eyes.

'I'll help with the harvest, too,' he said, voice rough, 'and we'll sort out the will and the rest of it. But after, I do have to go back to London, at least for a while. I'm in the middle of a few big projects. And you'll be on your tour anyway, then working in Brisbane.'

'I don't want to go! I'm staying here with you! I don't give two hoots about Brisbane.'

'I do. You're leaving today. No way I'm letting you abandon your dream for me.'

'You *are* my dream, Raff.'

'You're going, Fable.'

He brought her hand to his lips, his breath a hot stone in her palm. She shivered as heated slickness flooded between her legs once more.

'Again?' she asked hopefully.

He laughed. 'All day long, if it was up to me. I can't get enough of you. But you have to go back before we cause alarm.'

She sulked. He grew serious. 'Fable, I need you to understand, I *will* come back to Noah.'

'But – London?'

'Self-imposed exile doesn't serve me anymore.'

'What about your work?'

'I might have to design mango tree houses – at least until we figure something else out together.'

She hid her face in his chest. He stroked tendrils away from her forehead. 'But I need you to wait, once more. Is that too much to ask?'

Fable gave him no answer.

'Just one more time, I *promise*.'

She flew across the field to a cottage stark cream in mid-morning sun. Cerulean eyes followed her journey home. Three times she turned back to the forest figure, only to be waved firmly on. Her watching sentinel did not himself turn away until she'd made it through her window, and had blown a kiss from the sill.

Fable's gown fell in a leaf-strewn puddle at her bedside.

So, she would wait then . . .

369

Lamplight sputtered out, summer seared back. Stars receded under a blanket of furious charcoal. A tear struck her face, sliding forehead to chin. No, not a tear, but the first raindrop; warm as blood, solid as stone.

She tipped her face. The sky erupted.

CHAPTER 41

THE DELUGE

Sonnet held a hand under the veranda eaves, rain pounding through her fingers. The whitewashed world enclosed them entirely. Frogs sang in ecstasy, the roof shook under the hammering onslaught, plants stooped in greedy worship. The smell was like nothing else – months of longing emanating from the earth to welcome the flood hurled from on high.

Argillaceous odour: ugly name for the most beautiful relief.

'I should have made a break for it hours ago,' Sonnet bemoaned. 'I'm going to need a boat to get home now . . .'

'You know you can stay up here,' Olive said, working over a crossword.

'I'm tempted.'

'Why don't you?'

'I should go and get Fable, though.'

'She'll come up if she wants us. You've had the right idea giving her freedom to do her own thing. She's never been more open with us all.'

'Yes, funny how that worked out. I might take you up on the offer. Though, if it looks like Ceres is going to make a direct hit, I think I'll buckle down at the cottage with her.'

371

'Suit yourselves.'

Sonnet heard the twinge in her tone. She watched Olive's pencil scurry across the page, and sighed. 'Olive, I've been meaning to apologise to you.'

'What for?' Olive didn't look up, though her pencil trembled over its square.

'I was shockingly rude that afternoon. I said things I'm not proud of.'

Sonnet couldn't tell if the tight motion of Olive's head was a nod or a shake.

'It wasn't right or fair to attack your faith like that. You made your mistakes with Mama, but you've been nothing but generous and loving and compassionate to us girls – and I'll confess, I've resisted you and resented you, every step of the way.' Her eyes bored into the salted ginger of Olive's bowed head; more salt now than ginger.

'I think I just took all my sadness and anger about Mama's death, then discovering the truth of my father, and learning how she was treated here, and how Fable was treated, *all of it* – and I put that on you, Olive.'

Olive was trying to wave the words away, her chin tight. After all these years, Sonnet could recognise that particular Hamilton manifestation of pride. It had always been the chin. Sonnet was more Hamilton than she'd ever imagined.

'But I can't say there was any other way I might have coped. You were always as strong as a rock, so I leaned on you. I just didn't want you to know it, and I especially didn't want to admit it to myself. I'm *sorry*, Olive.'

Finally, Olive raised her eyes, pencil clutched awkwardly. Her face was a gaping wound. 'Oh, *Sonnet*. You girls were my second chance – my unearned, undeserved blessing. You're the daughters I always wanted . . .'

'Power's out in town, too. And the bridge out of Noah just went under,' Gav said, placing the phone back into its cradle. 'Our bridge *into* town will be next.'

'In less than, what, twelve hours' rain? Must be a new record, dear.'

Plum pressed close, eyes flying between aunt and uncle.

'Yeah, we'll be cut off in the valley for a week if this holds up. Weather Bureau says this system may be packing over forty inches of rain.'

'What about the cottage?' Plum asked, clutching at her uncle's arm.

'No fear, Plum-pie! Old Malcolm knew what he was doing. He drew a line in front of the cottage in nineteen twenty, and he told that old serpent – thus far, but no further.'

But Plum knew. The serpent was already there. She needed redoubtable Sonnet, and she needed her fast.

Sonnet was holed up in the candlelit bathroom, staring at herself, hands to cheeks. Plum hung back in the hallway, shocked by the vulnerability of her sister's expression, made grotesque by humidity's thick sheen, and the wavering light.

'Sonny, are you *crying*?'

Her sister turned at her timorous tone, without truly seeing Plum. 'Just got some things on my mind. What's the matter?'

'There's a snake at the cottage. And I don't want Fable and the baby to be down there with it.'

Sonnet gave an exasperated sigh.

Plum tried again, harder. 'I don't want Fable to be left at the cottage alone . . . in the cyclone. I want us to get her now!'

'We don't even know if it'll cross us yet, Plummy. It's just a lot of rain at the moment. Fable will come up if she wants us.'

'We can't leave her there!'

Sonnet was irritated now. 'Don't be stupid, we're not *leaving* her anywhere. She's more than capable herself to handle some rain. We'll go down later.'

Plum planted her feet. 'If you won't go save her, I *will*!'

'Now you're just being dramatic.'

'We *need* to go to the cottage!'

'For pity's sake, listen to the rain – you want to go out in that?'

'Pleeeease!'

Sonnet groaned. 'Fine! Go ask Olive for a flashlight, then. And umbrellas. And some bloody sense while you're at it, Plum. What a ridiculous idea...'

Sonnet swore under her breath as another wave of rain sought to sweep them off the hill.

'I should have given in and just let Gav go instead of us,' she cried. 'No wonder Fabes didn't want to come up – this is *awful*, Plummy!'

Her sister didn't answer, eyes fastened on the meek cottage glow below.

'Look!' Sonnet said. 'She's cosy and happy, probably reading a book by candlelight. You'd better tell Fable this was all your idea.'

Well, that wasn't quite true. Sonnet had pandered to Plum's paranoia and refused Gav as chaperone for her own reasons, too. After last night's discovery, curiosity was a nest of fire ants underfoot.

Had Fable turned her bedroom into a personal exhibition for Archer Brennan on *purpose*? How *could* she?! Whatever Fable knew, Sonnet would have it out of her by the time this storm blew over!

At the cottage, Plum ran ahead of Sonnet, scouring the garden from the safety of the porch, not the slightest bit relieved at what she didn't find. They sloshed inside on a blast of wetness. The lounge and kitchen were empty; filled with torrential roar. A single candle burned on the bench.

'Faa-bes!' Sonnet called, hauling off her raincoat and boots. 'It's only us.' She waggled her eyebrows at her youngest sister. '*Plum* just wanted to come and check on you.'

Her flashlight swept the darkness, finding the lounge and sunroom empty. There was a whimper, only the tiniest of whimpers, from the bathroom. Sonnet followed her beam of light into the bathroom, followed its track up the figure stooped over the sink, with face pressed against the faucet and arms braced against the rim.

'Fable?'

Her sister shook her head, without lifting it. Another tiny whimper escaped – with a hurried draw of breath after it. Plum came to stand beside Sonnet, her flashlight joining the first, illuminating Fable more brightly. Fable swayed, clenching at the sink, writhing on her feet. One last whimper came – softening – then she sagged heavily against the porcelain.

Sonnet took a step forward and Fable raised her head. The two women locked eyes: Sonnet aghast, Fable terrified.

Fable straightened, turning the low-slung ball of her belly towards them, gaping at a spot between her feet. Sonnet's torch swung down, just in time to watch the flood of water hit the floor. Fable gasped; one hand clutching at the sink, in case she was washed away.

'No!' Sonnet cried, finding her voice. 'It's too early!'

'Why are you weeing?' Plum whispered.

'It's not wee!' Sonnet cried. 'It's the baby! And it's coming now! Oh, Fabes, what are we going to *do* – we can't get out of Noah!'

Fable's eyes were wide, desperate rounds. Sonnet's hand flew to her forehead, raking hard through her hair. 'The cyclone! What if it comes in on us now? We don't have any power. We don't even have a phone!

Why the hell don't we have a phone?' Her voice had risen frantically. Fable's eyes mirrored her fear.

'We need Dr Fairley,' said Plum.

'Yes!' Sonnet cried, rounding on her sister. 'Yes! We have to get Jake – before it's too late! Plum, you need to go up to Heartwood. You need to *run*, and you need to tell Gav to take the Ford, before our bridge goes under, and get Dr Fairley!'

Plum's head shook violently, eyes bouncing between her sisters. 'I can't!'

Sonnet gripped Plum by the shoulders. 'You need to help me save Fable's baby. That's why we're here, remember? Because of you, Plummy. You knew something was wrong, and now we're got to make it right. *Go*, Plum!'

Plum's moving head changed direction, became an unsteady nod. She scampered from the room. 'I'm *going*!'

Fable turned again to the sink on another whimpering surge.

Olive blew into the cottage, with Plum stumbling after her, issuing a stricken demand – 'What can I do?!' Sonnet looked up from her kneeling position at Fable's back, bent over the bathtub's edge.

Olive's eyes remained fixed on Sonnet. From her hands dangled two garbage bags filled with towels and sheets and candles. A box of aspirin was tucked underarm.

'Just tell me you've already sent Gav to get Dr Fairley!'

'He's going full throttle!'

'Will he make it before the bridge goes under?'

'To be honest, I don't know. They'll be cutting it fine. I just … I don't want Gav caught on the other side of the bridge.'

Sonnet heard the quaver of dread. 'I *had* to send him, Olive. We need a *doctor*!'

'I know. Are you sure it won't fizzle out, though?'

Sonnet motioned towards the spill of amniotic fluid across the tiles. 'We're past the point of no return here.'

Only then did Olive finally allow herself to take in the form of her labouring niece. It was too much – her face quaked, a hand pressed against her lips. She turned back to Sonnet. 'Please give me something to do.'

'Light. We need light – everywhere!'

Ensconced in the bathroom, Sonnet nonetheless sensed Jake's arrival outside. It was warmth coursing into her solar plexus.

Thank you, she mouthed into the silence. Her hand trembled against Fable's sweat-soaked back.

She half expected him to come sprinting in. He arrived, however, with an unhurried ease which comforted when it should have infuriated her.

'Looks like we're having a baby, then,' he said, filling the doorway with height; the room with confidence.

Fable, slumped between surges, looked mutely up at him. Her face did not change – only Sonnet detected the relieved outbreath.

Jake's face was all calm professionalism. His eyes, though, lingered on Sonnet with compassion. The look made her feel like a cat inclining its head for a petting.

'You made it,' Sonnet said. There was a catch in her voice.

'And here I was thinking my first cyclone was going to be the only excitement of the evening.' He came to kneel on the other side of Fable, with only eyes for her now. 'How are you getting on here, Fable? Can you tell me how close these contractions are?'

Fable shook her head and dug her hands into the lip of the bath, bowing as another contraction reared up.

Sonnet pressed her hand hard against Fable's back, as she seemed to prefer, and they all waited in silence until the pain subsided.

'Is that one gone?' Jake asked, leaning to catch Fable's eyes. Fable nodded, eyes slipping away.

'She's been having these pains ninety seconds apart ever since I found her. Sometimes they seem to stampede in, one on top of the other.'

Jake nodded. 'And when did contractions start?'

Sonnet threw up her hands. 'She's not saying *anything*, Jake!'

'That's okay. Some women just prefer to go quietly into themselves. They conduct themselves in birth as they do in life.'

'But she's in too much pain! Can you give her *something*?'

Jake spoke directly to his patient. 'I can't give you any medicine here, Fable. I'm sorry; I'm not equipped for it tonight. Do you understand?'

Fable emitted a silent sob, hunching further over the bath.

'But we're going to make things as easy as we can for you. We can try some warm water next – the bath can be useful.'

Fable stiffened, breathing hard once more. She grabbed Sonnet's hand, whacking it against her lower back.

Jake watched quietly. 'Are you having pain in your back?'

'I think so,' Sonnet said, massaging firmly. 'This is the only thing that helps her.'

'OK, keep it up. Baby might be posterior.'

When Fable's huffing ebbed away, Jake leaned in close. 'Fable, with your permission, I'd like to check baby's position, and how far along you are. I'm going to have to work between your contractions, they're very close together. Would that be OK with you?'

Fable made a small, pained sound low in her throat. A lump rose in Sonnet's.

Plum stood back as Sonnet shut the door in her face, sealing off the bathroom.

What were they *doing* to Fable? Would childbirth just kill Fable – or the baby, too?

Plum wandered into the lounge-room, nursing a sob in her chest. Olive was shaking her head over a stubborn match, foot lighting up her calf on friction alone. Gav sat on the lounge, with his head in his hands. The emergency bulletin sounded, volume low, from the transistor radio.

'Uncle Gav? What will happen to the baby if the cyclone takes the roof off?'

'Already told you kiddo; this roof isn't coming off.'

Plum hated the weariness of Gav's voice. She tried, and failed, not to take it personally. 'But what *if*?'

'Fable's in the safest room in the house.'

'What if the creek comes for us?'

'It's not going to breach the flood line. That's a hundred-year mark.'

'But what if this is the hundredth year?'

Gav's big hands closed around his forehead.

'And what about the python? Is he still out there?'

'He would have gone long ago in search of shelter.'

'But what if he's sheltering in the cottage? Why would he go somewhere else when he could come in here?'

Plum imagined the serpent uncoiling from the rafters above Fable and the baby. 'Can't you go and check? Just to make sure he's not there?'

'Not *where*?' Gav said with a long exhale. 'If I check and he's not in the garden, how's that going to make you feel better? Then you're going to think he's in the roof!'

'Can't you check the roof, too?'

Gav ejected himself from the couch. 'Strewth, Plum! Just lay off it!' He thumped out into the storm, without looking back.

'He's only stressed, dear, he doesn't mean it,' Olive said from the kitchen, finally striking her match.

Plum cowered under the flimsy cottage roof – already lifting, and obviously hiding a python – and listened to the creek creeping ever closer. The bathroom door stayed barred closed.

When Gav returned, it was with bolstered resolve. 'Come here,' he said, drawing Plum to the window seat nook.

'See that sunbird's nest?'

'The one hanging from the wind chime?'

'Do you reckon they'd be stickin' around right now if there was a big flamin' snake nearby? Or if they thought we were about to get swept away? Not a chance!'

'Oh,' Plum said.

'Now look, this is *your* job, Plum-pie: I want you to sit right here and make sure nothing happens to that nest, OK?'

Plum pressed her nose against the bay window to see the bird's tiny beak poking out of the pendulous hanging nest. A gale made it sway violently, suspended as it was by the finest of grass cords.

'Uncle Gav, she's going to be blown away – the cord will snap!'

'Baloney! No way she'd build a home for her babies here unless it was safe.'

'You're doing really well,' Fable heard Dr Fairley say through a haze of pain and exhaustion. 'You're already dilated almost halfway and the baby is down low, too. It's all good news.'

Only halfway? God, this will kill me.

She broke into a silent scream, burying her face in Sonnet's lap.

Fable felt the looks exchanged once more over her head. She knew what they were thinking: Fable can't do it, and since no one else can do it for her, guess she's *done for*!

She would die in childbirth, in a muggy bathroom full of looks; the newest, saddest Hamilton tragedy.

The serpent crushed around her belly once more; its great mandible opening over her womb. Sonnet's hand pressed desperately against her back to release its grip on her. The fabric of her sister's shorts went in and out of Fable's mouth.

If she had to die, she'd do it quietly.

Olive dithered at the door frame. 'You must be tired, Sonnet. Do you want me to take over and give you a break?'

Sonnet looked around the figure braced and swaying against her. She could do with a toilet break. It was torturous being so close to a loo with such a full bladder. Fable's head shook violently against Sonnet's chest and her hands dug in.

'I think that's a no,' Sonnet said, with a wink.

'I need a job,' Olive pleaded. 'And don't say more candles. Place already looks like a cathedral.'

'Check on the cyclone again?'

'Done that. Ceres has been slightly downgraded, still coming in north of us, looks like she'll make landfall about two o'clock.'

No such downgrading was taking place in the bathroom. A shared question hung heavily in the air. Which would come first – cyclone or baby? Both women turned to look at the doctor leaning quietly against the window. Jake put his hands up, warding them off.

Sonnet spoke over Fable's head the way one might a truculent child. 'She's progressing *so* well, over halfway dilated now; doing *brilliantly.*'

The woman in question stamped her feet and kicked at the air, breathing like a bull.

Even Olive understood that. She slipped away.

381

Fable was naked in a blessedly hot bath – knees spread apart, buttocks bared brazenly to the rafters in front of her sister and her wannabe boyfriend. She had the vague sense she should be embarrassed, though the notion was from another life entirely. This world of obliterating pain was all she knew now.

'She can't go on like this, you have to do something,' Sonnet begged – whether to Dr Fairley or the baby itself, Fable was too far gone to tell. Sonnet sat beside her tub, hands tight on Fable's flagging fingers.

Fable whimpered in agreement. *Yes, do something. Drown me now, before the next one comes along.*

Dr Fairley drew near. 'Fable,' he said. 'I want you to remember this is *good* pain—'

'*Seriously?*' Sonnet muttered, voice dripping scorn.

'Hear me out,' he said, dropping to his knees. 'The uterus is a muscular organ, working hard each contraction to bring your baby down. And when muscle works over and over, it hurts. It's just your body doing its job well.'

'OK, that's better,' Sonnet said approvingly.

The immense maw stretched wide, and the python crushed again. Fable pounded her hands, wrapped in Sonnet's, against the porcelain, floundering for breath. She was drowning on dry land.

Sonnet's voice was a vine thrown from the safety of the bank. 'Fabes, just imagine you're climbing a mountain now. Do you hear me?'

Fable nodded, grasping tight.

'It's only a muscle burning, because you're going higher and higher, right to the very top. You beautiful girl, you're so strong, look how strong you are.'

Fable heard the roar of Moria Falls; saw, on the steep path ahead, a single hiker pushing just beyond her reach.

Wait, Raff.

Wind threw itself against the cottage in a demented rage. Plum started from the window after an almighty crash in the back yard.

'Hills hoist,' Gav said, not looking up from his *Reader's Digest*.

Plum realised she'd been dozing and glanced at the nest. The beak had still not moved – possibly because the stupid mother was already dead, and had smothered her babies beneath her.

The bathroom door whacked open and Sonnet hurried out to the sunroom. From the bathroom came the sound of a tired fist thudding on and on against the bath.

Olive rose hurriedly. 'Sonnet?'

'Jake said she's getting to the pushing stage. I need to make up her bed.'

'Don't be silly, I'll do that.'

Dr Fairley waited until Fable had come to the end of her grunting contraction – rearing up on her knees. 'Fable,' he said soothingly, 'I can't catch your baby in this bath, it's too narrow. Sonnet and I are going to wrap you in towels, and help you back to your bed – okay?'

Sonnet stepped forward, arms open in plush, towelling invitation.

Along the hallway Fable staggered, stopping twice to grunt against the wall.

'I'm just going to check to make sure you're fully dilated,' Dr Fairley said, pulling on gloves as Sonnet steadied her onto the bed. 'Then you can get in any position that feels comfortable—'

Sonnet's almost boyfriend or not, he was the only medical professional for miles; so what? Fable still really wanted to kick him in the teeth right then.

'All right,' Dr Fairley said, withdrawing. 'With the next one, you can go for your life.'

Fable turned on all fours, braced herself against the wrought-iron bedhead, and stuck her bottom in the air.

'Nearly there!' Sonnet said as her sister's knuckles went white, and the grunting began anew.

Nearly *where*? Fable was stuck at a chasm she could not cross on her own strength. Again and again and again the toil brought her back to this vast crevasse, and each time she fell feebly away.

Sweat poured from her body, soaking her hair. Her eyes struggled to stay open between contractions. All she wanted was for Raff to walk through that door right now, pick her up as easily as a doll, and carry her away from the pain, and effort. She didn't want a baby anymore.

Another expulsive urge took hold. Fable locked on Raff's face across the chasm – why did he just stand there looking at her? Why did he not reach for her hand?

Save me, Raff!

She collapsed against the iron curlicue as the surge drained away. If he didn't come soon, she would throw herself into that black hole.

'Oh, Jake, is she . . . okay?' Sonnet's voice – tiny, far away.

'Maternal exhaustion,' he answered. 'It's been over two and a half hours. If we were in hospital—' The sentence wasn't finished aloud. The looks flew fast and furious over Fable's swimming head.

She understood them, anyway: *Fable Hamilton isn't fit to be a mother – exhausted by motherhood before she's even attained it.*

'Fable, how about we try lying on your side, to give you a rest. We'll hold your legs for you.'

Fable shook her head, pushing their hands away. She gritted her teeth and bore down again.

Sonnet tore her eyes away from the unease now becoming perceptible on Jake's face, fixing instead on the painting above, of a three-tiered waterfall. The image swam hotly. She blinked hard, tethering her breath.

'Good girl,' Jake was saying on the other side of the bed. 'That was a great one. Next time, let's have another push like that!'

Sonnet stayed locked on the waterfall, avoiding the despair of her sister's eyes. In the glimmering candlelight, her father's name, a whirl in an eddy of water, leapt out. In paintings all over the room, his signatures – hidden in cracks and whorls and crevices – blazed now into recognition.

How had she ever failed to see it before? And who the *hell* hides their signature? What a pretentious, cursed man he was. When this was over, she was going to take an axe to every painting in the sunroom.

'That's it! Yes! Keep going, keep going, keep going, keep going – oh!'

Fable collapsed into Sonnet's arms. Raff's hand fell uselessly away, his eyes soft with pity; this chasm as wide as an ocean between them.

He turned to leave. Fable was never going to make it, and he knew it, too. He was going on now without her.

Sonnet murmured something fast and pleading to Dr Fairley, her lips moving against Fable's sodden head.

'She *can* do it,' Fable heard him reply. 'She has to.'

Sonnet raised the straw once more to her sister's lips, trying not to scream when Fable shook her hand away. Had there ever been a time in all her life when she'd wanted so desperately to bear another's struggle?

Fable groaned, clutching for Sonnet again, her head shake intensifying.

'Yes you *can* – you're doing it right now!' Sonnet said, watching in astonishment as the wet head pushed once more to a wide straining orb between Fable's legs. 'There it is! Keep going, keep going, keep going!'

Fable reared up, a hand flung out towards an unseen figure.

'*Raff!*' she cried, '*Raff, please – wait!*'

Fable's arms buckled. She bowed and buried her face, shuddering, in Sonnet's chest.

Across Fable's head, Sonnet saw Jake's answering grimace as white-hot, silent rage warped her own features.

'Fable,' Sonnet hissed against her cheek, 'you are the daughter of Esther Hamilton. You wait for *no* man. You wait *not one minute more*! Do you hear me? No more waiting! Never again!'

For a moment, nothing; only the trembling pant against her neck.

Then, a tiny nod.

Tears sprang to Sonnet's eyes.

'It's time,' she said fiercely. 'Bring your baby into your arms, Fable!'

'Plum! What are you doing?' Olive cried. She pushed Plum aside to slam the front door shut against the gale.

Plum seized at her aunt. 'I have to get the nest! I can't leave her there. It's going to fall. She needs our help—'

'She's safe,' Olive said, pulling Plum against her. 'She's going to be ok.'

A gust of wind swept up the hallway, shaking the sunroom door, guttering at the candles.

Fable felt the draught, robed in shimmering green, enter the room. Upon her forehead the cool hand laid itself. In her ear, she heard the whisper.

I'm here, I'm here.

'Mama,' Fable sighed.

'Yes,' said Sonnet, 'Mama wants to meet her grandbaby. Show Mama your baby, Fable.'

Fable gathered, and rose again.

For nine months, Fable had held his roaring release inside her. Nine months she had hidden that reverberating secret at her deepest centre.

It was time for her to let it go.

Now, Fable roared.

And in a cool, fluid burst, her baby slipped into the world.

'It's a baby,' Sonnet heard herself say in wonder, as the pale, blood-streaked shape was lifted onto Fable's chest.

'A big, healthy baby,' Jake said, towelling off that unfathomable creature with vigorous strokes.

A bleating cry lit the charge in the air. Sonnet and Fable broke into a shared sob.

Olive, Gav and Plum, transfixed by the primal birthing roar, held their collective breath. Seconds passed interminably. Plum pressed her knuckles into her eyes.

The lusty bawl of a newborn baby filled the cottage.

Olive and Gav turned to one another, already weeping.

'Oh, that *sound* – I never knew it!' Olive cried.

'My love,' Gav said, big arms absorbing her. 'Now you do.'

A quiet dawn was seeping into the world when Olive and Gav filed into the sunroom, with Plum trailing behind. Jake sat on the window seat, making notes in the grey light just beginning to dampen the candle gold. Sonnet was perched on the bed, Fable reclined against her shoulder. The new mother's face was pale with exhaustion, and resplendent with love. In her arms, with all eyes on it, lay a swaddled babe; mouth gaping frantically for the nipple.

'Our Fable,' Olive cried, going forward. 'You've brought life into a cottage that only ever knew death.'

Sonnet winced.

Fable, having attached that mouth to her breast, looked up. In her dazed smile, there was a fulfilment never glimpsed there before.

'This,' Fable said, stroking a pearlescent ear, 'is Rune.'

Sonnet added, with queenly pride: 'Rune, son of Fable.'

Olive's face split with joy. 'A boy?! We haven't had a Hamilton boy in three generations!'

Plum shuffled to the bed, eyes locked on her nephew. The room fell silent as she leaned close to study the suckling babe. When she drew back, it was with relief. 'I like him.'

'Phew,' Sonnet said, and the room erupted into laughter.

Only Plum stayed serious. She spoke, earnestly, to Fable. 'He's blue.'

'No, he's pink and healthy,' Sonnet interrupted.

Plum sighed. Fable tipped her head, patiently.

'Rune *has* blue eyes,' Plum said again.

Fable's lashes swept back tears. 'Yes, Plummy, yes he has.'

CHAPTER 42

LET ME COUNT THE WAYS

'Would you look at all this damage,' Sonnet groused from the porch. She surveyed a vale dishevelled and weeping after a late-night's revelling: fleeced of accoutrements, doused in confetti; her cape of green ruptured by landslides. The garden had been excoriated. Branches littered the ground, fence palings lay asunder; the faerie garden stones sat exposed, dark with moss.

'Count your blessings we didn't have a direct hit, pet,' said Gav, scooting up the hill after Olive. 'We'll see you up there, Doc!'

'Geez, we came close, didn't we?' Jake said, watching the river surge alongside the cottage, lapping at the gate.

Sonnet smiled. 'I used to think so in the Wet. I've learned, grudgingly, to trust the man who planted us here.' She followed Jake down the stairs, remaining on the final step as he laced his boots. '*Thank you*,' she said, voice run through with feeling. 'For everything, Jake. You were incredible.'

'No,' he said, standing to full height, stepping close. 'I just did my job. *Fable* was incredible – to pull that off, under those circumstances, after more than four hours of pushing. She's a strong woman.'

'And she did it *alone*.'

'She wasn't alone. She had one hell of a sister at her back, every step of the way.'

Her heartbeat stumbled over itself for a moment. Had Sonnet lost her roof to the storm last night, or should she, in any storm to come, she had the distinct impression Jake Fairley would carry it back to her in his own two hands. She fiddled with the messy bun at the nape of her neck, shaking her red locks free.

'So, I'm going to get cleaned up at the Emersons' now,' he said. 'Make some phone calls, and catch some sleep. Then see if I can make the crossing later today. Gav tells me it'll recede soon; they've hauled down the red pennant. But I want *you* to get some rest. Doctor's orders!'

Sonnet thought of the placenta left to bury, bathroom to sanitise, floors to mop, the linen still to wash. 'Definitely,' she lied. 'When will you come back?' She couldn't seem to remember how to affect a neutral air.

'I'll visit Fable in a couple of days for a postnatal check. I'm also going to send my nurse each day to see how Fable is getting on with the feeding and healing.'

'I don't want some gossipy old windbag coming here!'

'Rachael's a professional and will do her job in the strictest confidence.'

'But Rune *is* healthy – even though he's early?'

Jake chose his words judiciously. 'At that whopping size, without a skerrick of vernix, and as alert as that boy is, I think we might have some miscalculated dates.'

'Yeah ... miscalculated,' Sonnet said, with air quotes.

'*Rest*. No hounding would-be fathers!'

'Hound? I want to bloody *strangle* that Hull.'

'Try not to. Nearest correctional centre is too far way, and I'd want to visit you at least twice daily.'

Sonnet had no retort. She wiped sweat beads from her upper lip, a little tremble in her hand. Jake's expression was one of incalculable admiration.

Warmth flooded her gut. Sonnet stepped off the last stair, and into an embrace already waiting. Jake's arms were an extra set of lungs. Even in that tight constriction, even with her nose buried in his neck, she could breathe better. Why had she never realised how hard breathing on her own was before now?

I can't wait to fire you, Sonnet thought with muffled longing.

Plum had been left behind to sleep on the window seat – her feet were just visible beneath the curtain.

Poor thing, usurped as the baby.

Sonnet reached to tuck a burnished magenta curl behind an ear, marvelling at how lovely Plummy had grown, or rather, always stayed.

Do you see her, Mama?

Sometimes, Sonnet was convinced when she held Plum in her eyes like this, she was giving Mama a glimpse of her baby, from the other side.

Sonnet started as Plum's eyes snapped open, her first blush of the day just beginning.

'Sorry, didn't mean to wake you!' Sonnet said, about to withdraw when the tear-mottled condition of her sister's complexion struck her. 'Plum, are you OK?'

Plum motioned at the window. 'Uncle Gav told me to watch the sunbirds to make sure nothing happened to them.'

Sonnet looked with distaste at the nest hanging by, ostensibly empty. 'Oh, right. Well, try not to take it personally. That's just life in the tropics.'

One less filthy bird to worry about.

'No, look!'

Sonnet cringed as a yellow-breasted bird fluttered to the nest, food in its slender bill. Tiny chicks appeared, eager to receive.

'That's their dad,' Plum said. 'The nest and the chicks all survived the cyclone, and they have a mum *and* a dad.'

'And you're upset because Rune doesn't have a father bird?'

Plum rolled her eyes. 'Please. I'm not a baby.'

Right. So we've hit that stage again.

'No, you're not. But I only know what you tell me.'

'I'm sad because I'm . . . monstrous.'

Sonnet dropped to the seat beside her. '*What?!*'

'Never mind, nothing,' Plum said, turning away.

'Like hell I'll never mind! Where on earth did you get that idea from?'

Plum flamed silently for a long moment. When she spoke it was with sad, tired resolve.

'I found out I'm the "monstrous problem" born of premarital sex.'

'Don't be *ridiculous*!'

'It's true. I mean I'm summarising, but I read it in a science book.'

Sonnet's ire propelled her from the seat. 'What the hell! What *book*?' She only realised how hard she'd been gripping Plum's arm when she noted her grimace.

'Which book was it, Plummy?' she tried again, with unconvincing lightness.

'The one Olive gave me.'

'Not that bloody *Essential Facts for Young Women* book!'

Plum squinted, recalling the title. 'I think so, the cover was brown.'

'That stupid book was the one Olive gave Fable years ago. I purposely left commentary all through it, deconstructing that so-called doctor's propaganda. Weren't my notes still there?'

Plum shook her head slowly.

Sonnet gritted her teeth. *Bloody Olive*. 'Fable turned her nose up at that book, and you should have too. It was sponsored by a church some years back, and that's where it should have stayed – in the past. You need something modern. Books written *by* women, *for* women. Why didn't you ask *me*?'

Plum's silence was somehow damning.

Sonnet squirmed. 'I'm sorry, Plummy – I've been so focused on the baby coming, I just put you out of mind. I get so caught up with my own worries. And now I've failed you, just as I failed Fable years ago.'

Plum shrugged. 'I don't think the book was lying – even if it was written years ago. He is a doctor.'

'Wasn't *lying*? Plum, doctor or not, the book had an overt religious agenda. But we don't believe that stuff anymore.'

Plum chewed the inside of her cheek, watching the mother sunbird arrive, beak full. 'You definitely don't think I'm a *monstrous problem*?'

'Plum, you are the beloved daughter of Esther Hamilton, the most remarkable woman this town has ever seen.'

'Not *really*.'

'Really! She was spirited and brave and clever, and beautiful inside and out – like you. And Mama *knew* you weren't a monstrous problem, Plum. She wanted you more than anything in the whole world. She would just lie there for hours, stroking your little face; couldn't tear her eyes away from you. She loved to put her little finger right there in your dimple, and she called it "the mark of perfection".'

Sonnet watched one corner of Plum's lips twitch towards its dimple. Her voice grew thick. 'Is that why you've seemed so sad lately, because of that book frightening you?'

Plum shook her head slowly. 'No, it's not just the book. I feel afraid all the time, about everything. I wake up with a churning tummy, and I can't get to sleep at night for hours and hours – like my brain is broken. When Fable came home pregnant, I was just so sure something bad would happen to her, that she'd get punished for her . . . premarital sex.'

'Oh, Plummy! You don't get pregnant as punishment. I thought Olive explained how babies are made?'

'I know how Fable got her baby!' Plum cried in affront. 'I even saw her go to the forest that night—'

He dragged her off to the forest?! I'll kill him!

Plum drew back at the expression on Sonnet's face. She continued warily, 'I understood how she got pregnant. But everyone else was so worked up about it, too. I was convinced Fable would die in childbirth unless I kept her safe . . . It sounds stupid when I say it aloud.'

Plum slumped away. Sonnet reviewed this information.

'Plum,' she said gently, 'was that *you* closing the cottage windows all the time?'

'Yes.'

'And the gate tied up with vines?'

'Yes.'

'And the nasty tacks stuck all around my garden?'

'No.'

Sonnet burst into laughter. Plum blushed.

'And were those things to protect Fable? Or to try to ease your fears?'

Plum gave a small nod.

Sonnet was careful with her next words. 'You understand these are irrational fears . . . don't you?'

'They're not irrational to me.'

'No, and that's the problem. Before you were born, Mama constantly complained about her "nerves". And sometimes her "nerves" tipped into such suffocating sadness she wouldn't come out of her room for a month. I won't *let* that happen to you, Plum. I think it we should find someone to help us.'

Plum shook her head, looking smaller than she had in years.

'I'm talking about a physician who understands nervous illness.'

'But don't you have any books that I can read?'

'Absolutely, I do. But it's also important to talk to a psychologist. Oh, Plum, you've grown up right under my nose. You're not our baby anymore; you're a young woman. And I know you think of yourself as a scared, weird kid, but I happen to know you're courageous and resilient.'

Plum twitched, brows furrowing.

'Yes you are, Plum Hamilton. You lost Mama when you were still just a baby, and you've had to live every day of your childhood without her. I barely survived losing her as a grown woman! Every day I'm amazed by how much you've come through and how strong you are.'

Sonnet moved to place an arm about her sister, and was rewarded with an unstiffening sigh. 'Don't you have any friends you can talk to about big stuff like this?'

Plum began to weep. 'Mostly, the other girls don't talk to me.'

'Well now, that's something you have in common with both Fable and me in this place. But you'll be surprised how a best friend can just walk through the door one day, right out of nowhere.'

'I've only ever had one best friend – Jimmy.'

'Jim Taylor?'

'Yes. Except when all my fears got so big and weird, I pushed him away. I thought it would be better than to let him see how weird I am. And he doesn't even save me a seat on the bus anymore, much less look at me. He probably hates me.'

'I doubt that! But if he's your best friend, I bet he's hurting too. Hell, Plum. You've had all this going on, and no one to talk to about it. I am so *sorry*. Listen, this is what we're going to do. As soon as we can get into town, I'm going to load you up with *good* books on being a teenager. Then we're going to see a doctor about your fears.'

'Not Dr Fairley!'

'No, I hope to discharge Dr Fairley as soon as possible.'

Fable's room smelt these days like maple syrup and roast chicken – a not-unpleasant brume of bodily fluids. Or, perhaps Sonnet's sense of smell was thrown by the delicious meals accruing daily. Olive never came down at night without a dish or three, her payment for a hungry hold of Rune. Likewise, the nurse – sturdy, no-nonsense Rachael, to whom Sonnet had taken an instant liking – visited with home-cooked meals sent along by Dr Fairley. (That the man could cook so well on top of everything else was maddening.)

Olive, watching Fable feed Rune for the fifth time that hour, spoke with the quaver that never now seemed to leave her voice. 'You look so much like your mother, Fable, sometimes I sit here and imagine I'm sharing it with her. This has been such a blessing for me – getting to live it through you. How it might have been, if only I'd had your courage, Sonnet.'

'*Mine?*'

'Yes, you're the big sister I wish I had been to Es.'

'That's nice,' Fable said, tongue in cheek, 'but you do know Sonnet's only in it for my dishy doctor?'

Sonnet turned, straight-faced, to Olive. 'What – didn't you have dishy doctors in your day?'

'We had Dr Herbert, dear.'

All three women exploded with laughter. Rune snuffled, blinking, at the breast.

'Oh no, don't wake him!' Fable said, gently rocking.

In the settling silence, Sonnet's eyes went again to the waterfall above the bed. She asked, without preamble, and certainly without preparation: 'Fabes, did you always know whose paintings they were?'

Fable required no clarification. 'Yes, of course.'

Sonnet studied her sister. 'Which begs the question, why on earth did you want them?'

'Why shouldn't I? Frankly, his talent is wildly inspiring.'

'Because he's pond scum, and he ruined her life!'

'Or, he's an imperfect human and even in his misdeeds, he still gave her what she wanted most.'

Sonnet snorted. 'Which ruined her life. Look, I'm not going round in circles again.' She turned to Olive, accusingly. 'Did *you* know they were Archer Brennan's paintings, too? That I had *his* bloody artwork hanging in pride of place in *my* shop?'

'Well, no . . . . but I don't quite understand why you're so offended. He *is* your father. If anyone deserved to receive those painting from him, it's you—'

'But I didn't receive them!' Sonnet interrupted. 'They were languishing in the back rooms of a pub. Shouldn't they have been at least in a gallery?'

Olive mulled this over. 'Archer never exhibited his work anywhere in town, so he must have painted them after he . . . left teaching, and Noah Vale.'

'So, how did they come back to Noah? And why the pub?'

'It's a good point, I don't know.'

'Could you find out from some gossipmonger in town?' Sonnet asked, trying to curb her impatience.

'Why don't you just go and ask Brenton?'

'I'm not going near that bloody knave!'

'*Language!*' Olive said, nodding at Fable.

'Never mind Fabes, she's already had experience of her own with knaves.'

An odd smile played over Fable's lips. 'No, I haven't.'

Sonnet fixed on her with steady significance 'No? Can't think of anyone who should have known better but went ahead anyway and used their precious reputation and years of friendship to take advantage of a vulnerable girl, then ran away so he didn't have to face the music?'

Fable's gravity rivalled hers. 'No. I have no experience with anyone like that.'

Olive was already on her feet. 'All right, Sonnet, that's enough! Come and I'll help you fold those clothes. Let's give Fable some peace.'

Sonnet turned back at the door to deliver her coup de grâce, but found herself already dismissed.

Fable had eyes only for her tiny boy.

Fable didn't know how her next book was going to sell given it would be eighty pages of naught but Rune's perfection. Then again, she still didn't understand how she'd sold a book of faerie pictures with acerbic captions. Come to think of it, who *wouldn't* buy a tome comprised entirely of Rafferty Hull's son?

Raff's son.

If she didn't daily replay the inexorable ascent of Raff's lips along her innermost thigh, the lap of his tongue at her centre, and then the exquisitely tender way he had entered her and moved inside her, so incongruous with the thunder of his climax, she might have thought she'd dreamed Rune into life.

For he was Raff, in milk-drunk miniature.

Just as she'd filled notebooks with his father's eyes, now her pages abounded with details of Rune's beloved face: his tiny, elven ears (those alone, it seemed, were hers); ash-gold hair (Raff's); tiny cheek dimple (oh-so-Raff's); the gently serious way he looked at the world (who needed to spell it out?); and those blue, blue, blue eyes. Her favourite motif had been replicated, replaced.

Sonnet had tried to lord it over her with the choice between motherhood and creativity. But there was no choice. The creative juices Fable employed to bring forth new life and art were one and the same: it all flowed from her dreaming heart. She was still learning how to feed and draw one-handed, but each time her milk let down, prickling painfully across her chest, and as those languorous breastfeeding hormones coursed through her blood, Fable felt her creative powers surge.

For many years, Fable had believed inspiration flowed from her love for Raff, and her longing for Mama. But only in leaving girlhood behind, had Fable realised: each love served creativity, and never had it been the other way around.

She traced the tiny upturned nose feeding now at her areola, little hand clutching at her breast, and sighed. If she could have foreseen or imagined the contentment she would know as a mother – even in her thwarted passion and relinquished livelihood– she might not have worried quite so much. She had been engulfed by love incomparable.

Fable had more of Raff now than she'd ever hoped for. She had joined his life with hers, in a way that could never be undone, or taken back.

The only direction was forward, she saw that now. Rune would grow up strong and clever and oh-so-loved, with or without his father. She would always be Rune's mother, come hell or high water. And already, she'd faced both.

But Raff deserved to know the truth – to make his choice, as she'd made hers. Fable still had her quiet pride, though. She would not pressure Raff, or force him into any obligations, or drag him home unwillingly, to Noah. She did not need *rescuing*. She was worth more than that. If he genuinely wanted her – *them* – he had, now, to prove it.

Fable made a plan.

CHAPTER 43

CATHARSIS

Autumn 1965

Sonnet lifted her head from Olive's table to accept the black coffee.

'Six-week-olds suuuuuck.'

Olive smiled in commiseration.

'I mean, he's okay when he actually sucks, that's the irony of it, he's quite likeable when he's got a boob in his gob. But the rest of the time? I don't know how she stands it! He doesn't seem to sleep a wink when he should – she was walking the hallway with him all night. The crying – my God – I'm exhausted.'

'I wish Fable would let us help.'

'She will! You come down at three o'clock in the morning and she'll hand him over no worries. Then she follows you round mooning over how beautiful he is and how careful you should be, when she ought to be sleeping.'

Sonnet sculled the coffee and Olive promptly rose to refill it. Coming back with a fresh mug, Olive said: 'By the way, I solved your picture problem for you.'

Sonnet reached quickly for the cup. 'Seriously?'

'Yes, turns out the paintings were a gift to Noah Vale nearly a decade ago, following Archer's death. They were sent to the CWA for display in the hall, or otherwise marked out for exhibition and sale.'

'Who sent the paintings?'

'Archer's wife, after his death.'

'And how then did they get into the pub?'

'That one was a decision on the part of the CWA's then president.'

'Delia Bloody Hull!' Sonnet rolled her eyes at Olive's face. 'Language, got it.'

'Delia *and*,' Olive appended, 'other members of the CWA made the executive decision, in light of Archer Brennan's controversial history in Noah Vale, and in respect to recent arrivals in the valley, not to publicly display the paintings. It was simply deemed too shocking and, apparently, an "honour" he didn't deserve. So, they were donated to a newly bequeathed character building of historic significance.'

'The pub.'

'In short.'

Sonnet boggled. 'Why didn't they at least mention to me they possessed my father's artworks? Why hurriedly cover it up?'

Olive stirred her tea, looking towards the creek. 'The answer runs as deep or shallow as you want. They'd probably say because you're not a Brennan, your paternity has never been accepted, he never acknowledged you, you weren't mentioned in his will, the paintings were a public donation, and so on.'

'They did say all that, didn't they!'

Olive sighed. 'Yes, Marg made a few similar statements when I went to see her. Sonnet, the truth is more personal, though, I think.'

Sonnet didn't know if the steam billowing in her face was coming from her ears or cup.

'The choice was ultimately Delia Hull's, and it would appear she made that call based on her personal feelings.'

'Venomous bitch!'

Olive sniffed. 'Whether you like it or not, Delia Hull was very close to the Brennans in her day.'

'What?!'

'You know all this. We discussed it after your falling out with Delia.'

'I blocked most of it out of my mind.' (She hadn't.)

'Delia and William were fast friends with the Brennans. The Hulls and Brennans were the most charming and popular young couples in town back then.'

'Delia was never young; surely she was born an old shrew!'

'Far from it. For a long time, Delia was the most beautiful young woman in town – Miss Noah Vale herself in 1930. She and William were sociable and fashionable; scintillating company from all accounts.'

Sonnet made a choking noise.

'Delia Hardy grew up with Vera Logan, they vied for the crown of town beauty years before Archer rolled into town and chose Vera for his bride. Delia was married not long afterwards. They were bridesmaids for each other. Delia supported Vera through the birth of her boys, and those horrible diagnoses. You'd see Vera and Delia everywhere in town together – they were inseparable. When the scandal broke with your mother, whose shoulder do you think Vera cried on?'

'Satan's.'

'Sonnet, really. If you can't be serious . . .'

'So, Delia was more intimately involved in my father's life than I understood. No wonder she hated my mother's guts, and still does. I don't understand why you didn't explain this years ago!'

'On all those occasions you were willing to hear about it, you mean.'

'That couldn't be sarcasm from *Olive*!' Sonnet stewed for a moment. 'So, you think Delia was just punishing Archer and his spawn by refusing to show the works?'

'Most likely. Though, beats me why Vera thought anyone in Noah would want them here. I sometimes wondered if she'd had a change of heart in later years, even forgave him. You'd have to, staying married that long. You'd need to ask Delia herself about that.'

'Why would Delia know?'

'She and Vera have always remained friends, through everything.'

'Is she still alive?'

'As far as I'm aware. With those poor boys.'

Sonnet's next query was usurped by astonishment. 'Well, I'll be damned!'

Coming up the stairs, bundle in her arms, was an elegantly dressed Fable.

'Where are *you* going?' blurted Sonnet.

Fable looked only at Olive, fluttering neatly kohl-rimmed eyes. 'I want to go to church with you this morning.'

'Don't be *stupid*!' Sonnet cried, leaping to her feet.

Fable's gaze was unflinching. 'I need to get out of the house, Aunt Olive. It's time. I'd like to see some of the old faces from church, too.'

'No way,' Sonnet said. 'You're sleep deprived; you're not thinking straight.'

'We would love to take you,' Olive said, face beatific.

'Olive, you can't let her walk into that lions' den! She'll be eaten alive!'

'For pity's sake, it's church! You're thinking of the Colosseum.'

'Fable, don't do this. There are much easier ways to make a baby announcement than to prostrate yourself before every judgemental gossip in town.'

'No one will say a bad word to Fable,' Olive demurred.

'Not to her face, no.'

'Sonnet, the church *exists* to take in the fatherless and friend-less, with open arms. She'll get nothing but love and support. No judgement.'

'Certainly they'll judge, they can't help themselves. They're human ergo they're judgement-making machines! Fable, don't. I'll drive you into town myself and you can buy a milkshake at the Paragon. Start with something simple. Not ... *church*.'

'Thank you, Olive,' Fable said, refusing to yield to Sonnet's penetrat-ing glare.

Delia Hull is going to take one look at that baby and know it for her grandchild! He's the spitting image of her son!

Sonnet narrowed her eyes. And that was *exactly* her plan, wasn't it? The salvation Fable wanted wasn't from the pulpit at all ....

Fable lolled in enervated muteness as they journeyed home from church. Her aunt and uncle stuffed the silence with chatter, a near-giddy light in their eyes.

Well, good for them. The queasiness provoked by their elation was a small price to pay for today. She'd made her public declaration now: Fable would no longer hide in shame. Fable Hamilton would walk into any place in Noah she pleased, with head held high.

No more hiding; nothing to hide.

She had thoroughly underestimated how exhausting it would be to make such a statement. Showing up out of the blue like that; the pro-tracted walk down the aisle, flanked by Olive and Gav, all those familiar faces swivelling to gape, their greetings high-pitched and overcompen-sating. Adriana was there, front and centre, with eyes rapacious as ever, though her welcome had been breezy with indifference.

Fable slumped tiredly out of the car.

Sonnet was already three steps down and flying towards her. 'What happened? What did they say? Are you *okay*?'

Fable saw, again, Delia Hull's face behind the morning-tea table as she'd filed past, heart in mouth, to accept the proffered cup of tea and lamington. Delia had looked at Fable like she was carrying an eye-wateringly fresh pile of dog poo, and asking her to sniff it.

Sonnet's eyes drilled into hers. Fable read the question there: *Did Rafferty's mother recognise her own grandson?* There never *had* been anything she could hide from her sister.

Sonnet's brows were nearly at her hairline now. Fable shrugged. *No, Delia saw only the floozy she'd always known I was, just like my mother before me.*

Sonnet reached for Rune. 'Come here, our beautiful boy; Aunty Sonny missed you more than anything.'

Sonnet stewed for the rest of the afternoon. By dusk, she was over-cooked. With the abruptness of a timer going off, Sonnet charged out of the cottage door.

'I'm going to see her!'

Fable looked up from her nappy pile in abject terror. 'You *can't!*' She tore down the stoop and along the garden path after Sonnet, clinging to the gate as her sister marched beyond her.

'*Oh God—*' Fable whispered.

Sonnet felt not unlike the wrath of God as she emerged onto the Hulls' side, storming Summerlinn for the first time in nearly a decade.

Both the grand homestead and the woman who came, at leisure, to the discordant knocking had lost their proud gleam. Perhaps it was simply the distance at which Sonnet had held Delia Hull over those years, combined with the dramatic powers of memory. For the woman who stood before her now – slim as ever, immaculately dressed and elegantly tressed – had neither the talons nor scales she recalled. Grey threaded heavily through her dark beauty, and sadness had diminished her blue fire gaze.

Her face, however, was every bit as glacial as Sonnet remembered.

Without greeting, Delia hissed, 'I didn't say a damned word about her to anyone!'

'I didn't accuse you of anything—'

'Yet! Your presence on my doorstep is allegation enough. I've heard your lecture before, and I'm in no mind to hear it again.'

'I can't even visit a neighbour?'

Delia's lips pursed flintily. 'You didn't see fit to step foot on my property when we lost William.'

Point one to Delia.

'And I am truly sorry for your loss, Delia.'

'Mrs Hull.'

'Mrs Hull, it is a tragic loss, and our thoughts have been with you.'

'A simple card would have sufficed.'

Sonnet jutted her chin. This was not going to script. 'Mrs Hull, I have not come today to talk to you about my sister —' *Much less your grandson.*

'I have not the slightest interest in anything your sister does. I doubt *anyone* cares what Fable Hamilton does with her life.'

Well, this was a new tactic.

'I'm pleased to hear it. That will make a nice change for a Hamilton girl in Noah Vale.'

'Hamilton girls would do well to spend less time obsessing over the opinions of others, and demanding everyone else validate their poor life choices.'

Sonnet shut her hanging gob. 'You haven't changed a bit!'

'I've heard enough,' Delia snapped, the fly screen cracking shut in Sonnet's face.

'Delia, wait. I didn't come for a fight.' Only now did she appreciate the truth of this. 'I need information – about my father.'

The screen stayed closed. 'Why on earth would I have any information to offer you?'

'That's what I'm hoping you'll tell me. It's about the paintings, you see.'

The door squealed open. Light hit those shrewd, startlingly blue eyes. Sonnet thought of the boy who had inherited them, slumbering just beyond the vale of the creek.

'What paintings?'

Sonnet smiled. 'Yes, exactly, the ones you and the other CWA members tried to pretend didn't exist.'

'If I recall correctly, we were in receipt of paintings by a local artist, given to us by *my* friend. However, they were deemed unsuitable for public exhibition, given the artist's contentious history in our fine town.'

'And so, you just gave them away – rather than to the daughter who might have appreciated them.'

'You found a way to get your hands on them, anyway.'

The words were a punch in the gut. Sonnet remembered the accusation, dripping red, on her bookstore sign. Did everyone in town think Sonnet whored her way to everything she wanted?

Through her teeth, she said, 'Yes, I did manage to right that injustice.'

'What makes you think you're entitled to anything of his? You're unacknowledged, and illegitimate.'

'Then why did his wife – Vera, is it? – why did *she* send them to Noah Vale in the first place?'

'Why don't you ask Vera herself? If you ever dare to face the woman whose life you ruined.'

Sonnet smirked. 'Now you doubt my chutzpah?'

Delia sneered back. 'You girls have had years to make amends with Vera, it's clear to me you lack the moral conviction.'

'She's a stranger to me, how the bloody hell would I have made amends?!'

'A simple thank you for your mother's effects would have been the least you could have done, under the circumstances.'

'My mother's *what*?' A greasy, panicked feeling came over Sonnet. Already she knew the answer.

'The box of your mother's belongings, given to you many years ago, by a woman selfless enough to sift through the reprehensible communication between them and their dirty mementos, and pass it on to his bastard daughter. She could have destroyed it all! I would have made a bonfire of everything – all their evil lies, every last hair or toenail he ever shed – and I would have watched it *burn*.'

Delia quaked. Sonnet shook.

In her mind's eye, she read: *For Sonnet, from Vera*. She saw the cardboard box, already opened, filled with old books and useless junk. She remembered the tumble of those objects into a garbage bag; the books she had sold or left to moulder.

One hand went to the door frame, the other covering her stomach's revolt. Delia stepped back, breathing heavily.

Sonnet spoke in anguish: 'They were Mama's things? I threw them all out! It was just rubbish. I was cleaning up!'

When it came, Delia's reply was pitiless. 'That's where they belonged. It's what Vera should have done in the first place: taken out the trash!'

'But Alfred received her box, not me, and he died without telling me!'

Delia's gaze was narrow. 'You didn't read Esther's letters?'

'*What letters?!*' Sonnet was near to shrieking. Whether at Alfred, or Delia, she hardly knew.

'I can see you're shocked, but this hysteria! Lower your voice. If you weren't mooning over your mother's life of iniquity, then what *were* you doing in that shuttered bookshop for nigh on a year?'

'I was cleaning, and grieving! I felt unworthy of my good fortune. I didn't know if anyone even *wanted* me to reopen. Nobody reached out to me!'

'Now that's an outright lie. Marg herself went down personally to see how you were getting on, and if you needed help. The CWA would have been at your immediate disposal, if you hadn't been so full of pride and self-righteousness!'

Sonnet took stock of the woman before her, recognised her power and indignation for what it was.

'You!' she cried, clenching her fists. 'You read my mother's letters, didn't you?' Her voice broke.

Delia was unmoved. 'I certainly did. Death is the finish of all possession. They were as much mine to read as anyone's. Your mother and father thought they'd hoodwinked us all! But every secret comes out in the end. I only wish they'd been exposed when they were made to pay for it in this earthly life. You live a lie, you become a lie. Your mother made you what you are.'

A small, deadly smile settled on Sonnet's lips. 'You have no idea how right you are. Every secret *does* come out. Best be careful the bottom doesn't drop out of your world one day, too.'

Delia pulled the screen shut, dismissing her. 'It already has,' she said, turning coldly away. 'What have I got left to lose?'

'You'd be surprised!' Sonnet called after that proud, straight back.

Sonnet was raging through the row of mango trees when she saw Adriana Hull, coming over the paddock, hessian bag in arms. She was on Sonnet like a fury.

'What are you doing here?!'

'Seeing your mother about secrets and lies,' said Sonnet. It was a crow.

Adriana tossed her hair over shoulder. 'And I hope she sent you packing. You've got *nothing* left to say to my mother – now or ever.'

Sonnet's eyes glinted as she absorbed this. Ah, so *she'd* guessed. *Good one, Fabes, might as well have hung a placard on your back.*

Adriana's voice lowered to a vicious whisper. 'My mother has been through more than enough. We're fast approaching the first anniversary of my father's death. We're struggling to keep our heads above water on Summerlinn. I won't let her be hurt any further!'

Sonnet clucked. 'It's hard losing a parent, isn't it? Lucky *you* don't have a whole town set against you, as we did. I'd hate to see Noah ever turn on the Hulls.'

Adriana seemed almost pleased. 'We're in agreement, then.'

Sonnet gave a harsh laugh. 'Believe me, this is the most provisional agreement of your life! One wrong word against a Hamilton ever circulates in town, and—'

'Enough! I get it.' Adriana hoisted up the hessian bag.

'Glad to hear it.'

Adriana rolled her eyes. 'My brother's a fool.'

'No,' Sonnet said. 'My sister is.'

PART FOUR

'She had been forced into prudence in her youth, she learned romance
as she grew older: the natural sequel of an unnatural beginning.'

Jane Austen, *Persuasion*

CHAPTER 44

DYAD MOON

May 1965

The Hamilton girls were cruising up Main Street on the way out of town, windows of their red Morris Minor open to the golden breeze of an early-winter afternoon. It might have been a ticker-tape parade, with those Sugar Festival posters flapping from every post and shopfront. A tall figure on the pedestrian crossing, wrapped Paragon sandwich in hand, waved them over towards the footpath.

Sonnet ignored the low wolf whistle from the back seat as she swung her car, Moxie, kerbside.

Dr Fairley came, widely grinning, to lean over the driver's window. 'Hello, Hamiltons!'

Plum, in the front seat, blushed. Fable, leaning over a bassinet in the back seat, waved Rune's chubby arm in greeting.

'So, this is the new set of wheels, huh?'

'New to me, anyway,' Sonnet said, patting the dashboard. 'If Fable gets a baby, I can at least have a car. This acquisition was slightly less painful.'

'You look good in red. Did you end up getting old Ryan down on the price?'

415

'Too right!' Sonnet said. 'Told you I would. Not a dollar more than I wanted to pay. Now we won't have to rely on Olive's car to ferry Fabes and Rune around. We're just heading up to Cairns now actually, for our first appointment with the psychologist. Thank you for the referral.'

'No worries.' Jake leaned towards Plum. 'I think you'll like Carolyn. Fantastic approach with adolescents, and she has a lot of experience treating anxiety.'

Plum nodded tightly.

'And guess what!' Sonnet remembered excitedly 'We've finally got a phone on now!'

'You're joking. It's the End Times!'

'Certainly felt like the apocalypse trying to get the line. Do you want our number? Beats trying to talk to us in such a public show as this.' That was an understatement. All around them, faces devoured the scene.

'I've never wanted a phone number more!' Jake said, reaching for a pen in his shirt pocket.

Fable snorted in the back seat and Sonnet shot a dark look into the rear-view mirror, carefully avoiding the innocent baby boy.

Jake held out his free hand. 'Would you mind? I'll put it in my address book when I get back to the surgery.'

Sonnet took the proffered hand, resting it gently against the car door as she uncapped the pen. There was a tremble as she worked the pen into his tanned skin, and she couldn't tell if it was his or hers.

'Should you put your address down too?' Fable piped up helpfully. 'Just in case he needs to write you?'

Sonnet recapped the pen a tad too smartly. Jake left his hand where it was; almost, *almost* brushing Sonnet's skin. He looked past her at Fable.

'As much as you've been my favourite patient in Noah – wouldn't hurt you to do some doctor shopping in Cairns today, would it?'

Sonnet stared straight through the windscreen, hands gripping at the wheel.

'I'd do anything for my sister, Doc!'

'So would I,' Jake said, stepping back from the car, rapping his knuckles on the roof.

Plum chortled. The car sped away.

A few blocks later, Sonnet found her revenge. 'Look, Plum! There's Jim Taylor. What's he doing out of school?'

Plum was already following his course. 'He plays truant on Wednesdays.'

Fable and Sonnet shared mirrored bemusement.

Sonnet beeped the horn and waved as Jim stopped to stare. Plum shrank low in her seat, beseeching face turned towards Sonnet.

'Oh look, he's waving at me!' Sonnet said merrily. 'What a nice boy, he's so happy for me to have my new car. I might pull over and let him have a closer look.'

Plum's outraged cries were overpowered by Fable's cheering encouragement. The car came to a stop beside Jim. Sonnet leaned across Plum.

'Hey! Jim! Do you like my new car?'

Jimmy strolled over, eyes firmly placed on the passenger seat. 'Pretty cool.'

'She's *very* cool!' Sonnet said. 'Sorry I can't stay and show you, I have to take Moxie for a spin on the open highway now. But hey, we'll be at the Sugar Festival this Sunday if you want to come see. You could meet us at the Emerson–Hamilton table.'

'Would that be okay, Novella?' Jimmy asked, not looking at Sonnet.

Plum nodded, before turning flaming face to the urgent matter of her cuticles.

'I hate you,' Plum said as the car sped on.

'You're welcome,' Sonnet replied, eyes on the rear-view mirror. 'Wow, look, Jim's so taken with my car, he's just standing there watching me drive away.'

'Does he look sad, or mad, or . . . ?'

'Stoked, Plum. He just looks stoked.' Sonnet put her foot down as they cleared Main Street, exuberance creeping up on her.

'Right . . . so now we just need to find Fable a date for Sunday.'

Fable laughed. 'Already got one – best-looking boy in town, and he's all *mine*!'

Sonnet knocked off early on Friday afternoon – she hadn't seen a shopper all day, the whole town was prepping for the Sugar Festival. Even now, as she locked her front door, she could see bustling townsfolk setting up in Raintree Park: the long wooden trestle tables, fruit-and-veg stalls, livestock pens, children's rides in a miniature sideshow alley.

Sonnet smirked to spy the mayor and Olive's minister deliberating at the gate about the dark clouds fast rolling in, the forecast for unseasonal rain. Already the rain trees were packing up their leaves.

Hope it's a drenching!

Frankly, she'd be glad to skip this Sugar Festival as she had every year since they'd arrived. Sonnet had always used the excuse that the festival flowed out from Sunday services, and since she didn't attend those, it would be rude to rock up for the free food – even stupider to present for the polite public stoning.

This year, she was putting on a brave front. If Fable was courageous enough to appear in public holding her stupendously cute bastard while his unknowing grandmother swanned around nearby, then it was the least Sonnet could do to have her back.

But she would turn up as a single woman! And Jake could keep calling her three times a night, monopolising her new phone line for hours on end – she wasn't giving in! There'd be enough of a furore as it was, without adding further fuel to the fire. Jake was going to have to find his own bloody table.

Sonnet looked up the street to the doctor's surgery. A light was burning invitingly in the flat above Jake's rooms. He too must have finished up early. He was probably sitting down to start dialling her right now.

This time, Sonnet wasted no effort quelling a smile. Everything about that man made her beam. She glowed in his presence, became sweatier than even *she* thought possible; couldn't eat for the fire pit in her tummy.

Is this what you meant, Mama?

Sonnet's foot tapped an agitated beat against the balustrade as she contemplated the two-block dash to Jake's. So close, yet inconceivably far.

A spot of rain rolled down her nose. She held out her hand to catch the drops, turning back to Raintree Park, and the melee erupting beneath the trees. She jangled her car keys in her hand. Better get home before she felt guilty and offered to help with tarpaulins.

Jake's light burned against her back the whole way home.

The rain had set in heavily by the time Sonnet parked Moxie at Heartwood, called in on Olive and Gav, and hotfooted it for the cottage.

Fable had cleaned the whole house and cooked an early dinner. The leftovers congealed unappetisingly on Sonnet's plate. Talk about burnt offerings! *Fable should stick to making milk*, Sonnet thought. Her foot drummed an edgy beat against the table leg.

Fable herself was juggling a crabby baby from breast to shoulder and back again, on repeat. 'What's wrong with him?' Sonnet asked, leaving her fork to stand straight up in an untouched mound.

'I don't know,' Fable confessed. 'He's been unsettled all afternoon. I'm wondering if it's teeth?'

'Teeth! He's only three months old.'

'He's an advanced baby.'

Sonnet snorted, and went in search of sherry. Sherry would definitely help to settle *her* nerves; too bad for Rune there was no such cure. She poured a glass almost to overflowing, ignoring Fable's raised brow. The sherry might as well have been vinegar. She pushed it away to join her plate, with a sigh.

Rain pounded on the tin roof.

'Go on,' Fable goaded.

'Go on *what*?'

'"*Tell truth, and shame the devil.*"'

'Don't be stupid.'

Fable shrugged. 'I can think of much more enjoyable ways to be spending your Friday night than waiting for a phone to ring.'

'Yeah, and look how that turned out,' Sonnet intoned as Rune began to wail.

'What are you so afraid of?' Fable asked, standing to sway.

'Venereal disease, big-headed babies, pitchforks, a hastily set-up pillory on Main Street . . .' They shared a squall of laughter.

Fable grew serious. 'You're such a fraud, Sonny.'

Sonnet tried to take umbrage, but felt misery blanch her features instead.

'You pretend to be the strongest woman in Noah, who doesn't give a fig what anyone says, doesn't need anyone else, but it's all a cover. You bitch about the constant judgement and unsolicited opinion in this valley, but you are your biggest critic. You push us to follow our hearts, I mean you literally grabbed my dreams *for* me, yet you're withholding your own. Like you don't think you deserve anything just for *you*. You've been mothering us for so many years, I think you've forgotten to have your liberating youth. It's time you did! I'm a mother myself now. And Olive and Gav are going to approach you soon, with a view to officially adopting Plum—'

'They're *what*!' The table wobbled; her glass reeled wildly.

'She's lived up there for years! Olive is, for all intents and purposes, her mother. It's just the next right step to take. Yet, see, immediately you're getting your hackles up. You don't have to be the perfect guardian anymore, Sonny, or the perfect anyone. Now you can just . . . let go. Why are you holding back? What are you waiting for? Who really *cares* what they think anymore?'

'I do!' Sonnet cried, on her feet now. 'I care!'

'Exactly.'

They stared at each other across the table. Sonnet's face was knotted with the effort of holding back a wail.

Fable nodded, her eyes loving. 'Now, Sonny: *"Screw your courage to the sticking place!"*'

Mama's saying, from her sister's lips.

Sonnet stared at the rain-strummed attic ceiling, kicking her legs against the sheets, and each other. She could not sleep for the stubborn glow of a lit window burning still against her back.

With a snarl, she threw herself out of bed. She pressed against the dormer window, searching for the improbable sight of Moxie, head-lights flashing, beeping down the hill through the rain like a loyal steed. Below, she heard Rune's strident wail start up again, and Fable begin 'Somewhere Over the Rainbow', once more from the top.

Enough!

Sonnet yanked on a shirt and pants, then took the stairs two at a time, heedless of the already woken. At the kitchen bench, she scrawled a note with shaking hand, propping it against the sugar.

Faithful old Freya was already waiting on the porch. Soundlessly she rolled out into the rain. Sonnet didn't even stop to close the gate.

Through rainforest and cane and dreaming vale she pedalled, shivering with anticipation and the press of wet clothing against her. Rainwater ran into her eyes and mouth and down her heaving chest.

'"*Screw your courage to the sticking place*",' she repeated, through gritted teeth.

She rattled up Main Street, slowing only to fling her middle finger at the street-lit cassowary glowering through her shop window.

The lights were out at Noah Vale Family Medical. Sonnet threw her bike kerbside with a clatter. In the darkness she tripped through the spokes, swearing noisily as pain seared across her ankle.

The stairwell to Jake's apartment was behind a closed door. Sonnet braced herself against it, seeking air and nerve – both, it felt, in vain.

Screw. Courage. Sticking place.

Got it.

But if the door was locked now, would she have to turn and go home?

She would brook no opposition from a mere door this night – turning the knob and thrusting against the wood in one powerful motion. The door yielded inward, and Sonnet tumbled over herself into the bottom of the black stairwell.

She was climbing to her feet as a wide triangle of light spilled over the top step. A shirtless Jake stepped out, face pinched with concern. 'Son! What's wrong? The baby?'

Sonnet straightened, panting. 'No, Rune's fine. It's *me*.'

His brow furrowed with greater worry. He was three steps down before she could continue. 'I'm okay,' she said, putting up a hand. 'There's nothing seriously wrong. Unless you count insomnia.'

He stopped now, angling his head to the side.

Sonnet's own head, looking up, was impossibly heavy.

Sticking place.

Her words were light. 'Dr Fairley, what would you prescribe for a cynical nearly thirty-year-old virgin with control issues, a false sense of self-sufficiency, and an avowed distrust of men, who swore off romance years ago?'

He nodded thoughtfully. 'Ms Hamilton, as a doctor I'm going to have to pass on that one.'

She drew in deeply.

'However,' he continued, eyes dancing in striating lines, 'as the man madly in love with you, I can already think of a few ways to rectify the problem.'

Sonnet climbed to the step below his. 'Only a few?'

'If I have to go back to my textbooks to find more, I will!' He reached to take her shoulders in his hands. 'You're soaked to the bone! Aren't you cold? Come here.' He drew her into the dark, sparse curls of his chest, rubbing her arms.

'Warm me up,' she whispered, muffled hard against him.

Fable smiled all through Saturday, breaking into radiance each time her eyes fell upon the note propped up against the sugar bowl. She didn't need to read it. She grinned even though Rune's ornery fussing continued unabated, and not a speck of white could be traced by finger on his pink gums.

423

The drizzle eased late Saturday afternoon, though the baby grizzle did not. Fable rose, red-eyed, to greet the dawn of Sugar Festival day. She pulled on a favourite old sundress – holding her breath until the front button had managed its closing over breasts lush with milk. She gazed critically at herself in the mirror. Rune was still changing her figure, months after he'd left it; the demands of his hearty appetite whittling her back to girlish slenderness, albeit with the new softness to tummy and hips, the linea nigra fading from belly button to ginger mound. Fable's hair reached nearly to her waist now – split of end and rapidly beginning to lose the lustrous thickness of pregnancy – perhaps she should emulate Sonnet's bouncy shoulder bob? Tiredness was a permanent blue stain beneath her eyes, but never had her skin been so clear, or the fall of her features as serene. Fable also recognised the openness of her face; the maturity she had gained. She was much paler than she ever remembered being, though. What she needed was the touch of sun upon her skin, and *that* was one step she could take right now.

She slipped one of her handmade baby carriers over her body and reached for the grumpy boy on their shared bed. Using Olive's vintage sheets, Sonnet had sewn Fable a pile of wraparound baby slings – a clever idea she'd seen in a book. At the rate Rune regurgitated his milk, Fable needed a new sling for each hour of the day.

Rune slipped into the sling with a whimpering sigh and Fable gave thanks again for her brilliant sister. Who needed a daddy when you had an Aunty Sonny like his?

'Let's take a walk, Runey-boy,' she crooned, forgoing shoes at the porch step. 'Where should we go today – visit the Nanna tree again?'

Rune bellyached.

'No, we're not going to visit Nanna in a mood like that! What about to see Daddy's trees?'

More bleating.

'Someone needs a good rocking, then.'

Up the hill Fable bounced, body finding its instinctual shushing rhythm. By the time they'd reached the Orchard Hill, Rune had fallen into slumber. The sun was just hoisting itself over the mountains.

The Malay apple flowers were in bloom and a sodden, hot-pink carpet surrounded each tree. Rainbow lorikeets trilled and chirruped noisily in the branches, their nectar-feeding inducing a vivid snowfall.

'Oh, Rune, look what you're missing!' Fable sighed, floating through the apple grove. She lifted her face to the flowers, laughing as the pink sprinkles caught in her hair, gracing Rune's cheek and his tiny fist curled against it.

She sank to the ground against the papered bark of a Malay apple tree, scissoring her legs in the blossom dust, letting it run through her fingers. Her eyes glazed over; a new faerie already dancing into view.

Yes, she would wait here until Rune woke from his sleep cycle, then she'd show him the dancing birds, watch his laughter gurgle up.

What a life I will give you, Rune Hamilton!

Sunshine warmed her face and limbs as she gazed over the silver-pink ocean of cane. How many times had she conjured up the sunrise from this very hill? How often had she sat in dreaming wonder here and bid come the summer and Ra—

Fable started from the trunk, hands flying to shade her eyes.

There! Right *there*, coming up the long alleyway between canefields: a tall, striding figure, with large duffel bag slung over shoulder.

Who could that be at this hour on a Sunday?

But her heart was way ahead of her: trampling over the fields towards him, howling as it went. Fable launched herself out of the pink shade, after it. Down the hill she ran, pausing only as she became mindful of Rune's jostling. She held his head against the throb of her heart, slowing herself.

Look up, look up, look up!

The man raised his head, sweeping an arm across his forehead. At first sight of the woman halfway down the hill, he stopped.

Fifty yards lay between them.

He dropped his bag, a sigh forcing his shoulders into a slump visible even at that distance.

Tears burned in Fable's eyes. Only the weight of Rune's curled body restrained her from full flight. Sugarcane towered now on either side of her. The scent of molasses rose up. Long-beloved features began to distinguish themselves from the blur of distance and tears.

With only six feet left between them, she stopped. Light was in her hair, and heart. His gentle eyes ran all over her, searching out every broken place and joyful strain. She smiled, or tried to smile. It was a whimper, however, which broke from her lips – and in an instant he was upon her, falling to his knees in the rain-damp earth to throw his arms around her waist.

Fable steadied herself against the force of his embrace, hands flying into his hair. She held his face against the belly so recently filled with his son. Above Raff's head, Rune began to squirm and mewl.

'Shhh,' Fable murmured.

It was not her son who cried, but his father. Silent sobs racked his shoulders, drawing hot tears from her eyes, too.

'It's okay,' she murmured, 'I'm okay.'

He looked up, and she saw there the blaze of tenderness which had not, in a whole year, subsided.

'Forgive me, Fable.'

'Forgive *me*, Raff.' She drew him up, pulled his lips towards hers, tasting salt.

'If I'd *known*,' he said, breaking away to rest his forehead against hers. 'Fable, I love you. I would never, ever have left you.'

'That's just it! I was terrified you'd think I was just trying to trap you.'

'Trap me? I would *never* have believed—'

'No? We're together one single night, and then straightaway I'm pregnant and trying to tie you down with a baby. Noah's most eligible bachelor finally ensnared!'

'Wouldn't have crossed my mind, I'd have been here for you in an instant.'

'But I didn't give you the chance. I ran away, like I always do—'

'You had your book tour, your work in Brisbane. I *told* you to go!'

'No, I was hiding. It's how I cope.'

'When I didn't hear from you at all, I tried to call you, through your publisher in Brisbane.'

'I know, but I couldn't talk to you about . . . this. I couldn't. I had too much to lose, and I was just trying to hold on to him.'

'I thought you were done with waiting. So I wrote you that letter, once I got back to London.'

'A *letter*?' Her face was ashen.

'After it went without reply, I thought your answer was pretty clear. And I didn't want to keep hassling you.'

'Hassling? I thought you'd left me once and for all.'

He lifted her face to his. 'I'll never leave you again.'

Her hands fell from his neck to the babe grunting against her chest. Now there would always be this boy between them. 'Raff, before you go making sweeping promises like that, you need to meet someone first.'

Pain tensed his features.

'This is your son – his name is Rune William Hamilton.'

Only then did Raff lower his gaze to his miniature against her breast. His hand rose towards the small head, then fell away. 'I'm so sorry I did this to you.'

'*Sorry?* For Rune? You can regret whatever you need to, but never Rune.'

'I'm sorry you had to go through this alone.'

'I didn't. I had all my family. Then I had Rune.'

'And now you have me – if you still want me?'

Fable saw the doubt in his eyes, and felt anew the reversal of their roles. She had grown past him.

'I've *always* wanted you, Raff.'

His hands enclosed her face.

'I want a life here in Noah,' she said unbendingly.

'A home beneath our rainbow gums?'

'But I won't be your special charity project any longer. I can stand up for myself.'

'Less protecting – okay.'

'No more pedestals, either.'

'What about waterfalls?' His smile was wry.

Fable tried to look stern. 'And I'll never give up my creativity, or my Hamilton name.'

'I won't ask you to.'

'I want to make lots more babies like Rune, too.'

Raff nodded solemnly. 'We'll practise every day.'

Rune began to grumble, nuzzling for the nipple. 'I have to feed him,' Fable said, drawing free of his hands.

'How do we do that?' he asked, looking about.

Fable released a full breast from her dress with the flash of a button. On Rune latched, eagerly.

'Right,' Raff laughed, colouring, 'just like that.'

They watched Rune together.

'You're incredible, Fable,' he said, voice thick. 'Everything you do . . .' Raff reached to stroke his son's downy cheek.

'Feels like rose petals when you kiss it,' she murmured, her eyes languid with oxytocin.

'I remember very well,' he said.

Fable laughed. 'No, his *cheek*.'

'Well, I plan on kissing everything, all over again.'

Her womb undulated. 'When did you find out?' she asked, forcing her attention from that greedy throb.

'Bit over a week ago. I came on the next flight I could get.'

'But what about your work?'

'I walked out. I was treading water there in the end, waiting for any excuse to let myself come home. Then a little bird sent me a missive, ordering me back here in *no uncertain terms* to set things right. There may or may not have been death threats.'

'My sister,' Fable grumbled.

'No,' he said. 'Mine.'

'Adriana!'

'Yes. Adriana, it turns out, is quite the secret detective. Claimed she'd seen you with a baby that could only be mine. Said she'd known I was infatuated with you for years. And that she'd *always* known you were in love with me.'

'I can't believe it, Adriana hates me!'

'No,' he said with emphasis. 'She was only ever threatened by you. As it turns out, she was the only one in Noah who knew exactly why I insisted on staying away from Noah for so many years.'

Fable reached out to touch his face. 'If only I'd let you come back to the cottage that first morning, if I'd told my family about you right from the beginning – it might have saved us both a year of heartbreak.'

Raff rubbed the fine stubble of his jaw against her hand. 'Truth be told, I was on my way back over to see you that morning, under the flimsy pretence of searching for Eamon. I couldn't let you leave town before securing a way to contact you in Brissie.'

He sighed. 'But I ran into Marco on the way, and I realised how selfish it would be to put you on the spot in front of your family like that. I had asked you to wait for me – but it was then I realised I would be waiting for *you*.'

'I didn't want to miss my chance with you for anything in the world. Not even my book tour. I tried to stay! But everyone said I had to go, even you, Raff.'

'And as hard as this year was without you, I'm still glad I didn't stand between you and your work.'

'I went and tried to enjoy my tour,' she said, a little wobble in her chin. 'But I was homesick, so sick with Rune too, and frightened all the time that I was losing him. I wanted you, but after a while, I wanted my baby more. I had to *try* and put you out of my mind.'

Raff swept a long strand of hair from her face, pink dust falling between his fingers. 'You were never out of mine.'

'I didn't say I succeeded. That one night has . . . consumed me.'

They shared a heated smile.

'Absence,' Fable murmured, 'makes more than just the heart grow fonder.'

'You have no idea.' His lips hovered now above hers.

'I have good reason to get Rune down for a nap so you can show me,' she breathed back.

'It isn't . . . too soon? I don't want to hurt you.'

'Too *soon*? If you come back to the cottage now, I'll show you exactly how *long* you took, Rafferty Hull.' She glanced at the bag near his feet. 'Wait, have you just arrived?'

'Came straight here.'

'You haven't even been home to your family yet?'

'They're standing right in front of me.'

His mouth claimed hers.

CHAPTER 45

ESTHER SPEAKS

Sonnet woke to the sound of church bells, and rolled to smile at the man on his belly beside her. He cocked an eye open with an impish eyebrow raise. Sonnet slid her hand along his bare back to settle over a taut cheek, prickling with goosebumps. She shivered at the desire already turning molten in his brown eyes.

'*Callipygian*,' Sonnet murmured. 'Having well-formed buttocks.'

Jake moved his head to free his lips from the mattress. 'Marry me, Sonnet.'

Yes.

'Don't be stupid. We Hamilton women don't marry, we fornicate.'

'Well, if anyone was made for fornication, it's you. Seems like fornication might be your new favourite hobby.'

'It is. Better workout than running. You're one to talk, though! You don't like to go easy on beginners, do you?'

'Not when they're as competitive as you.'

'It's not my fault I get there faster than you.'

'No, it's mine.'

'You just like showing off how well you know your way around the female physique!'

432

'No, showing off my appreciation for the finest physique I've ever seen.'

'I do have a complaint about your bedside manner, though. Actually, more your on-the-windowsill-with-the-curtains-open manner . . .'

'Oh, were those complaints you were making?'

'How was I to complain properly in that position?'

'Want to air the rest of your grievances now, then?' Jake asked, moving smoothly over her. 'Because I'm all ears.'

'That's not your ear, Jake . . .'

Yes, yes, yes.

Sonnet emerged from Jake's shower to find her slacks and shirt from Friday night laid out on his bed – washed, dried and ironed. She had to laugh. 'I could get used to this!'

'I hope so,' Jake said, still ironing his own shirt.

'Will you come out to my cottage each morning to do my clothes?'

His eyes crinkled. 'If you want the laundry service, you'll have to move in with me.'

Yes.

'Shacking up with the town's doctor? That's one way to steal Fable's notoriety.'

'We could start by turning up together today at the Sunday service.'

Sonnet made a choking sound. 'I'd never step foot in that place! Bunch of bloody hypocrites sitting together polishing their throwing stones.'

'That's kind of the point, isn't it?' Jake said. 'We're all a mess of con-tradictions, in an imperfect world, with our favourite stones to cast.'

'Yeah, but most of the heathens out here don't hurl rocks from behind some self-righteous shield.'

'Is that your experience?'

Sonnet saw, again, a red-checked tea towel tossed over shoulder in a braying pub crowd. 'No,' she said, between closed teeth, 'women are shamed and blamed wherever they go. Damned if they do, damned if they don't.'

'Holds true for my mother. Devout member of a conservative church, and when she finally escaped my father, *she* was excommunicated. His sexual, emotional and physical abusing mattered less than her refusal to silently submit without making a dreaded fuss. It was easier for the church if the victim left than the perpetrator.'

Sonnet shook her head in disgust.

'The reception she got outside wasn't much better, though. She was a single mother single-handedly destroying the fabric of society, raising a delinquent, surely prostituting herself, who couldn't be trusted to rent a property much less get a loan, and who hogged welfare she didn't deserve.'

'Preaching to the choir here, Jake. And how much of those attitudes do you think stem from religion in the first place?'

'Or how much of our innate human nature infiltrates religions and societies?'

'You think oppression is *innate*?'

'I think human cruelty and lust for power permeates institutions setting out with even the noblest intentions.'

Sonnet, at first nodding, now cocked her head. 'Don't tell me you're a *believer*?'

'Merely a ... "reminiscer".' The iron hissed, in echo. 'I remember fondly the God of my childhood and how, according to my childlike trust, he was going to make everything right for Ma and me. But Ma had to save herself, and I haven't managed to find him since.'

'You *are* looking, though.'

'I was angry with the God I saw no rational sense believing in for many years, until it finally occurred to me maybe it was still okay to miss him, anyway, and perhaps my professional pilgrimages, from Asia to Africa, were my attempt at reconciliation. If I couldn't find God in a desert, I suppose he's no more likely to be found in a church. That doesn't necessarily stop me . . . wanting.'

Sonnet stared at Jake. She wondered how to explain her cassowary – her *firebird* – and how much she feared, despised and desired him.

'So, have you found anything yet?' she asked, not quite coolly enough.

'Yes.' He shot her a look of infinite warmth. 'The gift of our stubborn human need and yearning for each other, despite our incurable imperfections and the almost certain guarantee of disappointing, failing and hurting one another.'

Sonnet found herself with a solid, stinging lump to swallow. A whole folded part of her being strained at the seams to unfurl.

She watched the adept slide of his hand across plaid in silence.

'So, we can't share a pew, then,' Jake said, lightening; swinging his shirt off the board. 'But we can arrive at the Sugar Festival together?'

'Ha! I walk in on no man's arm today! It's bad enough I left my dirty-stop-out-mobile lying in front of your flat all weekend.'

Jake stretched into his shirt, saying nothing. Sonnet's hands ached to take it off again. Fastening the last button, he looked up. 'Honestly, Son? You won't get persuasion from me. I fell in love with a woman who knows her own mind, and runs her own life. That's sexy as hell to me. I'm not going to undermine your independence.'

'Not even a *little* persuasion?'

Jake came over to button her shirt, hands lingering at the top. 'Nope. I want to share the life you've created here for yourself, not demand you rebuild it over again to suit me.'

'There are some parts of my existence,' she said slowly, 'that more resemble siege ramparts than a life.'

He went to speak, but her hands moved to cover his, green eyes aglow. 'And those walls could certainly come down.'

'Now it sounds like you're trying to convince *me*.'

'Here, let me show you—'

'I do like it when you show me,' Jake said, as they retrieved rumpled clothing.

'And who knew,' Sonnet began, 'I had such talents for persua—' She trailed off, face grey.

'Son?'

'Persuasion.'

'Yes...'

'No, *Persuasion*! My mother's favourite book!'

'Oh, the Austen classic. Yeah, I don't think Jane ever wrote the kind of trick you just pulled.'

Sonnet leapt up. 'Holy heck, I have it! I still have *her* copy of *Persuasion*!' She didn't have time to elucidate, didn't have a moment to lose. Much less to re-button her shirt.

'See you at the festival,' she cried, hurtling past his bafflement and down the stairs, two at a time. She burst onto a street busier than she'd ever seen it. Cars were sardined in the gutters; footpaths flowed towards the park with townsfolk carrying blankets and baskets.

Sonnet was bending to retrieve her bike, in most inglorious fashion, when Marg and Ned Johnstone exited their car kerbside. Marg tutted loudly, sending Ned scuttling to the boot to retrieve their gear. Her son, Dane the Dickhead Dux, stood under the awning, leering. Sonnet followed Marg's eyes from Jake's apartment to the gape of her blouse, lace bra exposed.

436

Sonnet's hands clenched, desperate to mend the gape. She gripped her handlebars, instead. Sonnet Hamilton would not cover herself in front of this woman.

Marg passed her on a withering fume of Yardley, and *almost* kept her damned mouth shut. At the last second, she snapped.

'You Hamilton women just don't know how to leave a decent man alone!'

Sonnet threw back her shoulders. 'Oh, Marg, there's *nothing* decent about what Dr Fairley just did to me.'

She wheeled her bike to the centre of the busy road, shoulders still squared. Warmth flowed into her core. Sonnet stopped, turning to look up at Jake, who leaned over his tiny balcony with a hand mock-clutched to his heart.

A smile twisted the corner of her lips, wringing out bitterness. The last little thread of resistance snapped. Cupping hands round her mouth, Sonnet threw back her head to holler, 'I love you, Dr Fairley!'

The grin breaking over Jake's face sent her sailing down the road on a breeze of joy.

It was a different matter entirely in the privacy of her bookshop. From wall to shelf to ladder to discount rack she volleyed, cursing through tears.

'Where did you put it, stupid? You can't have sold it! You didn't! Come on, *think*!'

It seemed improbable that she would find it now, after all these years, all her ignorance. She'd probably waved it out of her front door in a paper bag years ago.

And yet – *there*! On the lowest shelf of Esther's Corner, amongst the Children's Classics, a soft dove-grey spine, and the word she'd been searching for in gilded curlicue: *Persuasion*.

It was, of all things, regret that seized her upon its discovery. It was no relief to open the cover, press back the dust jacket and find her mother's name scribed there – in the handwriting she had not seen for a decade, and yet would still have known after a hundred years.

How many of her mother's books had she relegated to obscurity among a thousand lesser books? How many had she *sold* for infinitely less than they were worth?

Sonnet traced the writing under her finger, and lifted her nose as though to receive her mother's floating scent. She pressed the book to her face and spun the pages beneath her nostril, still waiting.

An envelope dropped from the book, to rest between her feet.

Sonnet stared at it in sickened disbelief. Her first notion was to leave it where it lay, to run from what she already knew it to be.

Mama's letters had been hidden in her books.

Sonnet could barely hold the page straight as she unfolded the letter from its packet . . .

> *Archer,*
> *My love is a fever, longing still, for that which longer nurseth the disease.*

But Sonnet saw not her mother's pale, slender hand dancing across the paper; rather, a faceless, scorned wife gripping at the page; Noah's coven of witches poring over the words; Alfred's rheumy gaze treading down each line.

Nausea churned as she continued.

> *You have a daughter. A fat-cheeked little plum, with auber-gine eyes. Both baby and mother are well, or so they say – since no one ever asks me.*

438

Mama was still writing to him after they were separated? Sonnet's eyes flew to the top of the page, searching for a date. Of course there wasn't one – who dates a letter to an erstwhile lover? With a head-shake, Sonnet read on.

Her name is Novella, born of our shortest tryst of all.

Sonnet sank heavily to the floor. *Plummy* was his? She was years too late, a lifetime too slow to this discovery.

I bore her silently into the world, as every time before. Then I sat and stared at the ward door, defying the sister's canny eyes, and I waited. This time, I told myself, clutching tight our baby – this time he will come.
But you didn't come.
And I have waited long enough.

Sonnet thought of the paintings crowding Fable's sunroom as a living shrine to Archer Brennan; secret father who had bequeathed his talents upon her.

So, Fable already knew long ago then. But *how*?

I went home on the seventh day. I packed up my tiny flat, and left. You won't find me again.
I hear you, already: this won't last – we can't live long without one another, Es.
Come, then; find me. Fail. Turn back to the home you chose with her. We'll see who cannot live without.
You're already thinking this is another tempestuous Esther tantrum, nothing time cannot remedy. It's a familiar turn – the

months of parched and searing longing, then the conflagration of us. No one burns for love, the way we do.

But it is our daughters who will be, at last, our uncoupling. They deserve more than this. Sonnet – our brilliant daughter – is a senior and in her, I finally recognise my young self. I was old enough, but I wasn't wise enough. I understand now: I had a very girlish understanding of consequences then . . .

See Esther there? Flame-haired young woman in the library annex, come to study for her scholarship exams, with everyone's favourite vice-principal. How lucky she is, with those far-fetched dreams, and her unstable nature, to have such a prodigiously talented teacher take an interest in her. Dear old Alfred is thinking it this instant, as he prowls the aisles, guarding our scholarly endeavours from interlopers. He's made himself our alibi, and he hasn't got a clue.

For, look again: her skirt is up around her waist, with her bottom raised on a dusty tome, and her tutor stands now between her legs. In the quadrangle outside, marbles clack against each other, voices smash mutely against the window-pane. Watch her face as he plunges in, his hands cradling her gaping mouth – oh yes, her entreaties finally met, but did you catch that first sting of disappointment too?

It wasn't a love scene worthy of us.

Ours was a love grander, rarer, brighter than the sordidness we were limited to . . .

On your wife's bed, while she was at the doctor's rooms; under your desk, while your secretary tapped away outside; in your automobile, parked by dark canefields; and then, our new favourite – beneath the King's portrait on the school stage, hands gripping at red curtain, thrusts metered out by the clock's quiet outrage.

Someone must have discovered us there, long before the graduation ball. They were prepared. All the world's a stage, and on that night we were players in a larger tale of revenge. I obsessed over the culprit and their motives for many years. Was it dog-faced Margery? Or that seething Hardy girl? In the end, though, it doesn't matter who drew back the curtain. The point was our public shaming . . .

My favourite green gown in rustling protest, high on my thighs, my teeth latched on the webbing of your hand. But listen now, for that sudden winding rustle. There's a rush of cool along my legs, and our leaping shadows are starkly thrown. A single discordant piano note rings out, then that unearthly hush. I strain for a glimpse behind us, hissing your name. You pitch onto my bare back, and now I can see them over your neatly pressed collar. All of them, staring at us agape. My smothered cry turns to horror; yours erupts, and then the crowd begins to shriek, too . . .

How could we ever outlive such shame?

For nearly two decades, we've tried.

Before our discovery, I would beg you: Take me away! You thought I pled for the ecstasy which transcended slapping flesh in another woman's sheets. In truth, I wanted you to save me from the natural restrictions of my young life itself, and especially that small-minded, godforsaken town.

Eventually, we did escape – you first, with a forced resignation and your family's expulsion, a sleight of hand to reposition you, for my later arrival. In the anonymity of that city, beneath your wife's averted eyes, we believed we had a fresh start, and a love story to transcend it all. No, we were merely reliving the same tale: yearning and combustion, over and again. While ever in reach of one another; we were burning up, or out. I fled and you followed, you fled and I followed.

But you always belonged to your little boys, to her.

'Those who control their passions,' you would quote, to hush my jealousy, 'do so because their passions are weak enough to be controlled.' I pitied the dry, pallid loves around us, and in your marriage. I believed myself the true victor. Your wife kept only the crackling cicada shell, while I alone possessed your singing flesh, and hungering artist's heart.

So many years you've castigated yourself for your infidelity and faithlessness, and yet; you've never left her, refused to abandon them. I might have loved you all the more for that wounded nobility limping on and on, if we hadn't both depended so much on your weakness.

And what have our daughters had? A shadow man, refusing to be seen or known; little more than stolen kisses as they slept, notes slipped into my purse for their birthdays, new books hidden beneath their pillows. Only Fable has been blessed to meet you in any real sense – fleetingly, in disguise as a dispassionate art tutor.

But you never stopped promising; one day, you'd finally make a true family of us. When the boys might be easier to care for, when the war was over, when your finances were better, when it wouldn't hurt Vera so much . . . when, when, when.

Of all the things I might have been, I have become this: a covetous, kept woman. Not kept by the seasonal trespasses and steady donations of a bewitched benefactor – kept by shame, and the caged hell I have made of it.

How easily my life might have taken another turn, if only Alfred had taken three steps closer to the concertina door that first day. Or, when we were caught, if there had been just one person to say: Esther, there is nowhere you can go too far from home, nothing you have done so unforgivable; no place you cannot come back from. If I'd known that kind of love, how different my options might have been.

All my life I'd believed in my too-muchness – the blinding heat and black hole of my intensity. But I've met someone who doesn't buy it for a moment.

Her name's Maria. She's one of those earnest Christians so easy to mock, but I'll forgive Maria even her stubborn, stupid faith, for she is my first true friend. The only one who has never said, 'Too much, Esther, you're too much.' Maria is helping me to heal myself. She reminds me of Olive, and perhaps that's why I have grown so quickly to love and depend upon her, why I long now to go home.

I'm making a plan for my homecoming.

It always seemed preposterous I should ever take myself, and our children, back to Noah. But Noah calls, anyway.

Remember, Archie: the holy, harrowing night we glimpsed the cassowary – our last, stolen forest embrace, before you escaped Noah. Meeting there, we had disturbed that majestic bird from his plum foraging. Recall that look he cast on us – as though he meant to hold us ever in his thrall. The eye of creation trained upon us, and how we quailed beneath it.

There were handprints stinging on my face from days earlier, our ears still ringing from the howling hall, a hawk of spit long since washed from my chest – soiling me forevermore – and none of it mattered; for I had you in my arms, helpless as a boy, hand on my belly, sobbing your fervid vow: 'This is not the end. I'll fix what I've broken, I promise you, Es.'

Release me.

I will never write to you again. Close your secret post box, discard this last word, burn every chapter I mailed you – for I will begin my novel anew. If you kept all those many letters I wrote you of our daughters – of their insignificant, infinitely valuable lives – know they are all you have left of us.

'All our evening sport from us is fled,
All our love is lost, for Love is dead.'

Only the tales inscribed in our own blood will live on now, Esther.

Panic had frozen up the lobes of Sonnet's lungs. She turned and gaped, unbreathing, at her store of books.

Where were the rest of these lewd epistles? What chapters, what *novel* had she given him? And how many of Mama's most intimate writings, details of their innermost lives, had Sonnet peddled out, unwittingly, to townsfolk?

Mama's letter was a white flag quaking in her hand. Sonnet closed her eyes, unable to shut out the image of Esther Hamilton's secrets spreading through the town, burning on bookshelves across the vale; igniting scandal for years to come.

CHAPTER 46

SUGAR FESTIVAL

The swing band in the rotunda had started up and the jazzy mood swept beneath the giant rain trees, over the family tables. One tense, slender back resisted the ambiance. Fable, waiting at the Hamilton table alongside her bustling aunt and uncle, had not taken her eyes from the wrought-iron gate. Through an arching tunnel of flowering sugarcane, townsfolk merrily streamed. All the wrong people. Fable's eyes burned from not blinking, lest she miss him. Would it always feel this way – that she'd dreamed him into being?

They'd only been separated an hour, enough time for him to slip across the creek to reunite with and, moreover, *ruin* his family. Raff had wanted Fable to come with him. No, she told him, that scene was for the Hulls alone, she wanted no part of it. Not that her mind hadn't been fixed firmly on Summerlinn all this last hour, anyway.

Delia, Adriana and Eamon had arrived ten minutes ago, setting up at the Hull table, beneath the grandest rain tree of all, not looking a mite perturbed, or even once in her direction. Eamon hadn't even lowered himself to ogle her.

Why had Raff not come with them? If he'd already told them, why were they not this very second tearing her hair out?

Terror rippled beneath her skin. Fable's hand reached out as though to grip Sonnet's – a reflexive habit she had not been able to shake since Rune's birth. But her big sister was absent, and strangely late.

Where are *you, Sonny?*

Marg Johnstone passed by, en route to the Hull table, and her stage whisper landed with well-practised accuracy. 'Oh, look, another Hamilton with her breasts hanging out.'

Fable glanced at herself, and saw Rune had fallen from her peachy areola, fast asleep. She smiled, drew her blouse back together, and wiped the milk that ran from his lips.

Olive smacked Plum's reaching hand away from the fruit-garlanded pavlova, and sent her off to fill the water pitcher. Gav leaned over Fable's shoulder to stare at Rune's sleeping face. He nodded to himself and moved on again, whistling. Uncle Gav approved heartily of everything Rune did.

Fable's eyes did the rounds again, hurrying past the Hulls' table on a missed heartbeat. She sighed.

Doctor Fairley – no, she had to stop doing that – *Jake* arrived at their table, beaming, with cheek kisses all round, and a platter of his already-famous quiche. Fable had come to love Jake's meals. Could Raff cook? She'd borne his baby before she'd even sampled his culinary skills. Fable wanted to ask after Sonnet, but couldn't remember how to make her mouth open.

Hurry, Sonny, I need you!

At last, those Titian tresses, flaming beneath the sugarcane arch. Fable's hand clenched once more and the knot of fear began to unravel. Whatever happened next, they'd face it together. It was what Hamilton sisters did.

Sonnet had arrived several long minutes after her new lover, but where Jake had shone, Sonnet glowered. Cripes, had they fallen out already? No, far from it, judging by the easy abandon with which Sonnet threw herself into his embrace and how quickly his hands ran the length of her spine to scoop beneath her . . .

Oh come on, guys, you've got two sets of rooms for that now!

Fable strained past their schmaltz, and the blushing joy it kindled, to the gate.

'What did you shout at me on Main Street before?' Jake asked Sonnet, in a baiting tone.

'I said *yes*.'

'Yes to what?'

'Missing the mark, going down in flames, meeting with triumph and disaster – so long as it's all with you.'

Fable heard the deep well of feeling in Sonnet's voice, and chanced another look at the couple. Her sister was all over Jake like a strangler fig. Olive and Gav, two feet away, were studiously ignoring them. Plum, returning with her jug, offered to pour it over the pair.

Sonnet came then to gather Plum into her arms, enfolding her so tightly Plum mimed asphyxiation over her shoulder at Fable. Next it was Fable's turn – though at least she had the baby as some buffer against the ferocity of Sonnet's embrace, and the suppressed need in her own clutch.

What was *up* with Sonnet today? Her eyes were a reservoir of unshed emotions – yet happiness rolled off her, in waves. Must have been one intense lay!

Fable fixed her eyes again on the gate. And just in time – for there he was. Through the pink-turreted tunnel he came, a throng of people converging on him so quickly she had no time to even wave him over. Fable rose, eyes striving in vain for his. It was a returning

447

king's procession, his progress impeded by the back-slapping hugs and boisterous handshakes which came from all directions. Fable's heart hammered so violently, it seemed to move Rune's head against her breast.

From the stage, '*Bei mir bist du schoen*' began its whimsical quaver. The merry-go-round twirled to raucous laughter. Sausages popped and sizzled.

Beneath the rain trees, between family groups, Raff threaded. Not to her table, but the Hulls'. Still he had not sought her eyes, or acknowledged her at all. Fable sank back in her seat, scrambling to cover her sinking dread.

He went first to his mother. Delia stood, tall and regal, hands outstretched for her golden boy. He took her arms in his hands, and leaned to whisper in her ear. Her figure stiffened, but her face did not waver from its proud glory. He pulled her into a tight hold then, her silver-threaded head tucked against him. For the longest time they stood, just like that. He placed a kiss upon her cheek, then, with one final word, gently disentangled himself and moved away from the Hull table.

His blue gaze swept the crowd until he found his Glade eyes, already set upon him. He was deaf now to the friends and relatives pressing in – strode past them all, and straight for Fable.

She'd barely made it to her feet before he reached her. There was no time for a greeting, so swiftly did he take her face in his hands, lips swooping over hers. Fable heard, from some far-off quarter, a whooping cry and applause. On and on and on Raff kissed her, until the baby between them stirred and protested.

Raff straightened then and reached for his son, lifting Rune gently to his shoulder.

'Hello again, my little mate,' he said, nuzzling a rosy cheek. Fable's hand went to her heart, pressing back the ache.

He turned to Fable's family. Sonnet marched up. Eye to eye, she and Raff stood.

'If you *ever* hurt her,' Sonnet said, not even trying to keep her voice low, 'I'll tear you apart with my bloody teeth.'

Raff grinned. 'From you, I'll take that as, "Welcome to the family!"'

Sonnet harrumphed, eyes twinkling now.

Jake extended a hand. 'You must be Rafferty, I've heard nothing about you.' The two men shared a laughing handshake.

'And you must be the Doc,' Raff said, 'who crossed a flood to deliver our baby. I don't know how to thank you enough.'

Jake waved it away. 'I only oversaw the process. Your Fable delivered the miracle. You have quite a woman on your hands there.'

Fable heard the appreciative sound Raff made, low in his throat, just for her. She lifted a face, unmasked and refulgent, to his.

Olive and Gav, busting their guts to get their hands on Raff, pushed in.

'It's wonderful! Too, too wonderful!' Olive cried.

Gav squashed the new family, three at once, in a bear hug.

Only Plum dallied behind, unsmilingly. The family turned expectantly her way.

Jake noted, in an aside, 'Sorry to say it, but if you don't get Plum's approval, you're out!'

Raff pretended to smarten up. 'Right then.'

Plum came close. She squinted hard. 'You look like Runey.'

'Thank you,' Raff said.

'Did you know,' Plum continued, 'you both have the same blue—' She stopped, face red, as a young man decked out in brand-new, button-down shirt, with slicked-back hair approached the Hamilton table.

Everyone turned to gawk.

Jimmy waved, his hand falling away awkwardly. Plum moved quickly to his side, ushering him off towards the game stalls with a hand at his elbow. Rune and Raff were forgotten.

'But what about lunch?' Olive fretted after her.

'Not hungry,' Plum yelled back, without turning.

'Not hungry?' Olive muttered, watching the young friends disappear from sight.

Raff turned to Fable. 'Wait, does that mean Plum approves or . . . ?'

'Nope, you're still on probation,' Sonnet said. 'Hands off Fable until you pass.'

Raff tipped Fable's chin and bent down on her lips. Fable was a slender, bending branch. Rune smacked a dimpled hand against their cheeks.

A bottle popped and bubbled. 'I think a drink is in order,' Jake said, glasses clinking in his hand.

'Yes, please!' Sonnet said, taking a flute eagerly.

'Dear me,' Olive said, 'wine at a church picnic?'

'It's a miracle,' Sonnet replied.

Olive tutted as the glasses overfilled, running onto Lois's vintage tablecloth.

'What are we celebrating anyway?' Olive asked, waving the bottle away from her glass.

'Letting go,' Fable murmured into her own cheek. Aloud, she said, 'New horizons!' and smiled, as Sonnet was caught up in arms again.

'Such a *scene*,' Olive muttered, looking askance.

Jake broke away to raise his glass. 'While we've got an audience, I would actually like to propose.'

'No you bloody *won't*,' flashed Sonnet.

'A toast, that is,' Jake amended, grinning as Sonnet smacked his backside.

'So, here's to . . . coming home to Noah Vale!'

'Coming home to Noah Vale!' the circle cheered.

'Coming home,' Raff echoed, a moment too slowly, holding Fable with his eyes.

With a roar like thunder, Fable's eyes answered. His lips twitched. A hot, drawing ache, low in her belly, made her want to sink to the ground, and be carried off.

Sonnet sipped hard at her glass, eyes set above the arch of cane on her bookshop sign, picturing within: the books torn from shelves and scattered across the floor; the letters yet unfound; a mythical manuscript to forever now pursue.

'Coming home . . . to *no avail*,' she said darkly.

But Jake wasn't finished. He raised his glass again.

Sonnet placed a hand on his arm. 'Actually, may I?'

'Well, I *was* going to toast you next, Son,' he said, 'but it does seem more fitting you toast yourself.' The lines at his eyes striated, like rays.

Sonnet cleared her throat, holding aloft her stem. 'A *toast*,' she began loftily, but her throat closed over.

An unexpectedly stricken silence unfolded. Tears flooded, her lungs heaved. For she saw it now: the promise of a clean slate for the Hamilton girls in Noah Vale had not been real, would never come to fruition. They could not undo the story Archer and Esther had written here. Even now, all around them, new embers leapt – table to table.

Noah had never offered a brand-new life; only life.

And still – our *story to finish*.

Jake moved quietly to her side, placing a hand at the small of her back. Fable slipped in on the other side, a slim arm winding about Sonnet's waist. Sonnet looked gratefully to both of them in turn, pressing her head against Fable's.

Sonnet started again, on a half-breath. 'To . . . Mama.'

'Yes—' Olive nodded, lifting her empty flute '—to mothers.'

'No, Aunty Olive,' Sonnet said, reaching – *at last* – for her. 'To sisters.'

Olive stepped forward.

EPILOGUE

Neither eyes nor hearts bore witness on the rough eve that ancient tree, gowned in green and veiled by rain, finally fell, though the forest seemed to reverberate long after it had come to rest. A rotting book cover floated free, peridot crystal dropped away and tiny bone fragments settled on the creek bed.

A lissom, red-tressed figure, streaking barefoot through the forest at gilded dawn, was first to chance upon the Green Woman's Grove, where new sunbeams shafted now through draping mist.

Fable stood a moment, perplexed by the gaping new hole in the forest ceiling. Above her, the wind tossed raindrops, sparkling, from leaves. In the droplets, a rainbow glory had appeared.

Her eyes drifted lower then, to the Green Woman herself. Across the creek she lay now, like a bridge between two lands.

Fable dropped to her knees, hands crossing at her chest, a sob catching in her throat.

'Oh, Mama'

Light flamed in the understory, and on the serpent wended, through the slumbering vale.

ACKNOWLEDGMENTS

Those Hamilton Sisters is richly imbued with my experiences of motherhood, love, family bonds and growing up in the lush, enchanted tropics of Australia. Noah Vale is a fictional place, based on the rainforest valley I call home. The majority of magnificent locations described herein are inspired by real, sometimes secret, places in my beloved Far North Queensland.

This story was conceived fifteen years ago, when I was a new mother, living in a quaint villa overlooking a sea of sugarcane. Sitting up late at night, breastfeeding for hours on end, I would listen to ripe mangoes falling on our tin roof with a *whomp*, letting my overtired imagination run to wild imaginings. One such night I was gripped, viscerally, by the image of an amethystine python uncoiling from the rafters above me, and dropping down on my baby boy in his hammock. That motif would not let me go. In the tempest of sleep deprivation and postnatal anxiety, something else arrived then, too: a spirited character named Esther, with three plucky and resilient daughters she wanted me to take care of.

In the writing and publishing of Esther's story, so many generous and talented people have taken care of me, too . . .

First and foremost, thank you to my fabulous and amazing agent, Selwa Anthony, for championing *Those Hamilton Sisters*. In countless books read over the years, I saw Selwa effusively credited by authors in their Acknowledgments, and I still have to pinch myself that now she's *my* agent, working her magic for me.

I am also tremendously indebted to the brilliant Alexandra Nahlous for her editing genius and key guidance in the developmental stage.

To my beautiful Publisher, Tegan Morrison, thank you for falling in love with my story. Your vision for *Those Hamilton Sisters* has been wise, perceptive and truly elevating. You've made publishing my first book an utter dream.

Those Hamilton Sisters found a most wonderful home with Echo Publishing, and Bonnier Books UK. I have so much gratitude for the warm and passionate Echo Publishing team: Benny Agius, James Elms and Emily Banyard. Huge thanks to my UK editor, Claire Johnson-Creek, and my copyeditor, Sandra Ferguson, and proofreader, Gilly Dean, for their expertise and finesse.

Beta Readers are unsung heroes for wading through ugly early drafts, and I thank mine – Ally, Jenn, Lyndell, Jane, Libby, Karen, Amanda and Em – for their thoughtful feedback. Thank you especially to my Bossiest Beta Reader™, Kate DiGiuseppe, who has been my counsellor, cheerleader and 'unofficial' manager through everything. Kate Hardy is named after my Kate – because there had to be one surprise left in this book for her.

I was also blessed by the big-hearted encouragement of Annie Love, Life Coach extraordinaire, during my journey to publication.

For my research, I am most grateful to the Cairns Historical Society and Research Centre for their generosity, patience and expertise. Any blunders are entirely my own.

I am forever thankful for my husband's family – Des and Vicki Kenny, and Wendy Kenny – who shared their firsthand recollections of growing up in Far North Queensland during the 1950s and '60s.

I also drew intimately from my own birth experiences in writing Fable's birth scene, and I want to pay tribute to the book which prepared and empowered me for those births: JuJu Sundin's *Birth Skills*, with Sarah Murdoch.

My husband, Liam Kenny, has always been my first reader. Thank you, Wiam, for declaring me a 'famous author' when I was really just a teary, tiredly scribbling new mother, and for loving me, and my writing, at our rawest.

Thank you to my be*witching* sister, Aleta, for being my second reader. I hope I have been able to honour the absolute privilege of sisterhood in this. To my brother, Rowan, I just want to say: 'Roundhouse Bodalla, I saw it first!'

Mum and Dad, thank you for giving me a farm-girl childhood, deprived of television, with a bedroom full of books and grandparents in a tiny cottage just over the hill. Thank you, Mum, for modelling determined, resilient womanhood, and Dad for long poetry recitals, nature commentary and waiting for Mum to grow up. Because of you *Joy* is, both literally and figuratively, my middle name.

Finally, I want thank my children – Dash, Aurora, Eleanor and Teddy – who must sometimes feel like this *book* is my favourite child. Thank you, Kenny Kids, for endless cups of tea and your unswerving belief in me. Achieving my publishing dream might have taken longer for having birthed four of you, but this accomplishment is infinitely sweeter for being shared with you.

Don't miss the next irresistible story from Averil Kenny . . .

THE GIRLS OF LAKE EVELYN

You cannot force me to marry him.
I need to be free, to figure out what I want.
For once, please let me choose . . .

It's 1958 and Vivienne George is due to marry Howard Woollcott
III in the finest society wedding of the year. But when she realises
she can't marry a man she doesn't love, she flees, with the help of her
Uncle Felix, to a small town in tropical North Queensland.

Hidden away in a secluded lodge, Vivienne spends her days swimming
in the beautiful lake nearby and getting to know kind Owen Monash,
her only neighbour for miles. It may seem like the perfect place to
escape her troubles, but there's something about this mysterious lodge
and the lake outside which put Vivienne on edge.

When she meets Josie Monash, Owen's sister, she learns of Celeste
Starr, a beautiful movie star who tragically died in the lake and
spawned a curse that has plagued the girls of the town ever since.
When Josie decides to stage a play about Celeste with Vivienne in the
lead role, it sets off a chain of dark events. Is there any truth in the
legend of the girls of Lake Evelyn? And how will Vivienne find the life
she's always wanted when her past comes back to haunt her?

Coming 2022